5

The Black and White
Medicine Show

The Black and White Medicine Show

HOW DOCTORS SERVE
AND FAIL THEIR CUSTOMERS

DONALD GOULD

HAMISH HAMILTON
London

To Jen

First published in Great Britain 1985
by Hamish Hamilton Ltd
Garden House, 57–59 Long Acre, London WC2E 9JZ

British Library Cataloguing in Publication Data
Gould, Donald
  The black and white medicine show: how doctors
  serve and fail their customers.
  1. Physician and patient   2. Medical errors
  I. Title
  610.69'52   R727.3
ISBN 0-241-11540-X

Filmset by Rowland Phototypesetting Ltd
Bury St Edmunds, Suffolk
Printed in Great Britain by
St Edmundsbury Press, Bury St Edmunds, Suffolk

Contents

Introduction

There is a famous painting, now in the Tate Gallery, called *The Doctor*. It is the work of Sir Luke Fildes, an artist who flourished during Queen Victoria's reign, and only died in 1927. It shows a frock-coated physician seated at the bedside of a sick child. Respectful and trusting relatives decorate the background. The doctor is doing absolutely nothing, except for a ritual feeling of the pulse.

He is not injecting any wonder drugs, because there weren't any.

He is not ordering an ambulance to take the obviously gravely ill girl to hospital, for hospitals had little to offer the sick apart from shelter, soup and sympathy, which were abundantly to hand in the prosperous household of the picture.

He may well have known what ailed the child, because in his day the diagnosis of disease had already become a fine art, but the effective remedies he had at his command were pitifully few. He could give quinine for malaria, morphine for pain, digitalis for a failing heart, aspirin for fever, amyl nitrite for angina, mercury for syphilis, an antitoxin for diphtheria, but precious little else.

His surgical colleagues had a mite more power. They could save lives by treating wounds with Lord Lister's new 'antiseptic' method, or by amputating damaged and infected limbs. They could take out an inflamed appendix, remove certain cancers (but not with much chance of working a cure), repair hernias, deal with broken bones, and otherwise ease physical distress.

But on the whole doctors could do little to influence the course of disease. Their greatest contribution to the sick and suffering was to share the burden of illness, and to give their patients, and their patients' families, a sense that the best that could be done was being done, and that somebody knowledgeable was in control.

The physician acted more as a priest than a technician.

Times have changed.

Now doctors are the retailers of procedures and agents which can alter not just the lives of individuals, but also the pattern of society.

They can abort many dangerous and previously often fatal infections with a dose or so of antibiotic.

They dispense, by the million, pills and potions able to influence the mind, and they have well over 2000 other synthetic drugs at their command, many of which are truly effective in curing or relieving the distress of a wide range of ailments.

They can delay death and sustain life in grossly malformed infants, or very sick old men, and others who, not long ago, would have perished in a short time.

They can replace damaged organs, like hearts and kidneys and hips, with natural or man-made spares.

They have wiped out smallpox, and slashed death rates from other mass killers like malaria and yellow fever, and they largely control the means for birth control, and in these two manners they can significantly influence population growth, which is the largest problem facing the human race.

Shortly, by engineering the genes of 'test-tube babies' before putting the laboratory-fertilized egg back into the mother, they will be able to control the quality and characteristics of children born.

These, and other new powers of a kind undreamed of half a lifetime ago, are accumulating at an awesome rate. But are doctors, and the many others, including politicians, concerned in the delivery of health care, exploiting the medical armamentarium wisely and well?

Countless individuals and the world as a whole benefit enormously from modern medicine, but there are serious shortcomings in our attitudes to health and disease, and in the way our medical needs are served.

We have become obsessed with the curative approach, believing that we should strive to produce a pill for every ill, whereas the best hope for a healthier world must lie in identifying and attempting to abolish the causes of disease.

Some curative medicine will always be needed, and modern techniques and procedures can work seeming miracles. Others, like heart transplants, while dramatic in themselves, may be 'bad medicine' because they can make little impact upon the problems they are designed to solve. Some 'cures', including certain cancer therapies, enthusiastically pursued by the experts involved, may cause the patient more distress than the disease.

There are gross inequalities and inefficiencies in the distribution of health care, with whole sections of some communities, and some entire nations, lacking adequate aid. Within the richer nations the less glamorous and less profitable branches of medicine, such as the care of the old and of the mentally disabled, are ill-funded and poorly served, so that much avoidable misery and suffering occurs. The necessarily finite resources of money and energy and skills available for health care are too often mismanaged, with consequent waste and soaring costs which can make the economic consequences of illness disastrous for many.

Medical education, and the organization of doctors and other health workers, are still based on outdated attitudes toward diseases and patients, so that expensively trained experts have an inadequate grasp of their role in society, and of the tasks to be tackled, and of their potentialities.

The drug industry has made dramatic contributions to the wellbeing of its customers, but is the purveyor of powerful agents which are dangerous when misused, and sometimes both dangerous *and* useless. In the competition for sales and profits safety is sometimes ignored, damaging facts are suppressed, and the gullible and ignorant are exploited.

Richly equipped with the means to diagnose and modify disorders of the flesh, the new, scientific practitioner often seems to concentrate on the illness to the neglect of the person – a fact which, in part at least, must account for the growing popularity of unorthodox and 'unscientific' therapies like homoeopathy, osteopathy, psychic surgery and faith healing, which are usually dispensed with the aid of a highly developed bedside manner.

Some medical advances, such as artificial insemination, or the ability to keep bodies with irreparably damaged brains 'alive' for months or weeks on end, face society and the law with entirely novel problems, for the handling of which no precedents exist. Bitter conflicts have arisen, and we have yet to establish the means for monitoring developments, and for deciding, on behalf of society as a whole, how these new procedures should be used, and whether indeed some lines of research should be pursued at all.

The current medical scene is complex enough. The future offers prodigious opportunities for good and evil, disaster and success. How we shall fare depends upon whether we have the wisdom to exploit our cleverness to good ends – whether we can recognize and root out the faults and dangers and abuses, and appreciate and exploit the beneficial practices and trends. This is why this survey has been called *The Black and White Medicine Show*.

CHAPTER ONE

The Springs of Suffering

Given the will and the determination we could greatly reduce our heavy and growing reliance on medical care. So, to begin at the beginning, let's take a look at the size of the contribution which the medical trade makes to the sum of human health and happiness, and compare this with the manner in which we carelessly call down upon ourselves so many of the avoidable physical and mental aberrations which keep the bank balances of doctors in the black.

In 1963 I spent an exciting and highly profitable three months in Saskatchewan, the flat, sparsely populated province in Canada's corn belt. The local doctors were on strike, and I had gone there as a scab – a blackleg.

The provincial government had decided to organize a fairly mild form of state medicine whereby citizens paid a compulsory subscription to an official insurance scheme and then had the greater part of their medical bills reimbursed. The new legislation was fiercely opposed by the doctors, and their resistance had the moral and financial support of the powerful American Medical Association, across the border in the USA.

To the innocent, outside observer the violence of the dissent was difficult to understand. The doctors were still going to be paid for their work on a fee-for-service basis (so much for an injection, so much for an appendectomy, so much for a check-up, and so on), and they would be able to charge according to a comprehensive tariff of recommended prices already in existence, issued and periodically updated by their own state medical society. So how would they suffer? What could it matter to them if their customers got some of their money back from a caring government?

The overt objection of the profession to the new arrangement was that it was an intolerable state interference with the sacred doctor/patient relationship, and presaged the introduction of a full state medical service of a kind suffered by the unfortunate Brits. In truth the doctors' real fear of the scheme lay in their recognition of the fact that it would give authority (including the tax inspectors) precise information about their incomes, and about the extent to which costly and unnecessary 'services' were being foisted upon a medically ignorant public. Up until then the doctors had been getting away with murder, and in a literal as well as a figurative sense in that some of their patients died as a result of useless surgery done for profit.

It was for this that the Saskatchewan doctors went on strike. The provincial government reacted with a mixture of toughness and panic. On the panic side it assumed that the withdrawal of day-to-day medical care would be a disaster to be avoided at whatever cost, but being also tough it advertised in Britain, and other nurseries of orthodox Anglo-Saxon medical skills, for doctors who might be willing to act as strike-breakers. The pay offered was high – ridiculously high in British terms – but only equivalent to the average declared income of the striking natives. That's why I went – for that and the adventure.

I was sent out, together with a young colleague, to a hospital in a tiny prairie town consisting of a gas station, a general store, a cold store (where the ladies kept their fur coats for the summer), a drug store, a handful of offices, a hick hotel, a school, half-a-dozen grain elevators by the railroad track, two or three hundred houses, eight or nine hundred people, and nothing else at all.

There had been five doctors practising in the town and running the 40-bed modern hospital. Of course, all the high technology and abundance of medical expertise available wasn't supported by the tiny township within which it lay. The village acted as the medical centre for the even tinier hamlets and the many isolated farmsteads within the two or three thousand square miles of surrounding prairie, and the enthusiasm of the immediate locals for their temple of healing (which they supported with cash and managerial skills) sprang not from any hypochondriacal concern for their own health, but from the fact that the presence of the hospital and the doctors attracted a reliable flow of pilgrims seeking a cure for their ills who sustained the trade of the shops and the various service-mongers.

On the day the strike started all five doctors in the township went to ground. The previous day the hospital had been full to overflowing, with several extra beds put up in the corridors. But

on this day, D-day minus one, the doctors had found themselves able to send all the patients home, except for a couple
who had been transferred to one of the two or three hospitals in
the province which the warring medical profession had decided
to keep open for the sake of the desperately ill and its own
reputation.

During the three or four weeks for which the strike lasted,
and we two blacklegs staffed the place, we never had more than
half-a-dozen patients in our beds. On the morning of the day
that peace was declared we were still there with our six charges,
but almost before the sun had shown up the horizon, the five
local doctors emerged from the woodwork and told us to be
about our business.

It took us most of the rest of the day to pack, and settle up our
bills, and say our farewells, and by the time we hit the highroad
in our government-supplied cars, bound for Regina and our
friendly government employer, it was tea time. Already the
hospital was full again.

So had there been a tragic, uncatered-for need, which we
imported quacks had been unable to fulfil?

It seems not. During the period of the strike no single death
occurred which was attributable to the lack of availability of
instant medical care. Indeed the province's mortality figures
actually fell below the average for the time of year.

This brief experiment concerning the effects of the suspension or reduction of medical care did not of course even begin to
prove that doctors are useless and that we would be just as well
off without them, but it did strongly suggest that we may
habitually and grossly overestimate the importance of the
purveyors of curative medicine in maintaining health and
sustaining life.

A similar conclusion must be reached from studying the
results of a much larger experiment which has been taking
place in the United Kingdom ever since 1946, when the
National Health Service was launched. Since then Britons have
been privileged to enjoy one of the most comprehensive and
readily accessible systems of medical care in the world, served
by doctors and nurses and other health workers trained to a
pitch of excellence as high as may be found. And apart from the
existence of a mechanism for the delivery of medical care which
makes it a good deal easier to secure the services of a doctor

than those, say, of a plumber or a window cleaner, there have been major advances in therapy.

But despite this medical cossetting of the Great British Public, there has been no reduction in the total incidence of ill health. Indeed, the time lost from work due to sickness has actually increased, nationwide, by a prodigious 25 per cent since 1946.

In a remarkable paper published several years ago Dr Peter Taylor, chief medical officer to the Post Office, reported his analysis of the strangely few facts and figures known about this happening. He found that absenteeism due to sickness amongst the working population had increased to grossly different degrees across the country. The highest rates had occurred north and west of a line from the Humber to the Severn – in other words, in the part of the country containing most of the factories and mines, and most of the poor housing, and most of the unemployment. Wales headed the league with a massive mark-up of 52 per cent. North England scored 46 per cent, the East Midlands 26 per cent, and the West Midlands 16 per cent. Most of the other regions lying above the 'sickness line' produced figures somewhere in between. In dramatic contrast sickness absence rates for the predominantly agricultural East Anglia and for the prosperous white collar South East had barely changed.

However, while the incidence of ill health has shown small change (an increase in absenteeism doesn't necessarily mean that more people are ill more often than before), there has been a dramatic alteration in the pattern of disease.

In mid-Victorian times a man aged 50 could expect to go on living for another 20 years. Now, well over a century later, a 50-year-old man has, on average, 23 more years to live (women do a little better – they belong, biologically speaking, at least, to the tougher sex). This doesn't seem a lot to show for the explosive development in medical science which has characterized the latter third of the era.

On the other hand there has been a great improvement in life expectancy *at birth*. A hundred years ago a newborn boy could expect to survive to the age of 41, and a girl to the age of 45. These low average figures were due to the large numbers of deaths occurring among children and young adults, and especially to deaths during the first year of life.

Only six out of every ten children born survived to adulthood, and the infant mortality rate (which is the number out of every 1000 babies born alive dying before their first birthday) hovered around the 150 mark. That figure is now around 17 deaths per thousand live births, of which the great majority occur within the first week of life – that is to say, among infants who are born less than fighting fit, because of prematurity, or as a result of a difficult labour, or because of some congenital abnormality, or, rarely, because of acquired infection or inadequate care. (This doesn't apply in the Third World, where infection and malnutrition are the commonest causes of infant deaths.) As a result of the greatly reduced death rate among children and young people life expectancy at birth is now something over 68 for males, and just under 75 for females.

The greatly improved chance of surviving for the full Prayer Book allowance of threescore years and ten (you see, things haven't changed a lot since 1662) has, infant mortality apart, been largely the result of a reduction in the toll exacted by infectious diseases.

Since Gladstone first became prime minister, deaths from tuberculosis, typhoid, diphtheria, scarlet fever, whooping cough and measles have fallen by 99 per cent. Some of this improvement has been due to such factors as the widespread use of preventive inoculations, mass-radiography (for the early detection and treatment of tuberculosis before the victim could spread the disease), the development of penicillin and other anti-bacterial drugs, and similar instruments of medical science. But the trend was well under way long before such weapons became available. Our infant mortality rate, for example, had fallen to around 50 by the outbreak of World War II, when the therapeutic revolution had hardly begun, and the assumption must be that the major force for change has been a better standard of living – better housing, better nutrition, better conditions at work.

Marks and Spencer, offering excellent clothing at a price related to the national average wage, and successive governments enabling local authorities to build sound houses for rents also related to the national average wage, and companies like Sainsbury and the Co-Op and other providers of modestly priced foods for city dwellers, have probably, between them, had a larger impact on the health of the nation than all the medicines yet made.

But the erstwhile mortal diseases have simply been replaced by others which kill people just as dead. And the characteristic of the most important of these latter-day afflictions is their intractable nature, so that the best, modern, curative medicine is now paying disappointingly small dividends in terms of health restored and lives saved.

*

Heart complaints now kill about 170,000 people in England each year, and coronary artery disease, which is by far the commonest cause of heart trouble, is responsible for a quarter of all deaths, being ahead of cancer as the biggest single slayer of Western man.

About half a million new cases of coronary heart disease (CHD) are diagnosed in Britain annually, and for each middle-aged man in whom the condition is recognized there may be three more who would show signs of the trouble were they subjected to a routine medical check-up, including an electro-cardiogram (ECG), which is a record of the electrical activity of the organ, and which may show up faults before any symptoms have occurred. Strokes, which are due to a similar degenerative change affecting the arteries of the brain, are also a principal cause of premature disability and death.

Since the scale of this modern epidemic has been recognized a great deal of money has been spent on the provision of intensive care units (ICUs) into which the victims of CHD are wheeled after an attack, but following the first flush of enthusiasm for this fire brigade policy, some people began to wonder how well it was paying off, and made the sobering discovery that there is no difference at all between the survival rate of patients treated in intensive care and those nursed in the far more congenial atmosphere of their own homes. This is a statistical finding. It does not mean that no lives have ever been saved by the instant availability of the special machines, techniques and skills which intensive care provides. Certainly some CHD patients have survived who would have perished if left in their own beds. But a similar number must have been killed by the added stress of an ambulance trip and the awesome, unfamiliar surroundings imposed upon them during the immediate aftermath of a heart attack.

The finding does mean that the most advanced monitoring and corrective measures have made no impact upon the overall damage done by the disease, and it also provides an excellent example of the manner in which highly trained, percipient, and experienced specialists, and people involved in the provision of resources, and the public at large, may be misled and beguiled by the apparent logicality and promise of some new, highly technical approach to a medical problem without knowing, or even perhaps caring, whether it is truly worthwhile.

Experiment is clearly necessary if advances are to be achieved, and I am certainly not suggesting that no new techniques should be funded or otherwise supported unless or until it can be shown that they are going to work. But there is a need to subject what doctors do to constant, critical assessment. In the jargon of the trade, this process is called 'medical audit', and it is a concept which is slowly gaining ground.

But while attempts to cope with the results of CHD have not, so far, been encouraging (there are wonderfully effective ways for dealing with some other heart complaints), we do now know a good deal about the so-called risk factors which increase the chances of an individual suffering a coronary attack. These include cigarette smoking, obesity, lack of exercise, high blood-fat levels, high blood pressure, and choosing the wrong parents.

We can't do much about our parents. We *can* do a good deal about smoking, exercise, and eating habits.

Smoking causes as many heart deaths as it does deaths from lung cancer. Men smoking over 20 cigarettes a day are three times as likely to die from coronary heart disease or heart failure than non-smokers. Indeed, one study seemed to show that a high blood pressure or a high blood-fat level only increases the risk of a heart attack if the subject smokes as well. For reasons still not clear, pipe and cigar smokers run a very much smaller risk of damaging themselves through their indulgence.

Switching to 'low-tar' cigarettes doesn't seem to help a lot. Addicts who hope they can go on smoking with less risk to their health by changing their brand of cancer stick rapidly learn (albeit subconsciously) to take more and deeper drags per fag, so that they keep up their intake of the nicotine for which they crave. They also block the ventilation holes at the base of filter tips with their fingers, and so, one way and another, manage to absorb at least the same quantities of tar and carbon monoxide gas, which are the likely damagers of the heart and lungs. Numerous studies have confirmed that stopping smoking is the surest way of avoiding a heart attack, or a stroke, or lung cancer.

Exercise provides a powerful protection. In a survey of 17,000 executive grade civil servants, aged between 30 and 64, carried out by Professor Jeremy Morris and his colleagues of the Medical Research Council's Social Medicine Unit at the London School of Hygiene and Tropical Medicine, it was found that those who undertook regular spells of really vigorous exercise reduced their chances of developing CHD by about two thirds. The activities conferring this very large benefit included swimming, keep-fit exercises, digging the garden, planing and sawing wood, and moving the furniture around. To do the trick the chosen effort had to be undertaken for unbroken bouts of not less than 15 minutes. It had to be vigorous enough to raise the pulse rate and to make the performer feel that he (there aren't that many lady administrative grade civil servants) was extending himself. As the authors of the report put it, simply 'playing with the children' just isn't good enough, although, in the case of some children, no doubt, this caveat would not apply. The exercise indulged in seemed to exert its protective effect despite the fact that it had no influence on existing high blood pressures or high blood-fat levels. It even appeared to neutralize the malign influence of smoking.

Whether the newly fashionable activity of jogging, as practised by the trendies of Manhattan and Hampstead, does much good, is still a matter for debate. Any exercise is better than none for most people, but some joggers are so flabby and unfit that they would probably do better to put themselves in the hands of a good remedial gymnast, who could temper their effort to their capabilities, and bring them slowly, slowly, back into a state of active life. And I suspect that the majority of morning and evening trotters are doing no more than nodding obeisance to the goddess Hygeia, and are failing to produce that 15-minutes' worth of increased pulse rate and extended effort which Professor Morris found to be so valuable.

I do have my own solution to the exercise problem. When I was a young physiologist I used to do some terrifyingly dangerous and fairly fruitless experiments upon myself, and such colleagues and students as I could persuade to act as laboratory animals. We used to pierce arteries with needles in order to make continuous recordings of blood pressure, and we attached other devices to various parts of the body in question, and hooked them up to complex and costly recording machines in an attempt to establish the manner in which a wide range of influences, from injections of this and that to the inhalation of various gas mixtures, affected the circulation of the blood. We didn't discover much, but I was greatly impressed by the enormous increase in the rate at which blood was pumped out from the heart whenever one of our human guinea pigs, lying down, performed the simple manoeuvre of raising the legs and waggling them about in the air. It's what we used to call 'cycling' in the old days in the gym.

There are good and simple explanations for the dramatic effect which this exercise has on the action of the heart, but they don't belong here. Suffice it to say that for 20 years now I have 'cycled' each morning for about a minute before getting out of the bath, and I'm sure that this is the equivalent of Professor Morris' 15 taxing minutes per day, and that whatever else I die of, it won't be heart disease. I may drown of course.

A mass of evidence links atherosclerosis (the name given to the degenerative process which blocks the coronary vessels in CHD) with high levels of fats and fat-related chemicals in the bloodstream, particularly cholesterol and the so-called 'saturated' or animal fats. Therefore diets prescribing margarine made from vegetable oils instead of butter, and restricting the use of cholesterol-rich foods such as eggs, have long been in vogue – a fashion strenuously promoted by the manufacturers of the supposedly beneficial brands of margarine.

A number of protracted studies, lasting ten years or more, have been undertaken in an attempt to measure the effect of diet on the development of heart disease, and the results do suggest that people on a low fat diet do run a significantly smaller risk of suffering a heart attack, or of dying of a second heart attack within ten years of a first. However, it is the total fat content of the diet which seems to be important, rather than the type of fat eaten, and men seem to benefit from dietary control far more than women, since it appears that a woman's sex hormones in some way protect her from the ill effects of food fats. Recent work suggests that certain unsaturated fats or oils of a kind found in quantity in, for example some fish, actually protect against CHD. The one thing we can say with certitude is that the role played by fats is complex, and that other factors clearly play a part in modifying whatever damage a high blood fat level may bring about.

Other factors which have been accused of increasing the risk of heart attacks are drinking coffee (but not tea) and living in a soft water area. So far these are only statistical associations of cause and effect, and in neither case is there any convincing theory to explain the findings. It might be, for example, that coffee addicts also tend to be heavy smokers, or are more likely to be the tense, thrusting, go-getting types known to be more liable to CHD.

One school of thought strongly believes that emotional stress is a major influence in the genesis of heart attacks, and there is persuasive evidence in support of this idea, ably summed up in an intriguing book called *The Western Way of Death* by Malcolm Carruthers, a London doctor.

City dwellers are CHD victims three times more frequently than countrymen. American accountants are more liable to an attack during the spring when they have been grossly over-stretched by the rush of work at the end of the tax year. London bus drivers suffer twice as many heart attacks as their conductors (of course, conductors get much more exercise). The male coronary ward at London's Charing Cross hospital is usually largely filled by cab drivers. Airline pilots and senior detectives are often victims. British Labour Members of Parliament are more at risk than Conservatives (being, presumably, either more conscientious or less self-confident). There is a large increase in the incidence of coronary thrombosis during the months following the death of a spouse.

Dr Ray Rosenman of San Francisco divides mankind into two groups – those possessed of what he calls Type A personality, and those he describes as Type B. The Type A individual is the man or woman who works for 36 hours a day for nine days each week, who is a compulsive organizer but can't bear to delegate responsibility, and a perfectionist, constantly anxious lest a colleague or a rival steals a march. The Type B citizen may accomplish just as much or more during the course of the working week, but is able to roll with the punches, let others take their fair share of the strain, worry only usefully, and cast off care when day is done or there is time to spare. It is the Type A person, says Rosenman, who is most likely to be killed or crippled betimes by a heart attack, or a duodenal ulcer, or some other failure of the flesh.

All this is not to say that we would all live longer, healthier lives if somehow cocooned and protected from all the slings and arrows of outrageous fortune. A certain amount of stress (or pressure from the outside world) is essential just to keep the engine of the body running well. Witness the frequency with which men who have led busy working lives, never or rarely falling ill, go into a rapid physical decline and succumb to some mortal ailment within months or a year or so of retiring. I say 'men' rather than men and women, because wives never retire. It is not hard work, but frustration and anxiety and wrath which kill. Sometimes a well-known politician dies in harness. When this happens the eulogies heaped upon the deceased by his colleagues invariably include the claim that he died in the line of duty because of the unstinting manner in which he gave himself to a gruelling and over-demanding career selflessly dedicated to the commonweal.

Rubbish! Prime ministers are, presumably, the busiest of politicians, and yet they *never* die in office, and at any given time Britain is littered with ex-prime ministers who survive into a very ripe old age. They, of course, remain involved, and sought-after, and well rewarded for so long as they choose to go on living.

*

Next to heart disease and strokes, cancer is the major killer in the developed world, causing the death of one person in every five, and, as with CHD, the results of treatment have proved disappointing. Despite the fact that enormous sums are spent on cancer research, and despite skilled surgery, and despite the well-informed use of X-rays and other kinds of radiation, and the development of a range of powerful anti-cancer drugs, cancer cures are hardly more frequent now than they were half a century ago. A few cancers, including one form of childhood leukaemia, can be cured almost as a matter of routine, if tackled soon enough. But, unfortunately, it is the commoner cancers which have proved least amenable to treatment, and tumours of the lung and the gut and the female breast and the genitalia continue to kill more and more people every year.

There is a tendency to regard cancer as a malignant blight visited by a baleful Fate upon those unfortunate enough to catch her eye – an inevitable happening for those marked out for the disease. It is nothing of the sort, for, like CHD, many cancers are preventable.

Not long ago Professor Eric Boyland, then head of the Department of Biochemistry at the Chester Beatty Research Institute in London, stated that '. . . most of cancer in human subjects is due to external chemical factors that could be eliminated. . . . More effort should be expended in trying to find the cause of the more common forms of cancer. . . . The discovery of the causes and their removal seems to be the most hopeful way of solving the human cancer problem.'

Boyland's pronouncement was a greatly oversimplified statement of the case. Over the years a huge and diverse catalogue of physical and chemical agents have been shown to trigger off the cancerous process in *some* of the bodies exposed to their influence. These so-called carcinogens range from sunlight (the incidence of skin cancers is far higher in Australia than in Wigan) to (probably) a virus introduced into the vagina during copulation. (Nuns – at least, virtuous nuns – never get cancer of the cervix.) The list, which seems to grow daily, features such apparently wholly unrelated influences as asbestos fibres, cigarette smoke, sawdust (carpenters get cancer in the nose), maybe parsnips and red cabbage, nuclear waste, some human parasites (a liver fluke common in China makes liver cancer a leading cause of death in that country), nitrates drained into drinking water from fertilized fields, and a formidable menu of man-made chemicals, including some drugs, some once-popular food colourings, and many reagents used in industry.

In other words, we are all constantly exposed to a wide variety of carcinogens, and there are certainly many not yet recognized, in addition to those which crop up amongst the stream of novel compounds which chemists are creating all the time. So why don't we *all* get cancer? The answer is that a carcinogen is only one of the factors involved when a cell goes wild and becomes the parent of a monstrous family of murderous descendants. Often a second agent – a so-called co-carcinogen – seems to be at work. Thus asbestos workers who smoke are much more liable to develop cancer of the lung than either their non-smoking colleagues or smokers who don't come into contact with the dangerous dust. In addition constitutional tendencies play a part. A few cancers appear to run in families, and there is an increased incidence of the disease among the elderly bereaved, so that grief and other emotional disturbances may tip the balance. Indeed, it may well be that we *do* all develop cancers fairly frequently, but that usually the body's defence mechanisms destroy the aberrant cells before they have become a detectable growth, and that only sometimes, for some reason, do the rebels gain the upper hand.

Within the very recent past insights gained by molecular biologists give promise of an early understanding of the happenings within the cell which turn it into an anarchist, and when that understanding is complete it should be possible to devise the means for halting or reversing the process, but, in the meantime, shouldn't we be doing much more than at present to get rid of some of those carcinogens?

Unfortunately many of the known carcinogens are agents which work much toward our convenience or give us pleasure.

Sir George Godber, lately Chief Medical Officer to Britain's health department, and a remarkable civil servant, being amongst the most pragmatic and humane of men, admitted that much cancer might be preventable in theory by action aimed at limiting exposure to cancer-inducing circumstances or agents, but warned that such action would 'inevitably take a very long time and some of it would involve a limitation on the content of life that many would be unprepared to accept'.

But the fact that it may not be possible, or even desirable, to take the measures needed to eliminate the identifiable triggers of cancer altogether is no sort of excuse for failing to do what could be done without making life an exercise in total self-denial – a kind of continual Lent.

A great deal of cancer, like a great deal of coronary heart disease, is attributable to our life style, and to circumstances which we have created for ourselves. We could abolish much, probably most, of the invalidism, physical suffering, anxiety, grief, expense, and premature mortality caused by these two principal plagues of the developed world if we chose to apply the kind of energy and resources to the task as are now devoted to salvage bodies already crippled by avoidable disease.

Of course it would cost a lot of money, but in the long term prevention is always cheaper than cure. In 1982 Britons were spending £225m a year, the biggest single element in the national drug bill, on medicines for the treatment of CHD, and the total annual cost of the affliction, including treatment, lost productivity, and sick pay was estimated to be in the region of £1 billion. In the USA, where heart attacks were once more of a problem than in Britain, deaths from this cause have dropped by a quarter in the space of ten years. This encouraging, indeed dramatic trend appears to have followed an increasing awareness among Americans of the risk factors, so that many potential victims have paid serious attention to their weight and diet and behaviour. They have been subjected to skilled and sustained propaganda, notably by the American Heart Association, which now devotes half its budget to health education and to fostering a preventive approach to the disease.

*

Road accidents which, in theory, are totally avoidable cause 67,000 deaths in Britain each year (equal to about a quarter of the lung cancer deaths due to smoking), and result in 80,000 serious injuries. Some 6000 children are killed or injured while crossing the road. The estimated annual cost of the consequent medical care, damage to property, time lost from work, compensation or state support for the bereaved, and other direct sequelae, is now close to £2 billion, greater even than the cost of heart disease. No one has so far attempted to cost the pain and grief. Other developed nations pay a comparable or even larger price for our modern assumption that every Tom, Dick and Harriet has an inalienable right to pilot life-threatening machines around the countryside. Indeed a high proportion of any developed nation's wealth and industrial capacity is devoted to keeping people and goods on the move in motor vehicles, so that a significant reduction in traffic would now do serious damage to the economy. Hence, of course, the unpopularity of railways with governments and the industrial barons and financiers, despite the fact that trains can shift goods and people far more safely, and at much less cost to the environment, than do cars and juggernauts.

Apart from the determination of the automobile industry, and the oil industry, and the construction industry, and all their many satellites, to maintain and increase profits, and their share of the national wealth, we have, over the past half century, altered our life pattern in a manner which makes us utterly dependent on road transport, to the extent that oil-rich nations of the kind belonging to OPEC can hold the rest of the world to ransom, and risk their oil becoming the prize sought after when the super-powers launch the Third World War.

So it would be naive to call for a vigorous clamp down on automobiles simply on the grounds that they are by far the largest cause of death among the healthy young. However, much more could be done toward reducing the cost to health which our addiction to these machines at present exacts.

Heavy trucks are frequently involved in some of the most serious high speed accidents, and if their size and numbers are allowed to increase this must be at the cost of more lives and limbs. Government policy should encourage the transport of freight by rail, particularly in the case of goods which unlike, say, fish or milk, don't have to be shifted rapidly from door to door. The road lobby always argues that this wouldn't ease the traffic problem much, because even more vehicles would then be needed to shift freight to and from the railheads. But the time has surely come for keeping private cars out of city centres, and if this happened there would be ample space available for the safe and orderly movement of goods and a variety of public transport vehicles.

A study of what the lorries crowding our roads are actually up to would certainly show that great quantities of materials are shifted needlessly. Thus, for example, the costly folly of a great truck loaded with biscuits made in Edinburgh but destined for consumption in London passing an equally huge load of London-made biscuits bound for the homes and cafés of the Scots.

Reasonable speed limits, efficiently enforced (possibly by statutory devices fitted to engines) would produce a significant drop in casualty figures, as actually occurred in Britain when moderate, not excessive, limits were imposed to conserve fuel during a recent flexing of muscles by the Arab oil moguls. Nobody claimed that their lives had been disrupted.

Much more attention could be paid to safety aspects in road design and engineering.

More than one third of the drivers killed on British roads have a blood alcohol limit above the legal level, and driving 'under the influence' should be treated as the serious crime it is, warranting imprisonment just as much as rape, or robbery with violence, or arson, or other activities which hazard the health and lives of innocent victims.

Measures such as these would infringe some aspects of our cherished personal freedom, which was the argument successfully deployed to delay seat-belt legislation in Britain for so long, but unless vigorous, initially costly, and radical measures are taken, the toll of road deaths and injuries can only increase, and even at present levels we are talking of over 100,000 needless deaths, over one and a quarter million serious injuries, and a bill for over £30 billion, accumulating within the few years left between now and the turn of the century.

Motor vehicles don't just do harm by breaking bones and ripping flesh, they also poison the air, pouring out oxides of nitrogen, carbon monoxide (the lethal constituent of the old Town gas), and a peculiarly dangerous lead compound, from their exhausts. The nitrogen oxides can be removed chemically by a device incorporated in the exhaust system, and the USA authorities were forced some years ago to insist that cars used in that country are so equipped, because cities such as Los Angeles were being rendered almost uninhabitable by a permanent, eye-irritating, lung-inflaming, chemical smog resulting from an interaction between exhaust fumes and ozone in the atmosphere, catalyzed by bright sunshine.

The blood carbon monoxide level of somebody exposed for half an hour to London traffic fumes during the rush hour is raised as much as by smoking a couple of cigarettes.

Lead, projected from exhausts in the form of a tasteless aerosol, is the most damaging pollutant produced by cars. It is added to petrol to increase fuel efficiency and to act as a lubricant, but, at a modest extra cost (£40 or £50) engines can be built which run efficiently on lead-free petrol.

The need to reduce the level of lead in the environment is due to the fact that, swallowed with contaminated food, and breathed in from the air, it accumulates in the body and damages the brain and the blood. Children with above 'normal' blood lead levels (which would include at least some hundreds of thousands of children in the UK) have a lower than average IQ, and may have overt behavioural problems, such as an inability to concentrate, and hyperactivity. They are less accomplished readers and spellers. Other research has suggested that lead in the blood of pregnant women, which crosses the placenta and enters the foetus, may be a cause of stillbirths, and of damage to the chromosomes, leading to congenital defects.

Leaded petrol is certainly a major, and possibly the major, source of environmental contamination by the metal. Lead-laden exhaust fumes are not only breathed in by citizens living cheek by jowl with motor-ridden streets, they also fall on soil and crops, poisoning grass and cattle, so that lead from petrol is swallowed with food by millions who are lucky enough to live in places where the air is relatively free of automobile excrement.

Some countries, including the United States, Japan, Australia, West Germany and Sweden, have already committed themselves to a transition to completely lead-free petrol, and in 1982 the British Government announced that the permitted level of the poison in petrol sold in the UK was to be reduced by a little less than two thirds by 1985. This announcement led to anger among lobbyists who held that nothing short of a total ban on leaded petrol was acceptable in view of the accumulating evidence in support of the idea that there is no *safe* level of lead in the environment, or in the blood of people. But the Government remained firm, arguing that the cost to the automobile and oil industries of a total ban would be too great, and that in any case, owing to the multi-national nature of the motor industry, such a step would need the cooperation of other European countries.

*

Addressing a World Symposium on Asbestos, held in Montreal in 1982, Professor William Nicholson of Mount Sinai Medical School, New York, said that in that year 8000 workers in North America would die of cancer as a result of being exposed to the mineral dust, and that the death toll would rise to 10,000 a year by 1990. Three months later the US Manville Corporation, the world's largest asbestos firm, though economically sound, stunned the financial community by filing an application for technical bankruptcy to protect itself against some 70,000 current and expected claims made by asbestos-damaged workers, or users, or their surviving relatives, which could produce a final bill of US$2 billion. At the same time it was revealed that Britain's largest asbestos company, Turner and Newall, expected to pay out £6.6 million during the year in compensation to workers suffering from asbestos-related diseases.

That same year the British Government announced a general tightening-up of safety regulations, and a halving of the permitted level of asbestos dust in factory air, and in future manufacturers breaking the regulations could go to prison, instead of merely facing fines. But nobody suggested that further use of the uniquely valuable material should be banned altogether. That would cost far too much money. There are possible substitutes, but they are much more expensive.

That, unfortunately, is the trouble. Profits (or losses) always seem to be more tangible, and of more immediate importance, than any risks to our physical wellbeing. As a trades union lady said during a British television programme examining the relationship between the jobs people do and their chances of dying too soon of cancer, 'It is very, very unhealthy to be unemployed.' She was siding with the bosses in deploring too easy an attribution of cancer deaths to industrial environments, because she didn't want too many merely suspect processes to be banned. Prohibitions of industrial activities which have been proved bad for health don't just hit shareholders – they cost jobs.

Leaded petrol and asbestos are only two examples of agents causing death and disease which we have introduced into the environment, and which are therefore the cause of a significant amount of suffering which need not have occurred at all. Given the will, they are removable. Some other man-made causes of ill health, such as dioxin, which was released when the chemical plant at Seveso in Italy exploded, or plutonium, the long-lived radioactive carcinogen generated in atomic power stations, are not so easily disposed of. They are a threat to the health of future generations who will have had no say in their creation.

*

Every second, somewhere in the world, one, two, three, or even four people are catching syphilis or gonorrhoea. If the victim is lucky and receives prompt and efficient treatment, the infection may prove to be no more than a passing nuisance. But for the depressingly large number of the victims (many of them young) venereal disease results in prolonged sickness, sterility, or in extreme cases death.

Gonorrhoea is by far the commoner of the two principal venereal contagions, occurring (according to the country) 10 to 50 times more frequently than syphilis. In Britain, for example, there is now less syphilis than there was just after World War II. But this can be small cause for satisfaction in view of the fact that in the world at large over three million new syphilitic infections occur each year. And taking gonorrhoea and syphilis together, venereal disease is showing an alarming increase everywhere.

Now a new, so far untreatable, and uniformly fatal infection has been added to the list. AIDS (acquired immunodeficiency syndrome) first caused concern in the USA during 1982. The infection, a virus, progressively destroys the body's immune system so that victims eventually succumb to an overwhelming infection or may develop a peculiarly lethal cancer. Some 500 sufferers had been identified by the end of 1982, but by mid-1984 between 60–70 new cases were being diagnosed each month in New York City alone, and the disease has spread throughout the world. One expert predicted a toll of a million deaths from AIDS by the turn of the century.

Originally it was thought that the risk of contracting AIDS was confined to promiscuous homosexual men, but it soon became apparent that the virus could be spread through blood transfusions and the use of blood products of the kind needed by haemophiliacs, and by mid-1984 there were indications that it might be transmitted through heterosexual intercourse as well. A Yale University team had gained some apparent success by transplanting victims with pieces of thymus gland (which produces defence cells) taken from babies. The transplants were not rejected because the recipients had lost the capacity to react to foreign tissues, but it remained to be seen how long they would survive in an infected host.

In the immediate postwar years a dramatic reduction in VD was achieved within the developed nations, so while 45,000 new

cases of gonorrhoea were recorded in Britain in 1945, by 1950
the figure had fallen to 17,000. The newly available antibiotics
played an important part in bringing about this great improvement, for an untreated, or inadequately treated victim of
gonorrhoea can continue to spread the disease for months or
years. A penicillin-treated patient is generally safe within a
couple of weeks.

Then the picture changed again, and by the middle of the
1950s the graph of VD in Britain and elsewhere had begun to
take an upward swing, which has continued ever since. Over
the past quarter century gonorrhoea among men has increased
by more than 200 per cent, and among women by over 500 per
cent. Most disturbingly there has been a three or fourfold rise in
the proportion of infected girls still in their teens, who account
for over one-third of the total. There has been an even greater
increase of 'lesser' venereal infections, such as genital herpes.

How is it (since modern treatment is so effective and so freely
available) that sexually transmitted diseases have not become a
plague of the past, together with such previously common and
destructive infections as tuberculosis or smallpox?

There are some obvious contributory factors. Ignorance is
one of them. Thus, for example, the assumption that VD is an
affliction peculiar to rogues, vagabonds, and loose women, and
that the subject need not concern 'decent' members of society.
This is quite untrue. In Britain now only some five per cent of
venereal disease is traceable to prostitutes. They know their job
too well to court trouble by consorting with obviously infected
men, and they are also keenly aware of the signs and symptoms
which call for treatment. Most VD in the western world is
spread by amateurs who don't appreciate the odds. Promiscuity contributes a good deal. The highest incidence of
syphilis and gonorrhoea is found in the 18–24 age group, within
which young, unmarried men and women, at the peak of their
sexual activity, frequently change sexual partners. The way
people move around these days also helps. Wars, immigrations,
business trips, package tours, and long distance lorry driving
are among latterday activities which result in large numbers of
people, particularly men, finding themselves free from normal
inhibitions and restraints, so that, seeking to satisfy their sexual
needs in strange places, they pick up infections, and then
spread them around. In other words, VD is truly a social

disease, and not in the euphemistic sense in which the term was used a couple of generations back. VD is a fine example of an affliction which flourishes because of the manner in which people behave, despite the best (and it is a very good best) that curative medicine can achieve.

*

American studies have shown that high levels of unemployment within a community are associated with increases in heart and kidney disease, cirrhosis of the liver, homicide, and higher rates of admission to mental hospitals. (The higher incidence of liver cirrhosis is hardly surprising, since many unemployed, faced with idleness and hopelessness, are liable to drink more and eat less – a destructive combination. One British steel worker, sacked in 1982 because of the recession, told radio listeners how he had managed to spend the whole of his £10,000 redundancy money on drink in three short months.)

In 1981 Professor William Linford Rees, an eminent London psychiatrist, called for a long-term study into the precise effects of unemployment on morbidity and mortality. A few months later Dr Gerard Vaughan, then Minister for Health, confidently told the House of Commons that 'an excellent' pilot study had failed to demonstrate that unemployment breeds disease. He did have the grace to reveal that this momentous investigation had involved only 22 families.

The significance of this minor parliamentary happening lies in the fact that Dr Vaughan is also an eminent psychiatrist, who, before accepting political office, had been a consultant on the staff of Guy's Hospital in London. He therefore knows all about medical statistics, and would certainly have understood that the enquiry which he quoted (in defending his government against the charge that its economic policies were damaging the health of citizens) was far too small either to establish or rebut any cause and effect relationship between illness within a family and the breadwinner being out of work. Thus his stance provided not only a nice example of the manner in which politicians are willing to ignore the consequences to health of their acts of commission or omission when it is expedient so to do, but how, also, and for obvious reasons, they are anxious to hide any such callous proclivity. They will always strive to appear to be worshippers at the altar of Hygeia, quoting any 'expert' evidence which favours such an image, and disparaging work which puts their concern for achieving universal wellbeing in doubt. We can't rely on politicians to make the health of the community a top priority.

*

Around 14 out of every 1000 babies conceived in the United Kingdom die at some time between the 28th week of their mothers' pregnancies and the end of the first week after birth. They are either stillborn, or only survive as independent beings for a matter of hours or days. This may seem, statistically speaking (and ignoring the grief involved), an insignificant 'wastage' compared to the 150,000 foetuses destroyed by legal abortions every year.

But it is estimated that for every perinatal death, two or three badly constructed babies live on. And this figure includes only the overtly handicapped, such as mongols, or the victims of cerebral palsy, or spina bifida, or a cleft palate, or those who are blind or deaf or autistic, or who otherwise suffer from some demonstrable fault. An unknown but larger number of infants born into this world are probably less intelligent then they could have been, or more susceptible to infections and all manner of other ailments, or in other ways disadvantaged to the extent that their lives are the poorer for it.

Not so long ago all congenital defects were popularly regarded as acts of God, even if sometimes, perhaps, traceable to 'bad blood' in one or other of the parents, but unavoidable except by preventing 'poor stock' from reproducing.

The thalidomide affair made it tragically clear that, upon occasion, grossly deformed infants can be born to perfectly healthy parents as a result of some substance being taken by the mother during early pregnancy. Thus it is now accepted wisdom that pregnant women should avoid all unnecessary medication, and should (if they can) stop smoking, and stop drinking (some experts claim that even modest amounts of alcohol in the mother's blood can harm the foetus), and that before conceiving they should either have suffered or have been immunized against German measles, and that their bellies should not be exposed to non-essential diagnostic X-rays. That they should, in short, shun or be protected from a handful of agents *known* to be capable of damaging the foetus.

Far less general, however, is the view that most, if not all, congenital defects and perinatal deaths, and dangerous conditions such as prematurity and a low birth weight, could be avoided simply by paying adequate attention to the health and the way of life of parents (both mothers and fathers) *before* they conceive. This idea has its doughty champions, such as the members of a fairly new but vigorous British pressure group called Foresight, or the Association for the Promotion of Pre-Conceptual Care, founded by an enthusiastic amateur called Belinda Barnes, a Surrey housewife. Foresight has a lot of logic and a growing body of evidence on its side.

In 1980, for example, Richard Smithells, professor of paediatrics at Leeds University, together with colleagues from Leeds and elsewhere, published a preliminary report in the *Lancet* on an experiment designed to test the effect of supplying extra vitamins to women at special risk of giving birth to infants with neural tube defects (NTD). These are faults in the development of the brain and spinal cord, resulting in spina bifida or anencephaly (when the brain doesn't grow), and sufferers are born with paralyses of the lower part of the body (including incontinence), or mild to severe mental deficiency, or a mixture of the two. They may soon die, succumbing to infection, or survive partially or grossly disabled. Nothing can be done for anencephaly, but skilled surgery can preserve the lives of spina bifida victims who would have been beyond salvage not many years ago. (We shall consider the propriety of such operations later on.)

A mother who has given birth to, or aborted, one or more babies or foetuses with an NTD, has a much greater than average chance of producing a similarly deformed child if she becomes pregnant again, and may well seek medical advice before taking that chance. Smithells and his colleagues saw a number of such women, and offered them a multivitamin and iron preparation, to be taken regularly for at least 28 days before conception, and to be continued until the date of the second missed period, which is well after the developing nervous system has progressed beyond the stage at which the fault producing spina bifida can occur.

The incidence of NTD is greatest among women in social

classes III, IV and V, and such women are also more likely to eat nutritionally defective diets, so the suspicion arose that the malformation might be associated with inadequate vitamin levels in the mother during early pregnancy.

Of the women given vitamin supplements, 185 did become pregnant. A control group consisted of 264 women similarly at risk who had embarked upon a further pregnancy *without* seeking advice. The recurrence rate in the control group was five per cent, and in the treated group 0.6 per cent. There was thus the strong suggestion that the vitamins had done the trick. A larger trial has now been mounted, with government support.

At a conference mounted by Foresight only a week or so after Smithells' report on vitamins and NTDs appeared, Dr Roger Williams, a nutritionist on the staff of the University of Texas, said 'If all prospective human mothers could be fed as expertly as prospective mothers in the laboratory (he was talking about experimental rats), most sterility, spontaneous abortion, still-birth and premature birth would disappear. The birth of deformed and mentally retarded babies would be largely a thing of the past.'

He may have been overstating the case, but it does seem that a bit more 'preconceptual care', and a lot more attention to the nutritional value, rather than the cosmetic virtues, of the convenience 'junk' foods flogged in supermarkets could reduce the numbers of defective babies born dramatically.

*

Suicide, and particularly suicide among the young, has reached a disturbingly high level in the industrialized nations, but only within recent years, and this fact must say something about the communities within which such tragically needless deaths occur.

Clearly the make-up of the individuals concerned commonly plays a part, so that some people who appear to have everything going for them, like Marilyn Monroe, Tony Hancock, Kenneth Allsop, or Ernest Hemingway suddenly decide to end it all, while anti-heroes of the first class like Richard Nixon not only decide to soldier on, but actually make quite a go of it. Nevertheless, the fact that figures are rising suggests that some aspect or aspects of modern living swing the balance for many who destroy themselves.

Although suicide in Britain is commonest in the 55–60 age group, many adolescents do or attempt the deed, usually by poisoning. One Birmingham hospital alone admits at least 25 patients a year between the ages of 14 and 19 following suicide attempts.

An official Japanese report in 1978 revealed that 784 young people below the age of 20 had taken their own lives during the previous 12 months, with boys outnumbering girls by two to one. In about a third of all cases the fiercely competitive system of Japanese education was the overt cause. One 13-year-old schoolgirl jumped to her death from a 14th floor after failing to earn high marks in an arithmetic test. She left a note for her parents which read 'Papa, Mama, I have lost my confidence and the will to live. Please forgive me.' It is said that Japanese schoolchildren don't have friends any more, because they are all rivals. From the moment that they are capable of sensing the harsh realities of adulthood they are fed with the idea that if they don't do not just well, but very well at school, they're not going to stand a chance of getting the kind of job that will allow them to sustain their pride. In the USA 5000 young Americans between the ages of 15 and 24 now kill themselves each year.

Most of the young Japanese who seek self-destruction do so by hanging. The rest put their heads in gas ovens, or throw themselves under trains, or jump off high buildings, which implies that they all really do mean to end up dead. By contrast all the children admitted to that Birmingham hospital had attempted self-poisoning. Moreover girls outnumbered boys by five to one.

This suggests that many of the English children didn't really want to die, or, as a British psychiatrist has put it, they didn't 'want either to die or live, but do both at the same time', and that their act was a dramatic expression of discontent with the circumstances in which they found themselves – a gesture of the 'see what you've made me do now' variety, rather than a determined desire to be done with the world. So perhaps British children find themselves a bit less under pressure than Japanese boys and girls, but both seem to have departed tragically from the state of innocence anybody over the age of, say, 40, recalls as typifying childhood.

When I was a boy the very idea that a child would want to end its own life would have seemed an obscenity. Children, however poor their households, and however cold, hungry, and possibly even frightening, their day-to-day lives, were supposed to be immune from the kind of hopelessness that seizes an adult who knows (or feels) that he's failed.

Strangely, and in contrast to the trend in other developed nations, fewer British adults are killing themselves, although increasing numbers are making suicide attempts. Materialists have claimed that the fall in actual deaths is mostly due to the change to North Sea gas, which is relatively so harmless that the old, painless, wonderfully efficient, and erstwhile almost universally available method of *felo de se* – putting your head in a gas oven – is now denied despondent UK citizens. The less materialistic give credit to the Samaritans, the 'help-at-the-end-of-a-telephone' counselling organization, founded in 1953 by the Rev Chad Varah 'to befriend the suicidal and despairing'. Certainly the fall in successful suicide attempts has paralleled the expansion and use of the service.

But why the sickening upsurge in childhood suicides in the western world? One theory is that today's children are exposed prematurely to too many unpleasant aspects of the world of adults.

A year or so ago a senior physician, bemoaning Man's estate, told me that he believed that the most malign influence acting upon the nation within the past half century has been the British Broadcasting Corporation. I was appalled to hear such an obscurantist view, but I have since wondered whether the old-fashioned fellow might not have had some reason on his side. As a result of the flood of fact and fiction concerning an anguished planet now poured out in picture and sound during all the waking hours, seven days a week, even small children are invited to take a cynical view of the institution of marriage, and of kings and captains, and of the idea of justice, and of the belief that our destiny is in the hands of an omnipotent and beneficent God. You have to be fairly tough-minded, or else insensitive and unimaginative, to contemplate man's inhumanity to man without experiencing despair. The young do not lack imagination, and they are sensitive, and perhaps, nowadays, their minds are battered too constantly and too soon by a flood of ugly truths.

*

So-called iatrogenic disease – illness resulting from treatment – is now responsible, or partly so, for about five per cent of all hospital admissions, and one authority has claimed that some 30 per cent of patients, once in hospital, suffer some kind of unwanted effect from the drugs they are given. The numbers similarly affected in the community at large must be very much greater still.

Over-enthusiastic and injudicious therapy is no new thing. Louis XIII is said to have suffered 212 enemas, 215 purgations, and 47 bleedings in the course of a single year, and a canon of Troyes was once sued for the cost of 2190 enemas administered to him over a period of two years. However, modern drugs have a far greater potential for harm, and are far more widely available, and are far more recklessly dispensed than the ancient nostrums. We shall be looking at some of the ways in which surgeons, as well as physicians, manage to do their customers more harm than good.

*

Much of that disturbing 25 per cent rise in invalidism and sick leave mentioned earlier in this chapter, which has occurred in the UK over the past quarter century, is attributable to a catalogue of somewhat vague complaints such as sprains and strains, diarrhoea, nervous debility, headache, backache, migraine, and psychoneuroses.

Such diagnoses describe symptoms rather than identifiable faults in the functioning of the body beautiful. Somebody with appendicitis has an inflamed and infected appendix. Somebody with breast cancer has a growth of abnormal and destructive cells. Somebody with osteoarthritis has rough, grating joint surfaces, visible on an X-ray. But somebody with a headache or a backache has a pain, has a pain, has a pain, and somebody with diarrhoea has loose stools – an affliction suffered sometimes, for example, by students about to sit an examination who have perfectly normal guts.

Nobody would suggest that backache is never the result of a real fault in bone, muscle, or ligament, or that migraine is never the result of a true allergy to some substance which somehow sparks off strange happenings in the head. But the newly popular ailments are characterized by the fact that they are unpleasant *feelings* people have about themselves and their bodies.

The latter-day medical reasons for absence from work are largely complaints which the doctor can only assess on the patient's say-so. And there is good evidence that they occur most frequently among those who suffer less than satisfactory daily lives.

A study of London office workers has shown that those who have tiresome journeys to work, involving four or more stages (from bus to train to tube and so on) take 20 per cent more sick leave than their colleagues who enjoy easier rides.

Sickness absences plummet when imaginative managements ensure that workers are shown that they are valued, are told how their jobs contribute to a worthwhile end product, and are given some opportunity to use their judgement and make decisions.

Dons, judges, bookies, gamekeepers, and others able to do their own thing in their own way have the lowest sickness rates of all. Professional men take, on average, less than four days sick leave in a year. An unskilled labourer takes 18.

So while major stresses, like crushing debt, and bereavement, and thwarted ambition, and an unkind spouse, can, it seems, foster the development of killing conditions like heart disease and cancer, it also appears that the sheer dreariness of a wage slave's day can make people sick.

This doesn't mean that we have become a nation of lead-swingers. The out-and-out malingerer is probably a rare bird. But the large and increasing number of citizens who find their work onerous and a bore regard the rheums and aches and melancholies which afflict us all from time to time as acts of God which allow them to enjoy a brief unplanned respite from the treadmill with an easy conscience. They don't necessarily invent their afflictions. They simply make the most of them. And probably, more often than not, they convince *themselves* that they're unfit for work.

*

In this opening chapter I have set out to show that a very high proportion of the disorders afflicting the bodies and minds of people living in this last half of the 20th century are either caused or exacerbated by the way we behave and function as individuals and as a herd. So what are the chances of so reordering our attitudes and affairs that we (or rather our children and our children's children) can all live well and zestfully until we die?

In 1980 the *Guardian* newspaper in Britain published the main conclusions of a secret report on smoking and health produced almost ten years earlier by Whitehall officials, which had remained hidden until some 'mole' spilt the beans. It was a hard, cynical document which had been compiled by an interdepartmental committee of civil servants from the Department of Health and Social Security, the Scottish Home and Health Department, the Treasury, the Department of Trade and Industry, Customs and Excise, and (perhaps most sinister of all) the Central Statistical Office.

This committee of some of the more senior of our humble and obedient servants claimed that a reduction in smoking would be paralleled by an equal reduction in invalidism and premature deaths, but that the consequences of such an 'improvement' in the health of the nation would be unacceptable. The moguls of Whitehall pointed out that if only two out of every five smokers kicked the habit, the 'state' would have to face the problem of caring for an extra 100,000 old people every year. So any reduction in the cost of caring for the victims of tobacco poisoning would be more than offset by the extra cost of the retirement pensions which the state would have to pay to the unwanted survivors.

Moreover, if people stopped spending so much of their income on such a heavily taxed commodity as tobacco, they would have much more money left for the purchase of other and less revenue-producing goods, such as food, and videorecorders, and foreign cars, and so on. The committee calculated that over a five year period a 20 per cent reduction in cigarette consumption would reduce the balance of payments by a, to them, horrific £50m (and God knows what it would cost today). Thus were our Lords and Masters presented with several 'good' reasons for not trying too hard to alter the nation's smoking habits, in addition to the more obvious penalties of lost revenue and lost jobs.

In 1982 the London *Times* published extracts from advice given by a market research firm to Brown and Williamson, a

US subsidiary of British American Tobacco Industries, the world's largest tobacco company. Among other things, B&W were exhorted to present cigarettes to young people as 'part of the illicit pleasure category' and 'one of the few initiations into the adult world'. The firm was told that 'For the young starter, a cigarette is associated with introduction to sex life, with courtship, with smoking pot and keeping late study hours.' The researchers said 'To the best of your ability (considering some legal constraints) relate the cigarette to "pot", wine, beer, sex, etc. Don't communicate health or health-related points.'

In 1982, also, the British government, revealing the results of its latest round of negotiations with the tobacco barons concerning 'voluntary' agreements over the labelling and promotion of their murderous wares, boasted that the industry had agreed to give £11m over three years to fund a Health Promotion Research Trust, which would pursue its noble aims by all means 'other than studies designed directly or indirectly to examine the use and effects of tobacco products'. As (one imagines) part of a *quid pro quo* for this munificent gesture, the barons were able to reject a suggestion that packets of cancer sticks should carry a label saying that they 'cause bronchitis, lung cancer and heart disease' because they feared that this might give the survivors of deceased smokers grounds for claiming damages.

Alcohol is a poison which can kill directly, destroying the liver, or doing grave damage to the brain, heart, kidneys, gut, and other parts. Drink plays a part in over half of all violent crimes in addition to its major contribution to road deaths. Alcohol-related absenteeism, inefficiency, and accidents cost British industry maybe £500 million a year. The malaise is worldwide. Drunkenness is one of the major problems facing Soviet society. An estimated 700,000 Britons now drink to the extent that they suffer some palpable harm from the habit. The British government has refused to publish details of a report submitted to it in 1979 by its Central Policy Review Staff (the Think Tank) which recommended, *inter alia*, more restrictions on the licensing of liquor outlets, a big rise in drink taxes, tougher drink and driving laws, and an enquiry in the influence of drink advertising. (The report was leaked in 1982 by Professor Kettil Bruun of the Institute of Sociology at Stockholm University, who had got hold of a copy.) Instead, the government issued a heavily bowdlerized version of the document, entitled *Drinking Sensibly*. In 1980 the British Treasury garnered a massive £2500 million from duty paid on alcohol sold in the land.

In 1979 a British cabal called the Politics of Health Group (admittedly an association of persons with well-developed left-wing sympathies, but not to be disbelieved just because of that) published a booklet entitled *Food and Profit*, in which it was noted that processed foods now absorb more than half of the money we spend on edibles. It went on to explain that 'One of the most dramatic effects of this processing has been to *separate* appearance and taste from nutritional value. The nourishment can be removed, and colouring and flavouring, including sugar, added so that the object looks as good as or better than the real thing, and the taste can be made palatable. And, of course, many foods are put in packages so that they cannot be judged at all, except by the picture on the wrapper. The result is that our judgement of food – our so-called free choice – is more and more under the control of the food manufacturers.' In other words, we eat what we are persuaded to eat, and we buy food because it is available, or because it looks good, or perhaps because it tastes good. Hardly ever do we buy food because it *is* good. In that same year the US Federal Trade Commission stated that it would consider whether television ads for tooth-rotting confections should be banned during children's viewing hours (whatever those may be in this permissive age), and whether to require 'fun-food' advertisers (that is to say the people who flog seductively hued and titillatingly flavoured carbohydrate rubbish), to emphasize the need for a decent diet. An executive of General Foods said of the commission's ponderings that they were 'more than bizarre. This a frightening and dangerous enterprise'.

A year earlier a Mr Tim Fortescue, secretary general of Britain's Food and Drink Industries Council, had responded to suggestions that it might be a part of the government's job to persuade and make it easier for the masses to eat sensibly, by saying 'That means that someone else should decide what you have to eat, and the fact that you might like to eat this or that should not be paramount in your choice of food'. He seemed to forget what Tesco, Finefare, and Unilever have been doing with their massive advertising budgets all these years. In the event, of course, nothing whatever has been done by the governments of either Britain or the USA to stop their citizens eating themselves to death.

The so-called TT races on the Isle of Man, when youngsters drive motorcycles at excessive speeds round awkward roads, regularly cause deaths and dreadful injuries. A couple of years or so ago, when the practice run-ups to the event had already cost lives, a young competitor was asked on the radio whether the tragedies had given him pause to think about the sense of flinging his body into the dangerous joust. 'Well, not really,' he replied. 'After all, if you're goin' to coppit, you're goin' to coppit, ain't you? I mean, if you was lyin' down in bed, the ceiling might fall down and smash you.'

In the face of fatalism of that kind, and official inertia, and 'political considerations', and the lust after profits, and the pleasure to be derived from so many of the indulgences which do us no good, it seems unlikely that we shall change the way we live at any great rate, so we are going to have to rely upon doctors to patch up the damage we do to ourselves for some long time to come.

Let us, then, examine the way they go about the task.

CHAPTER TWO

Doctors and Disease

Most doctors are not particularly interested in health. By inclination and training they are devoted to the study of disease. It is sick, not healthy people, who crowd their surgeries and out-patient departments and fill their hospital beds, and it is the fact that the population can be relied upon to provide a steady flow of sufferers from faults of the mind and of the flesh that guarantees them a job and an income in harsh times as in fair.

Not so long ago even the treatment (let alone the prevention) of disease took second place to diagnosis and prognosis, since so few effective remedies were available. The great physicians became renowned for their ability to pin an accurate label on their customers' complaints, and for their success in foretelling the outcome of a sickness, rather than for any real capacity to influence the course of events. The sections on treatment in medical textbooks, even as recently as 30 or 40 years ago, were commonly both brief and padded out with vague platitudes such as 'attention should be paid to the bowels', or 'adequate rest should be ensured by the administration of sedatives as required'. Doctors were valued (and valuable) for their priestly rather than their therapeutic skills.

Times have changed, so that now, too often, powerful and potentially harmful agents and techniques are employed in an effort to deal with patients' 'complaints' *before* a firm diagnosis has been reached, or before the likely benefits to the sufferer have been properly assessed.

Thus many a family doctor will prescribe penicillin for every customer presenting with a sore throat without considering the chances that the discomfort may well be due to a virus or some other factor that penicillin can't affect. Anxious patients are sent away with a prescription for a tranquillizer without an attempt to discover the cause of the anxiety, or whether it could be removed. Victims of advanced cancer are subjected to distressing procedures, and filled with drugs which cause them added misery, in a vain effort to halt the disease, when they ought to be nursed to an easy death.

The trouble is that today's doctor, far from being short of effectual therapeutic weapons, has a huge armamentarium of remedies, and since 'masterly inactivity' requires a confidence and strength of mind not universally possessed, over-treatment or inappropriate treatment, rather than lack of treatment is the hazard now faced by many of the customers who go to the medical trade for help.

*

Lord Lister's concept of antiseptic surgery, which he developed 120 years ago, together with the slightly earlier introduction of anaesthetics, led to an explosive expansion of the surgeon's capabilities which shows no sign of slowing down. In Britain some two million surgical operations are performed each year. They are all, of course, designed to better the lot of the patients concerned, even if it is only a matter of relieving the nuisance of an ingrowing toenail, but a high proportion of them save or prolong life, or alleviate some serious complaint.

Within the long catalogue of routine procedures (routine only to the extent that they are everyday happenings) a few groups of operations stand out because they so frequently succeed in transforming the lives of the patients involved in a manner which they commonly describe as 'miraculous'. These 'miracles' include open heart surgery (particularly the replacement of faulty valves), the removal of cataracts, the cure of a certain type of deafness, and the replacement of arthritic hips.

The heart valves ensure the forward flow of blood, opening when the chambers behind them contract, and closing when they relax, preventing reflux. A valve may become distorted by disease so that the opening narrows and the flaps can't shut properly. The process is gradual and puts an increasing strain on the heart muscle, which has to work harder to force blood through an increasingly small outlet, and also in order to pump forward more blood per beat, or per minute, to make up for the quantity which leaks back in again when the chamber behind the faulty valve relaxes. At first the heart muscle thickens in order to cope with the extra load, but later weakens, allowing the organ to dilate, and fails to push out sufficient blood to cope with the body's needs. Heart failure has a domino effect, and disturbs the function of organs both downstream and upstream of the inefficient pump, but the principal disability of which the sufferer is aware is breathlessness. To start with any sharp exertion, like running for a bus, becomes distressing or impossible. The incapacity progresses until the victim lies propped up in bed, fighting for breath merely to stay alive.

The two valves most commonly affected are the mitral, lying between the left auricle and the left ventricle, and the aortic, at the root of the great vessel channelling oxygenated blood from the left ventricle to the body. Sometimes both are damaged.

Unfortunates who are crippled by heart valve disease, and who, untreated, face an early death (and they are often young, or in the prime of life) can be cured by having the faulty part or parts replaced by a metal and plastic substitute (some kinds are like the ping-pong-ball-in-a-cage valves on snorkel masks), or by a heart valve obtained from an animal (usually a pig), or from a human corpse. (Since natural valves have no blood supply, obtaining the little nutrition they need from the blood bathing their surface, they are not open to attack by the white blood cells which cause rejection of other transplanted organs like hearts and kidneys.)

Valve replacement demands great expertise. While the operation is in progress the patient's circulation has to be maintained by a heart-lung machine. The whole manoeuvre is at least as great a feat of surgical legerdemain and technological wizardry as a heart transplant operation.

The success rate is high, with up to 95 per cent of aortic, and 85 per cent of mitral valve replacements resulting in a full restoration of heart function (the battered heart muscle rapidly recovers once relieved of the unnatural load). Some 2500 of these operations are performed in Britain annually.

A cataract is a clouding of the crystalline lens of the eye, which is situated behind the pupil. The whole lens becomes increasingly opaque, causing a progressive loss of vision until total blindness occurs. Full vision can be restored by removing the affected lens. In this delicate operation a small semicircular incision is made in the tough fibrous capsule of the eyeball where the white of the eye meets the upper half of the transparent cornea which overlies the iris and the pupil. Special forceps are inserted through the cut and hooked on to the lens, which is pulled out. The incision is closed by fine sutures which were loosely inserted before the cut was made, so that, when tied, they produce an accurate closure. The lost focusing power is restored by the use of strongly convex spectacles or special contact lenses. In otherwise normal eyes the restoration of vision is uniformly excellent. About 40,000 cataract operations take place in the UK each year.

One common cause of deafness is otosclerosis, a disease which can occur at any age from young adulthood onwards, and which affects an estimated one in 250 of the adult population. Behind the ear drum lies a small chamber called the middle ear, and beyond this lies the inner ear, a system of curved canals set in the bone of the skull which house the organs of balance, and also the nerve 'microphone' which converts sound vibrations into electrical impulses suitable for analysis by the brain. The middle ear (about a centimetre in diameter) contains an articulated train of three very small bones (ossicles) which amplify the vibrations of the drum and convey them to the mouth of the inner ear 'microphone'. In otosclerosis the innermost of these ossicles, called the stapes (because of its resemblance to a stirrup), becomes welded to the bone surrounding the opening of the inner ear microphone by an abnormal growth of tissue, and gradually loses the capacity to vibrate. Deafness results.

In an operation called stapedectomy, which is one of the most delicate and intricate in modern surgery, the stuck stapes is removed and replaced by a plastic substitute, which is fixed at one end to the remaining ossicles, and at the other end to a flap of tissue from a vein, used to cover the opening to the inner ear which removal of the stapes has exposed.

Stapedectomy can restore normal hearing to people who have been profoundly deaf for decades, and some 80 per cent of the 2500 patients undergoing the operation in the UK each year are improved to the extent that they no longer need a hearing aid.

Osteoarthritis is, after diseases of the heart and vessels, the commonest serious affliction of the elderly. The smooth cartilage which lines joints roughens, and the friction slowly wears it away, exposing the bone, which grows spurs, and grates. The resulting stiffness and pain is particularly severe and disabling when a large, weight-bearing joint like the hip is affected. Drugs can help many patients, but may altogether fail to relieve the suffering caused by a badly damaged joint. The modern surgical approach is to excise the diseased joint and replace it with an artificial substitute, and the technique has proved outstandingly successful for hips.

The hip joint is deeply buried in thick muscle. After it has been exposed the upper end of the thigh bone (the femur) is removed, and a new metal or metal and plastic spherical head on a long shank is fixed into the marrow cavity of the sawn femur with cold-curing acrylic cement. The cement does little damage to the bone cells lining the cavity, and this is important because bone is a living tissue, which 'dissolves' and replenishes itself, changing its structure to meet the stresses placed upon it. The round head of the new part is seated in a plastic or metal cup which is attached to the site of the original hip joint socket in the wall of the pelvis. The new parts must be shaped and constructed to stand up to large loads, and to convey pressures, tensions and torques to the remaining thigh bone in as natural fashion as possible.

One successful and widely used artificial hip joint was designed by Professor John Charnley, of Manchester University, who died in 1982. He fused engineering, biological and surgical skills and understandings in producing an artificial hip which works, for which considerable achievement he became the first orthopaedic surgeon ever to be elected to a fellowship of the Royal Society. Every year some 19,000 dreadfully crippled British patients regain mobility and lose all pain as a result of hip replacements.

So, just like the Pickwick, the Owl, and the Waverley pen, surgeons frequently come as a boon and a blessing to men. Strangely, however, it seems to be their more perverse and ill-considered activities which gain not just the widest attention, but also the greatest adulation from the herd.

*

I shall never forget how I learned about the world's first transplant of a human heart. At the time I was editing *New Scientist*, and on a Monday afternoon I ran out of tobacco, so I walked out of my office in my shirt sleeves to go to the kiosk at the corner, leaving my glasses on the desk. That meant I was purblind, but I could still see enough to read the 72-point banner headline on the top copy of the pile of *Evening Standards* outside the tobacconist's door.

'FIRST HUMAN HEART TRANSPLANT', it read. 'Oh, the bloody fools!' I shouted out, to the discomfiture of passing Londoners, who resent overt demonstrations of emotion. My loud and reflex protest was made despite the fact that, without my specs, I couldn't tell who had done the deed, or why, or where. I just knew it for a silly act, bound to generate many more problems than it solved, and having small relevance to the task of medicine, which is the relief of suffering. That was way back in December 1967, and nothing that has happened since has caused me to change my mind.

The pioneer of heart transplants was, of course (and as I discovered as soon as I could get my specs back on), the soon-to-be-famous Dr Christiaan Barnard, and this ultimate folly of medical prestidigitation was memorialized in an issue of the *South African Medical Journal* which appeared within days of the event. The whole magazine was devoted to the happening, and, apart from the articles, the ads were mostly in praise of the miracle which had taken place at Groote Schuur Hospital, with messages such as 'Well done, Chris!' from the suppliers of the ligatures used, and so on.

But I treasure my copy of that issue of the magazine, because it brought to marvellous life the old joke that 'the operation was a success, but the patient died'. One of the articles, signed, *inter alia*, by Christiaan Barnard, was headed 'Successful Human Heart Transplant'. On the front page of the journal, edged in black, was an announcement regretting the death of Louis Washkansky, the victim of the great experiment, who had survived the surgery for a little under three weeks.

It wasn't really a joke of course. It was a tragedy. But the death of the patient did nothing whatever to diminish the awe accorded to Dr Barnard by the world at large.

A couple of days *after* Washkansky's death Barnard was lionized in Washington, met Adrian Kantrowitz and Michael DeBakey (then America's best-known heart surgeons, who described his feat as 'a very great achievement'), and was the subject of a nationwide television broadcast.

This enthusiasm for applauding the fact of the heart transplant adventure and ignoring the results still characterizes the public, and even much of the professional response to the undertaking.

Barnard (who had by then been voted third most popular man in the world after President de Gaulle and Pope Paul in a French poll, and named Man of the Year by *France-Soir*) returned to Cape Town on New Year's Day 1968 (ten days after Washkansky's disappearance from the circus) and, next morning, performed his second transplant on Philip Blaiberg, a 59-year-old dentist. Blaiberg survived to walk out of the hospital with his new heart, and to bask in fame, and to enjoy a free supply of beer for life from a friendly neighbourhood brewery, until he too succumbed to the infection which almost inevitably, sooner or later, kills transplant patients, unless their bodies reject the foreign flesh of the transferred organ first.

Once Barnard had taken the initiative, a heart transplant epidemic spread round the world. Two took place in America within 48 hours, then one in India, and three in quick succession in France. In May 1968 Frederick West became Britain's first heart transplant patient, and the surgical team responsible at London's National Heart Hospital held a press conference next morning in an atmosphere resembling that following the defeat of the Argentinians in the Falklands. There was a total lack of serious, objective comment. The principal actors, flanked by a supporting cast of nurses, porters, and technicians, waved miniature Union Jacks in the faces of the assembled mob of press, radio and television hacks, who shoved, shouted, and swore in the desperate competition to get 'quotes' and pictures. Frederick West died 46 days later from the same kind of infection that had killed Blaiberg.

At the end of July a Mr Gordon Ford became the world's 24th and Britain's second heart transplant victim. When he died, 57 hours later, only six of the remaining 23 were still alive, most of them having perished with days or hours.

During this heady period surgeons in Houston, Texas, put a sheep's heart into a 47-year-old man who died on the spot, the British team attempted to give two dying patients pigs' hearts, and Christiaan Barnard prepared to put a baboon heart into a five-year-old boy, but, having opened the child's chest, decided that a valve replacement would be enough to save the lad's life. There is nothing intrinsically wrong with the idea of using spare parts from other animals to replace broken down components in Man except for the fact that the rejection problem is magnified many times, and at that stage little was known about how best to handle it in the far simpler human to human situation. These somewhat desperate ploys therefore seemed symptomatic of a feverish anxiety among the new stars of the transplant extravaganza to notch up further triumphs, and fast. Suitable human donors were then, and still are, rather thin on the ground, and they couldn't wait.

After a third disastrous British transplant, no more occurred in the UK for four years. The Health Department, whose Chief Medical Officer was then the wise and compassionate Sir George Godber, effectively forbade NHS surgeons to attempt the trick in NHS hospitals. There was, of course, no publicly proclaimed proscription of the procedure, for that would have amounted to a gross and overt interference with the sacred cow of 'clinical freedom', which is the cherished but quite illusory rule that every properly registered medical practitioner may, at his or her absolute discretion, do whatever he or she thinks best for any customer. The surgeons concerned were, instead, invited to consider whether the cost in money and effort and time of heart transplant operations could be justified in view of the many unsatisfied but fulfillable demands on an overstretched health service.

Needless to say, the transplanters bowed to the official will. After all, they had research grants, and merit awards (see Chapter 3), and possible honours, and similar matters to think about, and they would surely have appreciated the need to keep their yardarms clean.

A minor revolt was staged in 1973, not by any member of the original heart-swap team, but by Mr Magdy Yacoub, a thoracic surgeon, at Harefield Hospital, London, who put the heart of a 15-year-old boy road accident victim into the chest of a 56-year-old office manager who died within hours. Most people were surprised, for nothing had occurred to alter the situation as it had stood in 1968. Sir Keith Joseph, then Secretary of State for Social Services, said he had been told of the intended adventure the day before it happened, and that while the medical profession was free to do what it thought best for its patients, he would prefer it 'to defer any vast enthusiasm for this subject until the immunological problems are cleared up'. The idea that officialdom should presume to tell doctors what they could and could not do enraged John Cronin, a Labour MP who also happened to be a surgeon, and who thought it 'intolerable' that Yacoub's 'skill and discretion . . . should be interfered with by any government body'. Nevertheless, that was to be the last British transplant for quite some time, and as recently as 1977 the Health Department's Transplant Advisory Panel recommended that there should be no more such operations, having concluded from experience worldwide that the game wasn't worth the candle.

Meanwhile an American surgeon, Norman Shumway, had been quietly beavering away at heart-swop ops at Stanford University Medical Center in California. Since 1968 he has been doing about one every three weeks, and turning himself into the world's most experienced and successful practitioner of the sport. To begin with only about one in five of his patients survived the operation for a year, but by 1978 he was claiming a 60 per cent one year survival rate, and results equal to 'those attained by the best kidney transplant units'.

Shumway's results were used in support of some high pressure lobbying in Britain's corridors of power, for in 1979, and only two years after the uncompromising thumbs-down verdict from its own advisory panel, the Health Department performed a small U-turn, and gave the go-ahead for another spate of operations. Strangely, none of the country's pioneer transplanters took advantage of the new green light. Perhaps they had learnt their lesson. Instead the rebellious Mr Magdy Yacoub, and Mr Terence English of Papworth Hospital, near Cambridge, plunged in. By the autumn of 1982 about 40 transplants had been carried out at each of the two hospitals. Many of the patients had died within hours, days, or weeks of the operation. Others had gone home on their own two feet, feeling better than they had done for years. (Partly, perhaps, because of all the attention they received, and the better life style they had, perforce, to adopt, and partly also because some of the drugs they have to take to stave off rejection produce euphoria, at least to start with. It must also be great fun to wake up from the operation and discover you are still alive.) However, only a very lucky few had lasted long enough to celebrate their new heart's second re-birthday.

The Health Department's contribution to the cost of these pricey operations (about £25,000 a time at 1982 prices, more or less, according to how you do your costing), was modest, but shortly after transplants were resumed Papworth was given £300,000 by one millionaire, and Harefield was given the same by another, and that's how so many came to be done.

Contrary to popular belief, a heart transplant is not a particularly difficult operation. Of course, to do the job efficiently, you have to be a good and experienced heart surgeon, but the skills required, and the technology involved (such as the heart/lung machine, which maintains the circulation and aeration of the blood while the patient's own heart and lungs are out of action) were being employed with great success in open heart surgery (some more intricate and demanding than a transplant) for a decade and more before Barnard took the plunge.

But despite the fact that the necessary techniques had been well developed, the early transplants were wholly unjustifiable because the surgeons involved did not know how to deal with the rejection problem, and knew that they did not know, and were thus unable to offer their chosen subjects a reasonable chance of an added span of worthwhile life. They nevertheless persuaded desperately ill patients, presumably frightened of death, to offer themselves as experimental animals on the basis of a hope whose slenderness must have been concealed from them. This may not have been a wholly deliberate deception, since experts of all kinds committed to some new and exciting venture tend to be over-optimistic, and in any case it would be a poor sort of doctor who, in explaining a proposed line of treatment to a patient, dwelt largely on the chances of failure rather than success. But the pioneers were not that innocent of what they were about, and immediately after his assault on Louis Washkansky, Professor Barnard is reported to have said, 'Even if the patient is lost, a great deal will have been learnt and achieved from the operation.' It has been argued on behalf of the transplanters, and in defence of their persistence despite deplorable results, that a start has to be made somewhere, and that only by attempting unproved remedies can progress be made, and experience gained, so that the goal of a procedure that will benefit the suffering is finally achieved. This may be true, but it is surely questionable whether doctors have the right to induce their patients to take risks, or even endure discomfort, for the possible benefit of others, and it is beyond question that experiments which may do harm are irresponsible, and a dereliction of the duty of care, unless the result at which they are aimed is worth achieving.

In the case of heart transplants this is not the case. By the end of 1982 some 800 transplants had been carried out in 74 countries throughout the world. Some progress had been made in some centres in the techniques of controlling the rejection process, but although the occasional lucky recipient of a new heart had survived the surgery for ten years and more, and had, indeed, been given a significant extra span of worthwhile life, the great majority had gained nothing from the physical and mental trauma to which they and their families had been subjected, and would have been better off left to end their days in dignity and peace. No doubt the improvement will be maintained (if these operations go on being done), so that a higher proportion of patients do get some benefit from the procedure. It might even be that the rejection problem will finally be solved completely, so that the operation becomes routinely successful, on a par with the replacement of damaged valves. But that is not the point.

The point is that heart transplants are bad medicine because the technique can never make more than an insignificant impact upon the toll of premature death and suffering exacted by heart disease. Approximately 350,000 people die from this cause in England and Wales each year. If only half of these lives could, in theory, be salvaged by the provision of a replacement heart, the total cost would just about equal the entire budget of the NHS. But even if the money could be found (as, for example, by abandoning the Army and the Navy and the Air Force – defence costs about the same as health), there would be the little matter of finding the surgeons and the nurses and the operating theatres and the hospital beds and all the rest of the labour and equipment needed to service some 500 heart transplant operations *every day*.

There is one other minor point to be considered. Every recipient needs a donor. The major contributors of healthy spare parts are young people badly injured on the roads who have been taken to hospital still alive but with irreparably damaged brains. Transplant surgeons and their supporters therefore have a vested interest in sustaining and even increasing the carnage wrought by motor vehicles. It is a matter of killing Peter in order to have the chance of a long-odds gamble on saving Paul. Of course, the transplanters don't recognize this sorry equation. Instead they accept road deaths as an inevitable part of modern living, and point to the sad 'waste' of all the hearts and livers and kidneys which are *not* plucked out of still living but 'brain dead' bodies for insertion into someone else. Those who see a growing and long-term role for transplant surgery in the treatment of any common disease of major organs are implicitly expressing defeatism in the matter of the increasing, but, given the will, largely preventable toll exacted by the motor car.

One factor militating against the success of heart transplants is that the arterial degeneration which has damaged the heart to be replaced is not confined to that organ. It is a general disease, and the lungs are commonly also affected. So grafting a new heart into the chest is like putting new wine in an old bottle. Replacement hearts that last long enough often begin to show signs of the disorder which had corrupted the original organ. In any case, the 'new' hearts have to cope with pumping blood through the narrowed vessels of unhealthy lungs. The apparently logical solution is to give the patient not just a new heart, but a full new set of healthy heart and lungs. Mechanically the task is rather less complicated than putting in a heart alone, but the rejection problem is significantly increased. And it is rejection, or the attempts to suppress rejection, which account for the rapid demise of most heart transplant victims. So leaping into the heart/lung transplant business while the handling of heart-only swops is still so depressingly unsuccessful is rather like a gambler who has lost a fortune by a talent for picking losers desperately striving to recover his position by doubling his stakes.

Two of the more recent extravagances in the field are worth recording. In July 1984 Mr Yacoub put a new heart, the size of a large plum, into a baby girl, Hollie Roffey, when she was ten days old. Hollie had been born with a severe congenital malformation of her own heart, which could not have sustained her life. She died 18 days after the operation from an accumulation of complications, including a perforated bowel, kidney failure and pneumonia. In October a similarly afflicted two-week-old girl, known only as 'Baby Fae', was given a baboon's heart by Dr Leonard Bailey at the Lowma Linda University Medical

Center in California. She survived for a remarkable three weeks.

The baboon heart transplant was widely criticized as a frank experiment with small chance of success. The British operation was also criticized, not only because of the many unresolved problems surrounding the progress and aftercare of so small and young a patient, but also, by one leading cardiologist, on the grounds that the mortally deformed infant of young parents can probably be replaced, and that 'the formidable call on resources' arising from such heroic rescue efforts was such that 'their place in the responsible delivery of health care must be questioned'.

*

Kidney transplants are a less evidently futile exercise for two main reasons. In the first place far fewer people face death each year from kidney failure than the number who perish from heart disease. In Britain it is something like 2000 as compared to 350,000, and of the 2000 only some 60 per cent are deemed suitable for treatment. So, if kidney transplants worked, the cure could be provided for everyone who might benefit from the technique. Four transplants a day, with no weekend work, would settle the matter. Secondly, people without working kidneys can be kept alive, and reasonably active, by the use of kidney machines, to which they have to be connected twice or thrice a week for several hours. These machines were once regarded as the answer to the kidney failure problem, but their use does impose severe limitations on the freedom of the patients, who also have to stick to a somewhat tedious diet, and many of them never feel really fit. However, the availability of the machine is a great help to the transplant surgeons. Ill patients can be restored to reasonable health before an operation, so that their chances of surviving the immediate trauma are improved. They can be kept well for months or even years until a fresh, well-matched kidney becomes available so that the need to take risks with less well-matched organs is avoided. Most importantly, if a transplanted kidney fails the patient does not die but is put back on a machine to await a second operation. Some patients receive three or four new kidneys over a period of time.

In some centres, such as Oxford, Cambridge, Minneapolis

and Melbourne, the advantages of having machines as an auxiliary method of treatment are skilfully exploited. Surgery is only performed on the most suitable patients, and provision is made for a return to an artificial kidney the moment a graft shows signs of failing. In an article published in the *Lancet* in 1975 it was revealed that the Melbourne workers were giving potential kidney donors drugs and extra fluids in the hours *preceding* death to ensure that their kidneys were in prime condition at the moment their hearts stopped beating. Treating the dying as transplant fodder before they are dead is not yet a practice generally accepted by society.

Under these very special circumstances the Melbourne team was able to claim that 80 per cent of the patients accepted for treatment were alive five years later, *either with a functioning transplant, or on a machine*. That is the point. The failures of the graft approach to the treatment of renal failure can be bailed out, time and again, by the waiting apparatus, and *still* be notched up as happily surviving beneficiaries of transplant surgery.

Now, an 80 per cent five year survival rate sounds pretty good, and the figure is far superior to anything achieved by the heart transplanters. But here are some less impressive facts. About 20 per cent of transplanted kidneys don't even start functioning. Only about half of all kidneys taken from unrelated dead donors are still functioning two years after transplantation, and losses continue thereafter. One third of all transplanted kidneys are rejected by the end of the first year. Results are much better with kidneys taken from living relatives, some two thirds of such grafts surviving for three years, but the ethics of taking an irreplaceable part (as opposed to, say, blood or bone marrow) from a healthy donor are questionable. In any case living donors can never provide more than a small percentage of the organs required for a full transplant programme, and unless they are carefully assessed for psychological robustness before being used, donors are likely to become unhappy and to develop hostility towards the recipient, whether or no the transplant succeeds. 'Good' results are only obtained at certain centres of excellence where a great deal of time, skill and money have been applied to perfecting the management of patients, so that whereas over 80 per cent of grafts last for three months in the best hands, only 14 per cent last that long in the worst. In most European countries and the USA almost all patients suffering from renal failure are treated by surgery or a machine at a cost which causes great concern. In Britain only good prospects (that is, otherwise physically and psychologically healthy adults, mostly under the age of 45) are taken on, and the rest are left to die. If British renal units treated the same proportion of kidney failure patients as the average European country does, then, by the time the demand had been fully satisfied, with the numbers finally dying balancing the new cases coming under care, the annual bill would exceed £200 million at 1980 prices.

Kidney transplant surgeons and their enthusiastic lay supporters frequently make emotive public statements suggesting that the procedure is a God-given answer to the problem of otherwise fatal renal disease, restoring valuable citizens like the mothers and fathers of young families to vigorous, productive and enjoyable life. They complain loudly that a parsimonious government and a lack of concern among potential donors combine to reduce the service that can be offered, so that many avoidable tragedies occur. In particular the surgeons castigate their medical colleagues for being ignorant of the need, and of the success of the technique, so that they don't bother to spot likely sources of spare organs among their patients, and don't notify the waiting transplant teams.

It is true that the procedure, combined with the use of machines, does postpone the deaths of around 1000 UK citizens annually, who then survive for varying periods, and often for several years. However, transplantation is far from being a once and for all salvage operation, after which the lucky recipients can forget their troubles and rejoin the herd. They are permanently on anti-rejection drugs which increase their susceptibility to infections and even to cancer. They face the prospect of repeated major surgery interspersed by spells on a kidney machine. Some patients enjoy interludes of wellbeing. Others are anxious, below par, and depressed, and find the extra life they have been given burdensome.

In short, transplants and machines are an inefficient and unpleasant answer to the problem of kidney failure, absorbing an unduly large share of finite resources of money, skills, energy and professional time which might be spent to better effect on other forms of care. I suspect that many doctors recognize this truth, and that this, rather than ignorance, is the cause of their lack of enthusiasm for the hunt for yet more spare parts. The public is being conned by the doubtless sincere champions of kidney grafts.

When I dared to propound this view in *New Scientist* a few years back I was rebuked in a letter to the Editor from three eminent Oxford medical academics, who sought to refute my 'irresponsible and inaccurate remarks'. (Enthusiasts, whether it be for nuclear deterrents or celibacy of the clergy, do tend to describe those who don't share their views as 'irresponsible'.) I don't think they did manage to refute any of my 'inaccurate' remarks. What they did manage was a revelation of the highly defensive attitude transplanters and their supporters adopt, which suggests a lack of confidence lurking somewhere down in the subconscious reaches of their minds. In particular, they boasted that the results of the transplant-cum-machine treatment of renal failure gives results which 'are far superior to the treatment of most types of cancer'. Others have used the same argument, and when you have to defend your performance by pointing to even less successful ventures, you are indeed showing symptoms of despair.

*

The results of cancer treatment *have* proved disappointing. The results of treatment for cancer of the breast, for example, are no better now than they were half a century ago. Faced with this grim situation, some cancer specialists tend to pull out all the stops in a desperate attempt to avoid defeat.

A year or so back a friend of mine in her forties developed cancer of the ovary. She was a cheerful, vigorous, hard-working jewel of a woman who raised the spirits of everybody she dealt with. Her breakdown was sudden. One day she was about her usual business, and on the next she suffered acute abdominal pain, and was taken to hospital. The pain soon disappeared, and never returned, but over the course of the next eight weeks or so she became progressively weaker, and thinner, and, most importantly, more and more discouraged.

Her cancer was inoperable. She was given chemotherapy. The pills made her sick and wretched far beyond any malaise that might be blamed on the disorder they were supposed to attack. She knew they were causing much of the distress and misery she felt, but, home again from hospital for a while, she faithfully and courageously swallowed the sickening tablets because of the hope held out to her that they would purge the poison in her belly, and put her back on her feet again, and let her return to the job and the associates she so clearly loved.

I say 'the hope held out to her', because I don't believe she ever really felt that hope herself. She said to me, once or twice in her sad time, 'They should just have let me go, and have done with it.' And she asked me more than once 'Are they doing me good? Are they going to work?'

When she said these things, I was with her as a friend, and not as her medical adviser, and since I didn't know exactly what she had been told, and since I knew I could only cause further worry and distress by contradicting whatever information she may have been given, I could not say what I believed, and I made such comforting and encouraging sounds as I was able to summon up, but felt my words futile.

After three or four weeks at home she was moved back to hospital again for the constant nursing care she had come to need. The pills she had learned to fear and dislike so much were stopped a week or 10 days before she died.

I don't believe she was ever told of her true state, and she was encouraged to think that the sickness engendered by the hated tablets must be endured because they could cure her disease. But I think that from the first she knew in her heart she was doomed, and I think she suspected, also, that she had to tolerate her distressing treatment more for her doctors' sakes than for her own.

This is not an unusual tale. Too many cancer patients have their last days or weeks or months made wretched by intensive treatment with drugs, or radiation, or both, when there is no reasonable prospect of a cure, and when they should have been allowed to die in dignity and peace.

Why does this happen? In part, perhaps, because the experts involved are unwilling to admit helplessness and defeat, and feel that they have to take some kind of aggressive action in the face of impending death. But there is a less emotional and, one might almost say, more cynical reason. The patients so treated are, to put the matter brutally, being used as experimental animals, and are being subjected to therapy with known ill-effects, not in the reasonable expectation that their lives can be saved, but because of a felt need to try this approach and that to a so far unsolved problem, in the hope that, eventually, a regime will be found that does relieve the distress and prolong the lives of future victims of the same disease.

Certainly there is a need for continuing trial and innovation, for only thus can skills be improved, and more effective help be offered to those in need, but the sick of today are just as important as the sick of tomorrow, and their interests should never be made subservient to the cause of 'progress'.

I believe that my beloved friend was ill served in her dying days, however well intentioned her advisers. She was a courageous woman, and had she and her family been told the truth, and had the high medical skills available been used to make her last weeks as easy as possible, and not in a vain attempt to deny the undeniable, then, I believe, those weeks could have been a period of richness and fulfillment for all concerned, instead of a time of increasing wretchedness and fear.

Heart transplants, kidney transplants, and the over-vigorous treatment of some terminal cancer patients, all demonstrate, to a greater or lesser degree, that many of our cleverest doctors still have to come to terms with death, that they cannot bear to remain inactive when some remedy, however unpromising or inappropriate, can be essayed, and that they have still to learn to treat their patients as people, and not simply as the vehicles of disease.

*

Drastic treatments are not a new phenomenon, and heroic surgery (the epithet is applied to the surgeon rather than his victim) is sometimes employed to deal with minor or even imaginary ailments.

The celebrated British surgeon, Sir Arbuthnot Lane, who died a rich man as recently as 1943, put forward the proposition, entirely without supporting evidence, that many of the ills of the flesh arise from poisons absorbed into the bloodstream from the faecal contents of the large intestine. Employing a kind of mad logic he cut out the last four or five feet of the guts of over a thousand trusting customers in an attempt to relieve them of the probably imagined symptoms produced by the certainly imaginary toxins they were supposed to be absorbing. His clients fared better than the recipients of transplanted hearts, and doubtless many of the survivors were convinced that the dangerous surgery had done them good, and were happy to suffer continual diarrhoea instead of the constipation which had previously been their lot.

More recently other surgical exercises of less severity but dubious value have been in vogue. In the 1930s between a half to three-quarters of all British children had their tonsils ripped out, often in bloody and painful 'production line' sessions, with a queue of unfortunates waiting in the corridor outside the operating theatre, new subjects being wheeled in at ten minute intervals. Apart from the totally unnecessary pain and suffering caused to the unfortunate victims of this surgical ritual, and the not infrequent tragic death from uncontrollable bleeding, an American study (in the days before mass polio immunization) revealed that after tonsillectomy children ran a fourfold increased risk of developing a particularly dangerous form of infantile paralysis. And much more recently another study has shown that people without their tonsils are three times more likely to develop Hodgkin's disease, which is a cancer of the lymph glands. So the 'might-as-well-have-a-go-at-it' approach, performed in ignorance of what was actually being done, was depriving countless children of an important part of the body's defence mechanism.

It is said that 85 per cent of the boy babies born in the United States are circumcised. Since there is no good medical reason for performing the operation on a normal penis, and since it is certain that only a tiny proportion of the infants so mutilated have been assaulted upon religious grounds, we have to wonder why it happens.

During the course of a long lifetime I have only once performed this operation. I did it while a blackleg in Saskatchewan, during the latter half of my time there, when I had been sent on my own to man a tiny, 8-bedded hospital in a remote prairie hamlet. The strike was over, but, the young and only resident doctor, having made his pile, had, like many of his colleagues, cleared out for good in search of the yet richer pickings to be had among the well-heeled, retired ancients inhabiting the West Coast. To my enormous delight (not having attempted the task for 20 years) I successfully delivered a couple of babies, and the mother of one of them asked me, indeed, expected me, to circumcise her boy child before they left for home. I was a bit put out, being reluctant to confess a lack of expertise in so simple an instance of kitchen surgery, but by great good fortune I discovered a patent circumcision gadget in an instrument cupboard. It was still in an unopened pack containing the instructions. As I now recall the happening, you slipped it on, and screwed it up, and sliced along the groove marked 'X', and that was that. Happily I deprived the small fellow of his foreskin without damage to the rest of his external reproductive parts, minute though they were.

Now, the mother was neither a Jewess nor a health crank. She was just a tidy-minded Canadian housewife who wished to have a routine matter allied to the birth of a boy baby dealt with in an expeditious and convenient fashion. And I performed the operation because I was anxious to show myself as a competent performer of the kinds of services doctors are supposed to provide. Apologists for the procedure have managed to dredge up the fact that circumcised Jews very rarely suffer penile cancer, but that is, in any case, an extraordinarily rare disease. There is also the possibility, far from established, that the bedmates of the circumcised may be marginally less liable to develop cancer of the cervix. Clearly neither of these considerations could have weighed with the tribal ancestors who invented the mutilation. That Canadian mother and I were simply and thoughtlessly conforming to a pointless, fashionable habit.

Unquestioning adherence to established practice, and an undue reverence for received wisdom, are important causes of much unnecessary and possibly harmful medical intervention.

Recently some surgeons have applied their minds and skills to the problem of obesity. Wiring the jaws together so that compulsive eaters are forced to subsist on slops for months is one imaginative ploy. A Manchester surgeon has kept an inflated balloon in a customer's stomach for months on end in an attempt to curb appetite. More drastically, abdominal operations have been carried out to short-circuit great lengths of gut with the idea of preventing much of the food eaten from being absorbed. Such simplistic mechanical approaches to what is a complex psychological and metabolic disorder take no account of the damage likely to follow from a gross interference with the normal economy of the body. They do reveal the fact that doctors who have acquired expertise as plumbers of the flesh may become bemused by their own dexterity, and that, having become mechanics, they tend to think of the human machine as an assembly of tubes and wires and parts, forgetting that each small fragment of every component is a community of microscopic cells, and that every cell is a highly active, tightly organized, precisely architectured, chemical plant, and that every such cell relates, directly or indirectly, to every other. In short, too many surgeons make too little use of the considerable book-learning of physiology and biochemistry which they are required to demonstrate before they are granted their higher surgical qualifications and certificates of competence. The real wonder is that so many half thought out surgical procedures leave those on whom they are practised relatively unharmed.

*

Doctors who now have some 2000 prescription medicines at their disposal, and who (especially in the case of general practitioners) rely almost exclusively on this resource when striving to meet their customers' needs, nevertheless have not been taught to ask themselves, 'What is my objective in using drugs?' – and then to go on to ask, 'Have I achieved it?'

A few years ago I wrote a long article for *New Scientist* on the manner in which we handle modern drugs, and interviewed many people concerned with the problem. Sir Ronald Bodley-Scott, then chairman of Britain's Medicines Commission (see Chapter 5) said to me, 'Doctors of my generation, particularly those in general practice (because hospital doctors do pick up a certain amount of information) have no idea how to use, I suppose, 90 per cent of modern drugs'. He did go on to modify that heartfelt statement by adding that, 'I shouldn't say "they have no idea", because they may very well have acquired some knowledge about drugs, but they were never taught at medical school anything very much in the way of clinical pharmacology or practical therapeutics.'

The late Professor James Crooks, then head of the department of pharmacology and therapeutics at the University of Dundee, agreed that most doctors are not capable of handling modern drugs wisely and well, explaining this on the grounds that up until 30 or so years ago physicians had hardly any effective remedies at their command, and so they concentrated upon perfecting the skills of diagnosis and prognosis. The therapeutic revolution had changed the physician's role entirely, but neither the medical curriculum nor the attitude of practising clinicians had kept pace with this change. Diagnosis is still regarded as the noblest medical skill, and treatment is still almost a secondary consideration. 'Modern drugs are such potent agents,' said Professor Crooks, 'that in order to use them rationally and effectively you really require special training.' He pointed out that only a handful of British medical schools have departments devoted to the study of drug treatment, 'and that even when they *are* established they usually exist only as a small appendage of the department of medicine'. The same is true in the US. 'One trouble is that the various specialists think they know it all already,' said the professor. Thus doctors are launched into the world lacking what should have been an important part of their education. 'So, into this vacuum comes the pharmaceutical industry.'

A past president of the Pharmaceutical Society, who is a dispensing chemist, bluntly described the prescribing habits of doctors as 'diabolical'. And the man in the High Street pharmacy is in a good position to know what is going on. 'It's obvious,' he said, 'that you don't control the use of medicines by making them "prescription only" unless you control the people who are issuing the scrips.'

Only recently he had come across an old man (not a regular patron of his pharmacy) who had been on three times the proper dosage of digoxin for three years. Digoxin is an old-established and extremely valuable drug in the treatment of various heart disorders, but it is also highly toxic, and there is only a small margin between the dose which will produce the desired effects, and that which will cause poisoning. When the doctor responsible was contacted he said, 'Oh, God! I remember the patient. He was only supposed to be on three tablets a day for the first *week*. Change it to one a day, will you.'

Patients receiving drugs of that kind (or any drugs, for that matter) should be regularly checked, so that the treatment is modified to suit their changing needs, and the pharmacist's tale provides an example of one of the commonest and least excusable causes of drug misuse. This is the habit many GPs have of leaving it to their receptionists to make out repeat prescriptions for patients on long-term treatment. The doctor signs a batch of the completed forms, and the patients collect them at their leisure without bothering the boss and cluttering up an already overfilled surgery. 'We get people coming in month after month for repeat supplies of powerful drugs when they haven't been seen by the doctor for maybe five years,' said the High Street chemist.

Old people are particularly liable to suffer from lackadaisical prescribing. Ageing is likely to produce a variety of symptoms and disabilities, and doctors wedded to the 'pill for every ill' idea tend to employ first this remedy, then that, for the different complaints of their more ancient customers, often without realizing how the burden of medicaments is adding up. Apart from the danger of unfortunate cross-reactions or additive effects produced by the cocktails of drugs consumed, the hapless patients are often incapable of managing the regimens so thoughtlessly imposed upon them.

Some of them attempt to solve the problem of coping with their many tablets by putting them all into one bottle and shaking out the proper number at medicine time. One of the patients admitted to hospital under the care of Professor Crooks had a mixture of thyroid, digoxin, diuretic, potassium, and sleeping pills in her medical ditty box, and all of them were white. She knew that she had to take five tablets at a time. One day she happened to shake out five digoxin pills and suffered acute digoxin poisoning. This type of accident is a fairly frequent happening, and was described by the professor as 'a kind of pharmaceutical Russian roulette'.

A young lady house physician in a London East End hospital shared the High Street chemist's view of the prescribing habits of family doctors, saying, 'The GPs round here are terrible. Every three months they'll prescribe large batches of the drugs the patients were on when they left hospital, and without ever seeing these old people. Sooner or later they're *in extremis* once more. Then they're readmitted, and we have to start all over again.'

Another house physician, working in a London teaching hospital, had a less discouraging tale to tell, more caution being shown towards drugs by his seniors than he had expected. He had soon learned (for example) that he'd be in trouble from his bosses in the morning if he had given instructions for some treatment over the 'phone from his bed during the early hours, instead of getting up and seeing the patient before deciding on the proper remedy. He had also been pleasantly surprised to find that brandy was sometimes sensibly prescribed instead of sleeping tablets.

But he *had* been worried by the manner in which some of the high-powered doctors for whom he worked would give a nasty and dangerous drug to correct some abnormality which had been discovered during the course of elaborate biochemical tests, even when the nuisance caused to the patient by the fault was trivial or nonexistent. Revealingly, he described a routine followed 'when a patient is looking really ill, and you're not quite sure what to do'. The drill was to withdraw all medication for 24 hours and see what happened. 'Sometimes patients who've been dull and drowsy and apparently on the way to death do come round. Then you realize the horrific fact that you've been poisoning them. This has happened three or four times in the past three months.'

But this was in a *teaching* hospital, those most sacred of temples to Aesculapius, within which the highest skills and wisdoms of the medical trade are supposedly to be found. The young lady doctor, in her ordinary NHS institution, had a more jaundiced view of her superiors. New to the trade though she was, the task of deciding what drugs patients should receive was left almost entirely in her hands, apart, that is, from the demands made by the nurses for the routine prescription of sleeping tablets in the hopes of ensuring a peaceful time for the staff at night. 'The surgeons don't know what to give, so they never ask you to prescribe anything. The physicians are largely interested in diagnosis, so they leave you to get on with it.' Of the three consultant physicians under whom she had served one seemed to have no interest in the drugs his patient was receiving, one was curious to know which medicines appeared to be having an effect, but only the third discussed treatment as if it was really a significant part of the business of having a patient in hospital.

This neophyte got by because most of her patients were old people suffering from heart failure, or bronchitis, or pneumonia, and the relatively few drugs she used were administered according to a standard, almost time-hallowed pattern which she remembered from her student days. 'I'm not up-to-date. We're all prescribing drugs that were prescribed ten years ago, except for the occasional novelty the consultant might have read about. I've never prescribed a drug which has been recently issued.'

And that is the quality of the guidance and 'training' in the use of modern medicines which the great majority of Britain's future family doctors enjoy during the year for which they must work in a hospital before being licenced to go it alone. Very few graduates destined for general practice succeed in the fierce competition for house jobs within the somewhat more informed and enlightened environment of a teaching hospital. Small wonder that they fall easy prey to the seductive advertising and promotional gimmicks of the pharmaceutical industry, which becomes virtually their sole source of information concerning the products for which over 350 million NHS prescriptions are issued every year.

A great part of the incidence of iatrogenic disease attributable to drugs (referred to in the last chapter, and accounting for five per cent of hospital admissions in the UK) is not just the unfortunate result of justifiable attempts to deal with dangerous or truly disabling complaints – that is to say, the occasional penalty to be expected from taking a calculated risk – but stems from overprescribing, and the dosing with dangerous chemicals of people who are unlikely to benefit from the nostrums so carelessly dispensed.

Over a recent ten year period the number of prescriptions issued in the USA rose by 50 per cent, and in France by nearly 200 per cent. British and Swedish figures showed a more modest but still substantial rise of around 25 per cent. Such statistics have, of course, no counterpart in any increased incidence of treatable disease, or in any improvement in general wellbeing due to the fact that hitherto neglected suffering is being dealt with. They are more likely to be related to more aggressive selling by the pill pedlars. (The figures for the different countries upset the widely held belief that an abnormally high consumption of drugs is encouraged by systems of socialized medicine under which they are supplied free or at a fraction of their true price – it seems that we will have our cure-alls at whatever cost.)

A UK study has suggested that more than half the adult population and almost a third of all children take some kind of medication every day. Moreover, 75 per cent of all the drugs being taken by the people involved in the survey had been obtained on repeat prescriptions. Certain categories of drugs, such as antibiotics and those which affect the mind, are particularly overused. In one American study it was found that out of more than 1000 hospital patients receiving anti-microbial preparations (drugs which kill germs) only just over a third actually had infections, over half were being given the drugs simply as a precaution, and in over a fifth the treatment being given was judged irrational, either because unsuitable agents had been used, or because no treatment at all appeared necessary.

Antibiotics are frequently prescribed for viral infections (the likeliest cause of a sore throat in children) for which they are useless. A busy partner in a well run group practice which provides a higher than average standard of general medical care told me of the temptation to order, say, penicillin for a child with a mild and probably transient sore throat 'simply to ensure against the possibility of having to see him again three days later when he might have developed a full-blown tonsillitis'. A majority of his colleagues in the trade probably do the same, only automatically, and with not the smallest pricking of the conscience, for every patient they see with an unexplained fever, or a nasty cough, or 'laryngitis'.

This is a particularly evil habit, for while the commoner antibiotics such as the penicillins and the tetracyclines are remarkably safe for most users (a few unfortunates do react violently and even fatally to the drugs), their wholesale and unnecessary administration is one potent cause of the rapid increase in antibiotic-resistant bacteria.

Anxiolytics – more popularly known as tranquillizers – are the most commonly prescribed drugs in the western world. Valium, the most frequently used of the so-called minor tranquillizers, headed the list of all drugs prescribed in the United States within ten years of its introduction. One in ten Americans over the age of 18 are given this emotional aspirin at some time during the course of a year for complaints ranging from chronic hangovers to painful sexual intercourse. In 1980 Sidney Wolfe, in charge of the American consumers' champion Ralph

Nader's health research group, claimed that in the US minor tranquillizers are prescribed some ten times more often than is necessary, which is, I would guess, a considerable underestimate of their overuse. In the same year the US Food and Drug Administration (see Chapter 5) ordered that Valium and its sister drug Librium and others of the same class (benzodiazepines) must carry warning labels stating that they should not be prescribed for 'anxiety or tension associated with the stress of everyday life' – a sanction likely to have as much influence as the British government's health warnings on packages of cancer sticks.

There is no excuse for the excessive and careless administration of drugs. Dr David Ryde, a south London general practitioner, is one doctor (and he has a few, but pitifully few, like-minded colleagues) who has demonstrated that the prescription pad need not be the linchpin of contemporary practice. He has reduced his prescribing levels to 20 per cent of the national average. Not long ago he told a conference how he had recently issued only 11 prescriptions during the course of 100 consecutive consultations, and that this, for him, was not an uncommon achievement. He explained that many of the conditions for which patients seek relief are either self-limiting or self-imposed, and that in such cases what matters is the patient's attitude to his illness, rather than the illness itself. The change in attitude needed to effect a 'cure', or to provide the sought-for consolation, is brought about by discussion rather than drugs. The doctor still pays an essential role, but informed and sympathetic counselling may be the most effective treatment for the many and undiagnosed minor ills a GP is called upon to deal with daily.

When he first took this line, over 20 years ago, his customers complained at not receiving the expected handouts of pills and potions, and some took their trade elsewhere, but now patients come to him precisely because they know they won't be subjected to inept and unnecessary medication.

We can summarize the reasons why a majority of doctors don't handle drugs in a similarly sensible and responsible fashion.

They are under pressure from patients who have been brought up to believe that health comes out of a bottle – a myth fostered by memories of grandma's treasured reserves of cough medicines, laxatives, and indigestion mixtures, and by the advertising techniques employed by the makers of patent medicines.

They are under pressure from the drug companies which mount costly campaigns aimed at persuading prescribing doctors that this or that product will speedily resolve awkward clinical problems (see Chapter 5).

They find that writing a prescription is the easiest way of bringing a consultation to an apparently satisfactory conclusion, and specially when the exchange between doctor and client has been cursory and brief.

They nurse a desire to believe that they are doing something positive for their patients, even when masterly inactivity, or some form of treatment other than drugs (such as simple sympathy or sound advice) would be more appropriate.

They tend to treat symptoms rather than patients (which accounts for the murderous mixtures of powerful pills so often imposed upon the old).

And finally, for want of the right training, too many doctors are largely ignorant of the potentialities, and the dangers, and the proper techniques for administering and monitoring the effects of the vast range of chemical weapons they are able to employ by means of a quick scribble.

All this is not to deny the value of modern medicines. Heart diseases, diabetes, epilepsy, mental illness, peptic ulcers, glaucoma, asthma, some cancers, unwanted pregnancies, pain, arthritis, high blood pressure, and a vast range of infections, including malaria, tuberculosis, leprosy and syphilis, are among the serious ills which can often be prevented or ameliorated or cured by the products of the pharmaceutical industry. We should be far worse off without them, and doctors would be far less capable of rendering effective aid. But profound changes are needed if the benefits of drugs are to be exploited to the full and their evil effects, both upon the flesh and upon our attitudes to health and disease, are to be minimized.

*

A characteristic of many of our more able, energetic, and imaginative doctors is an addiction to high technology. They are fascinated by the newest machines and procedures, and, like those infinitely dreary and humourless characters who crew the spaceship *Enterprise*, they are bemused by the idea of invading territory where no man has been before, regardless of whether or not the adventure is likely to add to the sum of human happiness (or even their own, for that matter). They are determined to be up-to-date, and, if possible, beyond-to-date.

A classic example of the nonsensical results that can accrue from such attitudes was cited by Erik Eckholm in his book *The Picture of Health*, published in 1977. He told of a hospital in Cali, Colombia, which possessed a well-equipped, expertly staffed unit for the care of premature infants. This excellent institution achieved immediate survival rates for its small patients as good as those obtained by special clinics in North America. But it was a hollow victory because, within three months of going home, 70 per cent of the babies whose lives had been so skilfully and expensively preserved were dead. They fell victim to contaminated water supplies, inefficient or non-existent sewerage, overcrowding, dirt and flies.

In the same year that Eckholm's book was published, EMI, the British conglomerate which makes everything electrical from music centres to the brains of satellites, announced with pride the sale of a second EMI-scanner to Siam. The scanner is a technological marvel. It uses X-rays and a big black box of computerized tricks to paint pictures of cross-sections of the body which show up organs and tissues with a hundred times more clarity than ordinary X-rays. The first machines, which came into use in 1971, were designed to detect tumours of the brain and other abnormalities inside the head. They were followed a year later, by instruments capable of scanning the entire body. Using the scanner it is possible to demonstrate the presence, say, of certain cancers, far sooner than by other means, and without causing the patient any discomfort or distress.

The trouble is that each machine costs about half-a-million pounds (at 1982 prices), and up to half the purchase price each year to run. The wondrous devices are very good at pinpointing faults of the flesh which can't be treated even after they have been discovered, and many of the treatable conditions which they can detect, when other methods fail or are less efficient, are fairly uncommon. In other words, the skilled enthusiasts who use them are devoting a substantial share of the time, money, energy and expertise which they have at their disposal to an enterprise which pays small dividends for the majority of the sick.

By 1977 some 800 of the magic cameras had been sold to hospitals and doctors in the USA, which fact caused that country's National Academy of Science's Institute of Medicine to call for an 'evaluation' of the technique in an attempt to discover whether it was all worthwhile. But by that time well over US$500 *billion* had been spent on the purchase of the capital equipment, and an annual liability of some US$250 billion in operating costs had been incurred, which seems a little late for wondering about cost-effectiveness.

Britain, of course, being so poor, lagged well behind the USA. By 1982 most of the 21 health regions in England and Wales had acquired at least one scanner, but more than half of these had been bought by public subscription. Glamorous projects of dubious value always stir the charitable instincts of the Great British Public far more effectively than, say, the plight of the indigent old or the mentally disabled. Unfortunately the good people who organize such generous gifts rarely make themselves responsible for the continuing costs with which the recipients have been saddled. There is no evidence that the comparative paucity of these miraculous aids to the diagnosis of rare or incurable conditions has caused the health of Britons to suffer in contrast to that of their wealthier transatlantic cousins.

But back to Siam. At the time of the purchase of its second scanner that country had 15 doctors for every 100,000 inhabitants. A high proportion of the medical care is provided by midwives and semi-skilled or traditional practitioners. Eminently preventable illnesses, including mismanaged pregnancies and childbirth, and infections in children, are the principal causes of death. There is one doctor to every 800 members of the population in the capital city, but only one to every 25,000 in the rest of the country. There is a medical school which provides a high level of training in medicine of the western, high-tech, curative kind (after all, the Siam General Hospital in Bangkok does have *two* EMI scanners), but almost 70 per cent of Thailand's new medical graduates emigrate in order to enjoy the richer pickings to be had from practice in the developed world.

There is not, of course, anything intrinsically wrong with the desire to exploit the latest tricks of the electronic engineers, and the chemists, and the physicists, and the molecular biologists for the relief of suffering and the promotion of health and happiness. (Take, for example, heart pacemakers – the implantable microchip gadgets which have most marvellously prolonged active life for hundreds of thousands of people whose natural heart-beat firing mechanisms have broken down.) It is a matter of applying new knowledge and techniques in a sensible and responsible fashion.

A secondary but important objection to high technology therapies is that they tend to glamorize curative medicine, and to divert enthusiasm and attention from more profitable methods of tackling disease.

In 1979, to the accompaniment of nationwide publicity, Anthony Nolan, aged seven, died in London's Westminster Hospital after years of heroic and costly effort to save a life which was never much more than an existence. He had been born with a defect of his bone marrow, which could not manufacture white blood cells, so that he was unable to resist infections. He was brought over to this country from Australia by his mother at the age of three because she had heard of a 'successful' bone marrow transplant which had been performed on another child, Simon Bostic, who suffered a similar disability. Unhappily all efforts to identify a suitable donor of the marrow cells which Anthony lacked failed. This was not for want of energy and initiative on the part of his devoted parents, or the doctors and nurses who looked after him. At one stage a 23-year-old New Zealand student was flown to London because he appeared to promise a perfect match, but, in the event, he proved unsuitable. Many other potential donors were sought out and tested and rejected, and attempts to process the cells of Nolan's father so that they would be 'accepted' also failed.

What happened during these costly and, in the end, vain years of endeavour?

A small boy was kept alive, but was only able to 'live' in a sadly limited fashion. Much of his time was spent in isolation. He was largely denied the company of other children (let alone of dogs and cats, or tadpoles, worms and beetles, marvellously seen and wondered at in ponds and grass and mud), and his knowledge of his fellow beings was mostly confined to a constrained and intermittent communion with his doctors and his nurses and his mother. He is said to have been the size of a two-year-old at the time of his death, and to have spent much of his brief life naked within an aseptic clinical cocoon because clothes proved unbearably painful rubbing against sore skin and swollen joints.

Denise Swann, aged 11, died a week after Anthony. She had been under treatment for eight years for the same kind of fatal disability, and had undergone two bone marrow transplant operations. Her story had closely parallelled that of Anthony, and the plight and battle for life of both children were used in appeals for funds for the support of research and, in particular, for the financing of a tissue-matching laboratory, and the maintenance of a register, with the aim of increasing the chances of finding the rare donors who could provide bone marrow which would have a reasonable chance of taking root in the bodies of other victims of their disease.

Was all that, and is all the continuing effort, spent on behalf of similarly afflicted children, justified?

It is comparatively easy to scoff at 'heroic', costly, long-odds gambles made in a bid to salvage dying adults. It is far more difficult (for me, at least) to argue against any measures that may be attempted in the hope of preserving the life of a child.

This is, I recognize, a reaction based upon sentiment rather than reason. Children are much easier to replace than grown-up parents and wage earners who have become essential elements of the family, so that others depend on them, and who possess experiences and skills needed by the community, and acquired during the years of schooling and training and sup-port for which the community has often paid quite heavily in cash terms. But I can think of no private hurt that would grieve me more than the loss of one of my own children, and I believe this feeling gives me at least some small right to suggest that the salvation of Anthony Nolan and Denise Swann should not have been attempted.

Speaking at a conference at about the time that Denise and Anthony died, Alan Williams, Professor of Economics at the University of York, explained that establishing priorities with-in a health service (or in any other department of life, for that matter), means asking who gets what at *whose* expense. He went on to express his amazement at the lack of any serious effort to assess the impact of the bulk of the exercises undertaken in health care upon the actual wellbeing of the nation. This, he said, leads to a general slackness in the system, and means that a hard-driving and single-minded consultant, with an interest in some esoteric branch of medicine, discovers that he has only to show that a costly adventure upon which he wishes to embark could do *some* people *some* good, for the necessary money to be made available to him. Few can argue effectively against the claims of such enthusiasts, said Professor Williams, because few are in a position to say what the other options are, and where any money available might be better spent.

A few days later Britain's Spastics Society claimed that at least a thousand babies are dying unnecessarily every year, and that many more are surviving with grave handicaps, because of the shortage of intensive care units for the newborn. Even if the Spastics Society was overstating the case, it is fairly certain that some hundreds of new lives could be saved annually by the expenditure of only a fraction of the energy and intelligence and cash now being spent on too often vain attempts to keep alive the rare victims of some of the more 'challenging' errors of the flesh.

Assuming that one young life is as valuable as another, then, in striving to preserve the Anthonys and Denises, and in neglecting the many unnamed infants dying for lack of an incubator, or excellent paediatric care, we are doing a wrong thing. It seems cold and unfeeling to think of the precious lives of children in terms of statistics, and 'cost-effective' procedures. But there it is. And it's a problem we have to face.

The need to establish priorities becomes more urgent and of greater consequence as the list of procedures available to doctors for interfering with the flesh and mind of man grows ever longer.

*

Not long ago it was generally assumed that babies in the womb were still in the hands of the Almighty, and that mere man, in the shape of obstetricians and paediatricians and health visitors and similar experts, could not begin to help a human infant with any physical problems it might have until it had been delivered from its mother's belly. But within the past 15 years the most remarkable advances have taken place, so that there is now a whole new science of prenatal medicine, and there are doctors who specialize in applying complex and ingenious techniques to the diagnosis and sometimes the treatment of foetal ailments.

As long ago as 1919 a German named Henkel had the idea of pushing a needle through the belly wall of a pregnant woman and into the womb in order to withdraw a sample of the amniotic fluid in which the foetus floats in its bag of membranes, but it was to be another 35 years or so before the technique, called amniocentesis, found a practical application. Then two Manchester obstetricians, Drs Bevis and Walker, started measuring the concentration of the bile pigment, bilirubin, in the amniotic fluid. Bilirubin is a product of the breakdown of red blood cells (RBCs), and is excreted in large quantities in the urine of foetuses suffering from haemolytic disease (the excessive destruction of RBCs) caused by rhesus incompatibility.

The rhesus (Rh) factor is a chemical found on the surface of RBCs in just over 80 per cent of people, and is one of several such substances which determine a person's blood group. Somebody whose red cells don't carry the Rh marker is called rhesus-negative. Such a person will develop antibodies against Rh-positive RBCs if they are introduced into the body, just as if they were invading germs or viruses or a transplanted kidney.

When an Rh-negative mother has an Rh-positive baby, some of the infant's red cells get into her circulation, particularly at the time of birth. She then develops Rh-antibodies. If she subsequently carries another Rh-positive foetus some of these antibodies will leak across the placenta into the unborn child and begin destroying its RBCs.

In the most severe cases the baby dies in the womb, or is born grossly anaemic and jaundiced, and can only be saved by an exchange transfusion, its own blood being almost totally replaced by bottled blood.

Before Bevis and Walker developed their technique the survival of an affected foetus often depended upon the skilled judgement of the obstetrician. The longer it remained in the womb, the worse it became. The process could be halted by inducing labour, or carrying out a Caesarian section, so removing it from the source of the destructive antibodies. But prematurity is itself a hazardous state, and, other things being equal, the nearer to full term a baby is at the time of its birth, the better is it fitted to cope with the dangers and stresses of life's first few weeks. So the obstetrician had to decide when the disadvantages of delivering the child three or four or more weeks early were more than outweighed by leaving a haemolytic foetus to suffer yet further damage in a hostile womb.

By periodic amniocentesis the Manchester team were able to assess the degree of red cell destruction as reflected in the bilirubin concentration in the amniotic fluid. They could thus leave premature delivery until the last, possible, safe moment, initiating the procedure when a sudden hump in bilirubin excretion showed that the danger point was near. Using this monitoring technique they were able to more than halve the incidence of stillbirths and neonatal deaths among affected infants (from 36 to 16 per cent), and to greatly reduce the need for exchange transfusions.

This was a promising start to the business of dealing with the problems of the unborn, but true prenatal therapy began in New Zealand in the early 1960s when Dr William Liley of the National Women's Hospital in Auckland delivered the first baby to be born alive after having received a blood transfusion while still in the womb. He has described the frustration he felt when the Bevis and Walker test revealed a progressive deterioration of the foetus while it was still too immatu. `or delivery to be contemplated. His impatience led to the birth of an idea. Why not have a go at treating the unfortunate infant's illness *before* it was born, instead of standing impotently by, watching it grow sicker by the hour?

'We were no strangers to putting a needle into a pregnant uterus,' he said. 'Sometimes we would even needle a fluid-filled, distended foetal abdomen. If we could do this accidentally, we decided there shouldn't be too much difficulty in doing it deliberately. You couldn't possibly do any harm to the baby. It couldn't possibly be worse off than it already was.'

The point of this remark lies in the fact that the foetus is able to absorb any red blood cells which may be floating around in its abdominal cavity into the circulation, and does not have to have them injected directly into a vein. Liley conceived the idea of transfusing a quantity of Rh-*negative* blood into the belly of a haemolytic foetus. The transfused red cells would enter the baby's bloodstream, and would *not* be regarded as 'foreign' by the Rh-antibodies present, and so would *not* be attacked, and might make all the difference, allowing a severely anaemic infant to keep a grip on life for a further two or three crucial weeks, until it could be delivered into the world with a sporting chance of survival.

Dr Liley worked out a technique for guiding a needle through the mother's belly wall so that its tip came to rest inside the baby's abdomen, and then went ahead with the great experiment. The first three prenatal transfusions, given to very severely affected infants, failed to save them, but the fourth was followed by a live birth, and when, after delivery, that baby's blood was examined, it was found that a full half of all the red cells in its vessels were Rh-negative. This showed that they had come from the blood which had been transfused, and also made it plain that the infant would have perished without them. For the first time in history a life had been saved by emergency treatment given to a baby (*not* its mother) before birth.

This exciting new approach to a problem which, at that time, was bedevilling about one in 200 pregnancies in the western world (not all nations suffered equally – very few Chinese are Rh-negative, for example) was soon taken up in America, and in the UK, and elsewhere, and many young people alive today owe their existence to the procedure. Its role in the treatment of haemolytic disease was soon to diminish, because the means were developed for preventing the formation of antibodies in Rh-negative women, but Dr Liley's pioneering work had demonstrated the possibility of breaching the privacy of the womb in order to treat sick foetuses.

The art of prenatal diagnosis established by Bevis and Walker has been greatly extended to include the examination of the chromosomes in shed foetal cells, to obtain samples of foetal blood and tissues, to view the foetus directly through a slender, flexible, glass fibre telescope, to study the heart action by means of a foetal electrocardiogram, and to monitor various other vital functions. Thus it is now possible to detect a range of abnormalities, including mongolism and spina bifida, and to sex the foetus. This means that women can be offered an abortion if they are found to be carrying a child afflicted by certain grave congenital defects, or if they run the risk of passing on hereditary diseases like haemophilia and muscular dystrophy which only affect boys.

The art of prenatal therapy established by Liley has also expanded fast. In 1981 a team in Boston, Mass., drained fluid from the ventricles of the brain of a foetus after ultrasonic scanning at the 24th week had revealed signs of hydrocephalus (water on the brain). They inserted a needle through the mother's abdomen and womb wall and into the baby's skull. The procedure was repeated six times over the subsequent nine weeks. The baby was born with some mental retardation because the brain was abnormal, but the doctors hoped that the technique could be used to procure the birth of babies with undamaged brains whose hydrocephalus is due solely to a blockage of the normal drainage channels which can later be relieved by surgery. Untreated, the condition can produce gross mental deficiency, which is often established at the time of birth.

In the same year New York surgeons destroyed a mongol foetus in the womb while leaving its normal twin unharmed to be born five months later (a similar operation was performed in Sweden in 1978), and a Californian team drained the distended bladder of a foetus suffering from urinary obstruction. Another Californian baby was removed from the womb for correction of the same kind of fault and then put back, but died after birth from severe kidney damage which had been caused by the obstruction before it was tackled.

Theoretically there is no limit to the scope of the surgery to which a foetus might be subjected, so that, for instance, attempts might be made to correct faults in the structure of the heart, or other serious anatomical abnormalities.

Drugs can be, and have been, administered to the foetus, either directly or through the mother. Some inborn biochemical disorders, such an enzyme deficiencies, might be countered by the injection of healthy cells which will 'take', and then manufacture the missing element, for the early foetus will tolerate and not reject foreign tissues. It will become possible to correct other abnormalities by taking foetal cells and fitting them up with desirable genes, afterwards replacing them. Such a technique might even be employed in an attempt to 'improve' perfectly normal infants.

So here we have a whole new branch of medicine which has developed within the course of a single generation. It is an excellent example of the manner in which an intrinsically admirable desire to innovate, which characterizes the ablest of modern scientific doctors, is so enlarging the scope of medical intervention that it is already becoming impossible to satisfy the new demands those selfsame doctors have created.

Over 15 years ago Dr William Liley said, 'We want to see that the unborn baby gets a better deal, right from the moment of conception instead of just from birth.' This is, on the face of it, a humane and sensible ambition, but does it make sense to spend an increasing share of our finite resources of skills, energy, time, money, and special equipment and accommodation, on attempts at salvaging imperfect foetuses when hundreds of thousands of immaculate conceptions are destroyed each year by 'therapeutic' abortions? Foetuses are easily replaced. Meanwhile much of the suffering afflicting already born and sentient members of our kind, and for which established remedies exist, remains neglected.

*

It has been asserted that countries like Britain, and even, perhaps, poorer nations, ought to support adventurous projects, however limited their application, simply for the sake of retaining the services of high flyers who, denied the opportunity to pioneer prestigious medical conjuring tricks in their homelands, might emigrate to exercise their talents somewhere else.

This is a feeble and specious justification for advancing the frontiers of endeavour in the wrong direction. There is no lack of challenging problems. The need is somehow to persuade our cleverest doctors to devote their energies to the practice of the best kind of medicine. And this must mean medicine of a kind which pays good dividends in terms of the prevention and relief of sickness.

CHAPTER THREE

The Medical Mafia

A quarter of a century ago Lord Moran, Winston Churchill's physician, who gained notoriety when he published intimate details of his illustrious patient's physical misfortunes, described GPs to a Royal Commission on doctors' pay as unfortunates who had 'fallen off the ladder' of professional achievement.

This was, and is, pernicious nonsense, and today not even the most insensitive and self-satisfied of medical moguls would dare to voice such sentiments abroad. Nevertheless, Lord Moran's patronizing view of family medicine is still held slightly secretly by many a clever hospital doctor, and even by quite a few of the targets of his scorn.

Way back in the Middle Ages there were three distinct branches of the healing trade. At the top of the pyramid sat the physicians – scholars and gentlemen who had received a doctorate in physic from one of Europe's ancient universities (usually Oxford or Cambridge), and who dealt with the maladies of the nobs. Next came the barber-surgeons, who, in addition to cutting their clients' hair and trimming their beards, would, when the occasion so demanded, let blood, or cut for the stone, and perform similar manipulations of the flesh. Finally, at the bottom of the pile, were the apothecaries, who made their living by dispensing the remedies prescribed by their betters, the physicians, and who also acted as the people's therapists.

There was bitter rivalry between the three castes, each wanting to maximize its share of the profit to be had from disease. But a kind of unity was finally imposed upon the different groups by the Medical Act of 1858. Thereafter, all who aspired to the title 'doctor', in the medical sense, and a place on the newly created Medical Register, had to undergo a pre-scribed course of training, and to pass a series of standardized examinations.

Thus, in theory, all doctors have been born equal since 1858.

But, as is very well known, laws can't change tribal attitudes and customs, and the old divisions still remain, with physicians heading the hierarchy, and surgeons running a close second, and GPs (the old apothecaries) coming a poor third. The only difference is that the sorting-out process now occurs after qualification, and not before admission to the guild.

For a time the Act of 1858 did have a levelling-out effect, for all those admitted by examination to the Medical Register were deemed competent to practise medicine, surgery, and mid-wifery, and largely took advantage of the fact. Thus, in the century preceding World War II, there was no essential difference between 'hospital' doctors and 'family' doctors. Most GPs were sturdy all rounders performing nearly all the tasks which are now the preserve of specialists. Every family doctor was accustomed to cutting out an inflamed appendix, either in the local cottage hospital or even on the customer's kitchen table, and was adept at delivering babies. He would also take full charge of the victims of heart disease, diabetes, pneumonia, syphilis, anaemia, and many another condition which is nowadays automatically regarded as demanding specialist attention. The Jack-of-all-trades nature of the family doctor's daily round was as much a matter of necessity as choice, for when World War II broke out there *were* only some 3000 consultants, compared to 20,000-plus GPs.

The consultants were drawn from among the more thrusting and ambitious graduates, who remained at their teaching hospitals, unpaid or on a subsistence wage, as the dogsbodies of their chiefs on the honorary staff. During this postgraduate apprenticeship they would take a higher qualification offered by one of the royal colleges – the FRCS if they wanted to be surgeons, or the MRCP if they aimed to become physicians. After 10 or 15 years of such gruelling vassalage, the neophyte might hope to become an honorary consultant himself. The same system operates today, except that the so-called Junior Hospital Doctors are now reasonably well paid. This is the 'ladder' which Moran accused GPs of having fallen off.

The chiefs were called 'honoraries' because that's exactly what they were, doing their work at the great voluntary hospitals for nothing, or for a token stipend of maybe £50 a year. They filled their beds with the sick poor who were 'fortunate' enough to suffer from some sufficiently interesting malady, or whose state made them 'good teaching material'. They made their living exclusively from the private patients whom they saw in their consulting rooms in places like Harley Street, or who were treated at home, or in nursing homes, or the private wings of their hospitals. These hospitals were their power base, and the place where they made their reputations, and their charity work was essential to their worldly success. They remained comparatively few in number because only the larger towns and cities sustained major voluntary hospitals and (just as importantly) a rich reservoir of prospective paying customers.

However, the humble GPs began to resent the competition for well-heeled clients presented by the hospital glamour boys, with their subtly advertised expertise. The threat of a really ugly internecine feud grew large, but this, in the end, could only have harmed business and damaged medicine's brand image, which, before the days of effective drugs, was one of the doctors' principal therapeutic weapons. So, something like a century ago, the 'provincial' doctors, represented by the youthful British Medical Association, came to an agreement with the royal colleges, which were the consultants' guilds.

The bargain was that the physicians and surgeons who set themselves up as specialists would not see any private patient except at the request of the customer's own personal or family practitioner. The provincial doctors now felt secure, and were happy to send some of their more puzzling patients (those who could manage the fee) to a consultant colleague for a second opinion. (Hence the title 'consultant', which is not found abroad.)

Family doctors still went on doing anything they felt to be within their competence (and maybe a good deal else besides), and not many people ever did see a specialist. But since the patricians were fairly thin on the ground, they did well enough out of the deal. Instead of having to attract their own patients, they were able to sit back and await the arrival of those referred by their ex-pupils, or by local practitioners who knew of their fame. Everybody was more or less happy.

This is the basis of the present British rule whereby specialists can only be approached through the good offices of your friendly neighbourhood GP. It has nothing to do with any rational idea that they ought to be protected from clients whose needs don't demand their peculiar skills (although it happens to be a convenient tradition for a state medical service). It is a trade convention, which doesn't apply in most of the rest of the Western world, including the USA, where its absence does no noticeable detriment to the health of the inhabitants. Its existence severely limits the customer's freedom of choice, and perhaps it should be proscribed as a restrictive trade practice. The arrangement became the final bar in the gate dividing the profession.

After the end of World War II Britain's Labour government, and its dedicated Health Minister, Aneurin Bevan, were determined to fulfil their election pledges and achieve an admirable aim by launching a National Health Service, providing full medical care, free to all at the time of need, and to do so with the least possible delay. This is why the existing structure, which was the result of 'happenstance' and history, and not the consequence of any kind of intelligent planning, was taken over wholesale by the state. In adopting this easy option our Lords and Masters fluffed a unique opportunity for setting up a system of medical care which would exploit the skills and resources available in a manner which would best benefit the needs of the nation at the smallest cost.

Even so, enormous problems had to be overcome, the greatest of which was the fierce opposition of the medical profession. Doctors of all kinds, from the most senior and powerful metropolitan specialists to the most humble and unassuming country family practitioners, were determined to maintain their traditional and accustomed way of life, and, in particular, were desperately afraid of any threat of government interference with their precious independence and 'clinical freedom'. They were scared stiff of becoming civil servants.

Nye Bevan is often accused by medical politicians of having divided the profession in order to rule. This is nonsense. The healing trade had already split itself in two, and in a fashion far more effective and complete than any outsider could have imposed.

To get the grudging cooperation of the consultants (who had powerful representatives at court, including the great wheeler-dealer Moran), Bevan had to make a number of concessions. They were to be given a proper professional salary for their work in the nation's hospitals, all of which (save for a special few) would become the health minister's property on 'the appointed day'. However, the senior and already established specialists were determined not to sacrifice their often extremely lucrative private work. Nye was forced to strike a bargain whereby any consultant could work part-time for the NHS and part-time for himself.

Since then about half have elected to work on the so-called maximum part-time basis, whereby they receive $9/11$ ths of the full salary appropriate to their posts in return for a notional nine half-day NHS sessions a week. For the rest of the time they can do their own thing. In effect this means that they can order their affairs pretty well as they choose, so long as the hospital work gets done. Many of the consultants who do opt for full time employment belong to the less fashionable specialties, such as geriatrics and psychiatry, where the chance of a steady flow of private work is small. (In the States, of course, many thousands of citizens employ private shrinks, but not, so far, in the UK.)

One result of this scheme has been to add to the heavy work load carried by the ineptly labelled Junior Hospital Doctors (the more senior of whom are experienced experts, sometimes better than their bosses at the job). Some of the less scrupulous consultants leave their highly competent 'juniors' to do much of the out-patient and ward work and operating which they ought to be tackling themselves.

The juniors daren't complain since, apart from passing stiff exams and otherwise proving their worth, their hope of ultimately joining the privileged ranks of the consultants themselves depends heavily upon the good will and recommendation of their elders. Their role as willing beasts of burden has also caused the top brass to resist fiercely all attempts to increase the number of consultant posts at the expense of some of the senior 'junior' jobs. Heavens! If *that* happened consultants might actually have to turn out at night themselves from time to time. *And* there'd be greater competition for a share of the finite supply of fee-paying customers, *and* less time to charm the guineas out of their purses. This wholly selfish obstructionism has led to frustration and resentment among the many mature and competent juniors who fail time after time in their applications for consultant posts, not because they aren't up to the mark, but because there may be 100 contenders for a vacancy.

Recently, and in the face of the pressure for enlarging their ranks, the princes of the profession have thought up a new self-protection racket. In the name of excellence they have produced a limited list of approved junior jobs, a selection of which must have been held before a would-be consultant can be considered for an appointment in one of the more popular and prestigious specialities. Needless to say, there aren't enough of these designated qualifying jobs to go round, so when, finally, the moguls have to give way, and more consultants *are* created, they will be able to claim that they would love to see them filled, but that, unfortunately, there just aren't enough candidates with the necessary background. Funnily enough, once a senior junior has finally made it through the eye of the needle and entered the kingdom of the blessed, where all power lies, he (occasionally it's a she) seems to forget what life was like below stairs, and keeps mum about the plight of erstwhile companions. There is a reason for this reticence (quite apart from any 'I'm all right Jack' attitude), as we shall shortly see.

Meanwhile junior hospital doctors will go on being grossly overworked, with, as is usual in any hierarchy, the leastest doing the mostest. Here's what one recently qualified healer told me of his day.

'I don't think we do too badly. I get a good six hours sleep most nights. Except, of course, on Tuesdays and Fridays and the weekends when we're on call. I manage at least one meal a day, and quite often two. I was foolish at first, and didn't eat at all if I was busy. Nobody *tells* you to go and have supper. So in the first two months I lost nearly a stone. But that didn't do me any harm.

'I get them to give me a ring at seven. I have a bath. I don't usually have time for coffee. I need to be on the ward by eight. That gives me half-an-hour before I'm due in the theatre.

'Once on the ward I'll do a quick round of roughly 30 patients. I'll examine the three or four who were operated on the day before. Our man mostly does guts, so a number won't be feeding by mouth. They'll be on intravenous drips. I'll have a look at the lab reports, and make sure they're getting the right amount of this and that, and if needs be order a change of the mixture in the bottle. Then I must say who can start taking fluids by mouth, or who can try taking more today than yesterday – or less. I listen to the sound of their guts. So long as they've got active, noisy guts, there's no need to worry.

'At 8.30 I belt up to the theatre. I'm normally a bit late, but I change and scrub up and start the main work of the day, which is mostly a matter of hanging on to retractors to keep holes open for other people to operate in. In one of the breaks between cases we'll get a cup of coffee if we're lucky. But the coffee lady is a nutty old harridan. She's very tight with "her" coffee, and turns nasty if she thinks you've asked to be served out of season.

'We've probably finished the list by two, except for one long day a week, when it may go on until six or eight. When the last operation's over I'll have forms to fill in, to go down to the lab with specimens. Then I'll have to see that any special instructions about patients reach the ward, and are understood. After that I might or might not get to the mess for lunch. The food's very cheap and rather nasty. We pay cash on the nail.

'Perhaps you're left in peace for 20 minutes to enjoy the soggy cabbage and braised heart, and perhaps not – the bleep goes roughly 30 times a day. Then it's back to the ward to sort out the problems they'll certainly have waiting for you. Somebody will have stopped peeing, or started vomiting, or have a fever. You have to decide what's wrong and what to do. Then the new patients start coming in. I have to chat them up, write down their histories, examine them, order any special tests, make sure they haven't any unsuspected troubles like heart failure or diabetes – and if they have, do something about it.

'If it's one of the two days a week on which emergency surgical cases come to my wards there'll be extra calls to casualty. One day last week I handled ten emergency admissions between two in the afternoon and five next morning. Two of them needed immediate operations. I have to arrange all that – book the theatre – find an anaesthetist – get any necessary tests or X-rays done – perhaps put up a drip or arrange for the right sort of blood to be ready for transfusion. And, of course, I have to assist at the operation.

'Meanwhile life goes on. If I can sneak ten minutes off I get a cup of tea with the nurses in their own little office off the ward. This is strictly forbidden. We're stealing from the NHS. It's "People's Tea", and "People's Sandwiches" we're using. I should go to the mess, and the nurses to their dining hall. We should pay for our cuppas. But it's a long trip. Five minutes

there and five minutes back. And we don't have that much time
to waste.

'We always talk shop. It's the only real chance we have to
chat about our patients. The people who think they're safe-
guarding the taxpayer's money by forbidding this kind of orgy
are bloody idiots. They simply don't understand what hospitals
are all about.

'In the evening I have to sit myself down at the desk in the
ward, and stick all the lab reports into the patients' files, and
write a progress note for everybody, and write letters to GPs. It
takes a hell of a time. Any half-sensible secretary could do most
of it just as well, and better.

'And it's my job to talk to the relatives, and tell them what's
happening. But a far worse job is talking to dying patients. On
the whole the doctors on this unit don't tell dying patients the
truth. If your boss has said something vague or comforting,
even if he knows a person's going to die, you can't just go along
later and contradict him. That would raise dreadful torturing
doubts. Sometimes I do tell a mortally ill patient what to
expect. I do it quickly before anybody else has had a chance to
tell a different story. And then I tell my bosses what I've said.
But you should be able to spend a proper time on this sort of
talk. For God's sake – isn't a dying person at least entitled to
half an hour of his doctor's time each day? But I can't find it for
them. In any case, this ought to be the consultant's task. *He's*
the chap who's supposed to have the experience and understanding. *He's* the chap who can best inspire confidence. And
will he do it? Will he hell!

'After supper the rest of the evening is taken in dealing with
problems of patients already on the wards. That's on a quiet
day. On a take-in day, of course, anything might happen. I've
usually finished by midnight, or one, or two o'clock. So then I
go for a last round on the wards, and I drink another stolen mug
of NHS tea, or Ovaltine, or Nescafé, with the nurses. And then I
put my bleep to bed in its recharging chamber, and then I go to
bed myself.

'The telephone might ring a couple of times in the night. If
we're not on take-in, the calls will be about patients I know,
lying in the wards, and perhaps I can answer a nurse's
query and go straight back to sleep. But on a Tuesday and
a Friday and alternate weekends, the call will like as not take

me down to casualty, and then to the ward, and then to the theatre.

'Officially we do get every other evening off, and every other weekend, and one half day a week. It doesn't work out like that, of course.

'The nastiest time comes just when you're turning in. You've parked your bleep, and you go along for a crap, and you're squatting there, and suddenly you hear a telephone ringing in one of the rooms. And you're convinced it's yours. And there's nothing you can do about it. That really is unpleasant.'

*

Since this matter of fact account of a work load which would send most of us screaming to the European Court of Human Rights fairly reflects what junior hospital doctors have to do, it is small wonder that the bosses don't want the burden reduced by shifting some of it upwards. Apart from their comparative immunity from onerous chores, there is another perk which the moguls cherish, and would hate to have diluted by any significant swelling of their ranks. This is the notorious system of merit awards, popularly known as 'Bevan's Gold', whereby one third of the country's consultants now receive a secret additional income in recognition of exceptional worth. This 'sweetener' was wrung out of Bevan by Moran (who else?) on the grounds that some inducement was necessary (apart from the opportunity for private practice) in order to persuade 'good' men to enter and stay with the NHS.

Over one hundred grandees of the profession hold so-called A-plus awards which double their considerable basic salaries. Some 3000 hold C awards, worth less than one fifth of the glittering top prize. In between, some 500 and 1500 hold A and B awards respectively, worth intermediate amounts.

About 60 per cent of all consultants will have achieved some kind of award by the time they retire, the top earners having worked their way up through the ranks. Broadly speaking, C awards go to those who have achieved a local reputation, Bs go to the nationally known, A awards to outstanding performers with an international reputation, and A-pluses to gurus like the presidents of the royal colleges and their cronies in the higher councils of the trade.

In theory every consultant is assessed each year for worthiness to receive an award or move up the scale. In practice it is a matter of being in with the right people who will champion your claim. Lord Moran who was (inevitably) the first chairman of the Advisory Committee on Distinction Awards, recalled, shortly before his death in 1977, how 'each autumn I drove round the regions and looked up the local medical potentate. Each neighbourhood had someone of importance whose views could be trusted.' More recently the choice has been made in a slightly less nepotic and haphazard fashion. Regional juntas made up of senior existing members of the merit club propose new candidates for C awards to the central committee. Teaching hospitals, and similar prestigious establishments, have direct access to the committee, and, moreover, are offered three or four times more 'places' per hundred aspirants within their patronage. The central committee dispenses A and B awards in its own wisdom, largely relying upon the old boy network for inspiration.

The result of this duce-dominated system is that a grossly disproportionate share of awards is collared by practitioners of the more revered specialities (like heart physicians and brain surgeons) working in high-hat places. Thus London, Oxford and Cambridge do twice or thrice as well as Sheffield and Leeds, particularly when it comes to the major awards, and chest surgeons do over three times as well as psychiatrists, with geriatricians hardly figuring in the lists. This bias can hardly be unrelated to the fact that the central committee and its satellites (whose members are nominated by 'Central's' chairman) consist largely of physicians, surgeons, and gynaecologists, this bracket of the clinical elite outnumbering humbler representatives of the trade (such as pathologists, psychiatrists and radiologists) by 14 or 15 to one on the patronage panels.

It has been argued that this apparent inequity merely reflects an unequal distribution of talent within the trade. It can equally well be argued that the system perpetuates such inequality. Excellent geriatricians are certainly of more value to the community than excellent brain surgeons, because while few of us ever need to have our heads sliced open, we all grow old (given that the Good Lord spares us for that fate), and it would be a good thing to have a lot of good doctors around skilled in ameliorating the medical problems of old age. But energetic high flyers are likely to go for the posts and activities offering the highest honours and rewards. Thus, for a start, the merit award system encourages a distortion of the pattern of medical care to the great disadvantage of the majority of the citizens who have to foot the bill.

The awards are secret. Recipients are not supposed to reveal their good fortune. There is no acknowledged parallel for this kind of disbursement of public money to unnamed beneficiaries. The condition was laid down upon the specious argument that, if identified, award holders would attract custom at the expense of their unhonoured colleagues. However, a survey carried out a few years ago found that while over two thirds of award *holders* wanted the secrecy maintained, less than *one* third of the unfavoured thought it appropriate. A measure pretending to safeguard the interests of the weaker brethren is, in fact, designed to protect the privileged from the jealousy and resentment of their neglected mates. It is, of course, absurd to suppose that patients, wholly ignorant of the devious ways of the profession, would nose around seeking out the As and the Bs and the Cs and the non-starters, distributing their custom accordingly.

But perhaps the worst feature of the merit award scheme is its deadening effect upon the imagination and the will for innovation which ought to be among the most desirable characteristics of the young (fortyish) clinicians newly elected to the consultants' club. If they are to have a reasonable hope of pleasing their superiors, so gaining a substantial pay rise, they must keep quiet about the legitimate grievances of the junior hospital doctors league, from which they have just escaped, and they must not be seen to disturb the rules and interests of the first division team they have just joined.

Two highly qualified psychiatrists, Stanford Bourne and Peter Bruggen, on the staff of London's prestigious Tavistock Clinic, uncomfortably aware of the raw deal suffered by their branch of the profession in the merit award stakes, spent their time and used their connections investigating the matter and uncovering unsaid things. They published their findings in the *British Medical Journal* in a paper which should have put paid to the whole sleazy arrangement. It didn't, of course. Evidence is of small value in the face of vested interest – witness Galileo. Anyway, they wrote, *inter* a great many pertinent *alia*, that the system 'means that elderly men continue to elect their own successors in perpetuity, and the repetition of existing patterns, right or wrong, is an inevitable consequence'. Their paper appeared in 1975. Nothing has changed since then.

So, as a student you have to toady to your betters in order to stand half a chance of obtaining a first job in a blue-ribbon hospital, which is the first rung of the Moran ladder. Then, for the next 10 or 15 years, you must sustain the sycophancy as you now slowly climb towards the consultants bar. And having eventually clambered over that (and while now safe from falling off, except by virtue of certified insanity, or conviction for murder, or some equally unignorable grave fault) you must carry on soft-soaping, and wearing the right ties, and voicing 'sound' opinions if you hope to climb any higher, and certainly if you aim to reach the top.

*

True enough, you have to be fairly bright and energetic to stay the course, but you have to be both those things to get a place in a medical school to start with. Young doctors who opt for general practice after their compulsory postgraduate intern year, and who then quit the hospital scene for good, are not all inadequates from the bottom of the class (although a few may be). They are mostly highly intelligent, hard-working, competent professionals, who may see the pastoral aspects of medical practice as being just as, or even more, fulfilling than the scientific. Or they may be independently-minded creatures who want to be able to do their own thing, and dislike the idea of spending half a working lifetime 'under orders'. Sometimes general practice recruits aspirant consultants who have indeed not 'fallen' but 'jumped' off the Moran ladder after some years, not because they are second rate, but because some personal trait (such as undue honesty, or too fine a sense of the ridiculous) has made them unacceptable to the godfathers, and they have realized that they don't, and never will, fit in. (Often these valuable nonconformists choose to emigrate instead.) But whatever the influence that draws the graduates of British medical schools into family doctoring may be, it is rarely because the choice is seen as a *faut de mieux* retreat, and Moran was an impercipient old fool to suggest that it was.

So, since it is served by men and women who are (originally, at any rate) as good as those who staff the hospitals, we have to ask why family doctoring in the UK is looked down upon by the medical moguls, and is indeed, too often, of an appallingly low standard.

The fault lies in the system.

When the NHS was founded the family doctors, working through the British Medical Association, struck their own peculiar bargain with the government. They were desperately afraid of losing their independence, and to prevent this happening they dreamed up an arrangement whereby they are not employed by the state, but undertake, as private contractors, to look after, on the government's behalf, NHS patients who apply to be put on their lists. The doctor is rewarded by a complex system of payments including a basic practice allowance, plus a few pounds a year per registered patient (with extra for old people), plus substantial further sums for seniority, contraceptive care, night visits, immunizations, taking on a trainee, maternity work, dealing with bleeding tooth sockets caused by the ministrations of office-hour-only dentists, catering for visitors, attending approved professional meetings and courses, working in designated difficult or unrewarding places, the reimbursement of practice expenses, dispensing drugs when there's no nearby pharmacist, and a whole ragbag of other activities and costs.

For all this (which in 1984 was calculated to produce an average net income of some £21,000) the GP is committed to serving the needs of his NHS patients for 24 hours a day and for 365 days each year. If your friendly neighbourhood practitioner wants to indulge in anything so hedonistic as a fortnight in Majorca, or even an afternoon watching McEnroe beating the living daylights out of the umpires and ball boys at Wimbledon, he must, at his own expense, provide a stand-in. If he falls down on the job, such as by refusing to visit a patient who merited attention and who then complains, he can suffer a substantial fine, maybe of several hundred pounds.

Since the great majority of GPs are wholly or almost entirely dependent on their NHS income they are, in all but name, employees of the state, and for the sake of an illusory autonomy they put up with conditions which no self-respecting salaried worker, such as a judge or an engine driver, would tolerate for a moment.

These days the more enlightened GPs, in areas where there is sufficient custom, organize themselves into group practices, working from purpose-built, well-appointed surgeries or health centres, and aided by a sufficiency of helpers in the way of receptionists, and a practice nurse, and perhaps, even, a practice manager. This way they can rid themselves of many tedious chores, and share the work load so that they can have *some* nights and afternoons and weekends off, secure from importunate clients.

However, even in the most felicitously equipped and organized group practice, the doctors daily round and common task can pall and irk.

When launching the NHS, Nye Bevan made known his ambition to 'universalize the best' in medical care, and this to him, and to many others, meant giving the entire nation easy access to specialists and hospitals. The training of extra consultants was begun at once, so that by the late '60s their ranks had swollen fourfold, and they, together with their 'juniors', had ousted GPs from hospitals throughout the land, not only taking over almost all in-patient care, but also running large outpatient clinics, where 'expert' attention could be sought by sufferers from everything from acne to apoplexy.

Thus family doctors were not only deprived of the satisfaction to be had out of performing routine surgery, like taking out an appendix or mending a hernia, but also came under an irresistible pressure to refer all their clinically interesting cases to one of the gurus in business at a hospital within a bus ride of the patient's home.

Now, there is much to be said for leaving all but the simplest surgery (including the administration of the anaesthetic) in hands well trained for the task, and the passing of the kitchen table and cottage hospital 'occasional' sawbones is by no means to be mourned. But the proliferation of experts in every variety of human ill has meant that family doctors have been deprived of much of their clinical responsibility, and are left to follow the advice and instructions of their 'betters' when it comes to handling their more medically titillating clients. They retain sole management only of the sufferers from vague aches and pains and anxieties and depressions (who, in any case, form the bulk of their clientele), and of not very sick children, and of symptom-prone but more or less functioning old men and women. They have become sorting clerks, form fillers, and agents of the pharmaceutical industry.

Good GPs in well run practices still manage to provide a valuable service to their customers, proffering sound advice on life's physical and emotional problems, truly filling the role of guide, counsellor and friend, and gaining reasonable satisfaction from their work, even although it's not nearly as absorbing as it should be.

But the less resourceful and resilient character, especially when working alone, or with a single partner, and from inadequate, ill-converted 'kitchen and parlour' surgeries, can soon find family doctoring frustrating and unrewarding, so that performance deteriorates, becoming worse as the years glide by. To begin with an effort to do the job conscientiously can result in fatigue and gross overwork. Later the losing battle to keep on top of the job is abandoned, and corners are cut, and standards of care slip dangerously. Consultations are rushed, physical examinations skimped or, just as likely, not performed at all, and many requests for visits are rejected or ignored. Patients clearly in need of urgent attention may be given a scribbled note to take to the casualty department of the local hospital, saying 'Dear Doctor, Mrs Jones complains of severe stomach pains – please see and treat.'

GPs of this kind, and even some far less sunk in the slough of professional despond, may have feelings of guilt, conscious or unconscious, added to their general discontent, so that, what with one thing and another, they actually grow to hate and resent the patients who sustain the pressures they can't handle. That is why too many GPs' receptionists are dragons, making the customers who approach them for appointments or advice feel themselves to be neurotic nuisances. These women in the front office are only reflecting the attitudes learned from their bosses at the back of the shop. In fact, when faced with the difficult task of choosing a GP it's not a bad idea to ask around about the performance of the local receptionists. The patient, helpful, comforting, cheerful ones usually represent good doctors.

Of course, the very worst practitioners don't *have* receptionists, for, apart from all else, they work from premises within
which no such bird could roost.

A long time ago, just before I abandoned the academic life
for journalism, I did a year's hard moonlighting. I spent my
days in the lecture theatre and the laboratory, and I spent
about three nights a week and most weekends cruising around
Islington and the East End of London in a Mini equipped with
a radio-telephone as a sweated labourer working for what was
then one of the capital's largest 'deputising' services.

These organizations, which now exist throughout the land,
answer calls from patients whose own doctors don't want to be
disturbed, and they began sprouting a quarter of a century or so
ago as a direct result of the absurd contract which GPs insisted
upon making with the NHS. They offered a tempting relief from
the 24-hours-a-day, seven-days-a-week commitment to which
family doctors had so thoughtlessly agreed.

A doctor using such a stand-in agency pays for each or a
contracted number of visits made on his behalf, and the
moonlighters who answer such calls (they all *are* moonlighters –
there isn't anything approaching a living to be made out of the
trade, except for the proprietors, of course) usually get a small
sessional fee plus an additional tiny sum per call answered.

In my particular setup we earned a handsome bonus – a
guinea, I think it was – if we managed ten visits or more in a six
hour shift. This was no easy task, since consecutive calls were
often from patients living miles apart, and in unfamiliar back
streets or vast, ill-marked, high-rise warrens. We were encouraged to get into the sick room and out again and on to the next
with the least possible delay. The less trouble you took the more
you earned, but it was never much. I remember calculating that
I'd be better off putting in the same time washing up dishes at a
Wimpy bar, and I hardly ever grabbed that glittering guinea. It
was a hard, exhausting grind, and I was delighted when it
ended, but the year's work did give me an insight into the
seamier side of the NHS.

Within my parish the deputizing service's largest customers
were single-handed practitioners who operated from lock-up
shops in places like Bethnal Green and Cable Street. The shop
part formed the waiting room, and the consulting room was at
the back. It contained the doctor's desk, a patient's chair, a

filing cabinet, a hand basin, and maybe a glass-topped trolley carrying a syringe tray, a tin of Elastoplast, cotton wool, a kidney bowl, an ear syringe, scissors, and a bottle of surgical spirit. There was probably an examination couch, more rarely a screen – and that was that.

There were no facilities for any but the simplest of thera- peutic exercises, such as giving a jab or bandaging a knee, but that didn't matter, since the doctor rarely found the need to move from his chair during the course of a surgery session, for many of the lock-up proprietors had long since abandoned the pretence and ritual of a physical examination. They might take a pulse or temperature or even a blood pressure, and perhaps lean forward to insert a symbolistic stethoscope through a gap in a shirt-front or blouse, but their chief aim was to get each customer out on the street again as soon as may be clutching the appropriate scrap of paper – a prescription, a sick certificate, or that note to 'The Casualty Doctor'.

Although their premises were mean and poor, the doctors themselves were not too badly off. They had large lists, and since their practice expenses were minimal they enjoyed good take-home pay. They never lived 'over the shop', usually having a pleasant pad in Canonbury or Dulwich or some other salubrious neighbourhood well away from the tower blocks and Peabody Buildings inhabited by their customers.

They couldn't be contacted by their patients after the even- ing surgery closed at six, or after lunch time on early closing day, or at weekends from Saturday noon until Monday morn- ing. A notice posted on the surgery door gave a telephone number for emergencies which was that of the deputizing service employed. Telephone calls to the surgery were rerouted to the same surrogate, and no way would these agencies reveal their clients' ex-directory home numbers, however dire the need.

A few of these lock-up surgery proprietors gave their patients a moderately competent service during ordinary working hours, undertaking day-time home visits, and at least spotting those who needed expert attention, and referring them to the right consultant. But others practised an appalling travesty of medicine, prescribing harmful or dangerous amounts of in- appropriate drugs, missing the signs and symptoms of serious disease, delaying response to urgent calls until it was time for the deputizing service to take over and neglecting altogether those patients too old or too ill to make it to the surgery.

Sometimes the moonlighters employed by the deputizing services were little better than the wretched 'principals' for whom they were standing in. Sometimes they knew their job, and were able to rescue mismanaged or neglected patients from dangerous situations, but for this they earned no thanks at all from their employers, and certainly not from the patients' own doctors, who resented the 'interference', and wished the deputies to provide the statutory cover, and nothing more.

It is apparent from reports which reach the medical and lay press from time to time that the quality of the rump of general practice has not improved since my own flirtation with the trade. More deputizing services have sprung up, some adequate, but too many still deplorable, and more use is made of them, partly, perhaps, because GPs now receive payments for visits made at night by them or on their behalf, which helps to offset the cost of a stand-in.

Every few years some politician gets an inkling of what the darker side of the NHS is really like. It came as a blinding revelation to Roland Moyle in 1977 when, as a Labour Health Minister, he went on a meet-the-people walkabout in Hackney. Moyle made noises, including protesting growls about absentee doctors, but nothing happened. The horrid truth was also revealed to a Conservative Health Minister, Kenneth Clarke, again, apparently, as a result of rubbing shoulders with the hoi polloi, this time during the election campaign of 1983. He, too, was disturbed by tales of raw deals suffered by patients left by their own GPs to the ministrations of fourth-rate stand-in agencies. Clarke asked family practitioner committees (the local statutory bodies which are supposed to regulate the conduct of general practice within the NHS) to check on what was happening, and to see that official guidelines were observed. Doctors are supposed to seek their FPC's permission to use a particular service, and to restrict their use of it to, say, two nights a week and alternate weekends. But FPCs, made up of appointed health professionals (local GPs, dentists, pharmacists, opticians) and lay worthies, are in no position to check on what the doctors under their mandate actually get up to, and in any case the idea of rationing the use of deputies is absurd, and no more than an expression of the Britisher's awkward nonconformist conscience, for if the principle of commercial stand-ins is accepted, and if a service is efficient, there is no reason why it should not be used every night, and if it's not up to scratch it ought not to be used at all. In any case, by mid-1984 it had become apparent that Clarke's reforming zeal was of little use in the face of the resistance and apathy of the professionals involved, and that little if anything would change.

*

Apart from settling for the sadly unsatisfactory method of contracting out the responsibility for family doctoring to 'independent' practitioners, which allows so many of them to remain isolated, antiquated, and inefficient, the state has grossly underfunded the so-called 'general medical services' ever since the NHS began. GPs represent roughly half the medically qualified clinical work force in the country, and they care for something like 90 per cent of all incidents of illness, and yet they spend and receive only some eight per cent of the NHS budget. In sharp contrast the hospital service – the power base of the influential consultants and the darling of the politicians – absorbs a massive two thirds of the vast sums which the nation spends on health care.

But putting a patient in hospital is a horribly expensive way of dealing with disease. The cost would be justified if it were essential, but several studies have suggested that something like one third of patients in general hospitals at any one time, and a far higher proportion of the mentally disabled, could just as well be looked after as out-patients, or at home.

Round-the-clock care in a medical factory is desirable for the acutely ill who need skilled medical attention continuously, or who are liable to need it at any time and upon the instant, and for the chronically ill of a kind who need constant nursing, and who simply can't cope for themselves for even a few hours at a time, but a high proportion of the patients occupying beds are quite well enough to move around and attend to their own personal needs. They can go to the lavatory. They can give themselves a bath (and a shave, if need be). They can feed themselves. Many could even do their own shopping and cooking and tidying up without prejudice to their physical wellbeing. And most of the remainder could cope quite well in the great outside world with minimal aid from a home help and, perhaps, a district nurse.

Many such 'walking wounded' are in hospital solely for the *imagined* convenience of the experts who have taken on the job of assessing their disorder and doing something to correct the faults discovered.

They may be seen briefly by a doctor once a day. Perhaps a lady in a nicely starched white coat comes along and takes a blood sample. Perhaps they are led by a probationer nurse down to the X-ray department (which is, of itself, a highly expensive way of getting anybody to an X-ray department).

But apart from the sheer convenience to the medical and nursing staff of having the patient actually on the spot, whenever his or her body might be needed for some item in the long, slow catalogue of events leading to diagnosis and treatment, there is often no other good reason whatever for keeping people 'in', except, perhaps, to help sustain the physical bulk of the empire of the consultant concerned.

The huge share of the available resources (human, material, and financial) preempted by the hospitals has had serious side effects, in addition to the near-fatal starvation of the general medical services, which should be the beefy chief purveyor of health care.

The first of these is the immense power it puts in the hands of the various health service unions (including the BMA). The NHS is the biggest employee in the land, having over a million workers on its payroll. They are well organized, and led by militants. The majority are involved in keeping the hospital service afloat, and since most hospital staff (apart from the administrators, doctors, and state-registered nurses) are wretchedly paid, they tend to be a rebellious bunch.

I once had a long conversation with Dr David Owen, while he was still Minister of State for Health, and amongst the many percipient things he had to say was this: 'There has been a powerful shift in the balance of power, reflecting a shift going on in the country as a whole. Nurses now have a voice to be reckoned with, and so do health service unions. No Minister of Health, whether Tory or Labour, can ever again handle the health service simply by squaring things with the BMA. There are other forces now – and they are there for keeps.'

But the muscle of the health service unions (NUPE,

COHSE, NALGO and ASTMS) is not applied simply to the task of securing better pay and conditions for their members, which is a legitimate and unhappily necessary activity. They, just like the consultants, are empire builders, with a powerful vested interest in keeping the NHS in its present form, although they often disguise the true purpose of their machinations by pretending that they are good-hearted, honest-to-God crusaders whose only concern is for the greater good of the sick and suffering.

Take the case of the Continental breakfasts. Just before Christmas a few years ago some 40 cooks working in the kitchens of hospitals in and around Liverpool went on strike. Not because a niggardly management had refused to pay them double time for slaving away over hot stoves while the rest of the world was paying libidinous tribute to the memory of the birth of our Saviour, Jesus Christ. Not because some Scrooge-like hospital administrator had summarily sacked some hapless scullion for indulging in the traditional seasonal activity of diverting a modest portion of the Christmas fare intended for patients to the use of some of the starving poor inhabiting his wretched home. No, it was for none of the orthodox causes of 'industrial action'. The cooks hung up their skillets and doffed their tall hats in protest against an order that thenceforth they were to supply Continental breakfasts, consisting of fruit juice, toast, and marmalade, to the patients lying in the wards above, in place of the customary offering of soggy bacon and coronary-clogging eggs.

You might have thought that the cooks would be delighted to find their early morning labours so eased, but not a bit of it. They were all members of NUPE (the National Union of Public Employees), and, on instructions from their union bosses, they became filled with indignation on behalf of the unfortunate invalids they served. The union described the decision as 'parsimonious and petty', and pretended that the strike was mounted for the protection of the bed-bound and inarticulate valetudinarians who could not battle for themselves.

The facts were otherwise. A survey had shown that a majority of Liverpudlians in hospital would *prefer* a light and tasty snack for breakfast, and since catering for this preference would save the Liverpool Health District some tens of thousands of pounds a year, the managers decided to make the change.

But how could NUPE get things so wrong, and so misjudge the will of the masses? The answer is, of course, that NUPE isn't nearly so stupid as the actions of its members sometimes make it seem, and a local NUPE official gave the game away completely when he conceded that 'the union would accept Continental breakfasts *if it was sure there would be no redundancies*'. So all the huffing and puffing turned out to be a load of hypocritical old nonsense. NUPE didn't give a damn about the patients. Its sole concern was to make sure none of its members lost their jobs.

This may seem a proper concern for any trade union, but it is an attitude which has implications far more serious than the pattern of a breakfast menu. All the health service unions, for example, have set their faces against private practice, not only within, but also outside the NHS. Within recent years NUPE and COHSE (Confederation of Health Service Employees) have frequently refused to serve meals, or sweep corridors, or wheel trolleys into operating theatres, or perform many another essential task, as part of a campaign to encourage the total abolition of pay beds within the NHS, and at one stage NALGO (the National Association of Local Government Officers) told its members working in Town Halls how to obstruct applications for planning permission for new private hospitals.

As in the case of the Continental breakfasts, these actions have been taken in the name of social justice. Rubbish! The health service unions want to prevent the growth of private medicine for one reason only. So long as the state has the virtual monopoly of the supply of medical care, then key workers in the NHS enjoy the same bargaining power as that already in the hands of miners and dockers and power workers, and other monolithic groups providing vital services. Any considerable flowering of private medicine would greatly dilute this strength, particularly since the great and the good of the land who govern our affairs, and all their well-heeled supporters, could readily safeguard their own health needs by paying cash, and could fight a general strike within the NHS secure from the threat of personal inconvenience or suffering.

But the worst consequence of the enormous power in the hands of the health service unions as a result of the present structure of the NHS is the obstacle it presents to any attempts at radical change. If all proposals for bringing about a large and essential shift of resources from hospital to community care are to be fought tooth and nail because of the loss of institutional jobs that must be involved, then the prospects for an improved, cost-effective, and modernized NHS are bleak indeed.

Some consultants and some junior hospital doctors have also struck or worked to rule upon occasion, and GPs have threatened mass resignation. Such gestures have always been, at root, about money, and have included resistance to proposed reductions of overtime pay (in the case of junior hospital doctors), or the abolition (under Labour) of profitable pay beds (in the case of consultants). They have greatly embarrassed those doctors who have managed to retain an idealistic view of medical practice, and the princes of the profession who have felt their dignity and status assaulted by so vulgar an exhibition of bellicosity. But even dedicated labourers in the medical vineyard have felt anger and the stirrings of revolt in the face of ham-handed actions and brash pronouncements by certain politicians, including the abrasive Mrs Barbara Castle.

However, the doctors are less tightly organized and more independent-minded than the various regiments of auxiliary health workers, so that their adventures into industrial confrontation have usually petered out with no clear result save for a damaging increase of ill will all round. Perhaps their gravest effect has been to encourage the less privileged members of the NHS work force to regard it as legitimate to hazard the welfare of the sick for short-term selfish ends. Only the state-registered nurses under the leadership of the Royal College of Nursing have consistently regarded strike action as abhorrent to their nature and calling, and this fidelity has sadly earned them more kicks than ha'pence from their employers.

*

The second serious side effect of the concentration of talent and resources within the hospital service is that this blatantly apparent consequence of official favouritism fosters the belief that the intensive application of high technology and esoteric learning to the diagnosis and attempted cure of disease is the medical profession's principal task and most valued contribution to the commonweal, thus diverting attention from the broader and much more beneficial role which medicine should play. And since the major hospitals are the training ground for the doctors of the future the chances for a change in outlook and attitudes are gravely diminished.

Hospitals are, in fact, bad places in which to teach the art of medicine, and the present medical course is a disaster. The curriculum has evolved to its present shape for historical reasons, having, like Topsy, just 'grow'd'. It has not been planned by people skilled in the art and theory of education, asking themselves what they hope to achieve, and then working out the most efficient way to reach their goal.

The preclinical years are devoted to an attempt to teach the scientific basis of medical practice – a task which long ago became impossible, since there is scarcely a branch of science or technology which is not now in some way relevant to some aspect of medical care. However, students are forced to absorb vast catalogues of facts and theories belonging to increasingly esoteric disciplines like physiology, biochemistry, microbiology and (perhaps most irrelevant of all) anatomy, when what they need is a broad understanding of the nature and problems of living things. Having crammed their heads with sufficient parrot-learning to pass an horrific examination they can then forget most of what they have engulfed and get down to the 'real stuff' in the clinical years.

In this second phase they are taught by serried ranks of experts, each of whom believes his own speciality to be the most important branch of clinical endeavour, but most of whom hardly appreciate even the existence of the kinds of problems most of the clients of most of their pupils will want to have solved. The schools do now pay lip service to the need for some tuition in the handling of sick people, as opposed to merely coping with disease, perhaps even employing a professor of general practice, and students may spend a brief period attached to a family doctor, and glimpsing what life in the trenches is really like. Most of their time, however, is spent at the feet of the hospital gurus, whose interests are narrow, even though their learning be profound, and none of whom will have had the least instruction in how to teach.

Thus bright and idealistic school leavers enter medical

schools at an immature age, and thenceforward are isolated from their fellows in other walks of life, to emerge, six or seven years later, their idealism weakened or killed by starvation, their brains made rubbery and set by overcooking, having been rigorously and vigorously 'processed', but educated hardly at all.

It could even be argued that the costly medical undergraduate training could be dispensed with altogether in favour of a much broader and shorter course in natural philosophy and human affairs, and on the grounds that useful vocational learning only begins after graduation, and once the apprentice is actually on the job. Certainly, if I were the dean of a medical faculty (as I have been, briefly, on a couple of occasions in the past), I would be gravely disturbed by the remarkable feats of various 'fake' doctors, whose deceptions are uncovered from time to time.

A certain John Shimmin from the Isle of Man who pursued a successful hospital career for several *years* had the advantage of an impressive medical background before he decided to join the profession. He had spent 18 months as a cadet nurse, a year as a nursing auxiliary, and a year as a plaster technician. Then, armed with forged documents, he got himself a post as senior orthopaedic house officer at a Margate hospital. He then chose to become an anaesthetist at the Isle of Thanet Hospital, his chief later explaining that young men, fresh from medical school, had no deep knowledge of the subject, so she taught them, and Shimmin (known to his colleagues as 'Dr David John Hart') 'was a quick learner' who 'rapidly became technically efficient'. She wrote to the court, when Shimmin came to trial, saying that he had become proficient at resuscitating patients, and frequently gave sound clinical opinions concerning patients awaiting surgery. He always showed great concern for his patients' welfare, and no surgeon who worked with him had ever criticized his ability. This lad went on to occupy several other anaesthetic posts, even acting as a locum consultant at the Luton and Dunstable Hospital. Moreover, during his unblemished clinical career he actually took and passed postgraduate examinations for diplomas in anaesthetics and in midwifery and gynaecology. He might have been a respected pundit yet, but for the fact that he foolishly diversified his business, branching out into insurance frauds, faking accidents, and collecting more than £1000 from four insurance companies who finally proved less gullible than his medical associates.

An Irishman, Francis Murphy, sometime commercial traveller for a meat company, got himself a certificate of good standing from the General Medical Council and obtained two 'genuine' false references, by representing himself to be a Dr A. J. Murphy, whom he knew had gone abroad. Francis worked as a junior hospital doctor in Ireland and England, posing, like Shimmin, as an orthopaedic surgeon. (Perhaps, after all, there is some truth in the canard, current in my youth, that the successful orthopaedic surgeon survives on brute force and bloody ignorance.) Anyway, Murphy ended up as orthopaedic registrar at Redhill General Hospital in Surrey, performing 17 operations in the course of 3½ weeks. He was soon sacked, but only for insubordination, having operated on a woman without his chief's consent. This incident caused more enquiries to be made, and the 'doctor' was arrested after his return from a flit around the world. Before taking up his appointment he had survived a job interview, and after his unmasking a Surrey Area Health Authority spokesman said, 'Since the case came to light the patients treated by Murphy have been seen by qualified medical staff and appear to be perfectly satisfactory.'

It's happening all the time, and the list includes several sham family doctors who, when discovered and arraigned, commonly attract round-robin testimonials from their erstwhile customers, lauding the tender loving care the miscreants have dispensed. (Real doctors don't often receive such accolades. Perhaps the falsies try harder.)

Now, the remarkable feature common to almost all the reported cases of medical impersonation is the fact that the impostors have done a thoroughly good job of work up until the moment of their confutation, and they are only exposed by the mischance of being recognized by someone who knew them in an earlier existence, or because of some act of folly unconnected with their principal fraud. They are not betrayed by any overt lack of skill, or an inability to rattle off the names of the twelve cranial nerves, or because they can't spell ectodermosis pluriorificialis, or for showing ignorance of any of the myriad esoteric facts which medical students are required to absorb and regurgitate before being granted a licence to practise. As I say, if I were a medical dean, such successful adventurers would cause me to think long and hard concerning the practical value of the elaborate and expensive 'education' provided by the learned members of my faculty.

*

A considerable part of the blame for the ossification of medical training in Britain must be laid at the feet of the General Medical Council. This Star Chamber of the profession was established by Act of Parliament in 1858. It was charged with the task of maintaining the newly created Medical Register, and, as a corollary, was made the legal guardian of medical education. For the next hundred years the council laid down detailed and inflexible rules concerning the courses to be followed – so many hours to be spent on dissecting paupers' bodies – so many lectures on compounding salves and rolling pills – so much time to be spent at the lunatic asylum, and the fever hospital, and in the labour ward. It was all carefully calculated so that (in theory, anyway) no gaps remained in the web of understanding owned by the graduating doctor. Any school departing from the course prescribed ran the risk of finding its degree or diploma made worthless, and so of course none did depart, and there was no room for experiment or innovation. Over the past quarter of a century this stranglehold has been progressively relaxed, so that the GMC's requirements are now couched in only the vaguest of terms, but the universities are only slowly recovering from the long tradition of stultifying conformity for which the GMC was totally responsible.

At the time at which the council wisely began to acknowledge its own incompetence in the field of undergraduate medical education, this illustrious body consisted of 47 sages of whom only 11 were elected by the medical hoi polloi by means of a postal ballot of the whole profession, the rest being appointed by the Queen, and by those universities with medical faculties, and by the royal colleges. Most of the appointed members were hospital-based luminaries of a kind who love committee work, and, indeed, any kind of opportunity for parading wisdom and exercising power, and who probably already had an

A or A-plus merit award safely tucked underneath the belt. Even the elected minority were of the same kidney, because Dr Pillmonger of Pinner would never have heard of Dr Softwords of Solihull, who might have got his name on the ballot paper, and so those members of the medical electorate who did trouble to return their forms (about one in three) almost invariably put their crosses against the names of candidates sponsored by the British Medical Association (the Ordinary Doctors' Org.), for want of any better guidance, and the BMA, of course, always put forward its own committee men and women – doctor-politicians who were more interested in the resonance of their own voices than the welfare of the profession at large – let alone its customers.

It was a thoroughly self-satisfied, almost self-selected, junta whose members exemplified an attitude lambently expressed by Lord Platt, President of the Royal College of Physicians from 1957–62, and a worthy treader in the footsteps of Moran. In an almost unbelievably arrogant statement, the noble healer said, 'It is important that the government of the profession should not be too democratic. It should be aware of the views of all its members, but should take its standards from the top, and clearly favour that small and not usually vocal minority whose professional standards, be it in practice or research, stand far above the average.'

However, this haughty conclave was soon to encompass its own deflation and dilution, partly by its handling of disciplinary proceedings, and partly because it started demanding money from the peasants it controlled.

Up until 1969 most registered medical practitioners rarely spared the GMC a thought. Most would have been hard put to name the president of the day. On qualification they had paid £5 to get registered – and that was that. Thereafter, unless taken in adultery with a patient, or otherwise found out, they had no further contact with the body. Hardly any of them imagined they would receive one of those awesome letters from the registrar, saying that a complaint had been laid, and coldly inviting a response. The other two functions of the council – maintaining a register and controlling the medical curriculum – appeared not to touch their lives. Then the council announced that it was deep in the red at the bank. It needed a lot of ready cash to clear the overdraft, and another lot of ready cash to finance its schemes for organizing postgraduate education and certification. (Yes, maybe it was better to leave the under-graduate stuff to the universities, but all the senior clinicians on the council would be just dab hands at working out how to train specialists, and at assessing them, and at putting their names in yet another set of scrolls.) Therefore the council proposed to charge each doctor in the land a trifling £2 a year for having his name kept on the register.

The profession shook with rage. Out of 12,000 doctors polled by the magazine *World Medicine*, 11,500 said they would not pay. This was no mere stinginess, but resentment at a charge designed to bring the council in an extra £130,000 a year which nobody believed would be profitably spent. Inevitably, the protesters caved in. It was easier to sign a £2 cheque, and send it off without the knowledge of your peers, rather than run the risk of finding yourself hauled up for posing as a registered medical practitioner when not entitled so to do. But, at a stroke, the council had made itself the most unpopular body on the medical scene, and thereafter its every move was keenly and critically scrutinized by its reluctant underwriters. In particu-lar the ordinary practitioner began to gag at the manner in which medical 'justice' was dispensed.

Since its inception the council has been empowered not just to register appropriately qualified persons, but also to strike off the register any of the certified chosen who subsequently backslide. To be cast into outer darkness a registered medical practitioner had to be found guilty of 'infamous conduct in a professional sense'. The beauty of this all-embracing charge was that it allowed the lords of the profession to chuck out any member of the trade they didn't like, for as Lord Justice Lopes said in 1894, 'If a medical man in the pursuit of his profession has done something in regard to it which will be reasonably regarded as disgraceful or dishonourable by his professional brethren of good repute and competency, then it is open to the General Medical Council, if that be shown, to say that he has been guilty of infamous conduct in a professional respect.'

And so it has been, and as recently as 1970, the council reminded the peasantry that a doctor (in the last century) had had his name erased from the register for keeping and exhibiting 'an anatomical museum containing waxworks of a disgusting character'.

Not all the victims of the council's wrath have been arraigned on such outrageous grounds, but in view of the fact that the overt purpose of the council's being is the protection of the public against incompetents, charlatans and rogues, it is interesting to note how its well-nigh open-ended disciplinary powers have been exercised over the years.

In theory the council does not initiate proceedings, and only acts upon complaints received, but it not infrequently gets round this annoying restriction by arranging for some other body (even, at times, its own solicitors) to lay the necessary information. It is also automatically notified whenever a doctor is convicted of a criminal offence. Immense and almost autocratic power lies in the hands of the president, who acts as procurator-fiscal, senior judge, and foreman of the jury. He it is who first considers complaints received, and chooses whether or not to take any notice of them. If he decides to go ahead, the doctor gets a letter outlining the allegation and inviting comment. The charge and the victim's response is then considered in private by a small penal cases committee, which may or may not decide that the matter should proceed to a full public hearing before the 19-strong disciplinary committee. This is like a court of law to the extent that the unfortunate prisoner in the dock is questioned before his accusers by an experienced advocate, witnesses may be subpoenaed, evidence is given on oath, and the accused may also be represented by a legal eagle. It is far removed from a court of law to the extent that the 19 judges (who are also the jurors) have no legal training or experience, may be wholly unsuited to the task of weighing the evidence presented by a cunning lawyer, and, in determining guilt, are not required to be satisfied that the poor wretch before them has broken some written or established rule, for it is sufficient that they should disapprove of what has allegedly occurred. It is true that lay magistrates may also sometimes dispense justice with less than professional expertise, but they *are* bound by a pretty comprehensive and detailed set of precedents and precepts, and they cannot deprive someone of his livelihood simply because they don't much care for the cut of his jib, and their crasser decisions can be readily corrected by a higher court. It is true, also, that a condemned doctor can appeal against sentence to the Judicial Committee of the Privy Council (the GMC is itself a committee of the Privy Council), but apart from correcting evident travesties of natural justice or the results of grossly negligent or unlawful proceedings, how can a bunch of eminent and elderly lawyers question judgements about what constitutes infamous conduct in the medical field arrived at by a bunch of eminent and elderly doctors?

And what have the 'small and not usually vocal minority whose professional standards stand far above the average' tended to regard as 'infamous conduct in a professional respect'?

From time to time the GMC issues a booklet to its vassals, outlining its functions and procedures, and its disciplinary jurisdiction. One such manifesto, distributed in 1970, occupied some 15 text pages, 12 of which were devoted to the punitive side of the council's work, which does suggest that the subject ranks large in the minds of the proprietors. But more interesting than the generous space allocated to this field is an analysis of the manner in which that space was parcelled out. Here, in ascending order, is an account of the number of column inches occupied by comments on the commonest infamies.

> Illegal abortions – ¾″
> Inexcusable neglect of patients – 1¼″
> Misuse of dangerous drugs – 1¾″
> Handing out false certificates – 2¾″
> Drunk in charge (of car or patient) – 2¾″
> Fiddling books to cheat NHS – 2¾″
> Covering (which means helping somebody not a doctor to do a doctor's job) – 3″
> Adultery with patient (or allied sport) – 6¼″
> Advertising (or knocking a competitor) – 12″

The careful reader will have noted that the largest emphasis is placed upon those crimes which could interfere with trade. Adultery interferes with trade because if people get the idea that their friendly neighbourhood physician may be a phil-anderer, they will be less willing to let the doctor come and go unhindered, and to visit, say, the mistress of the house while the master is at the office, and that would diminish productivity. Neglecting patients hardly upsets trade at all, and that's why it only earned 1¼″, while a chat on the evils of advertising received the full treatment. Advertising is enormously expensive, and, properly done, absorbs a great deal of time and energy which could be more profitably spent on earning fees. Moreover, if allowed to indulge in self-promotion, the smarter, more extrovert practitioners would have an unfair advantage over the grey majority. Better, for the general convenience and purse of the profession, to ban such vulgar activity altogether (except, of course, for the subtler forms of advertisement allowed to top doctors, such as writing letters to *The Times*, or being unwillingly photographed by the press on emerging from attendance at a royal birth.) Never mind the fact that the public would greatly benefit from knowing which doctors are interested in providing what kind of service. And it is clearly important, so far as it may be practicable, to keep the practice of medicine a closed shop, which is why a professional association with outsiders was regarded as a mortal sin. The essential hypocrisy of this prohibition is nicely revealed by the fact that a properly qualified and duly registered medical practitioner can indulge in whatever irrational quackery (such as homoeopathy or naturopathy) he chooses to espouse, without attracting sanctions of any kind.

In short, the medical criminal code, as expounded in 1970, was a set of deliberately ill-defined canons designed to protect the selfish interests and public image of the members (and, more particularly, the leading members) of the trade, and directed hardly at all (except by coincidence) towards the commonweal.

Two prosecutions mounted by the council in this era well illustrated that body's ineptitude in the field of jurisprudence, and the manner in which it allowed prejudice to interfere with justice. The publicity these cases received hastened the end of the savage rule of the many by the few.

Dr Richard Barker, a Hampshire GP, received a nine month sentence of suspension in February 1971, and appealed unsuccessfully. His crime was that for a period of 20 months before receiving a letter from the GMC asking him to explain his conduct, he had been living in peace and happiness with a woman who is now his wife. She had once been his patient, and later became his receptionist. But well before any emotional or sexual relationship had developed between the two of them she had removed herself from his list to that of another practitioner, feeling that to remain as both patient and working colleague might prove embarrassing. Both were married, and both had gone through family turmoil and distress, but felt themselves out of the wood and well launched upon a new and happier life. Both were liked and respected by Dr Barker's patients, whom he had continued to serve efficiently and well. Then somebody ratted on them.

Dr Barker was not particularly worried by the letter from the GMC, unpleasant though it was, for he was confident he could prove that no impropriety had taken place between himself and his new mate while she was still his patient. And he did so prove, but to no avail, because his judges and accusers nonetheless found him guilty of the undefined and wholly undefinable crime of 'serious professional misconduct'. (The Medical Act of 1969 had substituted this catch-all indictment for the pretentious 'infamous conduct in a professional respect' of earlier legislation, and also allowed the suspension of a doctor as an alternative to erasure.) They did not explain, and were not required to explain, how they considered this wholly private affair had brought his professional competence and integrity into question, or how depriving patients of the care afforded by a good physician for nine months could possibly be expected to serve the public interest.

As a result of the GMC decision the local family practitioner committee could have taken Dr Barker's practice away from him. It chose not to, and, instead, put in a locum. To cope with a particularly costly nine months during which he earned nothing, Barker had to borrow £9000 from the bank – a debt which, some years later, he had failed to reduce. So *his* fine was a mere £9000, plus an annual payment of £1400 which was the interest on his loan.

A few years ago, in an attempt to discover whether the moguls of the GMC were fully aware of the damage which their 'merciful' sentences of temporary suspension wreaked upon their victims, I spoke to a Mr Gray, who was the council's assistant registrar responsible for disciplinary matters. When I asked whether he knew what effect a suspension had on NHS contracts, he made the following extraordinary admission.

All I can say is that I know from people with whom I have discussed these problems, who are, for example, administrators of family practitioner committees, that they have a problem which they solve according to their rules and according to their lights. If somebody is suspended for a short period they can make one sort of arrangement for medical care for people who were previously on that chap's panel. If somebody is suspended for a long period, or an indefinite period, they might have to make other arrangements. The extent to which a contract is held in suspension is something about which I can have no knowledge. I have never seen such a contract, and certainly we have no occasion to see such a contract following any decisions.

If the resident penal expert had so little knowledge of the nature of the wounds inflicted by the crude knobkerrie wielded by his councillors, it seems unlikely that the amateur magistrates themselves (who mostly inhabited a world far removed from that of the average prisoner in their dock) were really aware of what they were doing. This, at any rate, would be the charitable view to take.

The GMC's ham-fisted and insensitive handling of Dr Barker was well publicized and scathingly condemned by a medical press catering for a readership becoming increasingly critical of the profession's Politburo, but, undeterred, the council staggered yet further into the mire.

The year following Dr Barker's martyrdom, the Inquisition made the grave mistake of attempting to crucify a Dr Caroline Deys. Dr Barker was (and I say this without the least intention of disrespect) a relatively obscure member of the healing trade, and had admittedly committed what a few of his starchier colleagues might have regarded as a venial, if not a mortal, sin. By contrast, Dr Caroline was something of a medical saint, well known, and, quite evidently, seagreen incorruptible.

She was (and happily still is) the wife of Dr Malcolm Potts, an internationally recognized authority on population control who was, at the time of her indictment, medical director of the International Planned Parenthood Federation. But she had no need of the support of his fame, because she was, herself, a right character.

She started her own family-planning career in a conventional clinic, but became dissatisfied with her efforts because she was seeing mostly intelligent and educated people like teachers and lawyers. She wanted to get to the sort of woman who desperately needs relief from repeated pregnancies, but who is overawed by the unfamiliar clinical ambience of hospitals and the impersonal, brisk efficiency of nurses. So Caroline Deys managed to obtain a small grant from local authorities around Cambridge, where her husband was a don, and for a year she drove round the countryside, taking the Pill and other contraceptives to the wives of farm workers and to caravan dwellers, meeting them in their homes.

Because at that time most women of that kind thought of the family planner as 'anti-baby' she used to take her small daughter on her rounds. The presence of this young person in her arms, or crawling around the parlour floor wetting her nappies, or grabbing at ornaments and pussycats' tails, completely shattered the 'us and them' attitude which so often prevents the humble and the inarticulate from seeking and getting the help they need from authority. Sarah, the daughter, was also useful as a living, damp-pantied demonstration of the contention that a woman could take the Pill and stop it any time she *wanted* to get pregnant. And just to prove beyond doubt her claim that the Pill was not some fearful poison, Caroline would time and again give Sarah one to swallow in the presence of a customer. (She might not be quite so keen to stage that particular variety act today.)

There were 114 women on the visiting list of this partnership, and in the course of a year's work Caroline and Sarah managed to reduce the pregnancies among their clients to four compared to the 84 which these same women had scored between them in the previous year.

Then Caroline Deys moved with her family to London, and began work at the Marie Stopes Memorial Centre, and turned her attention to men, performing vasectomies. She undertook two sessions a week, for each of which she received a modest, not to say derisory fee of £13.20, regardless of the number of customers served. One of the sessions involved treating patients in their own homes, and since she paid her own travelling expenses, the more work she had, the smaller her net cash reward. However, all this did not prevent the panjandrums of Hallam Street (where the GMC members swallow an excellent claret 'on the house' and dispense their rough justice) from charging Caroline with having acquiesced to the writing of an article purporting to show her medical skill, and that she did so for her own professional gain.

What had happened was that a few months earlier the *Sunday People* had carried a story by a woman reporter headed 'Their Sex Life in Her Hands'. There was also a picture of Caroline with her daughter. The headline was possibly not quite the sort of thing you'd find at the top of a *Lancet* article, but the story was a straightforward account of the way in which this excellent and dedicated woman was being happily accepted as their surgeon by a steady stream of men who had decided that their breeding days were over. Its effect and purpose was to show how easily the thing could be done, and how many ordinary working men had already become the doctor's satisfied customers. Dr Deys' defence rested on the fact that she could have expected no kind of pecuniary or professional advantage from the publication, and that she cooperated in the writing of the item because it seemed an ideal way of bringing a cause in which she fervently believed to the notice of the very kind of people she most wished to influence.

Because she was so well known, and, indeed, admired within the medical trade, her 'trial' was discussed in the medical press, and roundly criticized, before it happened, and somebody near to the heart of the Hallam Street Mob had the wits to see that a 'conviction' could be the final knock-out blow to the council's already battered and reeling credibility. She was acquitted of the crime of 'serious professional misconduct'. However, this last minute change of face (remember that the president and the penal cases committee had virtually already determined her culpability) came too late to acquit the council itself of the charge of stupidity and insensitivity, and of being fatally out of touch with the real world in which the doctors under its dominion were striving to do their thing.

But even before the Deys affair, dissatisfaction with the council and its oligarchic ways had reached a pitch which could no longer be ignored, and almost coincidentally with her acquittal, the government announced the setting up of an Inquiry into the Regulation of the Medical Profession under the chairmanship of Dr (now Sir Alec) Merrison, then Vice-Chancellor of Bristol University.

The pharmaceutical industry was in large part, albeit unwittingly, an agent in the fomentation of the peasants' revolt.

Around the beginning of the 1960s certain astute publishers realized that there was a lot of money to be made out of 'throwaway' journals sent free to doctors.

There is a convention, and it is nothing more, that 'prescription only' drugs (those you can't buy without the authority of a scrip from your friendly neighbourhood GP) can only be advertised to the profession. Therefore, if you can produce a periodical which doctors will be tempted to read, or at least leaf through, the pill makers, ever desperate to promote their products to the men and women who decide on treatment, will queue up to buy advertising space. They have always had the specialist publications, and the 'heavies' like the *Lancet* and the *British Medical Journal*, in which to push their wares, but GPs (by far the largest and most suggestible prescribers of the drug-makers' entrancingly packaged toxins) rarely read such esoterics. The throwaways, on the other hand, after some initial consumer resistance ('*I'll* choose what I want to read, *and* I'll pay for it myself, thank you very much') rapidly gained a wide audience, being attractively designed, cunningly illustrated, well and simply written, and ideal for perusal when sitting on the loo. And they contained not just boring old bits of clinical research and case reports, but lots of news and gossip and opinion.

Suddenly the numerous but scattered and isolated members of the medical peasantry had a press of their own, capable of discovering and publicizing and crystallizing views and attitudes which had previously remained hidden or ill-formed, and ready and eager to examine issues which the established and largely conservative journals had either ignored or reported without comment. (The *Lancet* was an honourable exception, having, since its foundation in 1823, used its editorial columns to castigate, whenever necessary, the follies and shortcomings of the medical Establishment, but since it was not much seen by the humbler members of the trade it lacked the campaigning power and unifying influence of the new populars.)

The GMC could not sustain its aloof and imperious dictatorial role once its nature and behaviour had begun to attract the critical attention of editors who had not the smallest respect for the medical aristocracy, and who were keen to print stories likely to appeal to the proles. But in addition to giving prominence to tales of hierocratic ineptitude, the populars eroded the dominance of Lord Platt's Olympians in another interesting and presumably totally unforeseen fashion. The names of the medical men and women whose by-lines and, often, photographs, began to appear regularly in these well-read publications became familiar to thousands of humble labourers in the medical vineyard. They constituted a new bracket of professional notables, possessed of views and values commonly strikingly different to those characterizing the traditionally-minded and ultra-orthodox 'dry' professors and royal college dignitaries and BMA committeemen who had hitherto been the only members of the guild able to establish some intra-professional fame. Various medical 'wets', lefties, and trendies (I speak, of course, in comparative terms) made their mark as the champions of ideas which would have kept them safely excluded from the conclaves of the Great and the Good in earlier times. Moreover the populars willingly gave space for electioneering propaganda to any doctor who wished to stand for one of the GMC places filled on the say-so of the mob.

Thus it was that in 1971 a newly elected and appointed council contained, for the first time ever, a handful of rebels who had had the temerity to stand for a place in competition with the worthies on the BMA's official list of favourite sons, and who had almost unthinkably defeated them. One of the successful mutineers was Dr Michael O'Donnell who had become known to thousands of doctors as Editor of *World Medicine*, the glossiest of the throwaways, and who had waged a just and merciless campaign against the Hallam Street Mob in the pages of his widely read and much appreciated organ.

Dr O'Donnell, now known to a much wider public through his radio and television activities (which might have got him 'struck off' 15 or 20 years ago) has remained an elected member ever since, providing a considerable civilizing influence, but he recalled in the Council's own annual report (no less) for 1982, how when he and his fellow rebels turned up for their first meeting 'some members were quick to express their irritation at our presence'. There was, however, nothing the irritated old-sters could do about it, and from that day on the council faced criticism from within as well as without. Hence the appointment of the Merrison committee.

If, during the 1950s and 1960s, the council members and its senior secretariat had been a little less willing to accept Lord

Platt's absurd proposition that 'the government of the profession should not be too democratic', and if they had not haughtily regarded themselves as being indeed endowed with 'professional standards . . . far above the average', so that the opinions of ordinary doctors (such as a desire for more elected members) could safely be ignored, major reforms might have been delayed for decades. But imagination and humility were lacking, and these deficiencies proved fatal.

Merrison recommended not just more elected members, but an elected *majority*. A new Medical Act was passed in 1978, and the following year a new council assembled, its membership enlarged from 46 to 93, of whom 50 had been chosen by the proles. The 50 included several doctors from overseas, so that the large corps of Commonwealth medical immigrants were represented for the first time. The throwaway journals had made an intelligent choice from a field of largely unknown, unofficial candidates possible. Among other changes the Disciplinary Committee was renamed the Professional Conduct Committee, in an effort to emphasize its role in maintaining high standards of medical practice rather than merely harrassing wretched sinners, and the council began to issue advice on standards of professional conduct, so somewhat reducing the open-ended and arbitrary nature of its penal activities. Also a Health Committee was established in the hope that it could deal in a humane and confidential fashion with doctors whose mental or physical state made them unfit to practise, such perilous operators having been previously ignored, unless their 'illness' (often addiction to the bottle, or some other drug) had caused them to behave in an 'infamous' fashion. (Incidentally, the old penal cases and disciplinary committees had always taken a peculiarly indulgent view of doctors reported for offences involving drink – perhaps because the members themselves were commonly enjoying the effect of, or the prospect of, the council's own excellent claret at the time such cases were considered, or perhaps because alcoholism is almost an occupational disease of the profession, so that too severe a response to its occurrence would have had an unduly disruptive effect upon trade.)

One delightful result of the 1979 election was the elevation to the rank of councillor of a Dr David Delvin. He, like Dr Michael O'Donnell, had become known to large numbers of GPs in his role as a medical journalist, and, in particular, as the medical editor of another well-read throwaway, a tabloid called *General Practitioner*. What made his election so pleasing to many was the fact that it was a nice example of poacher turned gamekeeper, because four years earlier the council had considered charging him (like Caroline Deys) with the heinous sin of advertising. Some anonymous wretch, doubtless moved by envy, had complained that the good doctor had allowed his name to appear (followed by his qualifications, which was supposed to make the matter worse) at the head of articles on sex and family medicine-type topics in various popular newspapers and magazine. Unlike Michael O'Donnell, who was a full-time journalist, Delvin also saw patients in the course of what must have been a frenetically active working day, and there is small doubt that the combination of his clinical availability and openly contrived personal publicity would have ensured conviction and erasure had his case come up a few years earlier. As it was, and in the face of growing impatience with the unevenly applied 'anonymity' rule, and the fact that the throwaways had made it plain that they were poised to create all hell should the lad be crucified, the council's penal cases committee wisely decided to drop the charge rather than risk a public trial which would have provided a stage for all manner of hilarious and damaging histrionics. (Much was made of the total lack of response by the council to the shameless razzmatazz indulged in by certain princes of the profession at the time of Britain's first heart transplant operation, and this embarrassing episode would certainly have been exploited to the full in Delvin's defence.) Since his dignification one of Delvin's publications, a sex manual entitled *Dear Doc*, has actually been advertised in girlie magazines. A council member's thoughts on sex promoted in a soft porn mag! By the beard of Aesculapius, it's enough to make the late lamented Baron Platt rain tears of bitterness and shame upon us from his doubtless senior position in that Great College in the Sky.

Thus has the council changed. It has become much more democratic, and a good deal less straight-laced. It's professional conduct committee is rather more concerned with shortcomings which patently prejudice good patient care, and rather less with private sexual liaisons, and allegations of self-advertisement, and associations which might seem to threaten the closed shop. There is more argument in the chamber, and less unquestioning acceptance of the dicta of committee chairmen and the secretariat. The members still enjoy their very good claret, but now must make do (at least when the full council assembles) with a buffet lunch in place of a sumptuous sit-down meal. The body is less offensive but just as ineffectual, being more 'in touch', perhaps, but far too large. No assembly that size can hope to wield executive authority in a consistent, resolute and expeditious fashion. The oligarchy of the patricians may have been broken, but the plebs who can now blarney their way on to the synod are no more likely to be blessed with Solomonic wisdom than their grandee colleagues. The GMC is a dodo that won't lie down. It should be abolished, such of its functions as are needful or useful being assumed by other, existing bodies possessed of the appropriate machinery and expertise.

A register of people suitably qualified to practice medicine could be kept in a computer at the health department. The universities (including the Open University) should be left to evolve their own, imaginative courses of undergraduate education. The various royal colleges (including the Royal College of General Practitioners) are best placed to lay down patterns of specialist postgraduate training, and to keep, if need be, separate and additional registers of those they consider competent to undertake the independent practice of the specialties they represent. The courts are well equipped to deal with malefactors, including those on the medical list. They already have first say in the fate of doctors who prescribe illegally, or cheat the NHS by putting in false claims, or who issue false certificates, or carry out illegal abortions, or drive while drunk, or otherwise break the law, and the civil courts offer a greater deterrence to the negligent and the incompetent than the GMC has ever attempted or achieved. It should be left to employing authorities, and to the customers, to dispense with the services of doctors who, while steering clear of illegal acts, behave in an unacceptable or inefficient manner. Purely 'professional' crimes, like adultery, canvassing, advertising, and 'knocking' a colleague should disappear from the calendar. The handsome premises in Hallam Street could be turned into an attractive and profitable medical museum, and the registrar of the day might be kept on as curator. He should, after all, be skilled in looking after fossils. The place might even sport a wine bar, where remaining stocks of claret could be sold by the glass to citizens in need of a stimulant after viewing the exhibits.

*

By giving a junta of top hospital doctors and senior academics control over medical education, and the right to destroy the livelihood of those among their lesser brethren who failed to observe club rules, the old, unreformed GMC played a significant role in perpetuating the division of the profession into Brahmins and untouchables already here described. This sharp division is not seen in countries where the practice of medicine is largely in private hands. Private practitioners are not keen on handing over their paying customers to a competitor, and so they make every effort to provide all the services within (and often without) their competence, passing on only those clients whose condition clearly demands the application of some special skill. You don't get only half the profession exercising true medical expertise while the other half act largely as form fillers and sorting clerks.

If, as some politicians and not a few doctors desire, the NHS was to be run down, providing only for the needs of the poor, and the old, and the chronically ill, and if most medical care was provided by independent operators, then the present injurious and inequitable malapportionment of resources and clinical responsibility and status within the profession would almost disappear. But this is not the remedy. One gross fault in the system would simply be exchanged for others, even more damaging to the interests of the patient – which are, or ought to be, supreme.

In Britain, happily, we don't have any idea of the hardships, problems, and even tragedies to which a reliance on private medical care so often give rise. In the UK private medical insurance schemes, which now cover around four million citizens, buy nothing more than convenience and a bit of extra comfort (and, perhaps, extra courtesy) for subscribers who fall ill. For an outlay ranging from about £5 to £10 a week (at 1985 prices, and according to your age) you can jump the NHS queue, and can be treated by the consultant of your choice (how does a common or garden citizen *know* which consultant to choose?), and can lie sick in a private room with your own telly and your own telephone. You might even be served with slightly better meals than you'd get in a public ward.

Membership is a luxury, and does not purchase access to medical care of a kind which is not available through the NHS. Indeed, the reverse is the case, since private schemes do not cater for large areas of need, such as the care of mentally handicapped children, chronic mental illness, alcoholism, or similar long-term and costly afflictions. Neither will the insurers pay for private treatment from a family doctor. They also set a limit on the hospital and medical charges they will meet, so that only by taking out a special and specially expensive policy can a client be sure that a serious illness in the family won't pile up liabilities well in excess of the sum that can be claimed. Some 10 per cent of claimants insured with the British United Provident Association (BUPA), which is the country's largest private health insurance scheme, find that their bills are not met in full.

But even with such wide-ranging limitations on their liabilities, the private medical insurance companies are now in deep trouble. In 1982 BUPA reported a loss, its subscription income of £190 million being exceeded for the first time by benefits paid and administration costs, only its investment income keeping it in the black. This state of affairs was partly due to soaring medical costs (well in excess of the rate of inflation – doctors' fees for private work had doubled over the previous four years), and partly to expanding business, and the inclusion among subscribers of large numbers of blue collar workers who are less healthy than the prosperous, middle-class clients at whom such plans were originally aimed. So the insurers are already faced with the need to reduce the range of benefits, or to increase premiums to an unattractively high level, or, more probably, to do both. Their problems would be magnified enormously were they required to finance the full medical needs of the greater part of the population, with the NHS acting only as a safety net for groups which couldn't possibly fund their own care, and it is easy to see why, in 1982, a Tory cabinet, ideologically wedded to private enterprise, reluctantly decided that proposals to shift much of the burden of paying for health care from the exchequer to insurance schemes were totally impractical.

Some faint idea of the scale of the problem can be judged

from two incidents which occurred at the end of 1982 following the government's decision to put an end to the provision of free medical care to non-entitled foreigners. An Indian visiting relatives in Bradford slipped and broke his thigh. Bradford Royal Infirmary sent his sister a bill for £7476. A Pakistani visiting relatives in Leeds was charged £973 by the General Infirmary for an emergency appendicitis operation. These were commonplace, almost minor, incidents of illness, and the fees were calculated on a highly conservative cost-to-the-country basis, with no profit or personal payment going to anybody.

Apart from the fact that only the massive resources of a tax-funded health service are sufficient to prevent illness from becoming a cruel financial calamity for many thousands of individuals and families each year, there is a second important reason for not looking to private health insurance to solve the problem of paying for medical care. It has a pernicious effect on medical morality.

The only way medical insurance schemes can work is by paying out the actual costs incurred by clients, having worked out a premium which will result in the lucky (healthwise) non-claimers providing sufficient funds to cover the bills of the stricken, plus a margin for profits and administration. This means that doctors and hospitals, and all the other rag-tag-and-bobtail hangers on of the medical supermarts are paid on a fee-per-item-of-service basis. Thus so much for an injection, so much for a simple consultation, so much for removing stitches, so much for taking and interpreting an X-ray, so much for every minute spent in an operating theatre, so much for a blood test, and so on and so on.

We all, even doctors, like money, and the fee-per-item-of-service system of renumeration is an open invitation to an indulgence in excessive investigation and treatment, which is not only wasteful and distressing, but often positively danger-ous. Patients are in no position to challenge the professional advice offered by the doctors they consult, and the insurance companies which foot the bills, while well aware of patterns of abuse, cannot possibly check the validity of procedures pre-scribed in any particular case. There is therefore nothing, except conscience, to prevent a doctor milking the system at the expense of his patients' safety and wellbeing. Overdoctoring is rampant in the USA, where the fee-per-item method of billing is ubiquitous. Recently the US Food and Drug Administration claimed that one third of X-ray pictures taken nationwide were unjustified, at a cost to the country of US$ 2000 million every year, and never mind the many extra cases of cancer which such massive exposure to unnecessary radiation must inevitably cause. There is also so much uncalled for surgery performed (notably hysterectomies and the removal of gallbladders) that in 1980 the US Health, Education and Welfare Department launched a campaign advising patients to seek a second opinion before agreeing to undergo any non-emergency operation.

The system also encourages outright fraud, with doctors claiming for services never performed. In the US the federal Medicaid and Medicare programmes, which help to pay the medical bills of the indigent and the elderly respectively, were almost regarded as fair game by many 'anti-welfare' physicians, and in 1982 an Australian Health Ministry report, leaked to journalists, stated that 2500 of the country's 27,000 doctors were suspected of cheating the national medical insurance scheme. There is no reason to suppose that British doctors, faced with a similar opportunity, would prove notably more honest.

The dependence of institutions and individual doctors on fees leads to treatment being denied to unfortunates who can't produce evidence of adequate insurance cover, or some other guarantee that charges will be promptly paid. In 1982 a Baltimore housepainter died from burns in a city 'poor law' hospital after 40 other institutions with special burns units had refused to take him because he was uninsured. A little earlier a white doctor in Alabama actually removed stitches which he had just put in to the wounded arm of a young black patient when the boy couldn't produce the $25 fee. Such ugly incidents are only particularly nasty examples of a 'no cash – no care' attitude which is commonplace in the USA, and we can do without the same sort of happenings here.

*

The answer to the money problems bedevilling the NHS is not to espouse alternative methods for delivering and financing health care – methods of a kind which have served other countries so ill – but to reorganize our precious, free-at-the-time-of-need, national service in such a way that the cash available for its support is spent to the best effect.

There must be a massive shift of resources from the costly and grossly overused hospitals to the front line, so-called, general medical services provided by GPs.

The absurd 'independent contractor' status of family doctors, and the pretence that this gives them a freedom of behaviour they could not otherwise enjoy must be abandoned. Instead they should become well paid, salaried employees of the state, just as hospital consultants are happy to be now (*they* certainly don't regard themselves as 'civil servants'). And, just like consultants, GPs must be given well-designed, well-equipped, and well-staffed premises from which to work, all paid for by the management.

This means setting up a network of health centres throughout the country, and accepting the idea that reasonably easy access to a health centre is a good deal more important to the average citizen than reasonably easy access to a hospital.

In addition to consulting rooms for the half-dozen or more doctors attached to the staff, each centre should have a treatment room (like a small casualty department), a theatre for minor operations and 'day surgery', a laboratory adequate for the performance of the most commonly required biochemical and bacteriological investigations (many of which can now be performed automatically by machines in charge of a technician), a diagnostic X-ray room, a physiotherapy room, a pharmacy, accommodation for nurses, an office for a practice manager and secretaries, a dental surgery, and a couple of rooms for the use of visiting consultants.

A small ward of, say, half-a-dozen beds, would be used for patients recovering from minor surgery, and other briefly upsetting procedures, and for those requiring observation and therapy and investigations of a kind needing more than a short lie down on a couch in the treatment room, but manageable within a working day, since the ward would probably be closed at nights and weekends.

Several studies have shown that most patients are very happy to be seen by a nurse in the first instance, only being passed on to a doctor when the need is apparent or whenever a chat with the boss is desired, so 'nurse practitioners', of which there are already some 15,000 serving rural areas in the USA, could deal with many of the problems bringing clients to the centre, and could also hold sessions in outlying parts of the centre's parish. A well trained and experienced nurse knows a lot more about practical medicine and how to handle patients than a tyro graduate not long out of medical school.

Consultants would remain based in general and special hospitals, which would continue to provide in-patient and out-patient care of a type beyond a health centre's scope, but the hospitals would be much smaller, and the consultants would do much of their out-patient work in the centres, which they would visit on a regular basis. There they would act *truly* as consultants, advising family doctors on the management of sufferers from ills of the flesh and the mind within their field of expertise instead of taking over altogether.

In my scheme the High Street chemist would disappear. Pharmacists undergo a training not much less onerous, and certainly requiring no less intelligence and application for its successful completion, than that imposed upon medical students. In the old days the dispensing chemist actually made up pills and potions according to the elaborate recipes scribbled out by doctors, and for this task special knowledge and skills were essential. Nowadays all he has to do is hand out the correct amounts of the readymade products of the pharmaceutical industry. His considerable learning is totally wasted on this mundane and mechanical task, which could be performed equally well by any literate, numerate, and conscientious school leaver. Moreover the cost of stocking and running his dispensary is so high compared to the dispensing fees he receives from the NHS that he can only survive by flogging lipsticks and cameras and hot water bottles and slimming foods to the shoppers who come in for their magic remedies – an activity not only unrelated but antipathetic to his professional endowment. He does provide a check on the accuracy of prescriptions (about five per cent of scrips presented to dispensing chemists contain some error which has to be queried), and he may spot the fact that a customer is taking an incompatible or even dangerous mixture of drugs. But a computer on the consulting room desk could instantly and unerringly detect wrong dosages, note side effects and necessary warnings, flash a red light if a remedy would react with other and previous prescriptions, and in all respects prevent mistakes more certainly than the most alert and knowledgeable of human dispensers. It could do better than that. Once it had vetted and approved the order typed in, it could pass this to another machine which would disgorge an error-free and immaculately labelled package of the drug prescribed.

Leaving that last slight fantasy aside, it is clear that the neighbourhood pharmacist is now a redundant animal. That's why my health centres will include a dispensary (every hospital has one), for it is costly, unnecessary, and inefficient to divide the prescription and supply of drugs between two different professions. In rural areas where doctors' surgeries are more than a couple of miles away from a chemist's shop, GPs already 'retail' the remedies they prescribe (collecting a dispensing fee), and with no notable detriment to the wellbeing of their customers. So let's get rid of dispensing chemists altogether. They really serve no useful purpose. And the disappearance of dispensing fees would much more than pay for the computers and attendants needed to ensure the competent supply of medicines at health centres.

Such a bold redistribution of spending and of medical man and womanpower from vast, almost unmanageable sickness centres to small, highly efficient health centres would greatly benefit almost everyone concerned, except for the unfortunate redundant pharmacists and the health service unions. (The executives of NUPE, NALGO, COHSE, and the rest would find it far more difficult to organize dangerous and oppressive disruptions of the delivery of health care if the greater part of the job was performed by many separate, close-knit teams, rather than large battalions of mutually mistrustful strangers.)

The customers (for whom, after all, the service exists) would have almost all their health needs expertly catered for by a friendly neighbourhood group of familiars.

The receptionists, managers, nurses, technicians, and cleaning ladies would have the pleasure and satisfaction of feeling and knowing that they were making a direct and valued contribution to the wellbeing of the community to which they belonged.

The consultants would doubtless at first resent seeing the physical size of their personal empires diminish, but should soon begin to revel in the relief they would gain from much routine clinical work and administration. Their daily rounds would become refreshingly more varied, and they would have more opportunity to ponder and busy themselves and experiment within their own special necks of the medical wood.

The family doctors would have their lives transformed. Instead of a dreary, repetitive ritual of three minute consultations ending with a dashed-off prescription or note to 'the hospital', they would enjoy the fascination of practising real medicine. They would have the time to treat their patients as individuals, and to get to know them and understand their problems, and to be supportive, and they would be loved and honoured for it. Their competence and enthusiasm would no longer fray and diminish with the passage of the years, for they would lose their corrupting isolation, and have the constant stimulation of membership of a multi-talented team of fellow professionals. They would have decent holidays and a proper ration of guaranteed leisure and privacy without having to arrange for and rely on unknown and possibly incompetent paid deputies.

The tax payer would have the satisfaction of paying for the cheapest and best health service in the world.

There would be no need to assail the personal freedom of either doctors or their customers by proscribing private practice, for the benefits offered by the NHS would be so excellent that few would want to pay for anything else, and the number who did would only support a modest structure which would not be large enough to grab any significant share of the total resources of cash and skill and energy available for health care.

Just to paint the lily I would establish regional medical colleges (or perhaps they should be called colleges of health). These would be buildings set apart from any hospital and would be as much a club as an academy. Each would have a restaurant, a bar, a lounge, and even tennis courts and squash courts and a swimming pool, as well as a library, seminar rooms, lecture theatre, and other accessories of learning. Membership would be open to GPs, consultants, nurses, ambulance men, schoolteachers, radiographers, parsons, policemen, nutritionists, accountants, drug manufacturers, journalists, milliners, and any and everyone sharing an active interest in the health of the nation. There they could meet on equal terms and learn a very great deal from one another.

The medical mafia would disintegrate.

CHAPTER FOUR

Unlucky for Some

Almost half of all Britain's hospital beds are occupied by people with some disorder of the mind, and one in every six girls and one in every nine boys now at school can expect to spend at least one spell in a mental hospital before they die. This means that most of us are likely to be affected personally by mental illness at some time or other, either as sufferers, or as the relatives or friends of patients.

That being the case, you might think that most of us would feel a selfish interest in making sure that the mentally ill are treated not only with humanity and skill, but that they also continue to enjoy as much liberty and capacity for self-determination as, say, motorcyclists, politicians, tight-rope artists, and others whose proclivities and attitudes pose a potential danger to the public or themselves.

It is not so. We like to shut lunatics away. We abnegate responsibility for their welfare upon the illusory and dishonest excuse that psychiatrists know best, so that we can leave our awkward friends and relatives and neighbours entirely in their hands. We are only too happy to forget them. This may partly be due to embarrassment, because while we can bring ourselves to sustain a relationship with the blind, or the paralysed, or even the dying, we just don't know how to react in the presence of irrational behaviour. But it is also a result of an atavistic fear of 'mad' people.

Introducing the White Paper which led up to the Mental Health Act 1983, David Ennals (who *is* enlightened, and was then Secretary of State for Social Services) said, 'There has been a dramatic change in attitudes to mental disorder.' This is only half true. Some of the myths have been dispelled. Some of the conditions under which lunatics are treated compare well with those current a couple of centuries ago (we no longer, for example, think it right to keep the wretched creatures in chains). But the fear remains, and the mentally abnormal remain second-class citizens, and are too often subjected to gross indignities, and even neglect and overt cruelty, without the rest of us lifting a finger or sounding even a muted protest in their defence.

Our lunatic asylums contain three kinds of patients. First there are the mentally handicapped. These are unfortunates who have a subnormal intelligence, and they range from the none-too-bright (who are just as capable as many of their fellow citizens who remain abroad and free), to idiots who can't dress or wash or feed themselves. Mental deficiency is predominantly a congenital condition, resulting from an incomplete or aberrant development of the brain, as in the case of mongols. Occasionally it is caused by disease or injury to an originally competent and well-developed organ. The mentally ill form the second group. These are people of normal or, not infrequently, superior intelligence whose minds have begun to function in an inappropriate fashion, such as schizophrenics who may hear voices or suspect they are the targets of death rays, and depressives who are plagued by gloom and apathy for no good cause. The mentally ill in hospitals can be divided into two further groups. There are the 'front ward' patients, in for a comparatively short time, perhaps only a matter of weeks, who respond to treatment, and can then get back to a more or less normal life outside, and there are the chronically ill (or often merely abandoned) 'back ward' inhabitants who may stay in the tender care of the psychiatrists for many months or years, or even a lifetime. Of these three groups the mentally subnormal and the 'back ward' mentally ill suffer incomparably the worse deal, but even the short-term patients are frequently ill served. A particular lunatic asylum may cater solely for the subnormal, or solely for the ill, or may enclose both.

It is important to realise that the huge Victorian institutions for lunatics and idiots which spatter the land were not built for the treatment of the mentally disabled, but for their containment. There is still no cure for subnormality, and such effective methods as exist today for the amelioration of mental disease are mostly the fruits of research within the pharmaceutical industry, and are not the result of psychiatrists knowing what has gone wrong with the mechanism of a sick mind, and therefore knowing how to put things right. Indeed, some of the major drugs now used in psychiatry are derived from compounds which were originally investigated with a quite different possible use in view, and which were observed, by chance, to have an effect upon the behaviour of rats or some other caged innocents during the many animal tests used in the screening of potential new medicines. A century ago, of course, when many of the asylums still in use went up, there were no such drugs, or any other kinds of valid therapy, available.

Before the Industrial Revolution there were few places for the custody of mental cripples. The weak-minded – the traditional village idiots – had got along well enough within their own small communities where their quirks and limitations were understood and indulged. It is true that some of the more bizarre and less engaging habits of schizophrenic spinsters earned them harrassment as witches, but on the whole it was a good time for the dotty. A system which we like to think we have just invented – community care – was working well.

Then the towns began to grow. A large proportion of the population began to live in novel and impersonal herds. The imbecilic and irrational became a peril to themselves and a nuisance to their bustling fellow citizens. So the asylums were hastily built, behind high walls, and well away from the homes of ordinary, decent, God-fearing folk. And the mental mavericks were quietly put out of sight and out of mind.

That explains why so many of our mental 'hospitals' look more like prisons, for that's exactly what they were and too often still are. And it explains why these isolated institutions have largely escaped involvement in the medical revolution which has totally changed the nature of every other sort of hospital, and why they are still a recurrent cause of scandal and the scenes of man's inhumanity to man of a kind that does not occur in any other sector of our national life.

*

For many years the appalling conditions suffered by long-stay mental patients remained largely hidden and unrecognized. Then, in 1967, the *News of the World* received, and forwarded to the Minister of Health, a statement by a former nursing assistant at the Ely Hospital, Cardiff (which deals with both the ill and the subnormal) alleging cruel ill-treatment of certain male patients by some members of the staff, the pilfering by staff of food, clothing, and other items belonging to the hospital or patients, an indifference on the part of the Chief Male Nurse towards complaints made to him, and a lack of care by the Physician Superintendent and one other member of the medical staff.

A committee of inquiry was appointed under the chairmanship of Geoffrey Howe, and it issued a report in 1969 confirming the fact that patients had been beaten and robbed, that children had been kept in filthy circumstances, that the nursing and medical staff showed 'an unduly casual attitude' towards deaths among the inmates, and that concerned nurses who complained were victimized and forced to resign. No attempt was made to train junior nurses, who were simply left to get on with the job. Nurses sutured wounds caused by their own rough handling of patients, and gave drugs to keep their charges quiet, without the knowledge or authority of the medical staff.

Here is one grisly item from a dreadful catalogue of malefactions, which nicely illustrates the almost unbelievably callous and slatternly attitudes then characterizing that miserable pound. The wife of a man suffering from senile dementia visited her husband and wanted to feed him a pear. She asked a nurse to bring his false teeth. The woman complied 'by endeavouring to fit a set from a bowl in which a number of unidentified dentures were kept together. The nurse probably also tried to fit (him) with a set of dentures removed from the mouth of a sleeping patient, after "rinsing them under a tap".'

Among the recommendations made by the Howe committee (apart from the basic need for 'the complete reconstruction of the hospital'), was the radical suggestion that 'Every patient should have a locker of his own. Patients can thus be enabled to have clothing that will be and remain their own'. And be it noted that the necessity for proposing such a great leap forward arose in prosperous Britain a mere quarter of a century after the publication of the Beveridge Report and the institution of the Welfare State.

By the time Howe had completed his investigations, Dick Crossman (far too honest a man to reach the top in politics) had become first holder of the newly created post of Secretary of State for Social Services, and was therefore the minister responsible. He decided to publish the report in full, when a lesser mortal might have decided to keep the shameful details secret.

But Crossman was determined to better the lot of the mentally disabled, and reasoned that telling the appalling truth, and so arousing the public conscience, would powerfully aid him in the task. Before the end of the year he had acted on one of Howe's major proposals by appointing a Dr Alex Baker as the first director of an entirely new body, independent of the Department of Health, to be called the Hospital Advisory Service.

Baker, a consultant psychiatrist of the better kind (and the good can be very, very good, even though the poor are horrid), assembled teams of experts – psychiatrists, nurses, hospital administrators, and social workers – whose task it was to visit asylums spending up to a week in each, in order to talk with staff and patients, and to look at their organization, and their practices and their facilities, and to identify deficiencies and problems, and also to take note of successful projects and good ideas. The teams went about their business with a will, and after each visitation wrote a detailed report, including recommendations for improvements. Copies went to the hospitals and health authorities concerned, and to the Secretary of State. In Crossman's own words, the visitors acted as 'the eyes and ears of the minister'.

The hope was that such a continuing programme of surveillance and constructive criticism would make it impossible for another Ely to happen ever again. The hope proved vain.

In 1971 an inquiry was ordered into allegations of cruelty and corruption at Whittingham Hospital in Lancashire, the country's third largest institution for the mentally ill. The committee was told, amongst many other scandalous items, of incontinent patients being 'bathed' with long mops used for cleaning floors, of bedridden geriatric patients being tormented and abused for the amusement of staff, of methylated spirits being poured on two patients and then set alight, of patients being locked all day in a coal house, and of 'difficult' patients being choked with damp towels twisted round their necks to 'quieten them down'. A male nurse told of how when he joined the staff he was offered £4 a week as his share of a 'racket' involving patients' cash and cigarettes. Government auditors had been unable to trace the fate of £49,000 of patients' money. A one-time assistant psychiatrist on the staff described how frightened patients sat 'mute and unresponsive' in a locked ward, dressed in drab clothes, and with nothing to do. Detailed complaints made by a concerned group of student nurses four years previously had been suppressed. When the committee reported its findings Sir Keith Joseph, who had succeeded Dick Crossman as Secretary of State, explained to the Commons that the Hospital Advisory Service had not been able to visit Whittingham because police inquiries had been taking place. All the remaining members of the hospital management committee were asked to resign, and Sir Keith said that the main hope of avoiding similar scandals in the future lay in choosing management 'with drive and ability'.

So what happened?

In 1972 an inquiry confirmed allegations of overcrowding, understaffing, cruelty and neglect at South Ockendon Hospital for the subnormal in Essex. At one stage the hospital group secretary acknowledged that he had received, via the Home Office, details of police accusations of negligence against one of his charge nurses, but said, 'I did not consider taking any action because I am afraid it did not occur to me.' He should have brought the matter to the attention of the hospital management committee, but although he had read the document involved, he 'did not examine it in great detail'.

In 1973 an official report on Napsbury mental hospital, near St Albans, revealed that a number of the inmates had suffered brutally harsh discipline and neglect as a result of a consultant psychiatrist's monomaniacal devotion to the idea that unacceptable behaviour of the mad could best be controlled by a system of punishments and rewards, or in other words that the patients in his care were best treated as though they were a kennelful of Pavlov dogs. Non-cooperative customers, who failed to 'improve' under this regime, were not allowed visitors, and were not given food if they couldn't get it for themselves, and were purposely allowed to live in squalor if they didn't attend to their own cleanliness and domestic chores. Visiting relatives spoke of 'row upon row of dirty plates with stale food slopping all over greasy tables', and of 'disgusting kitchens, filthy sheets and tattered old blankets', and 'the stench of unwashed patients wandering around in clothes they'd been wearing and sleeping in for weeks'.

The consultant concerned, a man with high academic qualifications, admitted using 'brutal' methods, both on patients and their parents, as a matter of policy. He told a local paper that 'We occasionally have to be brutal to parents in the patients' interests. They are feeling guilty, and in fact they like to be attacked. They know they are partly to blame for their child being in Napsbury.' The committee of inquiry acknowledged that the consultant and his team genuinely felt that the end (which was to prevent patients and their families abandoning themselves to the acceptance of prolonged institutional care) justified the means employed. Some might feel that the conditions revealed would have been marginally less horrifying if they *had* been the result of callousness and incompetence rather than a frighteningly misconceived missionary zeal. Sir Keith told Parliament that he accepted entirely the investigators' view that the situation they found 'should not exist in an NHS hospital'.

Similar reports, involving hospitals throughout the land, and telling the now familiar tales of brutalities, indignities, slum conditions, lax leadership, overuse of drugs, and so on and so on, received nationwide publicity in 1976, 1978, 1981 and 1982, and on each occasion some minister admitted that the conditions described were intolerable within a state medical service, and that steps would be taken to ensure that such scandalous happenings should cease.

In 1983 Mrs Thatcher ordered an inquiry into allegations of 'appalling conditions' at Botley's Park Hospital for the mentally handicapped in Surrey, the peripatetic inspectors having this time described the toilet areas as 'the most disgraceful we have ever seen'.

The percipient reader will have noted that Mrs Thatcher's determination to discover why patients at Botley's Park were disgracefully ill-served in 1983 was expressed a full 14 years after Dick Crossman, as a senior cabinet minister, had taken exceptional steps designed to ensure that the Ely Hospital scandal should be the last of its kind.

These post-Ely horror stories here recalled are only examples of a general and apparently incurable malaise which happen to have received publicity, either because of complaints by relatives, or by courageous or disaffected members of staff, or because of some unconcealable crisis such as a strike. There have, in addition, been numerous reports of acts of cruelty and neglect by individual nurses which have led to criminal proceedings. In July 1983 the *Guardian* published summaries of 18 reports (17 of which were either wholly or partly confidential), prepared by the Development Team for the Mentally Handicapped, and which dealt with 50 hospitals and 30 hostels or homes visited by the team between 1976 and 1982.

The confidentiality (which, in useful and characteristic fashion, the *Guardian* spoiled) was ostensibly applied not as a cover-up, but to encourage frankness and cooperation between the inspectors and the inspected. However that may be, the reports demonstrated that (with no more than a handful of honourable exceptions), Ely-type conditions are still the rule, and that a succession of visitations and ministerial lamentations have had no remedial effect.

*

Why is this so when, apparently, politicians do care, or are, at least, sufficiently embarrassed by each horrific revelation to pretend shocked disbelief and a determination to put things right? Why did almost all the dismal institutions dealt with in the reports leaked to the *Guardian* provoke the customary comments concerning 'filthy beds', 'appalling toilets without doors', 'unexplained injuries to patients', 'indefinite prescribing of drugs', and so on, while a very few, such as the Ryegate Centre at the Children's Hospital in Sheffield, earned praise, this particular establishment being described as a 'superb modern unit providing short stay and long term care. Homely, colourful and cheerful'? The rare exceptions demonstrate that high standards *can* be achieved with the resources available.

The answer is that staff – doctors, nurses and administrators – who find work in these wretched backwaters of the NHS are, in general, third-raters. Within the hospital service at large there is intense competition for a share of the finite amount of money and human effort and intelligence available, and the most energetic and ambitious and resourceful operators – be they consultants or nursing officers or managers – procure more for their own departments and communes and activities at the expense of their less forceful and dedicated colleagues. They get the best facilities, and the best assistants, and the best working conditions. Whoever heard of a kidney transplant unit with filthy beds, and in which 'difficult' patients were apt to be knocked about?

No government directive forces a regional or area health authority to limit the money and attention to be devoted to the care of the mentally disabled to such and such a proportion of its total time and budget, with the rest to be spent on the more glamorous, obvious, and therefore politically rewarding aspects of state 'given' medical aid. However, politicians, both at national and local levels, together with the civil servants whose job it is actually to get things done, are commonly disinclined to go out looking for trouble and making extra problems for themselves, and so, given an isolated institution, staffed by lazy, or inefficient, or demoralized doctors and nurses who wish only to be left alone and undisturbed, 'superior' functionaries in the NHS hierarchy, from officials concerned with the immediate district upwards, are happy to ignore the place. Meanwhile, back at the ranch, things go from bad to worse, the imbroglios stemming from physical and spiritual decay grow ever less tractable, and are therefore ever more studiously disregarded until and unless some kind of explosion occurs.

The primary fault lies in the poor quality of the consultant psychiatrists, for if they fail to provide vigorous leadership, and if they are patently unconcerned by low or disgraceful standards of patient care – if they walk past filthy beds and the miserable, ill-clad inhabitants of their joyless wards without comment, and never trouble to see how their charges are fed, or to cast a glance at where they wash or piss or shit – then, inevitably, the nursing staff will quickly lose heart, and not only give up the struggle to make the best of a very bad job, but, often enough, will come to resent and oppress the patients they know they are letting down. It is unreasonable to expect all the nurses in mental hospitals to be Florence Nightingales, and to kick against the pricks.

Many of the published adverse reports on mental hospitals take pains to stress that a majority of the nursing staff are making a brave attempt to provide ordinary, decent standards of care against impossible odds. Sometimes such statements may be no more than a considerate effort to cushion the distress which harsh criticisms of institutions must cause to those staff members – particularly juniors – who bear none of the responsibility for appalling practices and conditions. And often, of course, nurses and other ancillary staff of mental hospitals are good people who are made indignant and frustrated by a lack of resources and concern, and who do strive to minimize the effects of official neglect and inertia. But most mental nurses, however kind their hearts, and however noble the motives that drew them to the task, are not from among the brightest and best of their generation. While senior staff have received a training which is, in theory at any rate, equivalent to that undergone by the State Registered Nurses who run the wards and out-patient departments of general hospitals, mental institutions largely rely upon so-called State Enrolled Nurses for the care of the mentally ill – SEN(M) – or the mentally subnormal – SEN(MS). They become members of a health service union, and do not owe allegiance to the Royal College of Nursing. These grades have a lower educational requirement for entry, and a shorter period of tuition (two years instead of three). Moreover, the quality of training given (in line with the poorer standards of mental hospitals all round) is frequently deficient. In December 1981, for example, the General Nursing Council temporarily withdrew recognition of Rampton special hospital as a training school, despite opposition from the Department of Health. This grave step was taken following an inspection which revealed that 'training was not evident', and that pupils at that grossly understaffed institution were primarily used as extra pairs of hands.

Many mental nurses come from abroad. Would-be immigrants from countries like Spain can obtain work permits for service in mental hospitals if the employing authorities can show that they have been unable to recruit the necessary labour locally. Because of poor pay and horrific working conditions, the authorities can often do this in convincing fashion. I once heard a senior mental nurse complain how he, as the person supervising the night watch in a part of his own hospital, had the support of nine juniors – and between them they represented seven nations. Now, as everyone knows, there is nothing essentially wrong with foreigners. They are all God's creatures. But migrants with a strange background and culture are not likely to be best placed to empathize with what are to them mad aliens. Or, to put the matter in more brutal terms, we employ people who can't find a decent job in their own countries to look after our lunatics because we can't find sufficient native

Britishers to do the work. We employ, for this thankless task, the otherwise unemployable.

Many – perhaps most – of these semi-skilled workers could become effective guardians and therapists as members of disciplined and well lead teams within communities where compassion and carefulness and human dignity are held in high regard. They are particularly vulnerable to corruption when recruited into institutions where discipline is poor, morale low, and loving kindness difficult to discern.

*

Psychiatry, far from being an exact science, hardly merits description as a scientific discipline at all. We still have small idea of the mechanisms of intellectual disorders and deficiencies, and such insights as have been gained within recent years are largely the fruit of the work of neurophysiologists and other laboratory-based investigators, rath._ .han the results of the observations and acumen of clinical psychiatrists, and the experience gained in the course of their dealings with the mentally disabled. Thus it is possible for two distinguished, seasoned and successful psychiatrists, such as Dr William Sargant on the one hand and Dr Thomas Szasz on the other, to hold diametrically opposed views on the causes and proper handling of madness. Sargant is convinced that a disordered mind is the result of some physical or biochemical abnormality, and that effective treatment demands drugs or ECT or, sometimes, surgery, with the aim of correcting or interfering with the faulty function. Szasz believes that what we call madness is simply the socially unacceptable response of a normal mind to abnormal and insupportable circumstances, such as nagging or purblind parents who strive to force a child to behave in a manner contrary to his or her nature and desires. Szasz's patients, therefore, are not drugged or shocked out of their awkwardness, but shown the supposed external causes of their intellectual distress, and are taught to understand and accept them, or, if possible, to change them. It is as though a heart specialist at, say, St Thomas's, believed coronary artery disease to be a punishment by God for sin and that the remedy lay in repentance and prayer, while his oppo, over at Barts, believed the condition to be due to constipation, and treated all his customers with Epsom salts, neither 'expert' (or anyone else for that matter) having the first idea of the true roots of the malady.

Good psychiatrists are good not because they know what is actually happening in the computer circuits of the mind, and how the nerve cells work, and what is amiss in the functioning of the neurones of the mentally ill. They are good because they are humane, intelligent, empathetic, priest-like men and women who understand the problems of their fellow beings in distress, and can so give the support and encouragement their patients need. And it doesn't much matter whether they blame aberrant molecules or difficult parents for their patients' ills. Most of the 'special' insights they possess concerning the nature of the human beast are to be found, lambently proclaimed, in the Bible and the works of Shakespeare. It is true that *some* drugs, skilfully used, can bring dramatic benefit to *some* patients, so that a customer of a psychiatrist of the Szasz persuasion might, upon occasion, be ill served. On the other hand, he (or, more likely, she) would be safe from the gross damage which the ham-handed ignorant, and inappropriate or profligate use of dangerous remedies does to many who seek psychiatric aid.

Bad psychiatrists are bad because, while sharing their superior colleagues' ignorance of the brain's machinery, they lack their human virtues and intelligence and common sense, and in the absence of a teachable corpus of proven psychiatric wisdom (comparable to that which can, for example, make a competent orthopaedic surgeon out of an otherwise somewhat unimaginative hack), they are left without the resources needed for the successful performance of an exceptionally demanding branch of medical practice.

Good psychiatrists are attracted to the trade because they are fascinated by the personality of their patients, as opposed merely to the functioning of their flesh. Bad psychiatrists drift into the business after medical school because it provides a soft option to anybody happy to bumble along in bottom gear, for while good psychiatry requires dedicated effort, it is a specialty within which the incompetent are well protected against comebacks. Some choose it as a ready route to the exercise of power over their fellow beings. It is the easiest discipline in which to achieve an NHS consultancy. The best psychiatrists obtain appointments to the staffs of teaching and general hospitals and universities. The poor end up in the asylums. In particular, the asylums recruit many of their junior medical staff (well over 60 per cent) from the pool of immigrant doctors who come here from the nations which were once a part of the Empire (predominantly Indians and Pakistanis), in the hope of increasing their professional status by working in British hospitals and acquiring higher qualifications in medicine or surgery, but who find that the only employment open to them are the jobs that native graduates won't take. So it is that many of the doctors staffing our asylums (just like many of the nurses) are where they are not because they have the smallest interest in the problems of the mentally disabled, but because the mental hospitals are the only places willing to employ them. It is from amongst such reluctant alienists that a high proportion of the necessary corps of consultants must be found. Given the state of the art and the quality of many of its practitioners, it is hardly surprising that patients are often subjected to questionable treatments of a kind which frequently do more harm than good.

*

The big breakthrough in the handling of the insane came with the introduction of the tranquillizers, notably the so-called major tranquillizers, and in particular the phenothiazines, including such well known brand name preparations as Largactil, Thorazine, and Stelazine. These drugs, as their group title suggests, calm the troubled mind, controlling overactive and manic patients but without noticeably imparing consciousness. They relieve many of the symptoms of schizophrenia, and make patients more compliant. Their use has allowed many seriously disturbed psychotics to be discharged, after a brief stay in hospital, to continue their treatment outside. However, they are much abused.

Their calming effect makes a wardful of potentially disruptive and difficult customers – whether mentally ill or mentally subnormal – far easier to control, and, with staff shortage a 'normal' feature of lunatic asylum life, the prolonged and routine administration of these 'chemical straitjackets' or 'liquid coshes' is commonplace. Since they do not cure, but merely suppress some of the more troublesome manifestations of mental disability, their lavish use does not so much constitute treatment for the benefit of the sick as management for the benefit of the staff. This might not matter too much, were it not for the fact that the phenothiazines and other major tranquillizers exert some highly pernicious side effects. These include disorders of the heart and circulation, drowsiness, depression, indifference, a possibly fatal depression of production of white blood cells, liver damage (also sometimes fatal), breast enlargement in men, the suppression of periods in women, skin rashes (which may be severe), and a nervous complaint called tardive dyskinesia. This last resembles Parkinson's disease, or the 'shaking palsy', and involves distressing, involuntary, muscular movements, particularly of the face, lips, and tongue. The condition may be permanent, and there is no cure, although there are agents which can reduce the blatancy of the expression of the poisoned nerve machine. Unfortunately these 'anti-Parkinsonism' drugs have their own unpleasant side effects, so that their use to relieve one disorder may well lead to another.

Tardive dyskinesia is the most important of the more serious side effects accompanying the wholesale use of the major tranquillizers because it is so common. In 1982 a Canadian study, undertaken at the Royal Victoria Hospital in Montreal, suggested that one-third of all patients given such drugs develop the signs and symptoms of this fundamental damage to the brain, and the author of the report, Guy Chouinard, director of the hospital's department of clinical psychopharmacology, added his support to the several groups of experts who, within recent years, have maintained that these powerful and toxic agents should only be used for the *short-term* treatment of acutely disturbed patients. Such warnings have been generally ignored.

In November 1981 an inquest was held into the death of Mrs Jacqueline Shalloe, a once cheerful, healthy woman who became depressed after the birth of her third child. She had been under treatment for some years, during which time she developed epilepsy, possibly caused by medicines. She died in Long Grove psychiatric hospital, Surrey, as a result of what a pathologist described as 'a hazardous regime of drugs'. Her prescription sheet carried entries for eight different drugs which act on the brain, including three major tranquillizers and an anti-Parkinsonism agent. Five of these drugs, including two of the major tranquillizers were marked prn, the initials of the Latin phrase *pro re nata*, meaning 'as occasion arises', which authorized her nurses to give all or any of them at their own discretion. On the evening of her death Mrs Shalloe was given one of the so-called 'minor tranquillizers' (like Valium) as a sleeping pill, but remained agitated. Four hours later she was given a large dose (double the normally recommended maximum) of Sodium Amytal, a barbiturate. One hour after that she received an injection of Largactil. She had been given other drugs during the day. She died three and a half hours after the Largactil injection from hypostatic pneumonia, literally drowning as a result of a rapid leakage of body fluids into the lungs. This was directly due to the paralysing effect on her breathing of the drugs she had received within the previous few hours. Apart from their individual actions such agents also interact and potentiate one another.

The fatal mixture was administered by nurses who had not, it seems, appreciated the dangerous nature of their actions. The consultant involved defended the prescribing of hazardous drugs 'prn' on the grounds that this reduced medication to a minimum, no dose (in theory) being given unless apparent need arose. He said, 'We have to give discretion to the nursing staff.' However, his faith in the system of giving 'discretion to the nursing staff' seemed hardly justified in the light of his next amazing words. 'We work the dosage out. We do as best we can. *We do not know the qualifications of the staff* (my italics). It is not for the doctor to comment on what is a nursing administration matter.'

This is just one tragic incident arising from the ill-considered use of dangerous drugs in mental hospitals which happens to have been exposed in some detail, but inappropriate and damaging medication is commonplace. Indeed, the misuse and overuse of drugs is a familiar item in the catalogue of faults compiled by inspection teams. It is likely that many hospital deaths, particularly among the old, are caused or hastened by drug damage. It is certain that the mind-numbing effect of prolonged and heavy sedation is a major factor in the gross deterioration of intellect and spirit which characterizes the 'institutionalized', long-stay, mental hospital patient.

A few psychiatrists (fortunately their number is comparatively small) believe in 'chemical castration'. They give a female sex hormone (oestradiol) or a male sex hormone antagonist (cyproterone) with the idea of reducing the sex drive or libido of male sexual offenders – rapists and child molesters. Both drugs have serious side effects. Most experts believe that the urge to commit sexual assaults has little to do with ordinary sexual desire, and in 1975 a WHO expert report strongly condemned 'castration or hormonal demasculinization' as a means for preventing such behaviour, holding the treatment to be ineffectual. This view, however, has cut no ice with the enthusiasts.

In 1978, for example, the Home Office confirmed that over the previous decade more than 70 inmates of Dartmoor, imprisoned for sexual crimes, had been given oestradiol, in the form of implanted pellets, by a psychiatrist, Dr Otho Fitz-Gerald, a pioneer of the technique. Unfortunately oestradiol makes the breasts grow. Dr Fitz-Gerald had a simple answer to this tedious consequence. He sent his patients to a surgeon to have their unwanted breasts cut off. He claimed, at the time, that he had never pushed the treatment on his customers, all of whom 'came to me for help', and had signed a form acknowledging that they had been told what would happen to them. However, offering a drastic remedy of unproven worth to prisoners is ethically reprehensible, since such subjects are bound to have their judgement influenced by the hope that compliance with the suggestion of authority will attract favour, and perhaps procure an early release. In Dr Fitz-Gerald's defence it must be said that he didn't regard his offering as 'of unproven worth', stating that 'I reckon that I have saved dozens of children from sexual assault. This treatment is the only possible answer we have to this social problem.' He had, of course, no kind of proof for his assertions, for even if all his victims had subsequently led blameless lives (as opposed to merely telling the doctor what they knew he wanted to hear) it would have taken a massive and complex study to demonstrate beyond a peradventure that this happy result was indeed due to the administration of a havoc-wreaking drug, and not to some other factor, such as the unusual attention they received.

Apart from demonstrating the fact that some psychiatrists are perfectly happy to employ Draconian measures in the pursuit of doubtful ends, chemical or physical castration as a means for subduing socially unacceptable behaviour is a nasty example of a dangerous kind of abuse of medical skills, and is not so far removed from the Soviet habit of locking perfectly sane dissidents away in punitive mental 'hospitals'.

*

Electroconvulsive therapy (ECT) is frequently misused and overused, just as happens with drugs. Many knowledgeable doctors, including not a few psychiatrists, would say that it should not be used at all. One British brain pundit has described the procedure as the equivalent of 'kicking the telly when it's on the blink'.

The idea of 'shocking' lunatics out of their oddity (which is disturbingly reminiscent of earlier attempts to purge the mad of their possession by whippings or dunkings in the village pond) arose from a misconception. Certain percipient clinical psychiatrists had observed that epileptics never suffer from schizophrenia, and vice versa. It was later shown that this percipience was at fault. There is no such cross-immunity. The declaration of a great new medical truth had been based (as so often happens) upon an insufficiently rigorous examination of the evidence. But before the fallacy had been exposed the clever dicks of the psychiatric trade had already argued, in typically specious fashion, that if epileptic convulsions prevent the development of insanity, then the artificial induction of brain seizures should cure the mentally ill.

In pursuance of this illogical belief large numbers of schizo-phrenics and other psychotics were put into coma with insulin injections from the 1930s onwards, and until about 20 years ago, because this was one controllable way of giving the brain a 'kick'. Some early patients were subjected to painful intra-muscular injections of convulsant drugs such as the poisonous oil of camphor. But in 1938 a couple of Italians, Cerletti and Bini, were bold enough to induce fits in patients by passing a brief electric current through the brain via electrodes applied to the temples, and found that they could get away with it. The shock produces instantaneous unconsciousness and also causes generalized convulsions very similar to a major epileptic seiz-ure. The muscle spasms can be violent enough to break bones. Consciousness returns after a few minutes, leaving the patient confused, generally suffering from a headache, and with a loss of recent memory. Sleep follows, and on waking the victim has largely forgotten the event. This is called unmodified ECT. Usually, these days, the victim is first anaesthetized, given a drug which paralyses the muscles to prevent the hazardous convulsions, and is kept alive by artificial respiration until the paralysing drug wears off. Courses of treatment commonly consist of two or three sessions a week for two to six weeks, but some psychiatrists will subject severely disturbed patients to two or three electrical buffettings in the course of a single day.

It was soon apparent to psychiatrists who were honest with themselves that ECT was, to say the least, of dubious value in the treatment of schizophrenia – the condition which sparked the whole thing off – but a proportion of sufferers from severe depression, who have not responded to antidepressant drugs, show dramatic improvement after receiving their shocks. However, even after 50 years of widespread use we have no idea *why* disrupting brain circuits with the electrical equivalent of a cosh should restore the disordered mind, or indeed whether it ever actually does so. Numerous attempts at controlled trials, involving such manoeuvres as giving half of a group of patients the real thing and the other half an anaesthetic plus all the trappings but no actual shock, have produced conflicting or inconclusive results. This of itself is significant, because it is typical of investigations into therapies which are ultimately shown to have no specific impact on the troubles they were designed to alleviate, and whose apparent efficacy depends upon the subjective assessment of the treaters and the treated. (No doubt many of the patients of Sir Arbuthnot Lane, whose colons were cut out as a cure for their often imaginary ills, were persuaded that they had benefited from the operation, despite the fact that they had risked their lives and spent their money unreasonably. And no doubt many ECT victims, and their advisers, are persuaded that the malady so attacked is less after the event, whatever the truth may be. Perhaps it is just the persuasion that counts.)

In particular, the occasional, dramatic lifting of severe depression following ECT, which is often advanced as 'proof' of the procedure's efficacy, is nothing of the sort. It may be significant that the most rewarding subjects are those who have failed to respond to drugs. This suggests the possibility that there was nothing amiss with their brain chemistry or electrical activity in the first place, and that they were suffering from a form of hysteria, which might have responded to any kind of physical or emotional jolt (just as, for example, hysterical blindness may sometimes respond to a blow on the head).

But whatever the truth of the matter – whether the curative effect of ECT is a complete delusion, or whether the passage of a current through the brain does correct a disordered mechanism from time to time – there is not the smallest doubt that too many psychiatrists subject too many patients to unwarranted electrical assault, and do so, often, in a slapdash and irresponsible fashion.

At the end of 1981 the Royal College of Psychiatrists published a major report on the use and abuse of ECT, based on over 3000 questionnaires which had been sent to every doctor in the UK known to be using the ritual, and on the results of visits by college investigators to many of the 400 hospitals and clinics where the treatment is employed.

It was found that ECT administration is usually left to junior members of the medical staff who have received little training or guidance in the use of the technique, and who have acquired such know-how as they may possess, not from their psychiatric bosses but from the anaesthetists or attendant nurses who, just by looking on, had become familiar with the routine. (It is as though a neophyte brain surgeon had to learn his art from the promptings of the theatre sister.) Very few clinics displayed diagrams showing the correct positioning of ECT electrodes. The machines are made so that the strength and duration of the shock delivered can be varied to suit the supposed needs of individual patients, but in 72 per cent of the institutions visited the settings on the apparatus were never altered. In more than a quarter of the clinics the machines were obsolete and did not conform to accepted safety standards. Many of the older machines had no automatic timer, so that the duration of the shock delivered depended entirely upon the manipulations of inexperienced operators – a particularly serious fault since overdoses can lead to prolonged memory impairment. Many of the staff involved were bored, apathetic, and hostile to the technique. In about one fifth of the clinics visited the surroundings were quite unsuitable for patients, who were sometimes treated in an uncaring and cavalier fashion, *and this in the presence of visiting gurus.* Be it noted that this scarifying report was not the work of some pressure group, opposed to the rite, and anxious to discredit its practitioners, but was compiled and published by the psychiatrists' own professional body.

*

Psychosurgery has a therapeutic value at least as dubious as that attributed to ECT, with the added disadvantage that the results are irreversible, and that while it is questionable whether any patient's state of mind has ever been improved as a direct and genuine consequence of such interference, it is certain and acknowledged that many victims of this drastic stratagem have suffered grave and permanent damage.

The idea that slicing up the brain might ameliorate some forms of mental turmoil was advanced by a Portuguese neurologist, Antonio Egas Moniz, in a famous monograph published in 1936. He had harassed chimpanzees until they became neurotic, and had then found that he was able to reduce the severity of some aspects of the disturbed behaviour he had induced by severing the nerve fibres connecting the front of the brain (the frontal lobes) with the rest of the organ. The logic of this procedure (such as it was) lay in the fact that the frontal lobes are supposed to mediate the individual's intellectual response to external circumstances and to instinctual drives such as appetite, aggression and lust. A surgical colleague had performed the first human leucotomy (as the slicing of the white nerve bundles is called) a year before the Moniz monograph came out.

The unfortunate apes whose states of mind were reportedly improved by leucotomies were, of course, sane animals, until Moniz got at them, and it may be questioned whether monkeys, artificially driven to distraction, are comparable to 'mad' people (except, perhaps, Szasz's kind of essentially sane schizophrenics). But this small fault in reasoning did not prevent the psychiatrists of the world from hailing the Moniz monograph as a 'breakthrough'. In 1936 the major tranquillizers had not yet become the chief weapons of the trade, and psychiatrists everywhere were looking desperately for something they could do for disorders of the mind they didn't understand.

In 1949 Moniz received a Nobel Prize for his supposedly major contribution to the welfare of mental invalids, and by then some tens of thousands of patients had been subjected to mutilation of the brain. They had holes bored each side of the skull, just above the temple, through which a knife was inserted and waggled around to destroy the millions of fibres presumed to be carrying disruptive and inappropriate signals, and thus, as one eminent British neurosurgeon later put the matter, 'to break a vicious circuit of tension', a concept as vague and unsubstantiated as dear old Arbuthnot Lane's poison-absorbing colons.

It was not until the early 1950s that a few of the more thoughtful physically-minded psychiatrists began to question whether leucotomies actually worked. Everybody who believed in the organic (as opposed to the purely psychological) basis of mental disease had simply accepted as unquestionable the axiom that Moniz had been God's gift to the mind-healing trade, and the unwarranted Nobel prize had done nothing to diminish that conceit. Nobody had ever considered undertaking any kind of controlled trial, comparing the progress of the leucotomized with similar patients whose brains had been left intact, for it was felt wrong to deny wretched lunatics, including the multitude of schizophrenics, so ready a means of relief just for the sake of scientific meticulosity. However, when the results of the mass mind maulings *were* at last, and retrospectively, reviewed (some surgeons had routinely served their psychiatric colleagues by doing ten leucotomies in the morning, and another ten after lunch), it was found that schizophrenics, the type of sufferer most commonly so handled, had actually fared *worse* than others of their kind. They stayed in hospital longer. Their recovery was delayed. And these were the lucky ones. A good many patients of all categories died at the time of operation, mainly from haemorrhage. In one study, on top of their original troubles, it was found that every sixth leucotomized schizophrenic had become epileptic, as a result of scarring in the damaged brain.

When the operation was performed in an attempt to control disruptive behaviour such as aggression or obsessional self-mutilation it sometimes succeeded, not by restoring normality but by changing a previously difficult customer into a placid, spiritless vegetable, and patients of all kinds who escaped such severe damage still commonly suffered a marked and progressive deterioration of intellect, and a general blunting of the emotions. A reduced capacity for self-criticism often led to facetiousness, tactlessness, and a ridiculous surge in self-esteem. As recently as 1982 the Appeal Court was told that a burglar, seeking a reduction of sentence, had undergone brain surgery in an attempt to improve his state of mind, but, unfortunately, the result was that he had come to regard himself as a 'do-gooder criminal' – a latter-day Robin Hood who stole from the rich to give to the poor. It was decided that he ought to remain locked-up. A year previously a British woman had been awarded £95,000 damages because two leucotomies, performed some two decades earlier, had rendered her epileptic and incontinent. (Some psychiatrists had handed their victims over to the brain surgeons time and again in the desperate hope that the failure of one slicing operation could be transformed into success by a second, or a third, or even a fourth.)

Such unfortunate sequelae were commonplace (many of the worst results remained hidden behind asylum walls), and it is now acknowledged, even by those still practising psycho-surgery, that far more damage than benefit accrued from the worldwide epidemic of crudely performed leucotomies which marred the psychiatric scene for 30 years and more.

Things *have* improved. Instead of being prescribed with the kind of abandon which still characterizes the use of ECT, psychosurgery is now only performed by or on behalf of a relatively few enthusiasts. I say 'or on behalf of', because, of course, psychiatrists are not surgeons, and they have to get a knife-wielding colleague to destroy the parts of the brain which they, the psychiatrists, imagine to be the source of mischief. Some of the surgeons have themselves become keen devotees of the approach, and instead of just 'doing a Moniz' on demand, they have devised their own 'refined' methods for picking off a wide variety of targets within the brain. Nowadays most patients have their heads put in a clamp which, being fixed to certain standard bony landmarks of the skull, provides a reference frame, allowing an instrument to be inserted through a precisely placed hole in the bone in a direction and to a depth which will bring its tip to lie in a chosen spot. The cells or fibres round the tip of the probe can then be severed, or sucked out, or coagulated with an electric current, or seeded with radioactive pellets, or be disrupted in some other fashion.

Different surgeons and different psychiatrists develop likings for different targets, and go for spots within the brain which are supposed to be involved with specific functions and reactions. Thus psychosurgery has been used in attempts to correct such diverse departures from 'acceptable' behaviour as aggression, paedophilia, and anorexia nervosa.

Such procedures are, of course, a good deal more elegant from the technical point of view than the original Moniz mash, but while they tend to do less incidental damage than a freehand churning with a blade, there is small evidence that they have ever done much good. The fact that clever experimenters may have shown that a particular patch of brain tissue appears to be a part of the circuitry mediating anger or lust or greed in no way justifies the presumption that destroying this or that patch will free people plagued by unusual passions or appetites or attitudes from their aberrations. We may not know much about the mechanisms of the mind, but we do know that they are far more complex than the circuitry of the most sophisticated computers or artificial intelligence machines. An electronics expert would hardly imagine that a malfunctioning black box could be 'cured' by identifying *one* of the components in the circuits involved, and then destroying it with a red hot soldering iron, and without even knowing whether the part attacked was faulty. It is naive, almost to the point of irresponsibility, to suppose that the brain should respond favourably to such crude and illogical interference.

Some of the most ethically dubious operations have been performed on children, as young as eight years old, in an attempt to control aggression and antisocial behaviour. Disturbed prisoners at Rampton Special Hospital have also been thus assaulted with apparently (if not surprisingly) disastrous or equivocal results. In 1979 the neurosurgeon involved said to *New Scientist*, 'If you do find somebody who does understand the operation, perhaps you could let me know.'

Interestingly enough, about the only patients who have ended up grateful for psychosurgery are a few who have gained relief from severe depression – the same sort of sufferers as those who sometimes improve after ECT – again suggesting that the 'cures' may have been the result of a therapeutic slap in the face, rather than the rectification of any specific physical flaw.

The record of the psychosurgeons has been so bad, and their

arguments in favour of their stratagems so unconvincing, that a number of communities, including most of the USA, and, perhaps unexpectedly, the USSR, have made their work illegal. Here in Britain, where we seem to have an exaggerated faith in the superior understanding of doctors in general and psychiatrists in particular, psychosurgery is still undertaken, by those who believe in it, unfettered by any kind of legal or professional constraints. However, and happily, the British victims of the ploy are now to be numbered in tens rather than hundreds every year. The practice *ought* to be proscribed, at least until the doctors who wish to modify the mind by surgery can show that they know what they are doing. It is salutary to reflect that (as in the case of heart transplants, only more so) no drug which did so little good at the risk of so much harm would ever be approved for use, and it is at least entertaining to wonder why we, the customers, are so much more tolerant of dangerous surgeons than of suspect pills.

*

Some psychiatrists favour so-called behaviour therapy, or the use of carrots and sticks. One such was the Napsbury doctor whose wretched regime has been earlier here described. He was a fair example of the genre, but it is worthwhile describing two other adventures in the field which took place at about the same time, just to show how far committed practitioners of the approach will sometimes go.

In 1968 the *Lancet* carried a report of an horrific attempt at 'persuading' heroin addicts to kick the habit. Seventeen confirmed junkies were given a muscle relaxant drug, which, like curare, the South American arrow poison, produces a total paralysis, including the inability to breathe. As the drug begins to work the muscles start twitching, and at this stage the subjects gave themselves a heroin 'fix'. Seconds later, though remaining fully conscious, they became limp and inert, so that they had to be kept alive by artificial respiration. While in this helpless and presumably panic-stricken state, they were subjected to harrowing accounts of the dangers of addiction. The only good thing that can be said about this Machiavellian experiment in mind manipulation is that it didn't work. Scared into brief abstinence, most of the addicts were back to their old ways in a very short time. It's just as well, because had these essays in torture therapy worked, clinics for cure by terror might by now be commonplace.

A slightly greater degree of success was apparently achieved by an American psychiatrist who, unfortunately for the inmates, turned up at a mental hospital in Vietnam in 1966. He found they had problems. The patients, most of whom had been diagnosed as schizophrenic (whether they actually *were* so afflicted is, of course, entirely a different matter), were reluctant to work. They just sat around all day.

The psychiatrist, a certain Lloyd H. Cotter, had a bright idea. The patients were told that those who proved themselves by working well for three months could then go home. Out of a ward housing 130 men only ten took up the offer. In Cotter's immortal words, 'The reaction of the remainder was "Work! Do you think we're crazy?"'

Cotter then told these hard cases that 'People who are too sick to work need treatment. Treatment starts tomorrow – electroconvulsive therapy. It is not painful and there's nothing to be afraid of. When you are well enough to work, let us know.'

The next day the staff administered unmodified ECTs to all 120 recalcitrants. That is to say that they were convulsed without the benefit of a muscle relaxant or an anaesthetic. Comfortingly, Cotter noted that 'Perhaps because of the smaller size and musculature of the Vietnamese people, no symptoms of compression fractures were noted at any time.'

The unfortunates suffered these assaults three times a week, and, gradually, the number opting for work increased. Cotter stated his belief that the ECTs alleviated 'schizophrenic or depressive thinking and affect with some', but conceded that the change in heart in others 'was simply a result of their dislike or fear of ECT'. Never mind which, for as he complacently remarked, 'In either case our objective of motivating them to work was achieved.'

A wardful of 130 women proved less amenable to persuasion by electricity, but Cotter was not to be beaten. He said, 'If you don't work, you don't eat.' Twelve caved in at once, and by the end of three days without food all the rest had 'volunteered'. (The quotes around that last word are Cotter's.)

This type of 'therapy' is, of course, in the direct tradition of beating lunatics with chains, or douching them with cold water, or spinning them round in a 'whirling bed' until the blood flows from ears, nose and mouth, all of which remedies have had their vogue, and the frightening thing about the latterday advocates of 'driving out devils' is that they don't recognize their practices for what they truly are, and that they are actually proud of their achievements, and that journals of high repute, such as the *Lancet* and the *American Journal of Psychiatry* have been willing to print the authors' accounts of their grim experiments, thus giving them a false respectability.

The examples quoted may be extreme, but paltry rewards for good behaviour and unfeeling punishments for bad are commonplace in the handling of those labelled mentally disabled, so that minor tantrums or acts of disobedience lead to sentences of isolation in bare side wards, or the removal of comforting personal possessions such as radios, while (in the somewhat more humane institutions) good behaviour (meaning unquestioning compliance with orders and rules) may earn tokens which can be exchanged for small luxuries of a kind which ought to be supplied by right to the constrained. The cruelty implicit in this kind of Dotheboys Hall regime is excused, when complained about, on the grounds that it is part of the treatment, and based upon sound psychological theory, so that ignorant outsiders (like the parents of young persons thus maltreated in mental hospitals) should not presume to interfere.

*

Psychotherapy, or the talking treatment, is based, broadly, upon the assumption that disturbances of behaviour and the mind, and, often enough, the flesh (all manner of complaints from skin rashes to stomach ulcers), are the result of hang-ups concerning painful experiences in the past, and particularly (according to some schools of thought) mental bruising suffered during childhood, or even in the womb.

We have Freud and his associates, Adler and Jung (later, inevitably, his rivals) to thank for the idea that hurtful memories are suppressed, but not wiped off the cerebral tape. They keep popping up on the screen, but because we don't like them, we disguise them as something else. They emerge in code. Psychoanalysts allow their customers to ramble on, chatting about their thoughts and recollections and relationships and dreams, in the hope of identifying the disguised bad reminiscences. Once these have been unmasked for the impostors they really are, and once their true origins have been explained, then tension, conflict, confusion and distress will magically melt away, to be replaced by confidence, serenity, worldly success, bright eyes, and a good digestion.

Freud called one of his most famous patients 'the wolf man' because he had dreamt of a pack of white wolves seated in the branches of a walnut tree outside his bedroom window. Seized with terror at the prospect of being eaten by the beasts, he had screamed and woken up. It didn't take the Master long to sort that one out. He told his patient that, as an infant, he must have been asleep in his cot in his parents' bedroom one afternoon, and had awoken to see his father and mother making love. Naturally shocked, he had screamed and put an end to the disgraceful goings on, at which his parents' wrath had been visited upon his tiny head. The dream wolves were the distorted memory of the frightful, threatening scene, and their whiteness symbolized the lascivious oldsters' underwear. Freud claimed that this revelation cured his client, who, he maintained, had previously been an almost helpless bundle of nerves. However, the ungrateful fellow, who was a neurotic rake rather than a disabled wreck, spent the rest of a long life pestering psychiatrists, including several return trips to the Master, and died in a mental hospital, aged 92, asserting that the treatment had never done him the smallest good. Moreover, he reckoned he had never ever seen his parents making love.

Freud *et al* have, of course, spawned great regiments of disciples and imitators, and the fame and success attending their fanciful explanations of the springs of emotional turmoil have encouraged many other mind healers, both medical and lay, to invent and cash in on their own psychological theories and therapies, most of which are laughable.

I vividly recall having to take the chair at a medical society meeting upon the occasion of an address by a lady psychiatrist who dealt with unfortunate problem children in Birmingham. When I was introduced to her before the lecture, I had my pipe in my mouth, and she didn't even pause to echo my 'Pleased to meet you', but weighed straight in with, 'Ah! I see you're a pipe smoker. You know what *that* means, don't you?' I didn't, but she was clearly implying that it signalled some sad disturbance of my id, or my superego, or whatever, and I might have worried about it for years had her subsequent talk not made it plain that I need not concern myself overmuch with what she thought about anything, let alone me and my pipe.

She told the tale of a boy called Johnny. The poor little chap was an ice cream addict, and stole pennies from his mother's purse to satisfy his craving. His daddy had died when he was only three, and the good woman psychiatrist had soon perceived that this was the root of the problem. Clearly Johnny had hated Dad, regarding him as a rival for the affections of Mum, and had therefore wished him dead. When Dad *did* die, Johnny assumed, in his childish way, that his hate thoughts had been responsible, and that he was the murderer (all this taking place at a subconscious level, you understand). He couldn't tolerate such guilt, and so sought to escape from it by retreating to an earlier stage in his life – a stage at which everything had been hunky-dory – and that was the blissful bracket of months during which he had been sucking at his mother's breasts. But Mum's breasts weren't available any more. So Johnny had to find a substitute. And that substitute was ice cream. And so urgent was the little fellow's need for his breast substitute that he actually had to steal to fulfil his need – just like a hippy hooked on heroin.

The wretched woman claimed that her explanation of Johnny's thieving ways cured him then and there. Once he understood he stopped. I suspect that there may have been a different reason for his reformation, and that he refrained from wolfing cornets and stealing pennies simply to avoid any further contact with the appalling lady doctor.

Be it noted that this nonsense was propounded in all sincerity by a highly qualified and intelligent physician (she had graduated with honours), who was an NHS and WHO consultant, and that it was received, so far as I now recall, without dissent from her supposedly critically educated audience. Doctors just love explanations, and are not too fussed about whether they actually make sense.

This kind of psychiatry has, of course, little to do with medicine, and there is no particular reason why a psychotherapist of the Freudian or meta-Freudian persuasion should hold a medical degree. One lay operator, an American PhD called Arthur Janov, has evolved a form of treatment which he calls 'primal therapy', and which he believes bids fair to 'change the nature of psychotherapy as it is now known'. The pricey passport to salvation which he offers has gained some following in the UK. His simple (some might say simple-minded) doctrine is that all neurotic ills arise in people whose parents were beastly to them when they were children.

Janov gets his customers to chat about their early lives, and, particularly, their mums and dads, and thus far his approach is fairly orthodox. His unique contribution to the cause of mental health is the manner in which he purges his clients of their discovered hurts. They lie on the floor, alone or in groups, shouting 'Mommy! Daddy!' until they have worked themselves up into a right frenzy. Sooner or later they experience an emotional orgasm which is signalled by the emission of a piercing scream. One satisfied client has described the engaging ritual thus:

> So here's Janov, gingerly stepping over and around prostrate bodies, gently talking to first this person and next someone else, throwing private signals to his wife, and all around him people are screaming and crying out their pain. And he's drinking coffee through the whole bizarre mess.

The writhings and gaspings and sweating contortions of the communicants are supposed to represent the body's last desperate attempts to keep the revealed childhood injuries out of sight, but now the truth can no longer be suppressed, and the agony of it is the cause of that great cry – the 'primal scream' – which both acknowledges and banishes the pain. The mind is cleansed, the evil exorcised, and the body is free. A normal, healthy, well-adjusted, easy-mannered, fearless sample of the ideal All-American man or woman remains, purified of every blemish and ugly deed.

Actually, it's not quite so simple as that, because most customers will have suffered a *number* of ego-bruisings at the hands of Mum or Dad, and each requires a separate scream for its relief.

It is interesting to note the grave nature of the insults to young minds which Janov's probings have revealed. Typical of the examples reported by the guru himself is the case of a disturbed young man who complained of the disappointment his 'Mommy' had felt at producing a son instead of a daughter. So strong was her resentment that she attempted to 'demale' her offspring by treating him like a little girl, and he particularly recalled how she had once cruelly shown her hand by 'taking me into the ladies' toilet when in a department store'. It is tantalizing to reflect upon the horrific damage the little chap's psyche might have suffered from the scenes which would surely have ensued had his mother attempted to deal with his natural needs by taking him into the gents.

The rich variety of psychological explanations for mental and emotional disorder which now exist, ranging from classical Freudian dogma to the fantasies of Ron L. Hubbard and his Scientologists, are all incapable of proof, and hence (luckily for their champions) of disproof. To this extent they are all unscientific, and as with all cults and creeds based upon theory and apprehension rather than demonstrable facts, the disciples of the different prophets hold their beliefs with messianic certitude, and tend to deride and resent the followers of variant schools of thought with a good deal more feeling than they show towards rank outsiders.

It might be thought that the examples of fanciful psychoanalytical reasoning I have given are extreme, and so reflect unfairly on a majority of practitioners, but, absurd as they may seem to an unbeliever, they are typical of the explanations offered, and well illustrate the way in which this brand of psychotherapists think. This is not to say that the psychoanalytical approach is entirely without virtue. I am sure that many patients do benefit from the contact and encouragement and support involved, and that the wiser and less messianic members of the trade do help their clients sort out muddled thoughts and come to terms with suppressed emotions and unacknowledged fears. Moreover psychoanalysis has the great virtue of not causing tardive dyskinesia, or breast growth in the male, or epilepsy, or loss of memory. On the other hand it can be addictive and lead to dependence, and some patients do have their confusion worse confounded by the nonsense about themselves and the nature of Man which they are required to believe.

The different talking treatments are much more popular in the USA than here. This is because they are all time-consuming and demand the prolonged attention of the therapists. They are therefore much more attractive to practitioners with paying customers than to psychiatrists who have to serve the mentally disturbed seeking free treatment through the NHS.

*

So we have the druggers, the shockers, the slicers, the persuaders, and the talkers. We have the Sargants and the Szaszs. The amazing thing is that we continue to credit psychiatrists as a class with the ability to comprehend and handle the mentally distressed when they are in total conflict amongst themselves concerning the very nature of lunacy, and when the treatment a lunatic receives so largely depends upon the whims and prejudices, and even the fitness to practice, of the doctor who happens to gain control of a particular case, rather than upon the rational application of a soundly based, generally accepted, and well tested corpus of knowledge about the brain, and the way it works.

It is bad enough when trusting patients who are in a mental ward or hospital of their own free will fall into the hands of the less competent, cautious and caring members of the psychiatric trade. It is intolerable when people who have been labelled mad are *forced* to remain in stultifying institutions at the mercy of fourth-raters.

At any one time there are some 10,000 detained patients in Britain's asylums, of whom over a quarter are in the so-called special hospitals for those of 'dangerous, violent or criminal propensities'. These are locked and barred high security pounds, and while they are called 'hospitals', it is significant that their 'nurses' are members of the Prison Officers Association. They are the responsibility of the Department of Health and Social Security (one in Scotland comes under the Scottish Office), rather than Regional Health Authorities, so that their ultimate control is even more remote than that exercised over the generality of places for the mentally ill.

The English institutions are Rampton in Nottinghamshire, Moss Side at Liverpool, Broadmoor, Berks, and Park Lane, Liverpool. The euphemistically labelled Scottish State Hospital is at Carstairs, Lanarkshire. (Rampton, remember, is the place clobbered by the General Nursing Council as so badly run as to be unacceptable as a mental nurses' training school.)

The main differences between the special hospitals and ordinary prisons are that the inmates are accommodated in wards rather than cell blocks, that their 'sentences' are indeterminate, that the 'governor' and his assistants are doctors rather than arts graduates or ex-army officers, and that the use of drugs, brain surgery, solitary confinement, and so on, is called treatment and not punishment.

In the popular mind (and, I suspect, in the minds of a good many supposedly well-informed sophisticates like MPs, barristers, and judges), the unfortunates confined in these grim quasi-therapeutic penitentiaries, are all dangerous lunatics who have committed frightful crimes such as rape, murder, and arson. In fact, about one third of the residents have done nothing that would attract even so much as the penalty of a fine in a magistrates' court, and have not, indeed, appeared before any court, and have not been accused of any offence. They are there simply because some doctor, somewhere, has labelled them mad, and because their original nurses or medical attendants (it is usually the nurses who have the major say in such matters) have found them too much of a nuisance to handle. At a recent count the special hospitals housed over 50 boys and girls, some as young as 12, and nearly half these children were kept in adult wards for lack of sufficient proper space.

I know a good deal about one ex-Broadmoor patient. She was a bright, pleasant, Welsh schoolgirl. At the age of 14 she became a little difficult – once, for example, wrestling with her mother (the household had no father) about whether or not the television should be on. After one such family dispute, her mother packed her off up the valley to an aunt. There, at aunty's house, she went to bed at about 11, but at midnight her cousin found her getting dressed, and saying she meant to go home. The cousin tried to put her back to bed, and was bitten. Aunty panicked at the uproar and called a constable. The constable called a doctor. Then a mental welfare officer arrived. In next to no time the girl was in the local lunatic asylum.

The mother went to the hospital next day, and her tearful but percipient child said, 'Mummy, please take me out of this place. I'll be here for the rest of my life if you don't take me out of here.' In the event, and following that brief, hysterical episode at aunty's house, she stayed in the hospital for two-and-a-half years. She had her occasional brushes with authority, and, following some modest misdemeanour, sometimes spent periods alone in a side ward (not as a punishment, of course – heaven forfend! – but as an exercise in 'behavioural therapy'). That she was never regarded as a serious threat to anybody else's health and safety is clear from the fact that she was regularly allowed home at weekends, and for longer periods whenever her working mother had a holiday.

Then, one day, without the slightest warning, and very shortly after she had returned to the hospital from a perfectly normal home visit, her mother was informed that the child was to be transferred to Broadmoor. So far as anybody outside the hospital has been able to establish, this dreadful decision was reached after the girl had pulled a ward sister's hair, and because the nurses who looked after her were beginning to find the lively-minded, frustrated, and doubtless sometimes rebellious young woman, a bit of a nuisance. So they told the doctor in charge that she had become beyond their control, and thus they got rid of her. (A further likely motive for the move was that mother had also upset the hospital authorities by getting outsiders, including the local MP, to challenge the heavy-handed management of her daughter's allegedly disruptive state.)

She stayed in Broadmoor for the next four years, becoming increasingly 'institutionalized', and receiving, as treatment for her supposed mental illness, heavy doses of major tranquillizers, and the occasional spell of isolation (during which she was denied her personal possessions) for refusing to make her bed, or rejecting the doubtless delicious food put before her, or some similar peccadillo.

Perhaps she was, indeed, a victim of the schizophrenia with which she had been labelled, but, whether so or no, any young person would soon have shown mental deterioration, and have become socially 'awkward', under the regime she suffered. She was imprisoned for the best years of her youth, and for no obvious or compelling cause. Her mother desperately wanted her home, and could have given her competent, loving care. She could have received any *essential* drug treatment (if such there had been) as an out-patient, or during brief spells as a voluntary in-patient. Her progressive demoralization and spiritual and intellectual degeneration could have been avoided. Unfortunately she is only one of very many who have been, and are being, needlessly confined, and under circumstances which are positively damaging rather than helpful and restorative.

Certainly there are gravely disturbed individuals who must, for a period at least, be forcefully detained because they do pose a real risk to themselves or others. But it should be the task of a new kind of predominantly lay tribunal to decide, in open session, when so serious a sanction as the deprivation of liberty is truly needed. Such a body should act on the principle that compulsory detention is a last resort, which should rarely be ordered simply for the patient's own good (as opposed to the safety of others), since the 'treatments' at present available are of such questionable value. Psychiatrists would, of course, still offer their advice, but the state of their art does not justify the delegation to them of a final decision on the liberty of the individual.

Mental Health Tribunals, which are the patients' supposed safeguard against unreasonable compulsory detention, already exist, but they only deal with appeals from those who have already been incarcerated against their will, and who have had a request for release turned down by the doctor in charge. These tribunals consist of a legal chairman, a consultant psychiatrist from another region, and a third lay member, commonly a social worker. Needless to say, they don't order a patient's discharge very often, for there would have to be the grossest evidence of mishandling, or bad faith, or wrong-headed prejudice on the part of the hospital authorities, before a clutch of Establishment-minded outsiders would wish to assume the responsibility of overriding the 'expert' opinion of the man on the spot. These lunacy referees are far from being the kind of champions of civil liberties which those who have been diagnosed as mentally disabled so sorely need to have on their side.

Certain categories of patients at present routinely delivered into psychiatric care ought not to be handled thus at all. This is true for many of the offenders who are committed to special hospitals by the courts.

It is only reasonable and humane that the psychologically abnormal should not be treated as common criminals when they break the law, but a medical establishment is a wholly inappropriate place in which to confine a compulsive fire-raiser or a poisoner who kills for no apparent cause. These so-called psychopaths are often rational, well-behaved beings, save for their single, dangerous quirk. They are not mentally ill, and are not capable of benefiting from a medically-orientated approach to their problems. Judges who sentence such deviants to an indeterminate stay in places like Broadmoor and Rampton, remarking sententiously that 'there you will receive the treatment that will fit you, some day, to be at large in the world again', are talking through their wigs. Some criminal lunatics return to their evil ways the moment they are free, having conned their guardians into believing a 'cure' has been achieved. A majority stay out of trouble, having learned their lesson, or having undergone a natural sea change, or just because they do not return to the circumstances which sent them off beam in the first place. There is no way of distinguishing between the truly reformed and the plausible recidivists, and what happens after release bears no relationship whatsoever to anything done to, by, or for them while they were inside. We need a different, non-punitive, non-medical routine for attempting to keep identified psychopaths out of further trouble.

*

Similarly, it is absurd to put the mentally subnormal into hospitals under the care of psychiatrists. Just as with psychopaths, the mentally deficient are not ill and their disability cannot be cured. The deplorable conditions under which so many of their kind are corralled is in part due to the fact that their keepers have been trained in skills and attitudes which are irrelevant to the task. A very great deal *can* be done towards improving the intellectual and physical performance, and hence the morale and happiness and general well-being, of most mental defectives, but this requires the dedicated effort of skilled teachers and leaders, whose purpose and approach is poles apart from that of custodially-minded mental nurses and the pathology-fixated purveyors of curative pills and potions.

*

If left to the doctors, the general standard of psychiatric practice, and therefore the deal offered to the mentally ill, will not improve until we have gained some real insights into the mechanisms of the normal and disordered mind. Then, when the subject has gained a scientific respectability, a greater number of intellectually energetic and able and ambitious medical graduates will be attracted to the trade, and the less able members of it will have the benefit of sound guidance to help them handle their patients in a rational and helpful fashion.

As it is the only good psychiatrists are those who happen to have been endowed by nature with the kind of inborn wisdom, compassion, and understanding which would have made them equally excellent generals, managing directors, headmistresses, or priests. Their particular theoretical attachments (be it to the schools of Sargant or of Szasz) are irrelevant to their worth. Unfortunately such valuable persons are as much a minority within psychiatry as within any other branch of the medical profession, or any other calling or occupation, and their numbers are insufficient to have much influence on the whole. (There are probably more good psychiatrists among GPs than on the roll of the Royal College of Psychiatrists, simply because there are so many more GPs.)

It would therefore behove us well – public and politicians alike – to take an active interest in the welfare of our mentally disturbed compatriots, and not to leave their fate to the sole discretion of the experts. They are very far from being expert. And the figures tell us that there's a more than sporting chance that it will be you, or I, or our mother or our brother or our daughter or our spouse who becomes a victim of their ignorance before too long.

CHAPTER FIVE

The Pill Pedlars

The first thing to understand about the pharmaceutical industry is that it is Big Business. Its executives are not members of one of the pompously labelled 'caring professions', nominally devoted to the alleviation of human suffering (much as they would like to be so regarded in the public eye). They are tradespeople, and tradespeople of a particularly hard-nosed kind.

The drug houses are a branch of the chemical industry, which, a bare 40 years or so ago, tardily recognized a new and highly profitable use for its expertise in the matter of creating, and then manufacturing in bulk, new and patentable compounds.

Notable early achievements in the development of synthetic chemicals with a useful and sometimes dramatic effect upon human ills included aspirin, the barbiturates, Ehrlich's 'magic bullet' aimed at syphilis, and Domagk's original sulphonamide which revolutionized the treatment of many common and dangerous bacterial infections. These successes were made possible by the existence of commercial factories and laboratories which had already developed techniques for playing the game of molecular roulette – the manipulation of existing compounds to produce novel molecules in the hope of turning up a winner – but for quite different purposes, such as the search for cheaper and better dyes (although the discovery of the first aniline dye in 1856 was, in fact, a chance consequence of an unsuccessful attempt to synthesize quinine from coal tar).

The isolated and occasional emergence of a remedy from among the huge and growing catalogue of man-made molecules (aspirin was launched in 1889, barbital – Veronal – in 1903, Salvarsan in 1910, and Prontosil in 1932) pointed the way, and since the 5000-odd million inhabitants of the world are even more keen on swallowing elixirs supposed to benefit their health than they are on purchasing fertilizers or paints or plastic buckets, the chemical industry, slowly at first, but then with rapidly increasing enthusiasm, took on the invention and marketing of pills.

But finding a novel compound which has some desirable influence upon the diseased or healthy body, and then modifying the original molecule in an attempt to maximize its wanted activity and minimize its nasty side effects until a usable medicine has been produced, is an immensely costly and time-consuming process. Failures and false trails (often involving great expenditure and effort) are the rule. The final emergence of a saleable commodity is the rare exception.

Nevertheless, despite the fact that some 10,000 potential medicinal compounds are tested for every one which finally forms the basis of a new drug, and despite the fact that the one in 10,000 winner will have taken, on average, well over £50 million and ten years to develop to the stage at which it can be sold, the pharmaceutical industry prospers exceedingly, although it is virtually impossible to discover the true profits earned by the huge multinational concerns which provide the bulk of modern medicines, since they employ various powerful devices for keeping their financial manipulations opaque. But one figure which, for the sake of its public image and political clout, the industry is only too eager to advertise, is its contribution to the balance of payments. In 1982 British pill makers (most of whom are subsidiaries of foreign companies) exported medicines worth nearly £1 billion, and achieved a trade balance of over £600 million, coming sixth in the export league. They employed nearly 70,000 people, and made perhaps £300 million in profits from the NHS.

Such a chancy business, requiring such massive pre-sale investment, can only produce such glowing results if every nostrum that survives the long, pot-holed track to the point of vendibility is flogged with ruthless vigour and every last trick of the huckster's trade. There is not just the temptation, but an irresistible commercial compulsion, to maximize the sales of all the items in the catalogue, however dubious the value, suitability, or safety of some of them may be. This requires a costly, continuous, and relentless propaganda exercise aimed at the consumers who swallow, the doctors who prescribe, and the politicians and government officials who attempt to control, and who perhaps pay for, the thousand of brand-name medicines on offer.

The average drug company spends around 15 per cent of its total sales revenue on marketing its products, some US corporations devoting a massive 35 per cent of income to the task – a great deal more than the 10 per cent allotted to the development of new medicines, and several times the proportion of earnings which manufacturers at large find they need to use for promoting their wares.

In 1976 the British pharmaceutical industry was spending just under £50 million a year in attempting to persuade British doctors to prescribe named remedies (and never mind the promotional budget for exports). This sum represented 14 per cent of the home sales income, and since it was a deductible expense in the calculation of net domestic profits, and since these profits are used as the basis for agreeing the price which the NHS pays for its drugs, and since the NHS is the only significant native customer, the government felt that it might stand accused of, in effect, footing an excessive drug advertising bill. So David Ennals, then Secretary of State for Social Security, announced that he was requiring companies to prune their promotional budgets to 10 per cent of their home sales revenue by 1979.

This 'draconian' measure was greeted with the customary howls of righteous indignation, coupled with predictions of economic disaster, with which the drug makers' trade federation, the Association of the British Pharmaceutical Industry, invariably greets all efforts to curb its members' freedom to do exactly as they please. But, since the domestic drug bill soars annually, the 10 per cent still allowed for the purpose of soliciting custom continues to represent a fairly useful little sum, amounting, as it did, to £140 million in 1983. Even with this harsh government clampdown, the drug men were not actually prevented from pushing their wares as hard and expensively as they chose. They were simply denied the privilege of having the tax payer refund any expenditure over the permitted limit.

Almost half the promotional budget is absorbed by the cost of salesmen, or 'reps'. Every company of any consequence maintains a network of these travelling ambassadors, covering the country. They are well-educated, literate, articulate, expertly briefed men and women who tour the surgeries, hospitals and pharmacies of the land, pushing the virtues of their employers' products, with of course particular emphasis on new lines, and distributing largesse in the form of brochures, samples, scribbling pads, biros, and similar small gifts. These hardly amount to bribes. The days of free boxes of golf balls, stamped with the doctor's and the donor's name, are over, and the ABPI's own code of conduct (promulgated as a measure for preempting outside criticism) specifies that gifts must be of small cash value, and in some way relevant to the medical trade. However, they serve the valuable purpose of giving some slight pleasure and leaving the company's name on the doctor's desk after the rep has left.

Reps not only dispense information and persuasion but also collect valuable information for their bosses concerning doctors' attitudes, misgivings, desires, and prescribing habits. Some of this comes from the doctors themselves, and some is garnered from receptionists during the wait for admission to the consulting room, and some from the local chemists. Marketing managers place great emphasis on the value of knowing their victims' strengths and susceptibilities so that sales propaganda is applied to the best effect.

Most GPs welcome reps, and see about two each week, only some five per cent refusing to give the persuaders ten minutes of their time. This is because family doctors rely so heavily upon the use of the prescription pad in the struggle to satisfy their customers, and because the drug companies are the most dominant, and, for some, the only source of information about what's new, and what to use for what. And doctors do like to be aware of the latest and most fashionable pills and elixirs, for even if they have developed a healthy scepticism towards repeated claims of 'unsurpassed performance' and 'faster relief' and 'better tolerance' and all the rest of the oracular claptrap of the trade, they don't want to be caught short by inquiries from patients concerning 'that new medicine, doctor', which they've never heard of.

Individual companies often have their own methods for side-stepping the apparently saintly standards of behaviour demanded by the ABPI code. One disreputable trick employed by some reps from time to time is the pseudo-clinical trial. A GP is given a supply of some new drug and asked to try it out on suitable patients for a period, and then to send the company a brief report on the results (an exercise made seemingly more respectable by the request for comments on any unfortunate side effects observed). The doctor is offered an acceptable fee for each completed return, to 'compensate' for the additional time and effort involved. Apart from the fact that this provides an obvious temptation to pump the new nostrum into customers who may not really need it, or who are doing perfectly well on some rival's similar product, any information garnered from such an exercise is scientifically worthless, since any meaningful investigation of a drug's effectiveness requires the use of a carefully matched control group of patients who are given indistinguishable dummy tablets or capsules or whatever, neither the doctor nor the recipients knowing who is getting the real McCoy until the assessment is complete (the so-called 'double-blind' technique).

The real purpose of the manoeuvre is, of course, to get the doctors concerned into the habit of thinking of and prescribing the new remedy for years to come. In 1983 a GP wrote to the *British Medical Journal* claiming that he, and 40 other colleagues he had contacted, had each been offered £100 to take part in such a 'trial', and there is no way of telling what the cost and the scale of this particular example of the ploy might have been countrywide. The 'fees' paid are, indeed, thinly disguised bribes, and it would be a naive practitioner who regarded them in any other light. But then a lot of our intensively and expensively 'educated' doctors *are* extraordinarily naive, and are no match for the cunning moguls of the medicines guild.

One incidental benefit derived by the marketeers from the pseudo-trial is, presumably, that the cost can be entered in the books as 'research expenditure', instead of being added to the extravagant and much criticized promotional budget.

Apart from sending out reps, many pharmaceutical companies lay on cosy gatherings at some pleasant hotel to which all local GPs are invited in order to enjoy the illusory 'free lunch' and hear a talk or watch a video extolling a chosen item from their host's catalogue. These are generally well patronized, and one youthful and better-than-average group practice I know of regularly puts aside time once a fortnight to take advantage of these soft-sell happenings. The same is done for junior hospital doctors, on their home territory (they can't abandon the place *en masse*, and go *out* to lunch). I was told of one mess which had learnt the trick of organizing such affairs themselves for a good deal less than their benefactors provided for the feast, using the balance to pay for a later party of their own. My informant claimed that she and her mates were pretty immune to the accompanying spiel. But seeds so planted tend to take root and grow, however slight the immediate impact on the garden of the mind may seem to be.

Consultants are also targetted. They are valuable converts to the use of a particular preparation, not primarily because of the quantities they may prescribe themselves, but because, when their patients are returned to the care of a GP, it will commonly be with the recommendation that the use of a chosen medication be continued, and the GP is likely to take note of the expert's preference, and use the same brand product for other patients on his list who are afflicted in like fashion. This form of expansionism is particularly effective in the case of medicines for the relief (not cure) of chronic afflictions like arthritis, for which a particular anodyne, once started, is likely to be used for years. However, consultants are, or often see themselves to be, a cut above the type of fellow who can learn anything useful or new from a video 'commercial' or a company-programmed rep. But a scientific meeting – a gathering of master minds, bent on examining issues at the frontiers of knowledge – ah, *that's* more appropriate to their high estate. Therefore the drug houses contribute generously to the costs of such occasions for the sake of having their names associated with the jamboree, particularly when the theme is some mortification of the mind or flesh for which the sponsoring company offers some remedy or salve. There can be small objection to a tiny fraction of the drug trade's profits being used to cushion the costs of some of the thousands of genuine clinical and scientific gatherings which are staged each year, but sometimes firms will 'borrow' the name of some minor, respectable but impecunious learned society in order to stage a symposium which suits their interests, selecting (or, at least, strongly suggesting) the speakers and the topics, and generally controlling and paying for a debate which is ostensibly taking place under the aegis of an independent professional body. Manufacturers also often mount conferences of a suitably scientific and academically-flavoured kind devoted to the discussion of one of their own new wonder drugs. But when this is the overt purpose of the moot, some extra inducements may seem called for in order to tempt the desired gurus to attend. Hence the notorious case of the Orient Express.

In the autumn of 1982 Montedison Pharmaceuticals, the British subsidiary of a major Italian drug manufacturer, Farmitalia Carlo Erba, was given the job of arranging the UK launch of one of its parent company's new products, an anti-arthritic pill called Flosint. This was a fairly tough assignment for two reasons. In the first place arthritis is the commonest cause of disability among the elderly, and there is intense competition for a share of the large and highly profitable market for the group of medicines (the so-called non-steroidal anti-inflammatory drugs – NSAIDS), which are most effective for the long term relief of pain and swelling in affected joints. There were over 20 well-established preparations of this kind already in use. Flosint was just a variation on a theme. Secondly, a few weeks before the launch, Opren, an NSAID developed by the American firm, Eli Lilly, and marketed in the UK by one of its British subsidiaries, Dista Products, had had its product licence suspended by the government's Committee on Safety of Medicines (see below), and within a couple of days Lilly had withdrawn the drug worldwide. This followed reports received by the committee of 3500 cases of adverse reactions among British users, including 61 deaths. Toxic effects observed had included damage to the stomach and intestines, the liver, bone marrow, skin, eyes, and nails – a fairly horrific spread of evil activity. By association, therefore, all NSAIDs were under a bit of a cloud. However, this negative aspect of the Opren debacle was balanced by the fact that the product had been a market leader, so there was a tempting gap to be filled. In all the circumstances the task of promoting the newcomer, Flosint, clearly called for a more than ordinarily seductive sales campaign.

The favour of the influential rheumatology consultants was sought by an invitation to a one-day seminar devoted to expounding Flosint's superior performance. What made the summons somewhat special was the fact that the meeting was to take place, not in some musty lecture theatre at a provincial university, or at the cheerless London premises of a learned society, but at the Hotel Danieli in Venice. Moreover, the guests were to be wafted to their plush lodgings on board the Orient Express, with a smoked salmon buffet lunch *en route* and a modest banquet on arrival to cushion the rigours of the pilgrimage – all paid for by Flosint's kindly manufacturers.

The details of this sugar-coated 'academic' exercise, enjoyed by 100 serious-minded, seagreen incorruptibles from British centres of the healing art, were made known to a wider public in a BBC *Panorama* programme, a couple of months after the event. The rotters from that particular combat unit of the media (ABPI, like all self-seeking groups, hates the media), had got wind of the happening, and had sent undercover agents, with cameras and microphones, to accompany the innocents on their trip. Writing in *The Listener* about this and similar grossly extravagant drug promotions, Tom Mangold, who had reported on the industry's selling techniques for the box, said '. . . and I bet you a bottle of vintage Krug they'll have a long letter in this magazine next week. I hope their spokesman answers this point. Regulation Number 18 of the ABPI's Code of Practice for the Pharmaceutical Industry (Revised Fifth Edition, April 1982) states:

> '*Hospitality*. Entertainment or other hospitality offered to members of the medical and allied professions for purposes of sales promotion should always be secondary to the main purpose of the meeting . . . the level of hospitality should be appropriate and not out of proportion to the occasion; its cost should not exceed that level which the recipients might normally adopt when paying for themselves.

'My questions to the ABPI are these. Was or was not Farmitalia's launch symposium . . . a breach of this regulation? If it was not, why not? If it was, what action has been taken? And don't tell me you haven't received a complaint. Consider this to be one.'

In fact, Tom Mangold lost his bet. For once ABPI wisely refrained from its usual reflex response of righteous indignation against any whiff of criticism of its members' morals and machinations, because, of course, this particular breach of the code was indefensible, and therefore best left undefended, in the hope that the public's memory of the *Panorama* revelations would the sooner fade away. There was a later, semi-facetious note to *The Listener* from its secretary, David Massam, claiming that Mangold had declined an invitation to submit a written complaint to the Code of Practice Committee, and saying that he, Massam, was looking forward to receiving his bottle of champagne. In fact the committee did later deliver a formal rebuke to Montedison. The extent of the deterrent effect on such public and official reprimands may be judged by the fact that during 1984 ABPI's Code of Practice Committee upheld complaints against eleven member companies for breaches of the industry's own rules of conduct. Offences ranged from the offer of excessive hospitality and rewards in kind to the printing of misleading articles and advertisements.

There is an ironic footnote to the Orient Express affair. Opren had been launched to the accompaniment of trumpeting publicity just a couple of years before it was withdrawn, and the advertisements announcing its advent had claimed, among other things, that 'the side-effects story as a whole is very impressive indeed, as they are generally mild and transient'. Flosint was launched with equally strident confidence (quite apart from the Venetian jamboree), and the ads this time proclaimed 'major anti-inflammatory/analgesic activity WITHOUT (their capitals) an unacceptable level of adverse effects'. Flosint's product licence was suspended by the British government after 15 months, the Committee on Safety of Medicines having received reports of the deaths of seven patients given the drug, and of serious side effects, including internal bleeding, in over 200 more, the committee suspecting that the true incidence of dangerous damage was a good deal greater still. So much for Farmitalia's hopes of continuing dividends from its investment in the Venetian blind.

*

In addition to deploying reps and organizing shindigs, the pharmaceutical industry subjects doctors to an uninterrupted barrage of expertly designed and written printed propaganda, both through the mail, and as advertisements in professional journals, newspapers, and magazines.

When the high pressure production and marketing of novel pharmaceuticals began, direct mail advertising was the principal method of assault, and by the late 1950s GPs were receiving between five and ten promotional postal packages, often containing samples, every day. One reason for this letter-box overkill approach was the sad fact that a great many family doctors rarely if ever leafed through the medical periodicals available at the time, so that journal advertising missed out on a significant proportion of the nation's most prolific prescribers.

However, the sheer volume of literature cascading onto the doormat with each post tended to make direct mail advertising counter-productive, with doctors becoming irritated by the nuisance of so much impersonal commercial razzmatazz cluttering up their desks and diluting the final demands and other desirable items from the postman's bag. A lot of the stuff went straight into the bin, and various devices were dreamed up in an attempt to stop that happening. One trick was to enclose the product plug in an air letter form bearing a handwritten address and a glamorous foreign stamp, and great would be the rage of hoodwinked recipients who sliced open an unexpected billet-doux look-alike, expecting news from an old flame or long-lost friend, only to find themselves adjured to 'Prescribe Gutlax for your elderly patients – the *safe*, *gentle* answer to constipation'. There was also some general resentment aroused by the new phenomenon of prescription medicines being promoted with all the brashness and contempt for the potential customer's sense and sensibilities which characterize a soap powder campaign or a *Reader's Digest* special offer.

Therefore, although direct mailing remains to this day a substantial means of wooing prescribers, a large switch in expenditure from postal promotions to journal advertising occurred with the emergence in the '60s of a rash of controlled circulation 'throwaways' which rapidly became, and still remain, the average GP's favourite means for 'keeping in touch'. Unlike the *Lancet* and *The British Medical Journal* and similar 'heavies', throwaways with names like *World Medicine*, *General Practitioner*, *Pulse*, *Doctor*, and *Medical News*, are more the work of experienced and talented journalists rather than serious-minded medical editors, and instead of carrying turgid and polysyllabic 'original papers' by earnest researchers, they are filled with news, gossip, well written and expertly edited review articles, a good deal of practical advice on matters of the first importance such as maximizing incomes (as well as secondary matters such as treating patients), much pure entertainment, and lots and lots of photographs and colourful graphics. As a result of all this they get read, and because they are read they are favourite vehicles for the pharmaceutical companies' beguiling spreads. A typical issue of *General Practitioner*, for example (a tabloid weekly printed on shiny paper), consists of 76 or 88 pages, with well over half the space occupied by drug advertisements, the majority printed in full colour. And they are not only in full colour, but are given all the visual and emotional appeal of an invitation to conjure the genie of romance from a bottle of Hennessy Very Special Cognac. Lovely naked or carelessly clad ladies used to be a favourite 'come on' feature of the pill advertisements, until sour-minded, left-wing politicians began protesting at this denigration of God's honour and the medical art. Prudence has banished eroticism from the medicine mongers' sales ploys, at least for the time being, but their printed inducements still reach very far and very expensively beyond the simple need to keep doctors informed. I am looking, as I write, at a *four*-page four-colour spread promoting Tagamet, an admittedly effective agent in the handling of peptic ulcers. The useful information (such as it is) purveyed by this extravagant display (largely aimed at knocking a rival product) could have been well and legibly contained in a quarter-page black-and-white announcement. The industry's standard and basically sound defence of drug advertising, which is that it's no good making medicines if nobody knows they're available and what they're supposed to accomplish, provides no sort of justification for the kind and the scale of promotion that actually occurs.

Of course, the lavish spending on coloured insertions, commanding premium rates, is splendid for the financial welfare of the proprietors of the many free sheets which have mushroomed to take advantage of the drug houses' massive advertising budgets. But the patrons buy more than just space with their money. The free sheets are wholly dependent on advertising revenue for their profitability and survival. It follows that any publication which bit the hand that fed it by maintaining a critical attitude towards the pharmaceutical industry would very soon go out of business. There may be little in the way of overt attempts by advertisers to influence the editorial policies of the periodicals they sustain, but they don't have to go to such lengths, risking the odium of discovery. The fact that they are the sole providers of the publishers' and journalists' bread and butter is sufficient to ensure that the bulk of the medical reading matter enjoyed by GPs is sympathetic towards, or at least tolerant of, the pharmaceutical industry and its little ways. I am not accusing either side of deliberate suppression or deception or distortion (although I *do* know some American publishers of throwaways heavily guilty of these crimes). It is simply that, in the very nature of the symbiosis, the editors of pill-profit-dependent periodicals don't instinctively turn to the latest rumours of malfeasance within the drug industry when planning their next week's lead story. After all, *Horse and Hound* doesn't run editorials lambasting the morals of fox-hunting folk. The *Guardian* and the *Sunday Times* may be able to afford the luxury of sniping away at any activities of the medicine makers which appear scandalous, but *World Medicine* and *Doctor* and *Pulse* can't be expected to. The occasional critical item may appear, and may even be tolerated for the useful impression of editorial independence thus created (doctors no more like to feel they are being brainwashed than do any other bunch of self-respectful citizens), but it is not unknown for an offended manufacturer to cancel a remunerative series booking.

For a good many years now various drug houses have put up the money for valuable annual prizes (in the region of £1000 and more) for different categories of medical broadcasters and writers. There is nothing particularly sinister about this. The awards are organized by the Medical Journalists' Association, and decided by a panel of judges independent of the trade, but it all adds to the sweetness of relations between the industry and the people who are principally concerned with reporting on its affairs. Another company funds an annual MJA weekend symposium at which high powered panellists, such as the presidents of royal colleges, discuss weighty issues like 'Medicine, the Media and Society' before an audience of the association's members who have been lucky in a ballot, the occasion being staged at some pleasant country hotel, with everybody's bill, including travelling costs, being met by the sponsor. A variety of lesser MJA events throughout the year are also supported by drug money. All medical journalists, of course, just like motoring correspondents and wine and food writers, have frequent opportunities to join paid-for trips to interesting places to see the medicine makers at work and hear accounts of their contributions to the commonweal. I've enjoyed many such a freebie myself, and can't say my conscience hurts too much, for I've always imagined my good opinion to be unbuyable. Perhaps the moguls of the drug industry know better.

In recent years the funds available for medical research have fallen further and further behind the need, and here too the drug houses have used their money to good effect. Many important projects, including fundamental research in major fields like cancer, heart disease, and mental illness, would have to be attenuated or abandoned, or would never have got off the ground, but for drug company support. Some concerns (most notably the Wellcome Foundation, which, under the will of its founder-owner, devotes *all* surplus profits to funding research, via the independent Wellcome Trust) have long given valuable support to university and clinical investigators, including the massive costs of setting up and endowing hospital laboratories and university chairs. But now drug profits are not just a useful but a crucial source of finance for research. Therefore a large number of the nation's influential medical academics and clinicians are beholden to the industry, and must be, consciously or not, prejudiced in its favour.

*

Perhaps the most brilliantly successful of the drug makers' public relations exercises is the Office of Health Economics. This was set up in 1962 by ABPI 'To undertake research on the economic aspect of medical care. To investigate other health and social problems. To collect data from other countries. To publish results, data and conclusions relevant to the above.' This admirable brief has been fulfilled with distinction, and every three or four months for the past 20 years the office has produced an objective, well-documented, literate, and attractively presented booklet encapsulating the known facts about subjects ranging from suicide and rabies and heart disease to the cost of running hospitals and what the public expects from the NHS, always adding a few percipient comments and conclusions of its own for good measure. The office also produces fact sheets, statistical tables, and monographs on the economics and logistics of health care, and, of course, on various issues affecting the pharmaceutical scene.

This activity has earned the gratitude, and, indeed, the respect, of many people with an interest in medical affairs, including journalists, who have come to rely upon OHE's publications as accurate and wonderfully lucid source material. George Teeling Smith, who has headed the office since its inception, has achieved the status of a guru, and he enhanced the academic respectability of the operation when, a year or so back, he got himself made a part-time associate professor of medical economics at Brunel University, which institution he attends one day a week.

ABPI makes no secret of the fact that it is behind OHE. Indeed, the relationship is proudly proclaimed on the inside front cover of OHE literature (together with the nice little touch that 'The Office of Health Economics welcomes financial support and discussions on research problems with any persons or bodies interested in its work' – very good for the image of disinterested devotion to the commonweal, that one). And so George Teeling Smith and his staff have created a fund of goodwill for the industry, which is, of itself, well worth the £2 million or so a year it must take to keep the office and its works afloat (this figure is my guesstimate, because the ABPI annual report – the one for public consumption – wisely, doesn't include a balance sheet.) But there is, in addition, and as usual, a less obvious, but no less important dividend which the industry extracts from its investment in OHE. Every now and again the office produces a propaganda document, couched in the familiar OHE format and terms, full of arguments designed to promote the industry's aims of selling more drugs for more money with the minimum possible let or hindrance from interfering politicians and government officials. Thus, for example, a tract published in 1983, written by Teeling Smith, and entitled *The Needs of the Pharmaceutical Manufacturers from their Medical Departments in the 1990s*, in which he very reasonably argues that an increasingly sophisticated public, provided with alarming insights concerning drugs like Opren and thalidomide by the fearless investigators of *Panorama* and the *Sunday Times*, is going to demand a great deal more information about the many medicines which doctors so recklessly prescribe. (Those aren't quite the terms *he* uses, by the way.)

He goes on to say that in future the pill pedlars will not only have to show that their nostrums work, 'but also that they actually bring benefits in social and economic as well as purely medical terms'.

Now, this sounds like the responsible voice of sweet reason, and is the kind of statement calculated to appeal to the many critics of the industry who feel that these are the very consider- ations which the drug barons blatantly ignore in their stren- uous efforts to maximize the use of their every last marketable artefact.

But wait. How are the citizens to *get* the enlightenment they need in order to be able to judge for themselves which among the profusion of remedies on offer are worth swallowing and when, and which are best left to the birds? Here comes the crunch.

The professor makes the extraordinary claim that the cus- tomers are going to want 'more authoritative advice than their doctors can give. . . .' And how are they going to come by this 'authoritative advice'? Why, straight from the manufacturers, of course, for *they* are the people who know more about their products than anybody else. Mr Smith suggests, among other things, that the public might be made privy to the codes which doctors can now use to rustle up data on drugs on their TV screens. Anyway, one way or another there must, he asserts, be much more direct contact between the pill makers and the pill swallowers. Drug companies will have to start regarding them- selves as suppliers of health rather than just medicines, and 'in the extreme case' (whatever that term may mean) 'companies could possibly start to provide general health counselling' to accompany the use of their products.

Now, wouldn't that be lovely! For the pill pedlars, maybe, but not for anybody else. The present strict rule is that prescrip- tion only medicines (what the industry quaintly describes as 'ethicals') can only be advertised to doctors, although the spirit of this convention is widely ignored by drug houses which stage press conferences to 'inform' journalists of 'breakthroughs' in the treatment of this and that human ill achieved through the use of this and that 'exciting' new product (a news item or feature on the latest wonder drug in *Woman's Own* or the *Mail* having far more impact than a paid-for ad). But how much healthier it would be for trade if the convention could be abandoned altogether. The doctors may scatter their scrips into the laps of a drug-hungry nation like showers of autumn leaves, but they still act as an intolerable bottleneck between producers and consumers, the latter, poor souls, often not even knowing what wondrous remedies are to hand for the asking. If only they could be *told*, so that they went along to their medical advisers demanding a prescription for Roche's Nobrium or Squibb's Moditen, instead of just 'something for my nerves, doctor'.

Of course, if such a suggestion were to be made in the industry's trade press (such as the quarterly *ABPI News*, which is a frank propaganda sheet), it would be howled down on the instant as a piece of blatant and irresponsible hucksterism, threatening the essential function of the medical profession, and the safety and wellbeing of its clientele. But if it comes from a *professor* (be he never so part-time), and if it is propounded in a thoughtful and quasi-academic treatise from that nice Office of Health Economics – ah well, that's something different. We might not agree with it, mind you. But it has to be thought about, doesn't it? The seed has been planted.

*

Most of the promotional and public relations activities here described may seem reasonable enough, viewed in isolation, and except when overplayed (like the Venetian orgy, or, at a more modest level of extremism, the Tagamet ad), but taken altogether, they are a subtly but powerfully corrupting influence on the developing pattern of medical care. By regularly devoting a substantial slice of its very high gross profits to the task, the industry has purchased itself a dominant position in medical attitudes and thought. The drug makers certainly own the loudest and the most persuasive of the voices sounding in the ears of GPs.

Recently a family physician, Dr Peter Pritchard of Dorchester-on-Thames, told a meeting of his fellows about an experiment he had carried out aimed at assessing the effect of commercial drug promotions. For one year he refused all such blandishments. He then compared his prescribing habits for that year with his own previous record, and with the habits of four neighbouring practices. He found, unsurprisingly, that his use of new drugs, introduced during the year in question, fell to a quarter of the level of the new drugs he had prescribed during the previous year. The four 'control' practices continued to try out new products as before. Dr Pritchard admitted that he could not be certain that no useful new drugs had been overlooked as a result of his voluntary insulation from commercial persuasions, but said that on the evidence available this seemed unlikely. Now, the outcome of this modest little enquiry may not seem very dramatic, but it does, in fact, define a dreadful and avoidable result of the drug makers' determination to maximize profits by every possible means within the law, and without regard to prudence or the true interests and wellbeing of their clients.

In 1956 thalidomide was marketed as a sedative totally free from any nasty side effects, and therefore particularly suitable for women who were suffering from morning sickness and anxiety associated with pregnancy. Soon grossly deformed babies were being born because their mothers had swallowed a medicine considered so safe that it was sold over the counter in German supermarkets.

Before thalidomide (a term almost as significant to the drug industry as is the term BC to Christians) there had been little official control over the quality, efficacy, or safety of the medicines pushed down the public throat by the hucksters of the pharmaceutical trade. In Britain a number of Acts of Parliament, passed piecemeal over the years, regulated the use of a few notorious poisons and officially designated 'dangerous drugs' (like morphine) and the quality of certain biological preparations such as vaccines.

In other words, it was recognized that a very few sorts of therapeutic agents, if improperly prepared or used, might do much more harm than good. It was *not* understood that any medicament capable of changing the functioning of the flesh in one, apparently, desirable direction, must, inevitably , sometimes, and at the same time, muck up the works in an undesirable and possibly unforeseen fashion. The legislators and their expert advisers knew about the perils of opium and strychnine, and could quite see that vaccines made from dangerous germs made 'safe' could be killers if the germs were not, in fact, made safe. They did not understand that there can be no such thing as a risk-free remedy. The thalidomide affair changed all that.

The whole thalidomide saga was a chapter of accidents, and much of the public reaction to the tragedy in the years which have elapsed since all those hundreds of wretchedly deformed babies were born has been based upon a myth. This is that the companies concerned with the manufacture and promotion of thalidomide acted in accordance with the best advice and knowledge available at the time – that it was, in fact, not only an unforeseen, but an unforeseeable disaster.

This is simply not true. What is sustainable is the belief that Grünenthal, the German progenitors of the drug, acted in ignorance of the dangers surrounding any medication of a pregnant woman, and that this ignorance was shared by the British licensee, Distillers Company (Biochemicals) Limited (DCBL), and possibly, by Richardson-Merrell in America, and by such other firms as were involved.

Their 'ignorance' can be assumed, simply on the grounds that no company would deliberately land itself in the frightful trouble that resulted from the sale of these poisonous pills (although, as we shall see, many manufacturers have subsequently and wilfully suppressed or ignored information concerning less dramatic or less irrefutable dangers linked with the use of their products). The defence of ignorance gains additional credibility from the fact that, during the post-thalidomide years, a number of wholly disinterested 'experts' in the fields of pharmacology and toxicology propagated the view that the possibility of a drug taken by a mother during early pregnancy producing birth defects in her baby, could not, at the time, have been foreseen. These experts were wrong, and were themselves, almost inexplicably, apparently unaware of the fact that by April 1958, when medicines containing thalidomide were first marketed in Britain, some 400 chemicals (although most of them had never been used as drugs) had been shown to produce congenital deformities when given to pregnant laboratory animals, and a good deal was known about the circumstances under which such teratogens would produce their effects, and of the techniques necessary for revealing whether any new and untried agent possessed this dangerous property. At no time was thalidomide subjected to such tests.

When Grünenthal launched their new 'sedative' upon an unsuspecting public, their director of research was a man who had qualified as a pharmacist after war-time service as an NCO. There is, of course, nothing wrong with NCOs, or pharmacists for that matter, but a man who possesses only a certain amount of routine technical expertise, and who is used to obeying the commands of superior officers without question, is not necessarily the best kind of person to be entrusted with developing a product that may add a new dimension to the chemical assaults so prodigally made upon the cells and tissues of the human race.

The brute truth of the matter is that Grünenthal was an organization that was simply not competent for the task it undertook. It had a ludicrously small experience of the development and testing of the new generation of synthetic drugs. And the same applied to Distillers. This was a company practised in the business of producing whisky and other spirits, but totally innocent in the medicines trade. But the directors wanted to diversify, and were attracted by the apparently rich profits to be garnered from the pharmaceutical field. They had had a taste of the game during the war when the government enlisted their expertise in the matter of fermentation by getting them to help in the production of penicillin. But they knew nothing of the business of discovering new medicinal compounds, and so they looked for an already invented nostrum which they might make under licence.

It was, it can be argued, their great bad luck that they happened to choose thalidomide. On the other hand, it can equally well be argued that the choice was a product of their inexperience. Other companies who knew more about the medicines scene had looked at the stuff and found it wanting.

Richardson-Merrell in the USA had no such excuse, for although their fortunes had been based upon the sales of an over-the-counter, low technology, household remedy called Vicks VapoRub, they had already been briefly involved in trouble over another poisonous product, called Triparanol, which they had promoted for the reduction of blood levels of cholesterol, upon the then popular belief that high blood cholesterol levels were a major cause of heart attacks. Triparanol didn't noticeably reduce deaths and disability from heart disease, but it did make some of the people who took it blind, and produced other unpleasant effects. This had involved the company in large compensation payments, had cost it an $80,000 fine, and had resulted in criminal charges being brought against some of the firm's executives, in that they had given false information to the Food and Drug Administration when seeking approval for the drug. So Richardson-Merrell, at least, were well aware of the peril of promoting an insufficiently tested pharmaceutical.

In the event, the USA was spared any share of the thalidomide tragedy because an FDA executive, called Frances Kelsey, refused to licence the product. A second thalidomide myth maintains that she only saved perhaps tens of thousands of American children from dreadful deformity by acting in a slow and bureaucratic fashion. In fact, she did her nation a great service by refusing to accept the wholly inadequate material submitted to her office by Richardson-Merrell Inc. Her stubborn unwillingness to be hustled into giving thalidomide the green light was due not to inertia, but to well-founded suspicions born of her own percipience, and bolstered by reports from Britain that the sedative appeared to be the cause of nerve damage in some of those for whom it had been prescribed.

Excellent accounts of the bumbling inefficiencies and outright deceptions and evasions which characterized the whole disastrous thalidomide affair (including the obstructive role played by the British legal system) are provided in three articles by Dr Ephraim Lesser, a pharmacologist, which appeared in *New Scientist* during May and June 1974, and in *Suffer the Children* (André Deutsch, 1979), a book by the *Insight* team of the *Sunday Times* – the paper which fought so hard and effectively for a fair deal for the British victims of the drug.

But some good came of the calamity. It was the immediate stimulus for the setting up in the UK of an official mechanism for exerting some long overdue and badly needed controls over the rapidly expanding and primarily profit-orientated activities of the medicines men. The original body charged with the task was the so-called Committee on Safety of Drugs, which became generally known as the Dunlop Committee after its first and only chairman, Sir Derrick Dunlop, a distinguished professor of therapeutics and clinical medicine. Sir Derrick and his colleagues (who were appointed by the ministers responsible for health matters in the UK) set the pattern which is broadly followed to this day. No compulsion was applied, but manufacturers were invited to seek the committee's approval for any new drugs they wished to introduce. This involved the submission of massive reports (typically running to some 4000 pages) detailing all the information obtained during the development of a new product, and including the results of administering the material to animals and to human volunteers. The tests reported were designed to show as precisely as possible everything that happened to the new drug from the moment it entered the body until it was broken down or excreted, or had otherwise disappeared from the tissues.

The tests were also designed to demonstrate all the possible poisonous effects the drug might have, and, of course, the beneficial or therapeutic effects to be expected from its use. Because of the thalidomide affair, particular attention was paid to the effect of massive doses of the drugs on the foetuses of pregnant laboratory animals. The committee also required detailed information on the chemical and physical properties of any new material, including such matters as its stability during storage, and the methods and quality controls to be used in its manufacture.

If the committee was satisfied from all this information (leaving aside the sheer impossibility of members sensibly absorbing, let alone subjecting to a critical analysis, such an overwhelming barrage of required evidence) that the new material was likely to be both useful and safe, it would authorize the manufacturer to arrange for clinical trials, to be undertaken in a manner, and by doctors, and in places of which the committee approved. Absolute safety was not expected or required, but any dangerous or undesirable effects revealed by the tests already carried out had to be commensurate with the expected benefits. Thus a high degree of toxicity might be acceptable in a drug for the treatment of, say, leukaemia, but an indigestion tablet would need to be virtually harmless. Thalidomide would never have passed this test, because its benefits were doubtful, and possibly non-existent, so that even a hint of danger would have ruled it out.

The committee required that, whenever possible, clinical trials should be of the double-blind type already briefly described, thus nullifying any bias, conscious or unconscious, on the part of the investigators, and also neutralizing the influence of the 'placebo effect'. This is the powerful psychological response to the administration of a medicine which many people experience, irrespective of whether the stuff is actually doing anything inside the body. About a third of patients suffering from some real physical disorder, and an even higher

proportion of those whose troubles reside in the mind, are
convinced that they feel better after they have been given some
totally inert substance, like a chalk pill or coloured water. Even
genuine physical signs and symptoms, such as joint pain or a
rash, may disappear or diminish, such is the power of the mind
over the flesh. In the double-blind trial both investigator bias
and the placebo effect have an equal influence on the results
recorded for both groups of patients involved – those receiving
the drug under test, and those getting the look-alike dummies.
But because of these factors, and the many other imponder-
ables, which may effect the real or apparent course of a disease,
substantial numbers of patients must be included in clinical
trials before any ostensible benefit derived from the drug
concerned can be regarded as a true bill, rather than the
product of pure chance. Once a satisfactory performance had
been established – reasonable efficacy and an absence of side
effects incommensurate with any success achieved – the Dunlop committee would approve the new agent for general use. It
was a long, tedious, and extremely costly process, and the
industry hated it, and still does. Nevertheless, despite the lack
of compulsion, a very high proportion of the pharmaceutical
companies, and certainly all the major manufacturers, submitted all their new products for assessment. Clearly the pressure
to do so was extremely high, particularly since the NHS is the
industry's chief customer in this country. But there were a
sufficient number of small and less reputable companies
marketing unapproved drugs to cause concern, and the only
sanction which authority could employ was to say 'This
drug has not been passed by the Committee on the Safety of
Drugs'.

This was not enough to deter the determined entrepreneur
who had perhaps no worthwhile reputation to lose, and who
could see a profitable hole in the market which could be filled by
a substandard product. Mainly for this reason, the informal
control exercised by the Dunlop committee was replaced by the
provisions of the Medicines Act 1968. Under the Act no
medicine can now be made or sold without a licence from the
responsible Secretaries of State, and a number of official committees have been established to advise the ministers on how to
exercise their powers. The chief of these committees is the
Medicines Commission, which has an extremely broad brief. It

is charged with advising the secretaries of state on matters concerning medicines, with answering questions put to it, and with volunteering information. It is also required to advise the ministers concerning other expert committees to be set up, and how they should be constituted.

There are presently three expert committees – a Pharmacopeia Commission which has the job of producing the British Pharmacopeia (the official collection of formulae for the preparation of medical compounds), a Veterinary Products Committee, and the Committee on Safety of Medicines (CSM), which replaced the old Dunlop committee, and performs the same tasks (including the monitoring of side effects produced by drugs which may become apparent *after* general release), but with the important difference that its decisions (once accepted by the appropriate ministers) have the force of law. It may, and not infrequently does, revoke or suspend a product licence when a drug is found to produce unacceptable adverse reactions of a kind or to an extent which had not been appreciated during the long, prerelease investigations. These expert committees report directly to the secretaries of state. They are not subcommittees of the commission. This is an important distinction, because the commission acts as an appellate body for people aggrieved by the decisions which the expert committees make.

The Act imposes legal controls over many aspects of the manufacture, distribution, use, advertising, labelling and packaging of medicines which had previously been immune from any official interference. It makes it an offence, for example, for any drug advertisement to make false or misleading statements. It provides for the licensing, not just of products, but of the manufacturers and suppliers (including importers) of medicines intended for human and animal use, and it allows for the imposition of conditions under which such licensees must operate. The DHHS maintains a team of inspectors who attempt to ensure that the conditions (like proper record keeping, adequate storage facilities, and effective quality controls) are observed.

Subcommittees of the commission compile lists of medicines which may be sold in supermarkets, corner shops, and so on, and of others which may only be supplied on the authority of a doctor's prescription.

Regulations made under the Act require manufacturers to supply all prescribing doctors with so-called data sheets, setting out, in a sober and factual fashion, details concerning the nature and approved uses and recommended doses of any drugs they advertise. The sheets must also give adequate information about any contraindications, warnings, and known side effects. The essential facts recorded in data sheets must be reproduced in all advertisements which do anything more than 'remind' doctors of a drug's existence by proclaiming its name and broad field of use, as, for example, 'HEXOPAL FORTE – power plus simplicity in peripheral vascular disease'. (In practice this requirement is almost invariably met by printing the unglamorous and frequently off-putting details of a drug's true characteristics in tiny type, and often very tiny type indeed, so that the mandatory dose of reality has rather less impact than the government health warning on packets of cancer sticks.)

And there are further and severe restrictions on the freedom of the pill pedlars to sell what they like as they like (no drug, for instance, can be recommended for a use which has not been approved by the safety committee – although any doctor can employ almost any agent he fancies for any purpose, so that there is profit to be had from subtle nudges, hints, and winks about 'wider applicability').

*

All this being so, it might be thought that the capacity of the industry to market useless or dangerous medicaments had been effectively restrained. Sadly, otherwise is the case, which brings us back to the true significance of Dr Peter Pritchard's Dorchester-on-Thames enquiry.

Now that such measures as the British Medicines Act, and the regulatory powers enjoyed by the Food and Drug Administration in the USA, have made it unlikely that a non-starter drug (in terms of lack of usefulness or immediately obvious poisonous propensities, or both) will reach the market place, most of the nastier crops of adverse drug reactions, up to and including death, have resulted from the wholesale use of approved and novel medicaments which have seemed all right after being subjected to the tests at present required. However, much too much faith has been placed in the certificate of virtue issued upon the results of a successful clinical trial.

Clinical trials are conducted by experts on selected patients who are usually in hospital and who are suffering from a precisely diagnosed condition which is the one it is hoped the drug under test will alleviate. They are not (because they would be excluded if they were) suffering from the hotchpotch of physical inefficiencies which often characterize the customers, and particularly the elderly customers (the major consumers of prescription drugs) of family doctors. The physical state of the subjects of clinical trials is always carefully assessed. For example, nobody with kidneys working below full strength would be included in a trial of a drug which is eliminated from the body through the kidneys, because of the danger that an undue concentration of the agent might build up in the tissues, not only hazarding the subject's health, but also mucking up the results. Clinical trial subjects take precisely the right dose of drug under test at precisely the right intervals of time, and it is established that they aren't taking any other pills or potions which might interact with, or potentiate, or nullify, the agent under test. The patients of GPs may well be taking a grisly cocktail of prescription drugs, particularly if they are elderly, and may, at the same time, be treating themselves to all manner of over-the-counter remedies. They are prone to misunderstand or forget or ignore dosage instructions, and may, for example, decide to swallow double the proper amount of some nostrum in the hope that this will do them twice as much good. Finally, clinical trial participants are carefully watched for the first signs of any nasty side effects or adverse reactions, while somebody taking a medicine at home, and seeing the doctor briefly only once in a while, can be at death's door or beyond as a result of drug poisoning before anybody recognizes what is going on.

So the crucial question is, not whether a new prescription medicine is safe and useful in the hands of experts working under well-controlled conditions, but whether it is safe and useful when it rolls off the prescription pads of family doctors who happen to have been impressed by the latest four-colour, four-page spread in their favourite freesheet, or by the honeyed words and nice looking samples spawned by the latest visiting rep.

Good doctors appreciate all this, and while it may be a part of the function of a hospital consultant to beaver away at constantly striving to improve treatment regimes, which task will include experimenting with new drugs (and 'experimenting' is the proper term), the best general practitioners limit themselves to the use of a comparatively short list of remedies which they have found to be effective, and which they have got to know well – what response to expect and how soon, when to increase or reduce the dose, what signs of intolerance or unwanted effects to look out for, and what to do about it when they occur, and so on and so on. Such wise prescribers get the best results and put their clients at the smallest risk. They are *not* going to deprive their patients of the best available solution to their ills by refusing to hand out every newest nostrum, signalled by the makers as a 'notable advance in the treatment of chronic bronchitis' or whatever. Drugs which truly represent a 'notable advance' are pretty rare birds among the stream of newcomers constantly jostling for a share of the loot. As the OHE has recently proudly proclaimed (to show how go-ahead the industry is), no fewer than 40 per cent of the 2000-plus 'ethicals' available in 1982 had been introduced since 1970, but of these no more than a handful have made any dramatic contribution to the welfare of the sick (a probably larger number having had a tragically opposite effect). The cautious prescriber will very soon learn when something really good has hit the chemists' shelves, and give his customers the benefit of its use.

The drug makers are also well aware of these truths. They may be greedy, and they may be ruthless in pursuit of profits, but they are not fools, and they employ or have access to some of the best and most experienced medical brains (when Sir Derrick Dunlop retired, for example, he became a director of Sterling-Winthrop, a major pharmaceutical firm and in 1984 Dr John Griffin resigned as head of the Department of Health's medicines division, primarily concerned with drug licencing and safety, to become director of ABPI.) They therefore know full well that in spending lavishly on the task of persuading prescribers (who are too often injudicious and pharmacologically naive) to 'try out' new products on as many trusting guinea pigs as possible, and from the moment general release has been approved, they are encouraging the practice of bad and dangerous medicine. This is at best irresponsible, and, since the premature unbridled use of novel remedies has all too frequently resulted in avoidable deaths, and a great deal of physical suffering, promoting such profligate consumption of untried agents by high pressure selling simply for profit, and as though they were the equivalent of TV snacks or soapflakes, could even be regarded as wicked. The industry is deliberately taking maximum advantage of the major remaining hiatus in the system of controls operated under the provisions of the Medicines Act.

From the very beginning the Dunlop committee issued so-called 'yellow cards' to prescribing doctors. These are reply-paid postal forms designed to facilitate the garnering of information about suspected adverse reactions to recently introduced drugs and other agents, such as contact lenses (particularly reactions which are only suffered by a minority of consumers, and which therefore may have escaped detection during premarketing trials).

The system has severe limitations. In the first place it is a voluntary exercise, so that even if a GP (or a consultant, for that matter) is sufficiently on the ball to wonder whether an unexpected or nasty hiccup in the progress of a client is due to some nostrum being swallowed, he may not get round to reaching for a card and spending the ten minutes required for filling in all the blanks, various guesstimates putting the proportion of adverse reactions reported by this means at anything from a low one to a 'high' 10 per cent. Secondly, although the cards are franked for passage through Her Majesty's first class mail, this is a waste of taxpayers' money, since neither the Dunlop committee nor its successor have ever had the means to deal promptly with the information received, so that months may elapse before possibly crucial hints of unsuspected trouble get slotted into place. (Once a scare has arisen, of course, any relevant cards that arrive are given instant attention, but by then immense damage may already have been done.)

Thus, for example, in the 1960s at least 3500 asthmatics died from overemployment of a type of aerosol inhaler then in use (quite different from the present excellent and far safer aerosols), but by the time the cause of these deaths had been recognized, the CSM had only received six yellow cards suggesting the connection. In 1975 Eraldin, a widely used heart drug, was voluntarily withdrawn by its makers, ICI, from general use (i.e. by GPs) after it had become clear that perhaps 7000 consumers had suffered serious adverse reactions (including death, blindness, and a peculiarly nasty kind of peritonitis). When the more serious side effects began to be recognized, Eraldin had been in use for four years, and until then the CSM had received just one yellow card report linking the agent with any significant trouble – eye damage.

In the case of both the aerosols and Eraldin, published reports from individual physicians, and *not* the official safety checks, had first raised the alarm. It was also a lone consultant geriatrician, Dr Hugh Taggart of Belfast City Hospital, who first recognized the most serious adverse reaction to Opren (to wit, death) in some of his elderly patients, who suffered mortal liver damage, although the CSM had received an unprecedented number (1800) of yellow cards reporting lesser Opren side effects during its first year on the chemists' shelves. (It was later alleged that Eli Lilly had held back or 'massaged' some of the early information in its possession concerning an undue incidence of certain dangers, including abnormal reactions to sunlight, and accumulation of the drug in the elderly, associated with Opren's use.)

In March 1984, under pressure from the government, Ciba-Geigy, a huge multinational, withdrew two preparations containing oxyphenbutazone (Tanderil and Tandacote), and agreed that other products containing the probably slightly less dangerous phenylbutazone (known in the racing world as 'Bute') should only be prescribed by hospital doctors for those patients suffering from a form of arthritis of the spine for whom no other medicines bring adequate relief. The drugs (which are NSAIDs comparable to Opren, and which had been widely used for rheumatism and arthritis, and for the general treatment of painful muscles, ligaments, and joints) enjoyed annual world-wide sales worth some £65 million. They were highly effective (witness their popularity with trainers anxious to get injured horses back into the game), and were the first of their kind, and their introduction had represented one of the infrequent true advances in the chemical amelioration of distress. However, by the time they were withdrawn, after having been on the market for over 20 years, they had been responsible for many thousands of deaths, of which an estimated 1500 had occurred in Britain alone. The fatalities followed damage to the bone marrow (most frequently), or bleeding from the gut, or heart failure, or, occasionally, some other poisonous effect. Now, while the possibility of fatal adverse reactions had been recognized since shortly after the drugs were launched, the chance of a rare mishap, even though disastrous for the individual concerned, was officially regarded as an acceptable price to pay for the great relief enjoyed by the vast majority of users. There is no such thing as a totally safe drug, and there is nothing disgraceful about selling drugs which may cause trouble – even death – so long as the dangers are commensurate with the likely benefits, and both are fully and accurately portrayed. Unfortunately, there was no general awareness of the scale of the risks associated with the use of oxyphenbutazone and phenylbutazone until a Dr Olle Hansson revealed the contents of a confidential Ciba-Geigy internal report in an article in the Swedish press. The report, compiled by some of the firm's own medical staff, was dated September 1982, and recorded 1182 deaths known by them to have been associated with the agents. They went on to say that 'In the presence of many newer, equally effective NSAIDs now available on the market, with comparatively less toxicity, it is reasonable and necessary that the risk and benefit ratio for Butazolidin and Tanderil should be carefully reassessed'. Dr Hansson is reported to have said, 'These drugs should be taken off the market immediately. Warning voices have been raised, but have been effectively quelled by Ciba-Geigy's marketing strategy.' The document which he leaked had the effect of stirring various national authorities, including Britain's CSM, to make their own enquiries, aimed at unearthing evidence of past butazone deaths which might have gone undetected or unreported. The appalling estimate arrived at by the CSM led to vigorous remedial action which was long overdue.

These are just a small sample of the happenings which have made it clear that the present means for monitoring a drug's performance in the field are inadequate. There is a growing demand that this dangerous gap in the drug control system should be plugged. Several schemes have been proposed.

The identity of the first 10,000 or 20,000 patients prescribed a newly released drug could be registered, and each would be asked to complete a questionnaire designed to detect happenings that might spell adverse drug reactions. The information garnered could be looked at by agencies tuned to react to specific features in the replies. Thus, for example, the government Office of Population, Census and Statistics could use its computer to compare the fates of registered drug customers with those of the population at large.

Enquiries could be made into the drug histories of all sufferers from certain diseases, particularly those of still uncertain causation, and others (like bone marrow, liver, and kidney damage) frequently associated with drug poisoning in the past. Doubtless, otherwise unsuspected drug-linked maladies would be found.

The names of doctors prescribing a particular drug could be recorded (every NHS prescription finally lands up in the laps of the bureaucrats anyway), and the doctors could then be asked to report on the subsequent medical histories of the patients involved, being encouraged to tell all, and not just such incidents as they might have imagined to be the consequence of medicines dispensed. Put altogether these accounts would reveal causes and effects which seem unconnected in any individual case.

Official enthusiasm for such exercises had been noticeably pale, for any system, or combination of techniques, capable of providing substantially better safeguards than the present cumbersome and discredited yellow card machinery, would be both burdensome and expensive. This suits the pharmaceutical industry just fine. Professor Teeling Smith has attempted to back up the favourable effect of political inertia by widely quoting a figure of £55 million for every life saved as the price of the kind of controls which, might, in theory, have prevented the *acknowledged* drug-related deaths of recent years. He is also fond of the specious contention that drug deaths and injuries must be viewed 'in their true perspective' against the background of the hundreds of thousands of lives saved by vaccines, antibacterial drugs, and other remedies, implying that the bad luck of the few is the inevitable price that has to be paid for the much greater benefit enjoyed by the many, and that stiffer regulations would dangerously reduce the cascade of goodies pouring from the pharmaceutical cornucopia for the essential protection of a species otherwise defenceless in the face of pestilence and plague.

*

The industry has a powerful reason for resisting any restrictions on the high pressure marketing of drugs from the moment they have been approved for general use. New drugs are protected by a patent which lasts for 20 years. During that period the inventing company enjoys a monopoly. This not only means that no competitor can legally make or sell the same active ingredient, but also that the patentee can price the product at whatever level the market will bear. This, in the case of a medicine offering some genuine advantage over others used for the same purpose, can be many times the actual production cost. There is a hefty markup on patent-protected drugs sold in Britain to the NHS because, under the so-called Pharmaceutical Price Regulation Scheme, the government negotiates a price with the manufacturer (the profit element remaining secret) which takes into account the company's professed overall financial health, the value of the firm's contribution to the balance of payments through exports, a large element representing the general costs of research and development and marketing (including losses on non-starters), and other recondite factors which bear little or no relationship to what the company spends on making the product in question. (A device employed by the multinationals for boosting these 'agreed' charges is 'transfer pricing', whereby a company sells a British subsidiary raw materials from a manufacturing plant abroad for much more than their real value, thus making the apparent profits earned on the final product artificially low.)

But once a patent has expired, competitors will offer the identical nostrum for a fraction of its previous price. They can do this, and still make money on the deal, because they have not had to bear any of the huge development costs. The original producer must then also slash prices, or lose most, rather than just some, of the market.

The trouble is that a patent must be obtained as soon as a novel agent has been synthesized if rivals are to be prevented from cashing in on the discovery, and since the average time lag between first synthesis and first sales is ten years, half the period of protection has elapsed before the profits begin to roll. Ten years are left in which to make a killing. Any additional delays would cost a lot of money. Profits lost at the start are lost forever.

Supposing patent protection for new drugs to be justifiable at all (and it is difficult to see why hard-headed businessmen should be expected to invest large sums and effort in a gamble if they can't pick up their winnings when it comes off), then the cash penalties attached to hold-ups caused by necessary government controls could be reduced by a change in the law, giving, perhaps, a patentee a finite time in which to market a product containing the protected agent, and then, if he succeeds, a further period of protection (of whatever length is judged to be socially advantageous and commercially fair), dating from the time its use is finally approved.

Until something of the sort does happen it must be expected that the drug pedlars will use to the limit every permitted effort, and sometimes a few beyond, to maximize the sales of their latest cure-alls, regardless of the public interest.

But even if the damaging hyping of new products is thus made less necessary, there will still be an enormous temptation to dissemble. When you have spent £50 million and ten years of effort in striving to produce a new and saleable remedy, you're not going to be particularly keen to advertise any facts in your possession which cast doubts on its virtue. If, on the whole, it looks all right, but just the odd set of animal experiments or clinical reports seem a bit dicey – well, take them out of the records submitted to authority, or even falsify a few unhappy results. Pay a dishonest doctor or two to produce favourable reports on clinical trials when honest doctors have remained unimpressed. (There are even periodicals with high-sounding academic titles which are a favourite repository for dubious drug trial reports. Such testimonials cut no ice with the cognoscenti, but look good when quoted as references in advertisements or brochures aimed at the less sophisticated members of the medical trade.)

These and similar deceptions go on all the time, but the chicaneries are usually only discovered when enough people have been sufficiently damaged by a product to warrant an enquiry into the value of the credentials which gained it original approval, or perhaps when some disaffected employee decides to blow the gaff.

*

Not only does the industry scream with well-simulated agony whenever any fresh erosions of its liberties or profits are proposed, it also campaigns ceaselessly for a relaxation of the controls which already exist. It wants, in particular, a curtailment of the many tests which must be undertaken and reported before first human or clinical trials are authorized, so that drugs can reach the market sooner. The pretence is that the present licensing requirements are so needlessly onerous that the sick are being kept waiting for help they desperately need, and, but for bureaucratic hindrances, could have. The true cause of the drug men's resentment is, of course, that they eat into that precious post-release period of patent protection.

The government makes the regulations, and the industry attempts to use its beefy financial muscle to persuade the government to make things easier (or, at the very least, no more demanding). Its favourite ploy is to threaten that the multinationals (or as I think they are now called 'transnationals') which own by far the larger part of the British drug-making scene, will move their operations elsewhere if the controls which stifle their initiative and chances of scraping an honest living remain so severe, and *then* we'll be sorry as jobs and export earnings disappear. This is pure bluff. The multinationals have invested heavily here, not out of respect for the Queen but because it is a damned good place to be. We provide an ample pool of some of the world's best scientists (essential to the exercise) who can be hired at a third of the cost of employing their equivalents in the USA. Our regulatory agencies are *less* demanding and *more* efficient (in terms of speed) than most. The skills and integrity of British physicians are respected throughout the world, so that drugs approved for use after clinical trials here carry a widely accepted quality seal. It would take a great deal more anti-pharmaceutical aggro than any British administration has yet shown to shift the pill-peddling fraternity from our shores.

It is not of course unreasonable to suggest that elaborate safety precautions, designed during the emotionally charged aftermath of the thalidomide affair, and with the idea of guaranteeing, so far as was humanly possible, that no such tragedy should ever occur again, might have been overstringent, so that, in the light of experience, some requirements could be safely moderated or abandoned. But the argument that they unjustifiably cost lives and prolong suffering does not hold water. If, for example, a truly valuable new agent, such as a cancer cure, were to turn up, its passage from the laboratory to the clinic would undoubtedly be hastened by all possible means. In general, however, authority would be wise to err on the side of overcaution. The industry has shown that it will vigorously exploit every available slackness or absence of controls. To be assured of this fact, it is only necessary to look at how it behaves in the Third World, and in other countries lacking the disciplines imposed in places such as Britain and the USA.

*

The conscienceless exploitation by the multinationals of the ignorance, and of the lack of effective government machinery for supervision which characterize poorer nations has increasingly concerned the World Health Organization. Addressing the World Health Assembly as long ago as 1975, Dr Halfdan Mahler, WHO's Director-General, said 'Drugs not authorized for sale in the country of origin – or withdrawn from the market for reasons of lack of safety or lack of efficacy – are sometimes exported and marketed in developing countries; other drugs are promoted and advertised in those countries for indications that are not approved by the regulatory agencies of the countries of origin. Products not meeting the quality requirements of the exporting country, including products beyond their expiry date, may be exported to developing countries that are not in a position to carry out quality control measures.' He said that Third World nations commonly squandered pitifully inadequate health care budgets on expensive imported drugs, many of which were only modestly relevant, and others of which were totally irrelevant, to their true medical problems. Nothing significant has happened in the decade since those pretty restrained allegations were made to diminish their validity.

Two American companies, Organon and Winthrop, are among firms which have been involved in the Third World promotion of so-called anabolic steroids. These are synthetic hormones which, among other things, promote the growth of muscle. For this reason they became popular with athletes eager to put a shot or toss a caber further than their rivals. But such use was long ago banned by the authorities controlling sport, not only because they gave the users an unfair advantage, but also because they are dangerous drugs. They can stimulate the growth of certain cancers. They can produce virilism (that is, beard growth, and other 'male' characteristics in women), and when given to children they can encourage premature sexual maturity, including the early cessation of bone growth which normally occurs only at the end of puberty after a proper stature has been achieved. Put broadly, they distort the natural hormonal controls of growth and of bodily functions related to sex. They are a large spanner dropped into the works. They *can* be useful, in improving the health of patients whose bodies are working at low ebb following drastic surgery, or who are suffering from certain anaemias, or who are otherwise drifting downhill, but their use is only justified in a small number of sick people who are in the care of experts who know (or think they know) just what they are doing.

Organon's preparation, Fertabolin, and Winthrop's Winstrol, have been offered in Third World countries as a kind of tonic, able to make the weak strong, almost suggesting that heads of families have a duty to buy their infants these 'strength promoters'. What weakling Third World children need, of course, is good food and clean water. Trying to sell their caring parents an intolerably costly, totally false, and actually damaging aid to strong growth is a piece of cynical wickedness of a kind that even Colonel Gadaffi would hardly be able to think up. It is worth noting that in 1982 the Swiss firm, Ciba-Geigy, announced that it would stop production of Dianabol, a similar drug, on the grounds that 'the inappropriate use of this product constitutes a risk that far outweighs the benefit of the product's legitimate use'.

There are very many similar examples, such as promoting the use of antibiotics for quite wrong purposes. The ill-informed use of antibiotics (as, for example, the automatic prescription of penicillin for anybody claiming a sore throat or a fever) is not only bad medicine, but is also a hazard to the public health. The more that antibiotics are thrown around in a careless fashion, the more likely it is that germs will emerge that are resistant to their influence. Eventually the whole range of these life saving drugs could be rendered useless, as had already happened in the case of penicillin and a growing proportion of sufferers from gonorrhoea. A BBC investigation into what Halfdan Mahler has termed 'drug colonialism' was undertaken in 1979. This relatively brief and restricted exercise produced a long catalogue of grisly malpractices. They included the sale in Bangladesh of a combined injection of two antibiotics, penicillin and streptomycin, which was widely employed by unqualified practitioners as a cure-all for every kind of ailment, even including cuts and bruises. The researchers also came across a grotesque 'all-purpose' pack of pills on sale in Thailand. It contained two different antibiotic tablets, one steroid, one vitamin C, one paracetamol, and one Valium, its only virtue being that, while containing not enough of anything to do any possible good, it also contained not enough of anything to do any possible harm.

Taxed with responsibility for such immoral goings on, the drug companies commonly plead that they are acting within local laws, are catering for local needs, and are, in any case, not capable of enforcing the proper use of their products, which must be the task of the various governments concerned. This is hypocritical nonsense because the companies spend a lot of money on encouraging the kind of consumption of their wares for which they disclaim accountability. Huge posters proclaim the dubious virtues of their nostrums. In many developing countries there is a drug 'rep' for every four doctors, compared to one for 20 in Britain (another BBC discovery), and they push their companies' lines with a disregard for truth which wouldn't be either productive or tolerated in less innocent communities. In some Third World nations up to a quarter of the advertising revenue earned by radio stations comes from the pushers of medicaments.

The result of all this is that (quite apart from a wholly unknown incidence of drug-induced disease) many developing nations spend up to a half and more of their limited health budgets on buying overpriced and often inappropriate medicines from the West.

Companies take out patents on their products in Third World countries, not in order to manufacture locally but to stop anybody else from manufacturing locally, so that the patented elixirs have to be imported at prices set by the patentee.

In May 1982, in an attempt to curtail this kind of exploitation, WHO's World Health Assembly endorsed the secretariat's proposal for a list of just 246 essential drugs which could serve virtually all the needs of developing nations, and which, if observed, would reduce their dependence on large numbers of imported and expensive pharmaceuticals.

The following month Bangladesh became the first country to adopt the WHO guidelines, and announced legislation establishing a list of 250 essential medicines, banning 237 as dangerous, and directing that supplies of 1500 others should not be renewed. Within days the US Ambassador to Bangladesh, Jane Coon, had urged the government to reconsider the measures, and persuaded it to set up a review committee composed of military doctors. A couple of months later a group of American 'scientific experts' flew into Dacca to 'help' the committee and to see ministers. It included a representative of the Pharmaceutical Manufacturing Association of America, and executives from three of the corporations with a stake in the £35 million a year market.

The Sri Lankan government had taken vigorous steps, years earlier, and on its own initiative, to curb drug costs and their extravagant promotion. A State Pharmaceutical Corporation, established in 1972, cut the national drug bill by an estimated massive 40 per cent during its first year of operation. It managed this by taking over all drug imports so that it could buy in bulk from the cheapest source, by reducing the national drug menu from a few thousand to a few hundred items, and by ordering that all medicines should be prescribed by their generic (that is, official or chemical) names instead of by a brand or trade name. Next the government attempted to get a score or so of the most essential drugs manufactured within the country from raw materials obtained abroad, but was effectively frustrated in this aim by the determined obstructionism of the multinationals whose plants and skills would have been needed for the task. Finally, when the decision was taken to quell this resistance by nationalizing the recalcitrant concerns, the American Ambassador reminded Mrs Bandaranaike, prime minister at the time, that the USA was Sri Lanka's principal provider of food aid, and the scheme was quietly abandoned.

Thus and thus do the multinationals use the lever of their fiscal power to get politicians, who love the money involved, to brandish big sticks on their behalf. (Incidentally, the colour of the Sri Lankan government having changed, the pill pedlars there are now in full control of their own affairs again.)

The pharmaceutical barons are desperately keen to maintain their freebooting activities in the Third World, not only because of the vast export earnings involved, and of which they are so proud, but also, and perhaps just as importantly, because, if a poor nation was able to demonstrate that it could get along very nicely thank you with a strictly limited list of unbranded products, then the rich nations might begin to wonder what the hell they were doing spending so much on so many costly, marginally useful, and often dangerous drugs.

*

Nobody but a fool or a bigot would want to deny that the entry of the chemical industry into the medicines trade has brought immense benefits in terms of lives saved and suffering reduced. The scope and effectuality of both medicine and surgery have been increased beyond recognition over the past 30 or 40 years, largely (but not entirely) because of the invaluable tools, from antibacterials to safer anaesthetics, which the application of industrial research and manufacturing know-how and capacity to drug production has put into the doctors' hands. But the time is rapidly approaching when the unbridled, worldwide, and all-pervasive power and influence of the medicine makers, wrongly applied in pursuit of ever greater profits, could so distort the pattern of medical care that they will be doing us all more harm than good. Indeed, it might well be argued that this has already happened in many poor, large communities, where ruthless pressures, aimed at all targets, from governments to private citizens, have resulted in sadly limited resources being wasted on 'cures' of dubious worth, when the money and effort so spent could achieve far more if used for the provision of clean water, good drains, and simple health education of a kind that can be effectively dispensed by intelligent 'bare-foot doctors' after a pretty cheap and basic training. It could even be argued that the pharmaceutical industry has damaged British medicine by using its huge financial clout to encourage our own doctors to think, almost automatically, in terms of 'Now, what drug can I use for *this* patient's problems?', at the expense of a broader and, in the end, more fruitful approach to the task of attempting to change, for the better, the factors which influence health and disease.

We need a strong, adventurous, competitive, and (necessarily) profitable drug industry, but at the same time we need to keep it under strict control.

Politicians of a certain cast of mind would like to see the whole of the drug trade taken over by the state, pretending to find something grossly immoral and offensive in the idea that anybody should make money out of the medicinal needs created by physical distress. This is ideological nonsense, unless you happen to hold the view that nobody should make a profit out of anything at all. Food, for example, is rather more essential than penicillin, so that if people who sell things which ward off distress were all to be crucified, that would be Sainsburys gone for a burton for a start. On a rather more practical level, it is a brute fact that in countries like Russia, where all industry was nationalized before the pharmaceutical revolution began, not a single, novel, worthwhile medicine has emerged. And yet Russia houses as many clever chemists and medical scientists as may be found elsewhere. The profit motive, not a care for the commonweal, has encouraged the immense investment of money and effort needed to translate a potentially useful medicament from a gleam in a researcher's eye to a pill on a pharmacy shelf.

The first line of defence against the corruption of medical practice and the ripping off of the public purse by the drug pedlars must be the proper education of the medical profession in the uses and limitations of modern remedies. Doctors gain no material benefit from their prescribing (apart from the 'soft' bribes already noted, and the case of the few rural practitioners who dispense their own medicines), so that, vigorously trained to employ drugs with understanding, caution, and moderation, they could almost wholly prevent misuse, overuse, and the great majority of drug disasters. Such training must not stop at graduation, but must continue throughout a prescriber's working life by means of *compulsory* refresher courses, attended at, say, yearly intervals, to ensure that every practitioner authorized to scribble a prescription is kept thoroughly well informed. And as soon as it is possible, the power of computers must be employed, so that a medicine (which must be a potential poison) before it is channelled into a patient's flesh is checked against the intended recipient's medical and drug consumption history, and with the latest centrally available information on the drug's side effects and contraindications and possible interactions so that no avoidable mistakes are made. Failure to use such a procedure (a terminal being a standard item on every doctor's desk) should, except in the case of an emergency, be regarded as malpractice.

If this all seems a bit excessive, it should be remembered that many more people suffer death or injury each year from drug 'accidents' than from aircraft disasters, and that doctors are managing agents which, if mishandled, are as lethal as an ill-flown jumbo jet. We *force* pilots to keep themselves up-to-date and fit for the job. Why not doctors? Moreover, just like airline pilots, doctors should have a statutory *duty* to report, through their computers, all 'near misses' or other untoward events of which they become aware while in control of their useful but potentially harmful tools.

In addition to such positive controls, there should be proscriptions against the use of anti-education. The promotion of branded drugs to the profession could, for example, be limited to the circulation, by post or in journals, of the present data sheets, which set out the facts of a medicine's virtues and faults in sober terms. There is absolutely no case, in reason, for attempting to win the attention of professional men and women by means of four-page, four-colour spreads. The success of a drug in the market place should stand or fall on the basis of its virtues alone, and ought, clearly, to have nothing to do with the wholly irrelevant skills of marketing directors and advertising agencies and the size of the budgets at their disposal. Similarly, reps have no reputable place in influencing therapy.

A small concession to rationality was made in November 1984 when the government announced that from April 1985 a list of 31 commonly used medicinal substances would no longer be prescribable through the NHS by their trade names but would have to be ordered by their chemical or generic names (e.g. soluble aspirin instead of Solprin), thus obliging chemists to dispense unbranded but equivalent and far cheaper preparations. Most of the designated drugs were simple painkillers, cough mixtures, multivitamin pills, laxatives, tonics, antacids, and similar household remedies, many of which can be bought over the counter for less than the charge for a prescription, but the axe also fell on three prescription-only tranquillizers, including the immensely popular Valium and Mogadon. (Of course, all the agents named were out of patent, and could therefore be made by anybody.)

This 'tough' measure provoked protests from the BMA and the Royal College of General Practitioners on the grounds that it attacked a doctor's sacred right to prescribe whatever he thinks best (and never mind the basis of his thinking), and from the pill pedlars who foresaw greatly reduced sales of the several hundred proprietary medicines which contain one or more of the listed chemicals. The trade argued that whereas the prosperous could continue to buy their favourite brand-name nostrums in chemists' shops, the large number of old, young, and penurious citizens entitled to exemption from prescription charges would, if they wanted free medicines, have to make do with possibly less acceptable alternatives from the restricted list. The ABPI (always, of course, on the side of the underprivileged) claimed indignantly that the proposals would 'create an unfair two-tier NHS medicines plan'. The proprietors of the throwaways were also upset, since there would no longer be any reason for drug companies to advertise the no longer prescribable confections in the free-sheets aimed at doctors. Indeed, several publishers offered the industry free advertising space for the purpose of encouraging a revolt among GPs. But, apart from the immediate impact of the measure on sales and on advertising revenue, the industry and the free-sheet owners were desperately worried that, should the measures be implemented without obvious harm to the health of the nation, the principle of generic prescribing would soon be applied to a much wider range of patent-expired prescription-only medicines.

Such a happening, coupled perhaps with regulations forbidding the lavish promotion of still-patented brand-name drugs, would be the death of the throwaway sheets, and would greatly increase the cost to subscribers of serious journals like the *Lancet* and the *BMJ*, and would gravely diminish the number of column-inches open for grabs to medical hacks like me. But if so, so be it. There must be a better way of subsidizing necessary publications than that of having them act as billboards for the hucksters of dubious medicaments. Patients would *not* be deprived of excellent, available remedies if the four-colour, double-page spreads announcing their presence were to disappear. A good wine, as the old saying goes, needs no bush.

Of course, drug sales and profits would slump if the promotion of second-rate pharmaceuticals was curbed, but there would still be a lot of money to be made out of the invention and marketing of worthwhile remedies, and we need have no fear that the chemical industry would lose interest in the trade. The moguls might, indeed, be induced to concentrate their minds and resources wonderfully upon the production of agents which serve real needs, rather than those which can simply be sold.

The game must be to devise the means whereby the pill pedlars are properly rewarded for their endeavours at serving our best ends, rather than having our proclivities serve theirs.

CHAPTER SIX

Nonconformists, Mystics, Charlatans and Cranks

In Britain there are almost as many men and women making a decent and often a rich living out of the practice of irrational, unscientific, healing techniques, as there are family doctors dispensing pukka 'laboratory-tested', logical therapies and cures. Moreover, a fair sprinkling of registered medical practitioners are using homoeopathy, osteopathy, acupuncture, the laying on of hands, and other treatments of a kind which don't figure in the medical curriculum, in addition to the pills, potions, and manipulations which they have been taught to regard as the proper tools of their trade. Fringe medicine, as Brian Inglis, one of the more intelligent and educated advocates of mysterious remedies, has termed the industry, is on the up and up.

Why? Why pay out good money for a bottle of Potter's Ana-Sed tablets ('. . . a balanced compound of herbal nervines which afford relief by their calming effect . . .') when you can could enjoy a liberal helping of Valium supplied for next to nothing through our wonderful NHS? Why enrich the local bonesetter when you can have your backache attacked by a high grade orthopaedic surgeon at the local hospital? Why travel to Lourdes when you could go to Barts? Shouldn't the powerful therapeutic weapons now available to doctors, and the increasingly scientific nature of medical practice, have brought traditional and fanciful regimens into disrepute, leaving them to their place in history as relics of the days when effective therapies were scant, and any promise of a cure seemed worth a try?

The opposite has happened. At the end of 1982, Prince Charles, addressing the British Medical Association from the presidential chair, said that 'the whole imposing edifice of modern medicine, for all its breathtaking success, is like the celebrated Tower of Pisa, slightly off balance'. He urged members to handle their clients as whole persons rather than as bodies attached to a disease. He said, 'It is frightening how dependent upon drugs we are all becoming and how easy it is for doctors to prescribe them as the universal panacea for our ills. Wonderful as many of them are it should still be more widely stressed by doctors that the health of human beings is so often determined by their behaviour, their food and the nature of their environment.' A few months later, in a valedictory message, he openly invited the association to take note of and think upon the successes achieved by the practitioners of fringe medical techniques. A fortnight later still he presided at the official opening of the Bristol Cancer Help Centre (much to the annoyance of some worthy proper doctors), where treatment of the feared disease includes yoga, meditation, and a diet of vitamins and uncooked vegetables, and he again enjoined doctors and other kinds of healers to work together for the commonweal.

The Prince was only voicing an attitude shared by many of his mother's subjects, and because this was so, and also because a prince is a prince is a prince, the BMA set up an inquiry into alternative medical techniques, in an attempt to determine whether or not fringe practitioners were accomplishing something by means ignored by orthodox labourers in the medical vineyard. This apparent admission by the medical establishment that 'there might be something in it, after all', was, of course, simply a PR exercise, designed to counteract painfully obvious public discontent with the services proper doctors are offering their patients. As the chairman of the inquiry lamely remarked, when asked why the BMA had suddenly appeared to pay serious attention to techniques which it had scornfully derided in the past, 'If you elect someone president of your organization, you have a duty to listen to what they say.'

But why do the princes and the people flock to the providers of alternative therapies? There are several good reasons.

Modern medicine can alleviate many dangerous or distressing ailments, from plague to corrupted heart valves, which were untreatable half a century ago. But there are still numerous conditions, from cancer to migraine, which are often resistant to the most powerful scientific remedies. When proper doctors have been tried and have failed, many sufferers will look for help elsewhere.

Disasters such as the thalidomide affair, and the carnage and disappointments resulting from heroic and ill-considered surgery like heart transplants, have caused a reaction against high technology medicine, and a wish among many for a return to a simpler, blander, apparently safer, and less disruptive form of healing.

In addition to any positive mistrust of modern medical techniques, a great many people (Prince Charles and Brian Inglis apparently among them) have a desire to believe in magic and the supernatural. They are disillusioned with reality, and seek comfort in the belief that there are powers and forces at work beyond those outlined in the scientific text. Reason and evidence provide small hope that the human state can be rapidly and radically improved. Thus the temptation to abandon reason and depend for comfort upon faith.

In the good old days there were precious few diseases the healing trade could do much about. A handful of drugs, like morphine and quinine and digitalis, actually worked, and lives could be saved by surgeons cutting off infected limbs or snipping out a gangrenous appendix, but the heaviest shot in the doctor's locker was the confidence and hope he was able to instil amongst his patients and their families by taking command and appearing to be in control of a frightening situation.

He *did* contribute to the relief of suffering, because attitudes can greatly modify the effect, and even the course, of a disease, and the doctor's great skill was the encouragement of helpful and hopeful attitudes. He succeeded in this by getting to know his patients, and by talking to them, and, most helpfully of all perhaps, by listening. He dispensed the powerful magic of his personality.

The modern doctor doesn't do this much. If he works in a hospital he's too busy ordering X-rays, and considering the results of a nitrobluetetrazolium test, and writing up a paper for the *Lancet*. If he's a GP he's too busy writing out prescriptions. He can spare, on average, five minutes per customer. The contemporary patient is no longer a sick person (as Prince Charles rightly told the BMA), but the anonymous vehicle of a diseased pancreas, or a cancerous breast, or is a disembodied voice demanding a 'certificate'.

Patients miss the old-fashioned kind of personal support, and probably far more than most 'scientific' doctors realize. But 'fringe' practitioners of all kinds are in much the same position as that occupied by their orthodox counterparts 50 or 100 years ago. They all work according to the dictates of some theory of disease which, while it may be irrational or bizarre, is always magnificently simple compared to the real problems posed by the living flesh. And their methods of treatment are also simple, rigidly defined, and wonderfully undemanding in their application. You push a few needles into the skin, or you place a hand on a brow and think about eternal life, or you prescribe a nostrum or two from a short and harmless pharmacopoea, or you prod the spine to put a 'displaced' vertebra back where it belongs – and that's that.

Fringe practitioners have the time, and the spare intellectual energy, and (because their remedies don't, of themselves, affect the workings of cells and tissues) the actual *need* to provide the kind of beneficial persuasion now no longer available on the NHS. That's why they prosper.

There is a marvellous variety of fringe medical theories and techniques, offering wildly disparate explanations for our human ills, and for the 'efficacy' of the many and widely differing cure-alls available. Even if *any* of them contain some element of truth, they can't *all* be right. Your migraine or asthma *might* be due to an imbalance between the Yin and the Yang, as the acupuncturists would have us believe, or it *might* be the result of 'pressure on the nerves' caused by a misalignment of a strangely rickety spinal column (as a chiropractor would maintain). Both hypotheses are fancy-bred, but, even to a believer in the absurd, both can't be true. However, practitioners of fringe therapies achieve remarkably similar success rates, whatever the nature of their beliefs. Moreover, this logical dilemma doesn't prevent a fair proportion of unorthodox healers using, say, acupuncture, *and* homoeopathy, *and* naturopathy, or whatever – anything, so long as it isn't in the official rule book. They like to make a great play of treating the whole person, and not just the disease, emphasizing their superiority, in this respect, over your average proper doctor. The best proper doctors also adopt this approach, recognizing that a living organism is greater than the sum of its parts, but the term 'holistic medicine' has recently been hijacked by the fringers as a blanket term to categorize their peculiar brand of thinking about disease. It has overtaken 'fringe' and 'alternative' as the preferred epithet for dissident doctoring.

All this suggests that all fringe practitioners and all 'unscientific' therapies exploit a shared and powerful healing force which is quite apart from the particular theories and procedures involved, and to which needling, backslapping, and other ceremonies are merely ritual ornaments. Indeed, there is a strong bond of sympathy between all kinds of unorthodox healers, based upon an 'us' against 'them' communion (except in the case of osteopaths and chiropractors, who hate each others' guts because, like Protestants and Catholics, they only differ in the details of their beliefs).

A majority of healers, just like their customers, have sincerely espoused the ideas and practices they sell. A substantial minority know full well that they are preaching rubbish and exploiting credulity and fear for vulgar gain. So long as they are accomplished actors, the members of the second category benefit their clients just as effectively as the members of the first.

*

Faith healing is the most ancient and still the most popular of the instinctive medical arts. It depends upon the belief that some supernatural power, whether it be God Almighty, or some lesser holy ghost, can be prevailed upon to suspend the laws of nature, and to intervene upon the behalf of some living citizen.

Prayer is the cheapest and simplest of the rites employed. Thus, for example, a happening recently reported in the *The Times*. A boy seemed bound for death in Sheffield Royal Infirmary. Following an appendectomy he began both bleeding and clotting, developed renal failure, and went into a coma. 'But his family and friends refused to despair,' said *The Times*. 'They had prayed continually at home and at school every day for a week.' As he was on the point of death, unexpectedly, and against all the odds, the boy recovered. His father, described by the paper as a regular church-goer, said he believed 'quite simply that our prayers have been answered'. That family, and most of its friends and relations, will now be possessed of the unshakeable conviction that God can wave a magic wand when adequately nudged. They will not ask themselves how many people must pray for how long and how God-fearing they must be before the Almighty responds, or any other awkward technical questions of that kind. In particular, they will not wonder how it is that they, in their distress, had attracted the favour of a beneficent Providence when uncountable numbers of their presumably equally well-beloved contemporaries had been left to suffer torture, ruin, shame, bereavement, and all the other slings and arrows of outrageous fortune, without the smallest hint of help and comfort from above. But perhaps the most revealing aspect of this plain tale is the fact that *The Times* found space to report it. There is an enormous appetite for miracles.

Most faith healing involves a little more than simple prayer, and most commonly includes the good offices of an intermediary, whether it be a dead saint or a living possessor of 'the gift', who will intercede on the suppliant's behalf with whoever or whatever it is 'out there' capable of dispensing ghostly physic.

Perhaps the most celebrated of British faith healers was the late Harry Edwards, who ran a 'Spiritual Healing Sanctuary' at a spacious and elegant manor house in Surrey, where he dealt with 60 or 70 clients a week at small group healing sessions, and a further 7000 weekly (so he claimed) who wrote in to take advantage of his skills in 'absent healing'. He also spawned (or, at any rate, by-lined) a continuing flow of books, tracts, bulletins, and pamphlets, and conducted occasional spectacular public clinics at venues like the Festival Hall and Trafalgar Square. In other words he was, if nothing else, a first-class salesman.

Harry told me that he started off as a sceptic, who, being a bit of a conjuror as a lad, had taken to attending seances to see how it was done. 'But wherever I went they told me, "You are a healer. You should be doing healing", so I decided to give it a go.

'A lady friend of mine, who had similar interests, had a friend dying of consumption in the Brompton Hospital. He had pleurisy and haemorrhage, and was nearly dead. So we sat down and thought about him. And I had a vision of him lying on his balcony bed. I saw it all perfectly. Next day his temperature went right down, and then his haemorrhage stopped, and the pain from his pleurisy disappeared. Before Christmas he was back at work.'

Two more apparently miraculous recoveries quickly

followed, after Harry had 'thought' about the state of the invalid concerned. Then came his first physical encounter with a client. The sister of a consumptive girl came to see him, sent by a medium from another part of London. ('How this happened, I don't understand, because I was quite unknown.') Harry promised to visit the invalid next morning. 'I was feeling very self-conscious. I stood at the head of the old iron bedstead and put my hands on her head. The room was darkened, as the girl was dying, and the road outside had been softened with straw, which they did in those days to soften the noise of horses hooves. The mother was there, and I did a thing I should never do today. I said, "She'll be up by Sunday." I'll never forget the look on that mother's face – not shock – sheer disbelief. The girl did get up to tea on that Sunday. On the Friday she brought up a lot of stuff, and on the Sunday she was up. She never needed any more treatment. Her tuberculosis was cleared. She became a nurse at the sanatorium where she'd been a patient. That woman lived and reared a family. She's alive today, running her own healing sanctuary down in the West Country. I accepted the fact that these cures couldn't have been coincidence, and went on from there.'

Harry Edwards claimed that he was employing the medical wisdom of departed pundits on his clients' behalf, and that the spirits who so kindly cooperated in this fashion were wiser even than they had been when on Earth. He had some 'evidence' that Lister and Pasteur were among his principal heavenly collaborators, but he never attempted to 'tune in' to any particular spirit guide. 'I just tune in to Spirit. That way I can be sure that the right type of doctor to deal with the case is chosen and put in touch with the patient. Many healers do work under the trance of a single spirit mind, and they get good results, but I don't think that any one spirit mind has all the knowledge there is about the laws that govern us, and that's why we've learned to leave it open.'

The 'we' he referred to were his colleagues and principal assistants, a married couple, Joan and Ray Branch, who shared in the laying on of hands (Mrs Branch being particularly hot at dealing with eyes), and a corps of trusted workers who helped cope with the 7000 weekly requests for absent healing. Harry was vague about the strength of this back-up force ('There must be at least ten – I've never tried to count them') which seemed strange in view of the fact that they all had to be rather special bodies, capable of reaching instant attunement, both with postal clients and the spirit world, and were certainly not to be regarded as mere office hacks. Their method of working was, however, somewhat less than mystic and wonderful, the majority of replies being cobbled together from a bank of standard paragraphs 'which over the years have been found to work', a clutch being chosen to suit the case in hand. While ideal for computer processing, this method of dispensing inspirational advice would seem to limit the chance of the spirit doctors issuing original tailormade exhortations. But Harry assured me that attunement between client and ghostly prescriber was achieved the moment a letter was opened and the contents read, all actions thereafter being dictated from above. Difficult supplications were referred to him, and by 'difficult' he meant those requiring his special skills in 'penmanship and practical psychology' when it came to framing a response. Presumably he had access to the minds of more literate ghosts than those willing to work through the underlings.

I attended one of his sanctuary healing sessions. Although Harry always avoided direct references to Christian beliefs or to scriptural authority, both in his writings and his public performances, he made full use of Christian stage props, and the room in the manor where his physical contact clinics were staged had a stained glass cross in a circle in the centre of the dominant mullioned window, and devotional pictures on the wall, and a carved oak table bearing another cross, and flowers, and candles, standing before the fireplace, so that it looked like an altar, and (nice touch this) the wooden chairs arranged in a broad semicircle around the throne and two slightly set back semi-thrones occupied by the one major and two minor healers were of a chapel type, with a rack on their backs for prayer books, hymnals, and so on. They didn't actually hold any such breviaries, but the empty racks made them clearly identifiable as sanctified and not just ordinary seats. On the other hand, Harry and the two Branchs entered this quasi-shrine, to sit in majesty before their customers, dressed in long, white, well-starched coats, just like any NHS consultants. Thus, and without acknowledging any allegiance to either Christianity or scientific medicine, the Harry Edwards circus managed to convey the impression of purveying the virtues of both. The best of both worlds, you might say, and in a more than usually literal sense.

In dealing with his personal shoppers, as opposed to the mail order customers, Harry Edwards showed great skill in making the most of the opportunities offered by the emotional and physical states of the individual client. Thus an elderly gentleman with stiff, painful, arthritic knees was persuaded to move the troublesome joints more freely than he had thought possible, and was gently coerced into believing that the agony had lessened. He was assured that the improvement would continue in the weeks to come, and was helped back to his seat bravely demonstrating increased confidence and control – in other words, behaving in the manner expected of him by the healer and the anxious audience. On the other hand a lady with kidney failure was plainly told that, while she must have faith, the Master could not promise anything at all. I wondered what had happened to the powers of the youthful Harry, when the dying had been airlifted from the depths of the valley of the shadow of death. Had those powers diminished with age (the good old man was 82 when I met him)? Or had he learned, since becoming a world-famous and highly publicised figure, the commercial folly of giving guarantees that might be quickly and openly discredited? I even wondered, I fear, whether his recollections of the early 'miracles' might not have become coloured in his favour over the passage of the years.

(Louis Rose, a psychiatrist, who published an excellent book on faith healing in 1968, and who took a particular interest in Edwards, recalled how, on leaving one of the Master's London demonstrations, he saw 'a woman walking with the help of two sticks on which she leaned heavily. At other times this would have been a commonplace, though pathetic, sight. But I suddenly realized that this was the same woman who, an hour or so earlier, had walked down the steps from the platform to the auditorium without the aid of her sticks, glowing with joy at her 'cure' and taking her first unaided paces for several years.' Lord Soper, who might be regarded as being on the side of the angels in this matter, once remarked to me that 'there are a great many people who throw away their crutches in the evening at a mass meeting, and have to call for them the next morning.')

Rather more famous than Harry Edwards (although Harry was wont to claim superior results) is the sanctuary of Lourdes.

Some 50,000 sick people go there each year, hoping for relief, but they are only a tiny proportion of the three million pilgrims and tourists who visit this small French Pyrenean town during the season, making it the most popular and over-crowded of all Catholic shrines. The invalids are always vastly outnumbered by the healthy, but it is the sick who are the centre of it all, because the box office appeal of Lourdes rests upon its reputation as a place of miraculous healing.

In 1858 a sickly peasant child called Bernadette Soubirous had several visions of the Virgin Mary in a grotto by the river Gave which runs through the town. The original miraculous encounters bore no particular relationship to healing. Bernadette did not even ask the Virgin for relief from the asthma which troubled her so much. But according to the child's account of her experiences at the grotto, the vision repeatedly instructed her to drink and wash herself at a muddy spring nearby. Water has always been a ritual cleanser of spiritual and bodily blemishes, and so it is hardly surprising that, once Bernadette's story had spread abroad, the devout sick began to visit the place, and douse themselves with the lotion which the sacred apparition had so persistently commended.

Over the centuries countless believers have claimed a visionary sight of the Virgin, and most such claims have been discounted by the church. But Bernadette's experiences, after some initial haggling, were accepted as authentic, perhaps because the Bishop of Tarbes, within whose diocese Lourdes fell, and who had a reputation for advancing the importance of his see by all possible means, perceived the advantages of having a place of miraculous cures within his realm. But he can hardly have foreseen how his support for the tale told by an ignorant, albeit sharp-witted, adolescent girl would result in the growth of the largest, brashest, and most notorious religious fairground in the world.

Once the virtues of Bernadette's spring had been officially confirmed, the original muddy seepage was dug out to provide a free flow of clean water for the benefit of the invalids who began to flock to the spot. (The natural supply of healing fluid became inadequate long ago, and is now, discreetly, supplemented by connections to the town's mains.)

Although Bernadette did not see her vision until the latter

part of February 1858, before the end of March (according to an attestation by the indefatigable Bishop of Tarbes), three miraculous cures had taken place. A lady recovered the use of a paralysed arm, another had the health of an inflamed and distorted eye restored, and a man blinded by an injury became able to see. In all, seven such happenings were acknowledged before the year's end. However, once the initial enthusiasm, and its accompanying credulity (or opportunistic exploitation), had died down, the church adopted an attitude of extreme caution, and began to demand substantial evidence before recognizing any of the many 'cures' claimed by visitors to Lourdes as miraculous, and only 60-odd recoveries (including the early, readily accepted instances) have been certified as divinely engineered during the entire history of the shrine.

For a cure to be called a miracle, certain strict conditions must be fulfilled. There must be sufficient evidence that the person concerned was indeed suffering from a specific illness producing some observable abnormality in the body (proved by such means as X-ray pictures, chemical tests, physical examination, and so on) before the claimed cure took place. It has then to be shown that the main signs and symptoms of the patient's malady disappeared within hours of the supposed divine intervention. The original improvement must thereafter have been maintained for several years. Moreover, there must be no likelihood that the change could have been brought about by any physical treatment the patient may have been receiving at the time. In other words, the pilgrim must have made a recovery judged inexplicable in medical terms.

The responsibility for deciding whether such a thing has happened lies with two separate tribunals. The first is convened by the only medical member of the large bureaucracy which manages the many buildings, facilities, services and functions which now surround and relate to Bernadette's cave. He is called the President of the Medical Bureau, which is a modest office equipped not with resuscitators and bottles of penicillin, but with stacks of printed leaflets and mimeographed sheets concerned with the clinical aspects of the place's history and its customers. When a cure is claimed, the resident president calls together any other doctors who happen to be on hand (not the town's practitioners, who cater for the locals, but visiting physicians who are at the shrine as pilgrims, or attached to a pilgrimage of invalids). The nature and quality of the skills and experience guiding the deliberations of such juries are thus both variable and a matter of chance. The jurors will also, by their very presence, have a declared belief in the possibility of unusual help from above.

If a majority decide that an inexplicable recovery has taken place, the facts are reviewed by a second panel, but only after a lapse of several years. The 11 members of the second tribunal, called the International Medical Committee, are chosen by the Bishop of Tarbes and Lourdes. Each is a recognized specialist in some branch of medicine, and each is from a different country. This committee meets in Paris once a year. Again, a majority vote decides whether a lasting cure has been achieved and, if so, whether it can be explained in natural terms.

When, exceptionally, the experts decide that an inexplicable recovery has occurred (the international committee confirms only about a quarter of the findings of the first tribunal), the dossier of the case is sent to the bishop of the diocese in which the cured pilgrim lives, and if a canonical commission then concludes that all the evidence points to a divine intervention, the bishop may declare a miracle.

In view of the extreme rarity of officially acknowledged acts of grace, why do sick pilgrims continue to make the costly and, for the enfeebled, difficult trek to Lourdes in their tens of thousands every year? I found the answer to this question when I went there myself to look for it. Many undoubtedly go in the desperate hope that a miracle *will* occur, but a great majority are less expectant, and know that the trip will be well worthwhile because of the comfort and solace they'll receive.

I met a couple, Jack and Kathleen Ditchburn, on their third adventure to the shrine. Kathleen was 59 and her husband 71. She was a robust and boistrous Irish girl who had lived in England all her life. Jack was slightly but not much less agile than his mate, although he did have to carry a selection of strong medicaments (including a quart bottle of rum, from which he enjoyed a single, comforting nightcap). Their earlier journeys had been with and on behalf of a beloved priest and a brother. Kathleen was convinced that these expeditions had served both beneficiaries full well, and described their present sortie as 'a sort of thanksgiving'.

They were wonderfully representative of the pilgrims (or, if you like, tourists) who find a brief visit to Lourdes physically and emotionally sustaining. They were acutely sensitive to the religious significance of the place, but they were also out for a good time, and they had it. They delighted in the ceremony, the emotionalism, and the delicious, if half-frightening, belief that there was a kind of magic working all around them.

Along a 60-yard stretch of wall beside Bernadette's grotto there are a dozen or more brass, push-button taps, like the devices on the drinking fountains in public parks. The water that spurts when these buttons are pressed is supposed to be the issue of Saint Bernadette's spring. The faithful queue to get at the holy elixir. Kathleen and Jack refreshed themselves there two or three times a day.

'And it's beautiful – the water – did you ever drink it at all? Oh, it's a beautiful drink.'

Once, after offering a sip of the miraculous water all round, and having a slop of it left in her beaker, Kathleen laughed and tipped the dregs over her head, saying 'Shenanigans – that's the penicillin part of it.'

A couple of hundred Irish pilgrims were there at the same time. About a quarter of them were invalids. These were housed in one of the two hospitals within the miraculous domain. None were at death's door. There are no facilities for serving the desperately ill at Lourdes. The 'hospitals' are really hostels for the sick, who are bedded down in wards, and helped with their physical needs, like meals, and served by volunteers pushing wheelchairs and invalid carriages.

Most of these Irish sick were up and about, and although some of them were victims of cancer, and kidney failure, and other fell complaints, they were having themselves a ball. There was more laughter and warm companionship and rowdy optimism in those wards than you would find in all the bars and drinking clubs of their native towns. When I was there, with my tape recorder, striving to catalogue stories of human tragedy and despair, one pilgrim, managing somehow to make his voice heard above the babble of voices, broke in with a story.

'There was this Irishman going home from a holy journey, and he had a couple of bottles of poteen with him. So the customs man says, "And what have you got there?" "Holy water," says the man. So the customs officer sniffs at the bottles. "Ah," he says. "Another bloody miracle."'

Everybody roared with laughter, although they'd probably heard the tale a dozen times before.

Then there was Kathleen herself, who, after talking forever and again about the spiritual and physical afflictions of all manner of other people, finally let slip the information that she had been suffering the pain of a peptic ulcer for many years.

Had the miraculous water done her ulcer any good?

'Oh no. It still bothers me. But it gives me strength to bear it, perhaps, a bit more, you know.'

And that's what Lourdes is all about.

*

A purveyor of magical healing of a somewhat different complexion (although I suppose the difference to be not much more than skin deep) is Finbarr Nolan. He does not (like the late Harry Edwards) claim to tap the wisdom and beneficence of the spirit world, or, like the proprietors of Lourdes, to have a hot line to God. It is simply that he is the seventh son of a seventh son. This happy status confers upon the owner (according to legend) the power to heal by touch. I had the pleasure of meeting Finbarr while he was in London, generously dispensing his magic to such as might call upon him at the Northumberland Grand Hotel hard by Trafalgar Square.

When I saw him he was 21, six feet tall and lanky with it, dressed in an unremarkable brown lounge suit with a white, open-necked shirt, bearded, and sporting soft, long brown locks. He spoke in a quiet, rather flat voice, and the general effect was almost one of dowdiness. He had none of the charismatic presence of Harry Edwards, or many another successful healer, but that was clearly no great hindrance to success, for at the time the Revenue Commissioners of his native Eire were said to be taking a considerable interest in his career, having calculated that he had earned roughly £500,000 since the day, 19 years earlier, when, as a two-year-old infant, he began his healing career.

He told me that he had never had any ambition to heal the sick – he just found himself caught up in the game. It was the simple inhabitants of his native Gowna in Country Cavan who had insisted on exploiting the miraculous circumstances of his birth. When he was still in crawlers a neighbour persuaded Finbarr's mamma to allow her son to lay his tiny hands on the body of another infant supposed to be covered with a ringworm which no ordinary medicines had been able to cure. Within weeks, so the story goes, the young patient was completely well. Finbarr's fame spread and the demand for his services increased at a steady but modest rate until, as a teenager, he was featured on a local television programme. That did it, and from then on he was besieged by the maimed and the halt and the blind.

At first, in exploiting his new-found popularity, he used to pray and sprinkle holy water during healing sessions, but the church objected, and so he dropped the ploy, without, it seems, in the least diminishing his audience appeal. There is, after all, no need to invoke the aid of the saints when you are the seventh son of a seventh son. I watched his remarkably ordinary approach to his clients. He simply asked where the trouble was, laid his hands on the spot, and, without so much as a nod or a wink, moved on to the next customer. He told me that roughly 75 per cent of those so dealt with claimed themselves cured, or at any rate much improved, but refused to attribute this to any magic of his own, for it was, he said, they and not he who conjured with belief. That way nobody could accuse him of carpetbaggery or vain promises. He also had a sweet commercial sense. Like many healers (including Harry Edwards) he made no charge for his services, but invited the faithful to slip a freewill offering into a closely watched box on the way out, thus often receiving a far fatter fee than he could possible have asked for, many patrons reasoning that the larger their donations, the better their chances of receiving grace (the richest gift to which he admitted was £500). Better still, perhaps, with that kind of billing the tax men could guess away at his income to their hearts' content. At one stage in our conversation he asked me about the money to be had out of journalism. Why had I quit doctoring? When I told him that I'd taken to writing because I liked the job, but that it wasn't that much of a milch cow, he nudged me, and winked, and said, 'You ought to take to healing.'

I spoke to some of his satisfied customers. One had completely lost a crippling backache. Another had visited the healer just in time to avoid a gall bladder operation. A third had thrown away his asthma pills. They all thought him marvellous. Indeed, the most instructive feature of the Nolan circus was the reaction from the audience to a pretty dull act. Despite the lack of histrionics, or promises, or any hint of the religiosity sustaining Lourdes and flavouring the Edwards sanctuary, Finbarr's followers gazed upon him with a reverential awe, and I saw several reach out to touch him as he passed, as if he were indeed a holy man. It was plain that the seekers rather than their chosen saviour were generating any healing power that might have been abroad that day.

All other fringe medical techniques produce about the same incidence of benefits, in about the same sorts of invalids, as those achieved by the seventh son of a seventh son, and so, if you fancy a change from your friendly neighbourhood GP and his cornucopia of chemical cure-alls, but don't quite know which dissident medicine man to patronize, you can find reassurance in the fact that, whatever your choice, the reward is likely to be much the same.

*

Acupuncture was brought to the West well over a century ago by Jesuit missionaries returning from China, where it has been a major feature of the 'orthodox' Chinese medical scene for perhaps as long as 6000 years, and certainly since the beginnings of recorded history. Treatment consists of sticking needles into the skin at one or more of about 1000 precisely defined points, which have remained unaltered over the millenia. Each point represents a particular symptom or organ, but bears no obvious relationship to the part concerned. Instead the points are placed along the course of an imaginary network of 'meridians' in which are supposed to flow the two complementary life forces of the Yang and the Yin. Disease, says ancient theory, results from a local imbalance of these forces. Balance can be restored by puncturing an appropriate channel at the right place. A point on the forehead, for example, may be pricked to relieve piles. Acupuncture's elaborate lore includes the art of diagnosing any ill simply by feeling the pulse at both wrists. The two beats are alleged, between them, to demonstrate various permutations of textures and tensions detectable and interpretable through the fingertips of the skilled physician, but of a kind which have not yet been revealed by modern electronic hardware.

Chairman Mao Tse-tung was responsible for the boom in popularity which acupuncture has enjoyed in recent years. General Chiang Kai-shek had banned the practice as unscientific, and incompatible with his party's policy of modernizing the nation, but even before Mao had completed the 'liberation' of the Chinese mainland he decreed, for pragmatic and political reasons, that, under the Communists, traditional medicine should be restored to a place of honour in the land, and doctors trained in the Western mode were forced to acknowledge and embrace the use of herbs and needles. I happened to visit the Acupuncture Research Institute in Peking in 1956, a few days after it had opened. Housed in a by then redundant Buddhist temple, the institute consisted of an exhibition, open to the public, and half-a dozen rooms labelled Physiology, Biochemistry, Metabolism, Pathology, Bacteriology, and 'Analytical', in two or three of which white-coated 'scientists' were fiddling around in a desultory fashion with smoked drums, microscopes, and similar simple laboratory tools. The whole setup was designed to demonstrate that acupuncture could be explained and proved effective in terms of contemporary medical concepts and understandings. I asked several accomplished Western-trained physicians whom I met on that same trip what they thought of their country's renewed enthusiasm for the ancient thaumaturgy, at which they usually looked embarrassed, but invariably, if half-heartedly, replied, 'Well, it works doesn't it? So there *must* be something in it.'

During the 1960s acupuncture's supposed potency became the subject of serious scientific attention in the West following dramatic tales coming out of China about drastic surgery being performed on fully conscious patients under the influence of acupuncture analgesia. Physiologically respectable theories have been advanced to explain how the stimulation of nerves by needles or electric currents or other means in one part of the body might, indeed, interfere with the passage to the brain of pain impulses generated in another part, and it is not possible to dismiss out of hand the claim that in some subjects, and under some circumstances, acupuncture can be a risk-free substitute for chemical anaesthetic agents. However, the stories and eye-witness accounts of major operations undertaken solely with such aid lose much of their significance as evidence for the defence in the case of acupuncture versus the cynics when it is remembered that a little over a century ago, before ether and chloroform had come into general use, similar surgery was being performed at the London Hospital on patients rendered pliant by hypnosis. Moreover, the proportion of subjects who either respond to hypnosis or who tolerate pain when needled is the same, suggesting that suggestibility is the major force at work.

In 1980 two Chinese medical professors published an article in the Shanghai newspaper, *Wenhuibao*, casting doubt on the whole business, and denouncing the demonstrations staged for the benefit of visiting firemen. Claiming that doctors and their clients had been forced to use acupuncture anaesthesia during the Cultural Revolution, they described 'the enormous courage' demanded of the victims who 'even though in pain did not dare cry out' because of the 'political necessities of the time'. They told of patients 'forced' to shout political slogans, and to read aloud from Chairman Mao's *Little Red Book*, while undergoing open heart surgery, and asserted that many such traumatic procedures had in fact been carried out with the patient under the influence of chemical agents, the needles being stuck in for the benefit of the audience.

Allowing for the fact that such an article must have been politically inspired, as part of the powerful backlash against Mao and all his works, it nonetheless bolsters doubts concerning the value of earlier (and equally politically inspired) accounts of the miracles achieved by needles.

None of this worries the Western champions of acupuncture. Some of them profess (or simply parrot) a belief in the mystical concepts of the Yin and the Yang and the meridians. Others dismiss the traditional theories as irrelevant historical decorations to a system of medicine which they say works, and never mind exactly why or how. Either way, the use of acupuncture in the West belongs firmly in the realm of dissident doctoring.

The rest of the ragbag of fringe therapies need only shorter mention here, not (except for herbalism) being hallowed, in the manner of faith healing or acupuncture, by either ancientness or common usage.

*

Homoeopathy is the name given to a system of medicine or, rather, treatment, which was not so much discovered as invented by a German physician called Samuel Hahnemann, who was born in Saxony in 1755. He was a gentle and humane fellow who practised the orthodox medicine of his time for almost 20 years, but became increasingly unhappy with the services which he and his fellow physicians were offering the sick. Popular treatments included blood-letting and the administration of powerful drugs (or, rather, poisons) designed to produce sweatings, vomitings, and purgings. The highly toxic mercury was especially favoured as a medicine. The idea seemed to be that no remedy could be counted effective unless it gave rise to some dramatic and unpleasant response in the unfortunate patient. As a result of this philosophy a good many more patients perished under the healing hand than were ever helped towards recovery.

Hahnemann's homoeopathy rose out of this kindly man's distaste for inflicting additional distress upon his already suffering patients. He began searching the medical literature of the world in the hope of finding some better approach, and he began experimenting with various drugs, using them on himself, looking for agents which might comfort and relieve rather than torture and distress. In the course of his researches he had occasion to swallow a large dose of cinchona, the Peruvian bark which contains quinine, a specific against malaria, and one of the very few true remedies available at the time. To his surprise he found that the dose he swallowed produced achings, shiverings and sweatings remarkably like the symptoms of malaria – the very malady the drug was supposed to cure. From this observation, and by a process of leaping intuition, he evolved his new approach to the treatment of disease. He stated his belief that 'It is only by their power to make sick that drugs can cure sickness, and that a medicine can only cure such morbid conditions as it can produce when tested on healthy persons.'

His general argument was that the symptoms of a disease are not the expression of the damage done to the body by the disease process, but are a result of the body's natural and protective reaction against the fault or disorder producing the sickness. Thus any agent causing, say, diarrhoea and vomiting, would be a natural remedy for dysentery.

So, following his cinchona 'trip', he went on to search for

drugs which would produce the symptoms of other diseases, and soon accumulated a whole pharmacopoeia of homoeopathic remedies, which is still in use, and which is added to from time to time by the researches of latter-day practitioners. Gelsemium, for example, which comes from yellow jasmine, makes a person depressed and miserable and produces alternating sensations of heat and cold and a heaviness in the limbs and a weariness of the eyes – sensations remarkably similar to those produced by an attack of flu. Thus gelsemium went on the list as a flu care. Belladonna, from the deadly nightshade, produces the symptoms of scarlet fever, and was a popular homoeopathic remedy when that disease was rife.

All this may sound rather alarming, and might suggest that Doctor Hahnemann's new therapy was not much of an improvement on the horrific procedures which it was designed to replace, but a second remarkable feature of homoeopathic theory ensures that the patient is subjected to none of the unpleasant effects produced by the drugs employed. Hahnemann believed, for reasons which he never did explain, that a very highly diluted solution of his remedies was a more powerful medicine than a strong solution. While this was a welcome change from the contemporary fashion of giving very high doses of what were often dangerous and poisonous substances, Hahnemann did appear to fall overboard on the opposite side of the boat. He would make a solution of a drug and then take a little of the liquid and add it to a bottle of pure water so that the original was diluted, say, ten times. The mixture would then be thoroughly shaken for a given period using a certain appropriate, not to say mystical, number of agitations. Then a small part of this diluted solution would be taken and added to a third bottle of pure water to make an even weaker mixture, and the shaking (the process is called succusion) would be repeated. And so on for a fourth, fifth, sixth and seventh time or more, until, in the end, an almost infinitely dilute solution of the drug had been obtained, possibly not containing a single molecule of the original 'active' agent. (Homoeopathic pills are prepared in a similar fashion, but using powdered chalk or sugar or whatever as the diluent instead of water.) Hahnemann maintained that the virtues (but not, apparently, the evils) possessed by the chosen remedy were somehow transferred to the water molecules during the shaking ceremony. He didn't pretend to know *how* this happened, and neither do his living disciples. They are content to believe that it does, although, in line with the present fashion for seeking a scientific justification for irrational therapies, they like to refer rather vaguely to modern atomic physics, and the manner in which atoms and molecules are known to exert an influence on their neighbours by virtue of their charge and mass and other qualities.

To be fair to Hahnemann, he was well ahead of his time in preaching two important truths which have only recently earned general respect. He insisted on the need to treat the whole person and not just the disease (thus his choice of remedy would partly depend upon whether the patient was fat or thin, merry or morose), and he recognized that any medicine capable of doing good must also be capable of doing harm. He further invented the forerunner of the clinical trial, always testing out new products on healthy volunteers before administering them to the sick. (This so-called 'proving' procedure is still under-taken by homoeopaths who seek to add to their pharmaco-poeia.) It is just a pity that he chose to exercise his undoubted compassion and clinical wisdom through the agency of a wholly fanciful structure of invented lore.

However, the nonsensical nature of homoeopathic theory has not prevented the ghost of Hahnemann from recruiting many intelligent and erudite (as well as ignorant and credulous) patrons and practitioners to the cause. Indeed, the regimen's innate contradictions of much received medical wisdom may be a large part of its charm. Thus, in Britain, homoeopathy is the one fringe medical cult to enjoy official recognition and Treasury support. There is the Royal Homoeopathic Hospital in London, which is one of a handful of institutions within the NHS where Hahnemann and orthodox beliefs are practised side-by-side. GPs (the two or three hundred who are so inclined) can prescribe homoeopathic remedies for their NHS patients and the state will pay. A Faculty of Homoeopathy Act, 1950, gives legal status to the qualifications which the gurus of the art dish out. Much of this favoured treatment is the result of an enthusiasm for the mode shown by three successive generations of the Royal Family, including our present Queen who has a homoeopath on her medical staff. (Mind you, the royals turn to proper doctors soon enough when real trouble brews.) Of course, none of this validates the precepts of the curious craft – it simply shows how fond we are of mysteries. It may be that, with money getting tighter all the time, the orthodox quacks will soon succeed in ridding themselves of this embarrassing alliance. But, in the meantime, homoeopathy remains as one of the more respectable and respected Aesculapian quirks.

\

*

Osteopathy is an American invention, and while, like homoeopaths, its adherents accept conventional ideas concerning the pathology and diagnosis of disease, they hold wonderfully simplistic views on treatment. And, like homoeopaths, osteopaths base their approach to healing, not upon the difficult and tedious analysis and application of slowly, hard-won understandings, but upon a revelation granted to one man. Homoeopaths and osteopaths have in common the status of hagiolaters.

The particular saint who regulates the practice of osteopathy is a chap called Andrew Taylor Still, who practised medicine in Missouri. In 1872 he proclaimed his belief that the human body, having been formed in God's image, was a perfect machine, and that therefore, any faulty function required only a mechanical cure – the equivalent of a bonk with a hammer or the twist of a screw. Having failed to persuade any medical schools in his native land to adopt his ideas, he set up one of his own, and began conferring the doctor of osteopathy degree upon those who learned at his feet.

Still's quasi-religious approach to the amelioration of disease gave birth to a whole new tribe of medicine men who make their living out of twisting and thumping the human frame. And their customers love it. There are several reasons for osteopathy's appeal. The treatment involves some pretty positive action (often including the production of a satisfying 'crack' or 'crunch'), so that after a session on the couch the client feels that an instant and beneficial change in the body beautiful has been achieved. Many osteopaths are, in fact, skilled physiotherapists, so that, despite their curious views, their manipulations may often relieve symptoms which are, indeed, the result of trouble in the muscles, joints, or sinews (including muscle spasm – hence their undoubted value to backache victims who commonly form half their clientele). Their ministrations do no harm – there is no hangover, and no tedious, self-denying routine to be observed, and no side effects (apart from the occasional ache or twinge). And osteopaths frequently benefits sufferers from migraine, asthma, palpitations, indigestion, and similar 'symptom-dominant' complaints, with exactly the same and considerable degree of success as that achieved by all other kinds of unconventional healers, and so they soon establish a local reputation as menders with magic at their fingertips.

But perhaps John Lant, a Cambridge osteopath, unwittingly revealed the principal foundation of his own and many another fringe practitioner's success, during the course of a conversation. After telling me that his bread and butter was earned from clients who came to him after getting fed up with their own GPs (99 out of 100 being recommended by already satisfied customers), he explained that he gave each patient half-an-hour of his time. 'But manipulation is only a small part of the armamentarium. I spend perhaps ten minutes on the treatment, and the rest of the time I'm acting as a kind of uncle. You'll get the housewife who comes along with what she considers to be an absolute b. of a back, and which I regard as a moderate problem, and then you'll discover that what she really wants to talk about are her marital troubles. I get asked questions about social security – whether a pensioner can get a rent rebate, and so on. You can't go along to your doctor and tell him that your sex life is all wrong, or that your husband's beating you about the head, because he simply hasn't got the time. My patients pay me for a half-hour consultation, and they get half-an-hour of my total attention.'

John Lant made another revealing remark. He sits on a committee screening applicants for the limited places available at the British School of Osteopathy. The academic standard required is high, including the possession of A-level passes similar to those looked for by medical schools. 'But,' he said, 'I'm not interested in the geniuses. The few that there are in the profession are not, generally, good osteopaths. They are forever trying to answer every problem in scientific terms. They aren't good mixers. You have to be a good mixer. It's your personality that counts.' (Be it noted that many practitioners of osteopathy have not been through the rigorous training offered by the British School. You or I could put up our plates as osteopaths tomorrow. Here, in Britain – unlike the USA – it's an unrecognized profession, and anybody can join in.)

Chiropractors are allied to osteopaths to the extent that they use manipulation in attempting cures, but they hold narrower beliefs, and osteopaths generally regard their chiropractic brethren with ill-concealed scorn. The approach was invented by an Iowa grocer who had espoused other unorthodox methods of healing, including the use of magnets, before hitting on what proved to be a thoroughly saleable idea. The grocer, Daniel David Palmer, announced that all disease results from the malfunctioning of nerves which are pressed upon by dislocated vertebrae as they emerge from the spinal cord. His adherents claim that, by running their fingers down the spine, they can locate displacements, and that, by delivering an appropriate thump, they can put things right again. This is sheer nonsense. Vertebrae don't get displaced, unless you get yourself involved in a nasty car crash, or some other pretty violent event, or have your backbone eaten away by cancer, or tuberculosis, or whatever. And certainly a thump won't get things back in place. And while nerves may be important to the functioning of the flesh, their inefficiency is not the cause of most of the ills to which the flesh is heir. But the harshness of reality doesn't prevent the chiropractors from claiming, and, indeed, producing, their share of 'cures'.

*

Herbalism (whose practitioners commonly also espouse naturopathy, with perhaps a touch of acupuncture thrown in for good measure) is among the less irrational of the tools employed by dissident healers, for plants have been used in medicine since the dawn of time, and many do contain substances which powerfully and usefully effect the flesh, such as opium from poppies, digitalis from the foxglove, and atropine from deadly nightshade. Doubtless other vegetable drugs remain to be discovered, so that research on the pharmacological properties of plants (including those which have earned a place in traditional formularies) is a rational use of time and money. However, your committed latter-day herbalist works well outside the realm of orthodox medicine, caring (and knowing) little of pathology or the art of deductive diagnosis, and generally ascribing to his preparations virtues they do not possess. On the credit side, most of them are unlikely to do much harm. Naturopathy places faith in the healing properties of sunlight, sea-salt, vegetables grown without the aid of packaged chemicals, spa waters, mystical movements, the thinking of pure thoughts, and eschewing wicked pleasures like tobacco and adultery and champagne, which is all right if you like that sort of thing, and don't kill yourself (as has happened) with an overdose of carrot juice.

*

A whole further hotchpotch of dreamed-up and often ridiculous therapies enjoy a share of the market created by people who want to believe that some kind of elixir of life exists, or that miracles are not yet out-of-date.

There is Dr Peter Stephan (his 'doctorate' is an American 'degree' in homoeopathy from a correspondence college), who has waxed rich from a Harley Street address by treating well-heeled hypochondriacs with preparations said to contain cells from the organs of foetal sheep and other animals. If he decides that your troubles are due to a 'weak' liver, for example, he will give you a dose of liver cells, which are then supposed to make their way straight to the ailing part by a process of biological 'magnetism', where they support the sickly native cells with their youthful vigour. The sheep cells are either injected or administered by way of a suppository. The non-sensicalities inherent in this concept of so-called cell therapy are too numerous to detail, but, for a start, no cells would be absorbed from a suppository stuck up the rectum, and any injected, being foreign protein, would at once be attacked and destroyed by the body's defence mechanisms. At one stage (I don't know whether he still does it), Stephan had the brilliant idea of enhancing the potency of his healing soups by injecting them at the site of appropriate acupuncture points. Adenauer, Pope Pius XII, Charlie Chaplin, Somerset Maugham, and the Duke of Windsor are among the notables said to have been kept 'in peak condition' following the administration of puréed sacrificial lamb.

There are the 'radionic' enthusiasts (including a number of proper doctors) who diagnose disease by swinging a pendulum over a lock of the patient's hair, and then use a 'black box' consisting of dials and magnets and wires arranged in a manner unknown to the electrical trade in order to transmit details of a malady to some aetherial computer, and then to tap and channel to the sufferer a suitable cosmic anodyne. This system has the great advantage of being able to operate over any distance, so that clients don't have the bother of trekking to the black box owner's place of business. Moreover, it allows the agents of the paraphysical force concerned to serve a good many more paying muggins than might be found within journeying distance of their magic parlours.

There are the psychic surgeons, particularly abundant in the Philippines and South America, who fumble with their hands above the bellies of their victims, and then triumphantly hold up a gobbet of bloody flesh which has been the cause of all the trouble. And, miracle of miracles, not a trace of a scar remains to mark the spot from which the offending carrion has been dredged. Common sense apart, these gentlemen have, time and again, been shown to be outright frauds, the extracted tissues often having been identified as chicken gizzards. But such exposures haven't reduced the steady flow of pilgrims who spend vast sums, sometimes filling a chartered aeroplane, to cross the world to have their non-existent growths so painlessly removed.

*

And so it goes on. If you want to be assured of a comfortable living, all you need do is invent some panacea, and the less attached to harsh reality it is, and the more you can decorate it with pseudo-scientific gobbledegook, the greater will be your honour and your profit.

There remains the conundrum of why irrational remedies should work so well. Perhaps the most important factor is that the seekers after mystical healing *want* them to work, but there are additional circumstances favouring their sanctification and success.

Many illnesses are self-limiting, and disappear when they have run their course. Others produce symptoms which wax and wane, so that the victim of a duodenal ulcer, for example, may be in pain and misery one week, but feeling fit and well the next. Any kind of therapy, whether it be a modern drug or the incantation of a charm, which happens to be in use when such a spontaneous recovery or remission occurs, will get the credit for the 'cure', both from the grateful patient, and probably, also, from the doctor, or whichever other kind of healer may have been involved. And, of course, success breeds success, so that a homoeopathist, say, who happens to be administering one of Hahnemann's inactive potions to a sufferer from disseminated sclerosis at a time when that fell disease goes into one of its characteristic phases of recession, will gain an enhanced reputation, and thus his power to benefit other clients will be increased.

A good many sicknesses reside solely in the mind, and a neurotic person can suffer all manner of unpleasant symptoms such as prostrating headaches, frightening palpitations, or a crippling pain in the back when there is, in fact, nothing whatever wrong with any of the body's working parts. Such people are likely to be highly suggestible, and their distress can often be dramatically relieved by hypnosis, or any of a wide variety of other procedures or influences (from acupuncture to falling in love) which may persuade them that they'd be better off feeling better. Imaginary ailments apart, true disorders may have a greater or lesser effect upon their victims, depending upon the sufferer's psychological reaction to the fault. Thus a footballer can break a rib or crack an ankle, and then go on to finish the game before realizing he's even been hurt, while an inconsiderable bruise or sprain can keep a discontented factory hand off work for weeks. Similarly, of two people who have suffered comparable heart attacks, the first may only allow the incident to interrupt a busy life for a few weeks, while the second may become a permanent invalid, fearful, almost, to move. A good many 'cures' (including the administration of dummy pills) work by encouraging the owners of all manner of very real bodily defects to believe that they are not half so ill as they thought they were.

Sometimes the mind can generate not just aches and agitations, but gross disabilities, such as blindness, or paralysis, or deafness. An 'hysterical' paralysis of the legs was not uncommon during World War I among soldiers who became unable to face the repeated, senseless, and horrific business of 'going over the top'. But neither could they admit to themselves that they were afraid. A sudden inability to walk provided the perfect let-out. Such a hysterical suspension of a major physical function bears no relationship whatever to malingering, when the person concerned is simply pretending to some symptom or incapacity which he knows very well does not exist. The hysteric is convinced of the reality of the physical fault which his unconscious mind has invented. Somebody suffering hysterical blindness, for example, will walk over a cliff to destruction, rather than acknowledge to his conscious mind that the physical machinery of his vision is unimpaired. But an appropriate physical or psychological stimulus can break the block upon the instant. This is the basis of the recurring newspaper stories of people, deaf or blind or dumb or paralysed for many years, who have suddenly recovered their long-lost faculty following a terrifying thunderclap, or involvement in a traffic accident, or the shock of the unexpected reappearance of a supposedly dead relative or friend. If some healer happens to provide the necessary psychological jolt, then a miracle is declared by one and all.

Finally, people occasionally recover from a mortal illness, long after the doctors have labelled them incurable. Several careful inquiries, conducted with the strictest scientific rigour, have proved that this has truly happened in the case of cancer victims. Inoperable and untreatable growths have unexpectedly disappeared. More commonly, and before the days of effective chemotherapy, a small but significant proportion of sufferers from advanced tuberculosis would get better without the benefit of medicine. In such cases, and for reasons we still don't fully understand, the body's defence mechanisms, which appeared to have been overwhelmed, have rallied, and become more powerful than the invading germs or the anarchic cells. Tuberculosis, until quite recently a major cause of death and disability in the Western world, was the illness suffered by over one third of the pilgrims whose names appear on the list of miraculous cures at Lourdes. It seems unlikely that the Lord has a specially soft spot in His heart for consumptives. It is, on the other hand, entirely probable that, among the unnumbered TB patients who have flocked to the shrine, a couple of dozen would have made their pilgrimage at a time when nature was about to effect a spontaneous recovery. During the entire history of Lourdes only two miraculous cancer cures have been acknowledged. Even if it is accepted that in both cases the diagnosis was certain and the cure complete, there is no need for wonderment, since chance alone could account for even so rare a happening, having cropped up twice among the many hundred thousand supplicants with cancer who must have sought the Virgin's aid.

But there may be something more than chance involved when faith, or acupuncture needles, or other 'unscientific' therapies, apparently bring about improbable cures. A troubled mind can certainly cause tissues to malfunction. Mental stress seems to favour the development of the arterial damage which leads to heart attacks. The grief of bereavement is associated with an increased incidence of cancer. It could be that the immune system, which deals with infections and plays a role in controlling at least some cancerous growths, is depressed by changes in nervous and hormonal activity which accompany emotional turbulence. (There is some evidence that happy people are less likely to catch colds.) A serene, hopeful, and buoyant attitude might thus be expected to improve the body's capacity for dealing successfully with many a disease (it undoubtedly heightens the chances of a major operation producing a good result). Any external influence which engenders such an attitude (particularly, perhaps, an experience which fortifies a trust in God), might, therefore, just tip the balance in favour of a recovery which would otherwise not occur. But this, if it happened, would be a biological phenomenon, and nothing whatever to do with mysterious forces beyond the pale of human understanding.

*

Thus there are many rational and mutually compatible explanations for the popularity and demonstrable value of irrational therapies, and there is no need to invoke any of the fanciful notions offered to account for their success. It's a matter of applying Occam's razor. Moreover, by some strange instinct (which *is* somewhat mysterious), the sick seem to know when a dissident doctor can best serve their ends, and when the help of a down-to-earth practitioner of the strictly scientific kind is what they really need. So a major criticism of unorthodox healers, often advanced by the medical Establishment, which is that they lure customers away from proper doctors with the result that serious but treatable conditions go undiagnosed and undealt with until it is too late, is rarely supported by experience.

All this being so, it might seem sensible to agree with the Prince of Wales, and to campaign for the greater recognition of the fringe merchants and to make better use of their services, perhaps even following China's example and recruiting nonmedical practitioners of some of the less fantastical cults for the treatment of patients within the NHS. They do little apparent harm. (Probably a good deal less than is wreaked by drug-obsessed physicians and scalpel-happy surgeons. What if a few sharp operators milk the credulous? Their customers feel they're getting value for their money. What if, say, cancer victims are offered false hope? Isn't it better for the process of dying to be accompanied by optimism, rather than resignation, or anxiety, or despair?) They clearly dispense much comfort and healing power of a kind which proper doctors, these days, don't deliver. Why not make the most of what the nonconformists have to offer, and to hell with uncharitable logic?

There is, I suggest, a powerful reason for rejecting this easy and superficially attractive option. Truth is a fundamental value. If we accept uncritical thinking in one department of our lives, for the sake of convenience, or because of the popular appeal of a seductive myth and the short-term comfort to be gained from a belief in the unbelievable, or because the false answer lets us pretend we are competently coping with a painful problem which we haven't truly tackled, then we are all the more likely to adopt the same strategy in other situations, from dealing with the family to managing the national economy, and from chairing the parish council to handling arsenals of nuclear weapons. The result is likely to be unhappy, and stands a decent chance of proving a disaster. Irrational beliefs are always dangerously corrupting, even when they only relate to the cause and cure of piles.

No, there isn't much of a case for embracing the preachers of crackpot ideas and the practitioners of weird rites within the official medical fold (there are enough of that kind within it already). There is an excellent case for having the proper doctors take a long, hard look at the manner in which there dissident competitors operate, with a view to adopting those features of their approach which are of such patent value to their clients – empathy, demonstrable concern, making an effort to reassure, simple courtesy, and, above all, treating the person as more important than the disease.

CHAPTER SEVEN

Doctors in the Role of God

In 1978 a consultant surgeon, Paul Vickers, told a BMA meeting that 'what the public and we are inclined to forget is that doctors are different. We establish standards of professional conduct. This is where we differ from the rag tag and bobtail crew who like to think of themselves as professionals in the health field.' Three years later he received a life sentence for murdering his wife with a poisonous anti-cancer drug.

Now, there is no reason to believe that the medical register contains a higher proportion of criminals and hypocrites than are to be found within the ranks of other trades and callings, but it is clear that doctors are pretty ordinary people, being no better than the rest of us. Yet, increasingly, they are achieving and using powers which allow them to manipulate life and death and the fate of individuals in a manner previously reserved to the Lord. The more arrogant and less thoughtful among them do believe that their training and status gives them a divine right and duty to exercise these newly acquired god-like capabilities, if not entirely at their own discretion, then certainly without let or hindrance from lesser beings outside the medical fold.

Thus an extraordinary letter to *The Times* from Sir John Peel, sometime Surgeon-Gynaecologist to the Queen, concerning arguments then being bandied about in the public print to do with the controversial handling of a baby born with spina bifida. Should it have been 'allowed' to die, or should every last technical trick have been employed in an effort to keep it alive? Sir John wrote, 'In our modern society we have an obsession that public debate will solve every problem whereas in fact it not infrequently means that the judgement of the ignorant and ill-informed takes precedence over that of those with experience and special knowledge. The practice of medicine is about caring for patients individually and their families. I have a strong feeling that too much public debate only makes matter more confused, where difficult and delicate decisions have to be made which primarily concern the individual.'

Doctors of a humbler and wiser mien, and many potential customers of medical care, believe that the client, and society as a whole, should have more rather than less say in what is done, and what is best left undone.

*

The Abortion Act of 1967 virtually gave British women (better say women in Britain, for so many foreigners have taken advantage of its liberal terms) access to abortion on demand. This is by reason of its so-called social clauses, which allow the possible impact of the birth of an unwanted and unplanned child upon the long-term physical and psychological wellbeing of a woman or any existing family to be taken into account, and also because of a clause which allows termination of a pregnancy if its continuance would pose a greater risk to health than would its stoppage. Since childbirth does involve a small but significant threat to life and health, while an early abortion, competently carried out, is wonderfully safe, a termination performed on these grounds alone is legally okay.

The champions of the Act (including, I suspect, David Steel, whose Private Members Bill it was) must have known that its passage would, in effect, allow abortion on demand, although it well may be that many of the MPs who voted the measure onto the statute book were not so percipient. However, and wisely, it was not so propounded, and to make the whole thing more acceptable to conservative and religious opinion, the successful Bill required that two (not one, but *two*) members of the all-wise and seagreen incorruptible medical trade must certify that a proposed termination was necessary 'on health grounds'.

This, of course, allows any seedy practitioner and a surgical colleague (he doesn't have to be much of a surgeon) to wax rich on running an abortion business, serving all comers, purely for gain. It also allows thousands of decent and humane GPs and gynaecologists to be (without any extra monetary reward) the agents for relieving a vast amount of suffering and distress. It also allows a minority of doctors, who hold views on the sanctity of foetal life and the idea that sin should reap its just reward (to which they are perfectly entitled) to impose those views upon their customers.

At one stage, the ease with which women could obtain an abortion varied widely in different parts of the country, so that in Newcastle, for example, over 80 per cent of all terminations took place in NHS hospitals and within the patients' own residential areas. In other words the women there did not have to shop around away from their home territory in search of more sympathetic doctors, nor did they have to go outside the state service. In Birmingham, on the other hand, and in the South West and North West Metropolitan regions the proportion of women who could get the help they sought from their local NHS hospitals was under 40 per cent, and in the London borough of Brent was only 26 per cent. Hence the establishment of the still widely used British Pregnancy Advisory Service, a charity which started its operation in Birmingham, arranging cheap, or free, expertly performed, legal abortions for women who had been turned away by those officially employed to meet their needs.

This disparity was due entirely to the attitudes of the senior consultants in the different regions. We have already seen how the hierarchical system of hospital medicine makes dissent a dangerous indulgence, and where the top gynaecologist happened to disapprove of the Abortion Act his reluctance to operate its provisions would be reflected right down the line. In the Birmingham region the head of the obstetrical priesthood was Professor Hugh Cameron McLaren (now retired) who had been among the most politically active of the members of the medical establishment opposed to David Steel's Bill. His view of women and their nature and their needs was made beautifully plain during a seminar at which four gurus discussed the rights and wrongs of the case of an unmarried, 19-year-old, diabetic, orphan, Jamaican girl, living alone in a single rented room, who had been aborted and sterilized. McLaren thought the abortion uncalled for, though clearly legally in order (pregnancy poses a special risk to diabetic women, and the girl had been pregnant twice before, miscarrying the first conception, and suffering two diabetic crises while carrying the second).

He dismissed, in contemptuous terms, the worth of the judgement of the GP, who had referred the girl to a gynaecologist, supporting the request for an abortion, saying that 'the general practitioners are entitled to their opinion of course, but their total experience of diabetes in pregnancy must be almost negligible so that the decision to abort rested with the obstetric specialist'. By this statement he showed that he was largely insensible to the girl as a person, and simply regarded her as a clinical problem, who could successfully have borne her child, given skilled medical care. But he was not entirely blind to the social implications of the case, saying that while he could accept the judgement of a social worker that 'the father of the child in the womb would not marry the girl' it was possible that 'on the other hand, the Jamaicans' love of children might have led to a postnatal marriage', which pious hope showed what he thought of the nature and the purpose of the wedded state.

But perhaps his most revealing remark was the declaration that he would never 'advise sterilization simply to arrange sterile coitus. I might by such advice lead the unfortunate girl into prostitution!'

By no means all authoritarian gynaecologists share the professor's distaste for sterilization, and on many occasions women physically capable of coping normally with further pregnancies, but regarded by their 'advisers' as wayward and feckless, have been pressurized into accepting sterilization at the time of, and sometimes even as a condition of, being relieved of an unwanted child.

Religious and ethical objections are not the only basis for the unsympathetic attitude shown by some consultants towards supplicants for abortion. I once spoke to Ian Donald, a fervent anti-abortionist, when he was Regius Professor of Midwifery at the University of Glasgow. After retailing the stock objections to the procedure, he said, 'Well, you see, I'm a doctor. And therefore I will only do the operation for doctors' reasons. I'm blowed if I'm just going to have something (sic) sent up to me with a note saying "Just get rid of this – it's inconvenient".' He could not tolerate the idea of playing the role of a mere technician. (He also said, 'A woman with eight children doesn't mind having a ninth.') In similar vein Hugh MacLaren wrote to the late Dick Crossman when Dick was, briefly, editing *New Statesman*. MacLaren was worked up about the number of abortions being performed on foreign (largely German) girls at a nursing home within his bailiwick, which, since it was a private and perfectly legal venture, he could, of course, do nothing whatever about, and exclaimed that during the great debate surrounding the passing of the Act 'no one ever suggested that 14 years of training to be a young gynaecologist should end up in a booth at the end of a Heathrow runway, or above Coventry station in an "advisory" centre!'

So here was the reaction to the problem of unplanned and disastrous pregnancies shown by two of the country's most senior and influential obstetricians, in which an apprehended threat to their professional dignity and jurisdiction seemed to weigh almost as large as moral and societal issues. (Some gynaecologists – although, I'm sure, neither of those quoted above – seem, by their actions and attitudes, actually to dislike and despise the sex they have chosen to serve, so that you wonder why they ever went in for the trade. Could it be in order to assert a dominance over women they fear they may not naturally possess?) Fortunately a large majority of family doctors, and a majority and growing number of obstetricians and gynaecologists, are now thankful for the 1967 Act, after seeing it in operation for almost a generation. Dr George Morris, as secretary of the organization Doctors in Defence of the 1967 Abortion Act, has described how original feelings of hostility have given way to solid support. Before the Act his own practice would deal with four or five tragedies a year among women who had undergone illegal abortions. Some would be made sterile. Others would become chronic invalids as a result of infection. There was the occasional death. 'Now we see none of these things, for nobody in North London, thank goodness, has to resort to illegal abortion.'

Dame Josephine Barnes, a preeminent consultant gynaecologist, has said, 'I never enjoyed carrying out abortions, but my years on the Lane Committee' (appointed by the government to report on the working of the Act) 'convinced me that there was no alternative to a humane Abortion Act, the biggest reason being that it does abolish back-street abortions, which are now few and far between.' (Before 1967 illegal abortions caused 30 or more deaths every year, and led to at least 30,000 hospital admissions for the treatment of unpleasant and dangerous sequelae. A great deal more suffering and damage must have remained undetected. Before the antibiotic era the annual death toll from amateur abortions was 400–600.) But

Professor Richard Beard of St Mary's Hospital in London expressed the view which most directly conflicted with those held by Donald and McLaren when he said of abortion that 'it should be seen as a social service in which the gynaecologist is involved as a technician, and to a slightly lesser extent as a doctor.'

Beard was, of course, dead right. The fact that a man or woman has acquired expertise as a plumber of the female reproductive tract, together with some learning (however profound) in the matter of the physiology and pathology of the sexual apparatus, cannot, of itself, endow the possessor of such understandings with any peculiar wisdom concerning the human situation. Indeed, family doctors are usually much better placed to know what an unwanted pregnancy may do to a life or a family, even if 'their total experience of diabetes in pregnancy must be almost negligible'.

But why drag doctors in at all except for actually doing the job? The present Act is in effect, even if not by intention, a hypocritical instrument, because it does make possible abortion on demand, while pretending that a 'medical' justification must be established before the deed is done. What has medicine to do with assessing the impact upon an already hard-pressed family of a new infant who needs not just to be fed, housed and clothed, but also demands intensive care when the capacity to care has already been stretched to the limits of endurance? Any half-sensible and half-sensitive citizen could make that judgement, and, best of all of course, the unwilling mother-to-be concerned. The honest solution would be to give every woman a right to have a pregnancy aborted should she so choose. Or, alternatively, to go back to the harsh old attitude which proscribes the destruction of a foetus altogether, except, perhaps, when the mother's physical survival is at stake.

The second alternative is unthinkable. The first is unlikely, given the vociferous political clout carried by organizations such as the Catholic church and the Society for the Protection of Unborn Children, which are only prevented from imposing their views upon society by the weight of medical opinion now in favour of a liberal law. So, for the time being, doctors will retain the godlike, if unasked for, duty of deciding which unwanted foetuses should perish, and which should be allowed to survive. The question is likely to be resolved quite soon when safe, effective, abortion pills become available. Then no law, and no doctor, will be able to prevent women from making the choice themselves.

*

Sterilization has long been regarded by some as a proper means for preventing the birth of children who, though not perhaps unwanted, would possibly be second-raters, particularly in the matter of their intellectual capacity, and who would thus be a burden on society, and who, even more importantly, would themselves give birth to inferior citizens, and so contribute to the erosion of the quality of the 'genetic pool', or, in simpler terms, the excellence of the human race.

It is self-evident that vast improvements in housing, nutrition, social services, and, to a lesser extent, effective medical aid, have allowed the survival to reproductive age of countless thousands of individuals who, in crueller times, would have perished during infancy or childhood. It is arguable, but entirely unproven, that this has resulted in a lowering of the viability of the herd, and that, allowed to proceed unchecked, the progenitiveness of the unfit will lead us all to destruction. Hitler was wedded to this idea.

However, people are not cows or crows or cauliflowers, and genetic traits of a kind which might make a vegetable unsaleable in a greengrocer's shop, or prevent a bird from surviving once out of the nest, are not to be equated with transmitable faults in human organisms. Our society has a great capacity for not only accommodating, but also benefiting from, all kinds of mavericks. It is not up to doctors (as opposed to plant breeders or stockmen) to decide which of the living things under their care should be allowed to reproduce. But some doctors don't accept this view.

A recent example of medical arrogance in this field was revealed by the Sotos syndrome affair. A few years ago a Sheffield paediatrician and gynaecologist decided, between them, that an *11-year-old girl* should be sterilized. This grotesque plan was decided upon because the child in question was diagnosed as suffering from a rare disease which the doctors involved believed could be transmitted to any children she might one day bear.

The victims of this genetic disorder are said to be unusually tall, to experience an early puberty, to be liable to epileptic fits, and to suffer a greater or lesser degree of mental retardation. However, the Sotos syndrome, apart from being rare, had been first described only ten years before the Sheffield case hit the headlines, so that very little was known about the course and prognosis of the condition. This did not prevent Ronald Gordon, a paediatrician, and Sheila Duncan, a gynaecologist, from persuading the child's widowed mother that her daughter ought to be sterilized on the grounds that her intellectual impairment was such that she could never hope to hold down a job or care for a child, that if she did become pregnant there was 'a very high chance of her producing a very abnormal child', and that although she was only 11 her 'sexual' age was 14, which put her in imminent risk of conception. At a press conference called shortly after the plan to sterilize had aroused public interest, Dr Gordon remarked that 'any girl who has reached puberty is at risk of becoming the mother of an illegitimate child, and if you don't know that your eyes must be very tight closed'. He also claimed that the operation was going ahead at the wish of the mother, and with the child's understanding and consent – although how an 11-year-old, supposed to be too dim to hold down a job, could possibly give her informed consent to such a procedure, the good doctor did not explain.

The alarm was raised by the girl's teachers. She did have some physical defects, including a tendency to epilepsy, but this was well controlled by drugs, and she could swim, ride a bicycle, and dress herself. She was attending a special school for marginally subnormal children, and had been described as a 'dull normal' with the understanding of a nine to nine-and-a-half-year-old, but was said to be doing splendidly, and to be just about ready for transfer to a normal school, so that the good people looking after her were appalled when they learned what was going on. They made their feelings known to Dr Gordon, but he remained obdurate, insisting that the operation must go ahead on the planned date. In response to the fuss created he claimed that the girl's condition was incurable, which was, of course, true, but hardly to the point. He also attempted to mollify critics who expressed disquiet at the finality of the operation by saying, 'Nonsense. Of course the operation is reversible. We just stick the tubes together again, but we can't give a 100 per cent guarantee of success.' A few days later he was forced to withdraw this statement upon discovering that his critics were not just ignorant yokels, and were well aware of the cold fact that attempts to repair divided egg tubes rarely succeed. The suspicion that his original assertion was a deliberate evasion, and no more *lapsus memoriae*, was heightened by the later revelation that it was the intention to sterilize the girl by cutting out her womb, and so far the surgical whizz-kids have failed to find a way of annulling the effects of *that* particular surgical assault. It was further reported that one of the doctors concerned explained the decision to operate on an 11-year-old, not on the grounds that the child might become pregnant at any moment, but because 'later on she might become truculent'. (Incidentally, it was afterwards admitted that the girl had, at the time, shown no interest in boys, and that her opportunities for promiscuity, if she became so minded, were virtually non-existent.)

In short, Drs Gordon and Duncan were not to be moved, and parried every argument against their sad intent, despite opinions voiced at the time by Walter Bodmer, professor of genetics at Oxford, who said that he doubted whether the Sotos syndrome *was* inheritable, and from Graham Snodgrass, a consultant paediatrician at the London Hospital, who believed that the chance of the girl producing a physically normal baby would be very good indeed. So, the operation would have gone ahead save for the determination of Margaret Hubberly, an educational psychologist connected with the special school. After vain appeals to the Area Health Authority, and with only a week to spare, she wrote to the *Guardian* and contacted the National Council for Civil Liberties. The *Guardian* gave the story nationwide publicity, and the NCCL advised Mrs Hubberly to see a solicitor to have the child made a ward of court, which she did. In the face of the legal action the operation was cancelled, but it was a damned close run thing.

Some months later Mrs Justice Heilbron in the High Court decided that the wardship should continue, and that the operation was to be forbidden. She was satisfied that the girl had already reached 'a fair academic standard', and that her interests, which included the worship of a well known pop star, were 'those of a normal girl of her age'. Her Ladyship also referred to 'the basic human right' of a woman to reproduce.

The most frightening aspect of this grisly tale was Dr Gordon's refusal to admit that he could possibly have made a wrong decision, or that anybody else had the smallest right to question his opinion, and this in a man whom the judge had felt moved to commend as a doctor 'who had always taken a most compassionate interest in his patient'. He told Mrs Justice Heilbron that in his view of such cases 'provided the parent or parents consented, the decision was one to be made in pursuance of the exercise of clinical judgement, and that *no interference could be tolerated'*. (The italics are mine).

Her Ladyship luckily thought otherwise, saying, 'I cannot accept, and the evidence does not warrant the view, that a decision to carry out an operation of this nature, performed for non-therapeutic purposes on a minor, can be held to be within the doctor's sole clinical judgement.'

In making this statement the excellent lawyer was, of course, delivering a body blow to a principle cherished by many worthy and honest medical practitioners who sincerely believe that their 'clinical judgement' is sacrosanct. They seem unable to understand that decisions made in the light of their technical expertise often have implications and consequences of a kind which they don't have any special competence to evaluate, and that the 'side effects' of medical intervention (or the refusal to intervene) may be much more important to the individual or society than any immediate 'clinical' result. This dangerous professional insularity was well illustrated by a letter to *The Times* from Nigel Harris, an orthopaedic surgeon, during the early days of the Sotos syndrome affair. He wrote, 'I will never tolerate interference from administrators, MPs, social workers and the like. . . . We do not need additional safeguards which is just a euphemism for interference. Our moral and ethical code is quite sufficient to protect the public.'

*

But the final destruction of the conceit that the medical profession's 'moral and ethical code is quite sufficient to protect the public' began not in any court of law, but in a Cambridge laboratory, nearly 20 years ago, when an unknown physiologist started a development which has *forced* 'administrators, MPs, social workers and the like' to 'interfere' with what the doctors are about.

In 1965 a Dr Robert Edwards published a paper in the *Lancet* describing the 'apparent fertilization' of human ova by human spermatoza on the laboratory bench, and stating his belief that the successful cultivation of human embryos in test tubes could not be long delayed. Although it may sound a simple enough achievement to take some eggs from women's ovaries, removed by a surgeon for some good cause, and to mix them with spermatoza (much more readily obtained), so that the sperm penetrate the eggs, and fertilization occurs, it is not an easy thing to do. Precise conditioning of both eggs and sperm must have occurred before the magic union takes place. Medical scientists had been attempting the trick for decades prior to 1965, but without success, so that Edwards' claims, if confirmed, constituted a dramatic advance in Man's capacity to manipulate nature. However, his article and its title were couched in obscure technical terms, so that Fleet Street and the broadcasters missed the significance of the publication, not having on tap the kind of highly educated specialist newshounds they now employ, and it actually fell to me to be the agent through which the significance of the Cambridge experiments became known to the world at large.

This happened because I was at the time, the first editor of the newly established *World Medicine*, a glossy throwaway magazine for doctors of the kind described in chapter five. Excited by the *Lancet* article, I sent a reporter down to Cambridge to interview Bob Edwards, and she came back with the full story which we published in plain, readable language under an arresting headline, and which contained his thoughts on the possible future applications of his work, including the birth of test-tube babies, the use of the technique to allow a choice of the sex of a child, and the implantation into the womb of a fertilized egg obtained from another woman. Within hours of our press copies going out the Cambridge Physiological Laboratory was besieged by men with notebooks, flash bulbs and television cameras. Edwards took refuge in the library, amazed, bemused, appalled, but also a bit excited by his sudden, unexpected fame.

However, the real interest in this tale of my early brief

involvement in the test-tube baby saga lies in the fact that, reckoning we had a pretty portentous story to print, I telephoned a number of eminent scientists, including a couple of Nobel prizewinners, to get comments which I could publish alongside the account of the Cambridge happenings.

I spoke to Sir Peter Medawar, who is one of the world's most respected natural scientists. After explaining how useful early human embryos would be for the study of chromosomal abnormalities of a kind which produce grave congenital defects, he added, 'Some people might look at this work and start thinking in terms of "test-tube babies", but test-tube babies are out, and this isn't the importance of the discovery at all.'

I spoke to Dr Alexander Comfort, poet, novelist, medical researcher, and author of *The Joy of Sex*. He said, 'This could be a very useful development from the point of view of embryological research, but otherwise I cannot see that it can have any practical importance whatever. There might well be an uproar, arising from the fear that we shall now start culturing human babies from embryos in test tubes, but the people who protest will never ask themselves why anybody should want to do this. The normal method is more fitted, I think, to most of our purposes. It seems to me to be entirely a work of supererogation.'

I spoke to the Reverend Hubert Trowell, a distinguished physician who retired from medicine quite late in life to become the Perpetual Curate of Stratford-sub-Castle in Wiltshire. He said, 'To grow a human being outside the body is theoretically possible, if not now, then in the future, and this raises very big problems from the point of view of bringing up the child afterwards. Every human being, so far as we know, needs maternal love, and also needs a father to back up the maternal role. How are you going to lay on these?

'Have we the right to kill this sort of thing in the test tube if it turns a bit bad? Normally a being is only fully protected by law when it is born from the mother. A developing foetus has some degree of protection before the law, but it gains much more once it has been extruded from the mother, at which stage we believe we have no right to kill it. We have nothing to guide us when it comes to the possibility of producing human embryos *in vitro*.

'At what stage does the foetus start to have some life of his own? This is a very, very difficult issue. The Church has chosen the moment of conception, because no other stage – that of quickening, or of viability – has got a clean watershed. Penetration of the ovum by the sperm does represent one convenient point of definition, but I think the Church has been wrong in maintaining that this is the time at which you really become a separate being. I don't think we can talk in terms like that. All that we can say is that the fertilized ovum is entitled to a good deal of respect. You see, in many cases, it won't turn into a human being in the end.

'I think we shall soon be faced with some of these problems, and we should start thinking about them now.'

On 25 July 1978, the world's first test-tube baby, Louise Joy Brown, was delivered by Caesarian section at Oldham General Hospital in Lancashire. By mid-1984 some 250 test-tube babies had been born worldwide, including twins, triplets, and quads, and in Australia a woman had given birth to a child which had begun life as a frozen embryo. Four more such babes were said to be on the way, and 250 fertilized human eggs were lying in a freezer at Monash University, Melbourne, awaiting their fate. Two of them were already orphaned, their wealthy 'owners' having been killed in an aircraft accident, although exactly whose orphans they were was not quite clear, since when the question arose as to whether they should be implanted into the womb of an unrelated woman so that they could develop to a stage at which they might claim their inheritance, a lawyer acting for an earlier and conventionally manufactured child of the embryos' 'mother' alleged that the eggs in question had been fertilized by sperm from a man other than her husband. The by then famous partnership of Edwards and Steptoe, with their flourishing private test-tube baby clinic at Bourn Hall in Cambridge, had announced that they were almost ready to give their clients a choice as to whether they would like a boy or a girl to result from the unit's costly manipulations. An Australian woman had given birth to a baby grown in her womb from an embryo generated in the laboratory from her husband's sperm and an egg donated by another woman. Doubtless, by the time these words appear in print, further fantastical results of Edwards' original experiments will have been reported.

So much for the dismissive comments of Sir Peter Medawar and Dr Comfort. These two exceptionally thoughtful, intelligent and learned men were rapidly shown to have been entirely wrong, and Dr Trowell, the physician-turned-priest, has been proved entirely right.

*

The moral of all this is that, once some new manipulation of nature becomes technically feasible, whether the object of the interference be the weather, or the atom, or the human body, or the human mind, somebody, somewhere, is bound to have a go. If a thing can be done it will be done, and success will stimulate imitation and competition, with rival experts striving to cap the achievements of their peers, and it's no good asking with Alexander Comfort 'Why should anybody want to do this?'

'Why did you want to climb Mount Everest?' they asked Sir Edmund Hillary. 'Because it's there,' he said.

Enthusiasts, from Enrico Fermi to Christiaan Barnard, will always find ample and noble justifications for doing their own thing, but, with eyes and mind wonderfully and necessarily concentrated on the challenging task, they will often be insensitive towards, or actively impatient with, opinion which questions the value or the wisdom of their cherished aims.

That is why Sir John Peel was so misguided in asserting that 'too much public debate' is undesirable, and why Nigel Harris fell so far short of the mark in claiming that the medical profession's 'moral and ethical code is quite sufficient to protect the public'. It was not until 1982 that a state investigating committee in Victoria took a brief and half-hearted interest in the goings on at Melbourne University, putting a temporary ban on research into egg donation, and only in 1982 did the British government appoint the Warnock committee to review the legal, ethical and moral problems surrounding the new techniques of bench fertilizations, experiments on early embryos, artificial insemination, sperm banks, egg banks, embryo banks, womb leasing, surrogate motherhood, and all the other fruits of scientific interference with the natural processes of reproduction. This was 17 years after Hubert Trowell had foreseen the kinds of difficulties likely to arise, and had said, 'We should start thinking about them now', and by the time the Warnock committee issued its report in 1984, many developments had proceeded beyond the point of no return, and the members were only able to recommend tinkering controls, such as a ban on commercial surrogate motherhood agencies, and the establishment of a standing committee to keep an eye on future developments, and a licensing of establishments dealing with bench embryos and AID (just as abortion clinics have to be licensed now). The Warnock report may or may not result in legislation, but it certainly won't turn back the clock.

A couple of decades is a very short time for the birth of a technique in a laboratory to bring about political reaction and widespread public concern, and the test-tube baby saga is a salutary demonstration of the fact that the advance of science and technology is now so swift that we, the people, have got to know what the experts are *thinking* of doing, instead of what they have managed to do, if we're to stay ahead of the game and have the opportunity to encourage or prevent manipulations of our way of life.

*

One important reason for not leaving the dispensation of expert services to the discretion of the experts concerned is the fact that they cannot long retain a monopoly as providers of such care, so that soon less principled operators than the doubtless high-minded pioneers of clever scientific conjuring tricks will start to exploit the skills the gurus have evolved.

In 1975, for example, Melville Kerr and Carol Rodgers, writing from the Department of Obstetrics and Gynaecology at McMaster University in Canada, contributed a paper to the *Journal of Medical Ethics* in which they reviewed 'the technical and social problems concerned in donor insemination', describing, *inter* a lot of *alia*, the 'non-medical criteria' they employed when faced with the task of deciding whether to 'service' a woman in this fashion.

They wrote that 'The couple must have a stable, mature relationship. We would at present consider only married heterosexual unions, and would not consider either single women or lesbian couples as prospective parents. The couple must be seen to communicate freely and honestly with each other . . .

the man should have come to terms with the fact of his subfertility. He must be tolerant of the idea of not being the biological father of his child, and have an appreciation that it is in the social role of fatherhood that fulfilment lies rather than in the biological role. A pregnancy should certainly not be sought as a means of holding together an unstable marriage. A sense of complete trust must be present between the couple and the team. If this is lacking donor insemination should not be attempted.'

All good, sound, common sense, no doubt, but whose job is it to weigh and assess such matters – the doctors' or their clients'? Apart from the impertinence of attempting to assess a couple's fitness for parenthood, just because they need some technical assistance in the matter of procreation, when the vast majority of citizens are able to reproduce without the prior approval of the Kerrs and Rodgers of this world, it is a piece of pointless pomposity, or, in Comfort's immortal phrase, 'entirely a work of supererogation', for any customers turned down by such as K & R would only have to nip round the corner in order to get the job done by a less judgemental medical journeyman. Indeed, were they rich enough and silly enough they could go to the Repository for Germinal Choice at Escondido in California and buy themselves some frozen sperm allegedly drawn from the loins of a Nobel laureate or some equally superior sire.

In 1979 the BMA appeared to take a more liberal line than that adopted by the Ontario pair, the doctors at its annual meeting defeating by a slim majority the proposal that providing an AID service for lesbians should be banned on the grounds that the practice is 'unethical and destructive of the family unit'. But was the rejection of a motion which might have been thought attractive to the conventional medical mind symptomatic of a developing realization that the profession may have been ordained by the Lord to serve rather than dictate? Not a bit of it. Michael Thomas, chairman of the association's ethical committee, vigorously urged a divided and uncertain house to throw the motion out on the grounds that accepting such a rule as a canon of the official faith would erode each doctor's right to do exactly as he pleases with his patients without let or hindrance from his peers, or authority, or (least of all, perhaps) the patients themselves.

It is, of course, perfectly proper for a doctor to *advise* his clients that they should, perhaps, think twice before having a baby (or even before getting married) because the wished-for birth or union would be likely to give rise to problems of which they might be unaware, but should interference go further than advice? In 1978 an eminent Oxford psychiatrist stopped the planned marriage of two of his out-patients by lodging an objection with the registrar the day before the ceremony on the grounds that they were both of unsound mind. He might well have been right in believing that the somewhat eccentric pair were looking for trouble (although the man's GP had signed a statement denying that they were unfit to wed), but had the psychiatrist any right or duty to wield the big stick in this fashion? Apart from all else the couple were well past child-bearing age, the thwarted bride-to-be being 63.

*

But while some doctors choose to assume godlike responsibilities, others have what was once a divine role thrust upon them.

In 1981 the late Dr Leonard Arthur, a Derby paediatrician, was committed for trial charged with the murder (later reduced to attempted murder) of a three-day-old mongol boy who had been rejected by his parents. After the baby's condition had been diagnosed the mother and father decided that they did not want him. He was placed in a side ward, and the mother discharged herself from hospital and did not see her son again. Dr Arthur wrote on the case notes, 'Parents do not wish baby to survive' together with the instruction, 'Nursing care only'. He further prescribed a morphine-like drug which, it was said, favoured the development of the pneumonia from which the child died, although he told the police that the drug was given solely to reduce suffering, and not to kill.

At the end of a famous trial the judge and the jury were able to set the doctor free (the judge's summing up had as much to do with the 'innocent' verdict as the jury's compassion and common sense), but the jury might not have found it so easy to clear the name of the good and conscientious physician (which they did after a remarkably short two hour retirement) if the principal medical witness for the prosecution had not had the value of his evidence brought into question by the defence.

Professor Alan Usher, a Home Office pathologist, at first maintained that, apart from mongolism, the child had been born healthy, and that his death from pneumonia, 69 hours after birth, had been directly caused by the treatment employed. He later, showing considerable integrity and courage, admitted that he had been wrong, after examining specimens prepared by another pathologist Professor John Emery, on behalf of the accused. These showed damage to the heart, lungs and brain of the infant which must have occurred before birth. Nevertheless, it was estimated that, given food and other active treatment, the baby would have stood an 80 per cent chance of survival, and it was clear, although of course never conceded by the defence, that Dr Arthur did intend an unwanted and mentally handicapped child to die peacefully and soon, rather than face a lifetime in an institution.

Dr Arthur had been charged as a result of information given to the police by the chairman of LIFE, the extremist 'right to life' organization, orginally founded to fight the 1967 Abortion Act. LIFE had in turn been tipped off by an anonymous worker at the hospital where the baby died. The Lifers encourage nurses and others sympathetic to their cause to report late abortions, failures to resuscitate or treat the handicapped, and other similar apparent breaches of the law they may observe in the course of their work – an activity which Sir Douglas Black, then President of the Royal College of Physicians, described at Dr Arthur's trial as 'destructive for the confidence of the medical and nursing professions'.

It is widely acknowledged that several hundred severely handicapped newborn babies are allowed to die each year, sometimes by withholding curative drugs and food and giving generous doses of a sedative, and sometimes (as often in the case of spina bifida) by not performing an operation which might procure survival, but which would leave the patient still miserably crippled in body and mind. It was a cruel injustice that, at the instigation of meddling zealots, Dr Arthur should have been subjected to the horrors of a trial for the gravest of crimes when he had only done what hundreds of his honourable colleagues had done before and will do again. These doctors are showing a humane response to a tragic situation for which no wholly impeccable solution can exist. Dr Arthur's acquittal meant that no further such prosecutions are likely to be sanctioned, at least for some years, but while the outcome may have reflected the weight of public opinion in the matter, it did nothing to alter a law which was framed at a time when the possibility of salvaging lives which nature would not sustain had not been envisaged. Sometimes the law has been used to force the performance of life-saving operations on grossly deformed and mentally handicapped babes when the parents have withheld the necessary consent, with local authorities obtaining guardianship and assuming responsibility for the decision. Unfortunately, when bureaucrats choose to intervene in such cases they do not seem to recognize their incapacity (it may be even unwillingness) to provide the exceptional and demanding care which the cripples so saved should enjoy for so long as they survive. It is not enough to consign them to a wardful of similarly afflicted mortals, and provide barely adequate food and shelter and clothes. Great love is needed too. We do indeed all have a right to life, but life consists of a great deal more than the possession of a heart that continues to beat and lungs which continue to breathe.

*

Following the Arthur trial pleas were heard for a change in the law from, at the one extreme, those who wished a disabled infant's right to every last aid to survival to be written into the statute book, to, at the other pole, those who wanted the parents of abnormal babes to have the legal power to say whether their imperfect progeny should perish or survive. But nobody could possibly devise laws which, even if their objects seemed desirable, could be reasonably interpreted or enforced in such a field. What court or lawyer is to say that some drastic surgery, left undone, ought to have been attempted on, say, a pair of Siamese twins sharing a single heart or liver? What if parents wanted to dispose of a baby born with a hare lip? It is impossible to draw lines, and, for all kinds of reasons, the case of every abnormal baby born is unique. This does seem to be an area in which, for the time being at least, doctors will have to accept the role of God, deciding who shall die, and who shall be, by all means, kept alive.

This doesn't mean that they should regard themselves as the supreme and sole arbiters in such matters. Apart from the influence that must belong to parents, the informed opinion of all kinds of people outside the medical trade should be used as guidelines when awesome and transcendental decisions have to be made. That is why Sir John Peel was misguided in claiming that 'too much public debate' is to be deplored. The more the better. Maybe it wouldn't help to have busybodies, however well intentioned, forever attempting to mediate the handling of individual cases, but doctors should read the correspondence columns of *The Times*, and listen to the radio, and watch TV, and otherwise keep themselves *au fait* with the feelings of the world at large. That way perhaps they can act, when they must, not so much as gods, but rather as archangels, or the agents of God. (Always assuming the will of the Lord to be found by searching in the minds and consciences of all His creatures here below.)

I do recognize that in condemning LIFE for harassing Dr Arthur, while praising Margaret Hubberly for her intervention in the Sotos syndrome affair, I am demonstrating both inconsistency and prejudice, but that, surely, simply serves to illustrate the thankless task doctors face in their attempts to make the right decisions in such sad cases. Whatever they do, they are bound to win support from some observers while outraging others. Legislation is too blunt an instrument for the resolution of individual problems. There is a superficial attraction in the idea of local ethical committees which would assume the responsibility for approving or rejecting proposed courses of action, but a little thought will show that, in practice, such bodies could only increase and prolong the agonies involved without in the least improving the chances of a 'right' decision being reached, and there is something intrinsically more evil in the concept of objective referees, rather than the principals concerned, making life and death judgments. It would be a move towards giving society rather than persons control over quintessentially personal affairs. Perhaps, before too long (particularly if scientists like Dr Robert Edwards are allowed to continue and expand their experiments on early 'surplus' embryos), this particular doctors' dilemma will largely disappear, as we find the means for preventing grave congenital deformities.

*

Much the same difficulties as those surrounding the handling of grossly abnormal newborn babies (and foetuses) are attached to the management of the mortally ill.

General Franco of Spain perished in 1975, and perhaps in the medically induced and sustained wretchedness of his dying days he repaid some of the debt he owed humanity, for the grotesque efforts of the Spanish doctors to keep him alive, and his consequent suffering, had the important effect of drawing popular attention to the manner in which medical skills and resources can be misused.

On his deathbed the general was attended by 32 doctors, who, in their efforts to delay his end, had, among other things, used a kidney machine and a respirator, performed at least three major abdominal operations, and administered an unknown number of gallons of blood. Yet very soon after a series of heart attacks heralded this old and sick man's final illness it became apparent that he had no prospect of recovery, and the desperate measures subsequently employed never stood a chance of achieving anything but a wretched and painful prolongation of the act of dying.

Five years later the same kind of treatment was accorded to President Tito of Yugoslavia. For a quarter of a year this 87-year-old head of state was, as a matter of political convenience, kept going by a variety of machines. He was plumbed in to an artificial kidney, his heartbeat was sustained by a pacemaker, his breathing was taken over by a respirator, and he was 'fed' by an intravenous drip. For over three months before his 'death' he had not been a person at all, but a laboratory animal.

But you don't have to be a head of state to attract this kind of attention. At the time of the cruelly extended death of General Franco, newspaper readers were being regaled with the heart-rending story of Karen Quinlan, who was lying mindless but alive under intensive care in a New Jersey hospital.

About eight months before General Franco fell ill Karen Quinlan, a lively, good-looking 21-year-old, swallowed a murderous cocktail of alcohol and tranquillizers, not in an attempt to kill herself, but just for kicks, and over the course of several hours during a day which ended, for her, at a local tavern. There, after a single drink at the bar, she started to nod off, so a boyfriend decided to drive her home. By the time they arrived she was unconscious and had stopped breathing. He started mouth-to-mouth resuscitation, an ambulance was called, and she was taken to hospital where she was put on a respirator. She has been in a coma ever since.

For some six months she was kept alive with a tube in her throat and other tubes putting things in and taking things out of her body. At the end of that time her adoptive parents, having been told that there was small prospect of consciousness ever returning, asked the doctors to switch off the respirator so that Karen might be allowed to die 'with grace and dignity'. The doctors refused. The parents went to the New Jersey Superior Court to seek authority to have the artificial life support measures withdrawn, but the judge ruled that 'judicial conscience and morality' persuaded him that 'the treating physician' was in the right. The father appealed to the state's Supreme Court where it was held that in such cases an individual's right to choose death takes precedence over the state's interest in preserving life, and that through her father (who was made her guardian) Karen could so choose, provided the father could persuade 'competent medical authorities' to agree formally that there was no reasonable chance of recovery. This concession he achieved, but the doctors, instead of simply pulling the plug, weaned Karen off her respirator, so that she (that is to say, her body) gradually got used to doing without it, and, against all expectations, she (that is to say, her body) survived. Thus the doctors managed to frustrate the wishes of the parents, and also what (in their sincere opinion) would have been the wish of their daughter, and also the clear intention of the court. The distressed mother and father found themselves involved in a grim, new dispute concerning the definition of what constituted 'extraordinary means' in the efforts of the physicians to keep their daughter 'alive'. Is her artificial feeding different in quality to the artificial respiration which was thought to be essential? Should antibiotics be used to ward off the infections which pose a constant threat to her life?

At the time the respirator was withdrawn Karen was described as a 70lb, motionless, skinwrapped skeleton. She later developed contractures of her muscles which brings her knees up to her chin, and bedsores which expose her thighbones. As long ago as 1975, when this whole horrific mockery of 'medical care' began, Karen was costing New Jersey State, which is footing the bill, around £225 a day, so that by now the sustenance of her wretched and meaningless frame must have absorbed well over £1m.

Dr Barney Clark, a dentist, died at the University of Utah Medical Center in March 1983, 112 distressful days after being fitted with an artificial heart. During his brief period of notoriety he was frequently labelled by the media as the first person ever to be given an artificial heart. This was not correct. During the heart transplant epidemic which swept the so-called developed world following Dr Christiaan Barnard's first Cape Town adventure, several crude pumps were sewn into the chests of unfortunate American citizens, all of whom promptly succumbed. Doubtless the number of victims of this particular form of surgical homicide would have been greater but for the American Food and Drug Administration whose officials promptly and wisely proscribed the procedure.

The FDA can't tell American surgeons what they can and cannot do to their customers. (Had it this power there might be a dramatic fall in the incidence of hysterectomies, gall bladder removals, and other operations performed in that great country for profit rather than the client's greater good.) But the agency does have the job of approving materials and devices (as well as drugs) intended for the treatment of disease, and way back in the 1960s it rightly concluded that none of the artificial hearts available was fit for the job.

But by the end of 1982 the FDA was persuaded that the Utah Medical Center had evolved a plastic and aluminium 'heart' (known as the Jarvik 7, after its designer, Dr Robert Jarvik) which stood a chance of sustaining some kind of life, and permission was given for a series of seven experiments employing the new toy, after which the instrument's worth was to be reviewed.

So the boys in Utah went ahead. The manoeuvre was different in kind to a heart transplant, for while, with a transplant, there is at least a chance (albeit a slim one) that the victim will walk away from the hospital and enjoy a period of tolerable life, there was never even the possibility that Barney Clark could ever be more than a wretched cripple. His future, should he have one, involved being permanently connected by two six foot hoses to a massive power unit weighing 375 lb. His life would be forever and literally hanging by a thread, except that the thread would be a couple of plastic tubes.

In the event Barney Clark 'enjoyed' a few lucid intervals after his operation, but, in general, went downhill, and certainly died at a far greater cost and with far more distress than would have been incurred had his own failing heart been quietly allowed to finish him off. The likelihood of the misery he might face following this unconscionable operation was foreseen and acknowledged in a lengthy legal document that he was required to sign before the deed was done, one of the grotesque provisions it contained giving him the 'right' (on whose authority – God Almighty's?) to terminate his own life if he found his state unbearable.

Despite the seven-up clearance given by the FDA, nothing more was heard of the artificial heart in Utah. But two years later, in November 1984, Dr DeVries, who had operated on Barney Clark, performed the same manoeuvre on a Mr William Schroeder at the Humana Hospital in Louisville, Kentucky – one of a chain of commercial clinics. The event was accompanied by massive publicity, which included the hiring of satellite time for the 24 hours surrounding the operation in order to ensure that a blow by blow account of the exercise should reach the nation, and the Humana organization announced that, provided satisfactory progress was made, it would finance a further 100 such implants at a cost of up to £200,000 each. The University of Utah had, it seems, decided that it could not support another Barney Clark affair, but a bunch of hard-headed businessmen had been persuaded that, properly exploited, the procedure might pay financial dividends, even if its clinical promise seemed bleak.

*

Unlike the malformed baby problem, the postponement of death predicament cannot be eased by any conceivable advances in medical science, for it is the increasing cleverness of doctors that created it in the first place. It can only become more thorny as that cleverness improves. Whereas, just a few decades ago, a physician could rely on the assumption that he was remaining true to his calling and his patients in doing everything he could to save a life, this convenient principle no longer holds true. But traditional attitudes die hard, and the travails faced by the dying are often and sometimes frightfully increased by the belief shared by many doctors (perhaps more by specialists than GPs) that they have lost a point in the Great Professional Tournament whenever a customer under active care hands in the chips.

However, we all have to die, and that is the only certain item in our lives, and should the scientists ever manage to destroy that certainty we should be in a pretty pickle indeed. So the question is, how fiercely should the battle to postpone the ineluctable be waged? Apart from the pointless distress so often caused by heroic attempts at salvaging the unsalvageable, the cost must be considered. Perhaps it is distasteful to attempt to put a cash value on a life, but, accepting that cash is only a symbol of real resources and endeavour, and in face of the fact that such commodities can never be in limitless supply, there must be a point at which efforts to preserve an individual become too expensive for the rest of us. The money spent on Karen Quinlan might have saved a thousand lives elsewhere. Similarly, the resources absorbed in the lifelong care of a severely subnormal mongol child might be used instead to increase the still woefully inadequate number of hospice beds where cancer victims can have their last months on Earth made not just painless and peaceful but rewarding. If we can't manage both might it not be positively wrong to keep the mongol alive?

There is, of course, already rationing of medical care. In countries like the USA where private medicine is the mode this is largely achieved by price. Under our own state system the best served customers are often those in need of the skills of experts in prestigious fields like neurosurgery, or cardio-thoracic surgery, or the treatment of leukaemia, because the doctors involved are highflyers with the energy and influence needed to grab for their specialties substantial slices of the medical cake. But even such plutocrats have to choose who shall benefit from the resources they command, and who shall be left unserved. Thus many victims of kidney failure in the UK whose lives might be saved or prolonged by dialysis go untreated because there aren't enough skilfully manned machines to go round. Most centres have an arbitrary upper age limit for new patients, and others who qualify by age may be excluded on the grounds that their prospects of returning to active life are not sufficient to justify tying up facilities that might be better used. Even the 'social value' of the candidate may be taken into account. Of course the rejects are not told that their lives are not considered to be worth saving. They are just not allowed to know that they could have been rescued from their fate.

*

While too many doctors too often strive officiously to keep the clearly doomed alive, many others are willing to give death a helping hand when suffering is harsh and no hope of recovery exists. Even those who would hesitate to administer a lethal overdose of a painkilling drug are often happy to refrain from vigorous efforts at resuscitation when the heart or breathing falters. In 1967 the then-Physician Superintendent of Neasden Hospital in London, Dr William McMath, won himself instant fame of a painful sort by having committed such a policy to paper. Some months earlier he had issued a memo detailing the categories of patients in his wards who were 'not to be resuscitated'. They included the very elderly (which he some- what hurtfully described as those over 65), and sufferers from cancer, chronic chest disease, or chronic kidney disease. Unfor- tunately for McMath a BBC team got hold of a copy of the document and broadcast it to the nation. There was turmoil. *The Washington Post* (that's Washington, DC, USA – not Washington, Tyne and Wear, UK) carried an article headed 'Britain in Uproar Over "Let Die" Directive'. Outraged MPs were assured by Kenneth Robinson, then Minister of Health, that no such regulations existed in other NHS hospitals and that an immediate inquiry had been ordered. The inquirers re- ported within a few *days* (which shows how much panic the 'revelations' caused), stating that no patient had died at Neasden needlessly, commending McMath for his courage in trying to tackle a difficult problem, but rapping him over the knuckles for botching things up by being too honest – that is to say 'by distributing a memorandum which rendered it liable to public view over a considerable period'.

And that's the trouble. We don't want to know.

McMath was only guilty of putting down on paper guidelines which half the hospitals in the land did then and do now observe, and those which don't (in which nurses and junior doctors are not told by their elders and betters what to do) are simply pretending that a demanding problem doesn't exist.

So, quite often, doctors decide when their fellow citizens, from the still unborn to the disintegrating old, should die. Since they have no legal right to take such decisions (except with parental consent in the case of some of the unborn), their actions occasionally land them up in trouble, but on the whole we're happy to leave them with a power over life and death the rest of us don't wish to have to exercise. It's been suggested that victims of kidney failure denied dialysis should sue. This hasn't happened yet. But in the USA a number of couples have been suing doctors, on behalf of a child, for 'wrongful life' following the birth of a diseased infant when an abortion was held to be unwarranted on the grounds that a normal child was to be expected. Clearly the responsibility, so far informally accepted by the medical trade, of advising or conniving or deciding in such matters, may soon become too perilous to be borne. And what shall we do then?

Within the past half century there have been several attempts in Britain to change the law so that the distressed and terminally ill should have the right to demand to be put down. Suicide or attempted suicide, with or without 'good cause', is now no longer (thankfully) a crime. So why shouldn't those of us seeking death be able to ask for skilled assistance in doing a job we could legally do for ourselves but might well mishandle to our own and our loved ones' greater distress?

There are all sorts of reasons why. Death is pretty final, and the distressed and confused might make a decision they would later regret, were they later capable of regret. Invalids, burdensome to their relatives, might be overpersuaded to seek an exit they didn't truly desire. The BMA has taken the line that the knowledge that a doctor was legally entitled to destroy you would be fatal to the faith a patient should have in the physician. Euthanasia might be too readily accepted as a cheap and easy way out of the burdensome duty of giving the elderly sick the care they have earned. (That great and good woman, Dame Cicely Saunders, who founded the hospice movement, has repeatedly said that none of the 'hopeless' patients under her skilled and compassionate charge have ever asked to be allowed to die before their appointed time.) Could doctors be properly asked to play the role of executioners 'on request'? And, as always, the moralists and theologians would assemble their arguments denying the right of mere humans to make law as preempting the will of God.

But the dilemma has to be resolved, and the only workable solution is to remove the task of making life and death decisions from the doctors, and from the courts, and to put them in the hands of the individuals concerned. I therefore predict that, not long after the turn of the century, chemists' shops (if there are such establishments), and even supermarkets, will have on their shelves, not only safe and effective non-prescription abortion pills, but also suicide pills.

*

Meanwhile, apart from taking a hand in determining survival, doctors are busily engaged in striving to prescribe how those of us who remain should conduct our lives.

Medical opinion was decisive in bringing about the seat-belt law for motorists. This was a sound measure because the assaults on personal liberty and choice involved were trivial compared to the benefits derived, which have amounted to at least a 25 per cent reduction in deaths and serious injuries suffered by motorists. This is not just good for the saved, but also for the rest of us, because people crippled or bereaved in road accidents are a costly nuisance to society.

Less justified is the BMA's avowed intent, confirmed by its annual meeting in 1984, to campaign for the legal proscription of both professional and amateur boxing. It is a vile sport (if sport be the term), and there is no doubt that its supporters and practitioners choose to ignore the horrible damage done to minds by point-winning blows to the head, so it is right for doctors to draw their attention to the truth of what they are about. But should the doctors try to stop them doing it, if, being well informed, that's what they want to do?

Medical paternalism can go too far, and we should beware of giving the medical establishment too much legal power. Take, for example, the remarkable trial, in 1982, of Mr Brian Radley, at the instance of the West Midlands Regional Health Authority.

Mr Radley was found guilty of the heinous crime of 'attending' his common-law wife in childbirth, contrary to the provisions of the Midwives' Act, 1951, which stipulates, among other things, that only a certified midwife, or a midwife in training, or a doctor, is permitted to provide any such 'attention', except in an emergency.

The birth of Radley Junior was not an emergency. Brian and his wife wanted to have their baby at home, and they believed in 'natural' childbirth. They asked whether a home delivery could be arranged, and were told that officialdom would not object so long as a midwife was present, plus a trainee. 'Necessary equipment' would also have to be available, and the 'labour room' (bedroom) would have to be fumigated (why?), and an ambulance would have to be at hand in case of the need to transfer the happening to a hospital.

Radley's wife, Michele, had suffered the birth of a baby in an NHS hospital two years earlier, and said, 'The whole process was like a production line. I was disgusted and determined never to let it happen again.' But to avoid that happening, the Radleys were required to turn their home into an obstetrical unit, which, of course, they couldn't do. So they went ahead unaided. Mr Radley read books on natural childbirth and did the job himself. It was a job well done, resulting in the easy birth of a thriving child.

Now, if Mr Radley had sat in the parlour watching television while his wife laboured alone and uncared for in the bedroom, nobody could have interfered, for it is not (and clearly could not be) illegal for a woman to give birth unaided. But he did give aid, and that was his sin, for which he was fined £100.

A year earlier a 25-year-old Scottish woodworker called Keith Emslie was similarly prosecuted, and was fined £50 by a person called Sheriff Muir Russell at Stonehaven near Aberdeen for a comparable 'offence'. Keith had successfully delivered his wife of a child after the local doctor had refused to attend the birth when the mother had said she didn't want to go to hospital. Sheriff Muir Russell told the unfortunate Keith that he must 'come to terms with your principles, and think of the child, and do as the law requires'. As a matter of fact it was never intended that the law should require a doctor or midwife to conduct every birth. The clause of the Midwives' Act under which these charges had been brought was designed to prevent latter-day, unqualified Sarah Gamps from muscling in on the midwives' trade.

We have come to a pretty pass when the health authorities (who instituted these proceedings) not only use but abuse the law in order to force the rest of us to behave in the manner the medical cartel sees fit. It's time for the rest of us to have our say, and so we must, however much the good Sir John Peel and his ilk may resent such questioning of their wisdom and authority.

CHAPTER EIGHT

Brave New World

Today's doctors wield powers which they are not always competent to handle wisely and well, but tomorrow's doctors are going to have yet tougher and more complex decisions and judgments to make as they strive to benefit rather than exploit and manipulate their clients and society.

Aldous Huxley borrowed the beauteous phrase 'brave new world' from Shakespeare as a title for a novel, published in 1932, which foresaw how scientists would give politicians such powerful means for influencing the minds and bodies of the rest of us that none would be free, but that all would, instead, take their appointed places uncomplainingly in a fully regulated, trouble-free society. The fantasy included baby farms in which bench-reared embryos were engineered to produce the needed number of tailor-made citizens in various categories, ranging from the highest intellectuals to the humblest workers.

A quarter of a century later Huxley wrote *Brave New World Revisited*, in which he looked back at his prophecies, and expressed the fear that some might be coming true much sooner than he had imagined. That was in 1958. If he was still alive today he would have to be appalled, for since his death, in 1963, Edwards and Steptoe and their imitators have made the baby hatchery idea a looming likelihood.

And that's the way it's going. The science fiction writers are having a hard time of it just keeping pace with reality, let alone amazing us with concepts we hadn't even dreamed about.

Here are a few predictions concerning medical happenings within the next few decades. They owe nothing to poetic imagination. They are a sober and reasonable assessment of the probable consequences of developments now begun.

*

By not long after the turn of the century a single medical college might be capable of supplying all the doctors of a sort equipped with practical skills and expertise who will be required by the nation, because machines will be providing most of the health care. In the essential matter of diagnosis electronic doctors have been shown to perform at least as well as a skilled physician, provided of course that they have been programmed with physicianly skill in the first place. Patients answer questions displayed on a screen, commonly by pushing a 'Yes', 'No' or 'Don't Know' button, and the response evokes the logical next query in the detection trail. If the interrogating screen uses friendly, informal language, couched in the idiom of the people it's designed to serve (including such apparently trivial but actually important details as kicking off by spelling out 'good morning' or 'hello') then it is much liked by customers. In an experiment carried out in Glasgow as long as 15 years ago, many of the patient guinea pigs said they preferred the questioning machine to a session with a live consultant, because (presumably unlike its human counterpart) it was 'polite, considerate, and understandable'.

Computers are also used for such skilled chores as analysing electrocardiograms, and screening the lists of drugs prescribed for patients to spot the danger of interactions.

Only the will, rather than any so far unachieved technology, is needed to employ machines to not just diagnose but prescribe, and to follow the course of a disease, modifying the recommended management in the light of day-to-day (or even hour-to-hour) results. When everyone has a computer terminal in the sitting room it will be a simple matter to tap the finest medical expertise available. A micro-multi-analyser attached to the terminal, and connections for skin electrodes, and perhaps a microphone stethoscope, would make it possible to add information about the blood and urine, and the electrical activity of various organs, and the quality of the heart sounds and the breath sounds, to the information upon which the central computer was required to make up its mind.

I don't quite envisage a computer attached to a robot surgeon which would instantly perform an appendectomy, but there is no reason why a computer shouldn't tell you to *have* an instant appendectomy, and at the same time find and notify a hospital able to do the job, and tell you where to go, and, if need be, lay on an ambulance to take you there. A machine could certainly dispense necessary drugs, perhaps by providing a code to be keyed in at the board of the 'drug dispenser' set into the front wall of your friendly neighbourhood chemist's shop, where the appropriate electronic authority for the one-time-only delivery of the right quantity of the drug in question (labelled with the right instructions) would already have been received.

With the advent of the parlour physician there would be no more time-consuming visits to crowded surgeries, no more missed diagnoses, no more agonizing waits for 'emergency doctors' who don't turn up, no more inappropriate prescribing of antibiotics or over-prescribing of tranquillizers, and no more withholding of vital facts by patients too embarrassed to tell a living doctor the truth.

These electronic 'home doctors' will not only perform cheaply, efficiently, and at great speed, most of the tasks now carried out by general practitioners and hospital physicians, but will also lead to a considerable reduction in sickness rates and the demands for medical services. This valuable effect would accrue from the fact that all the information garnered from the 20m or so terminals in the kingdom would be continuously correlated and analysed by a central computer, so that the causes of ill-understood afflictions, including many cancers, would become apparent. Unexpected drug side effects and looming epidemics would be spotted early, and vigorous preventive and remedial measures would be machine-prescribed before much damage had been suffered.

All this, and more, could certainly be achieved by the determined exploitation of the present generation of computers. All we shall need is a small corps of experts able to provide the information needed by the programmers, and a somewhat larger corps of experts able to perform the functions still outside the range of the machines.

It will be interesting to see whether a few very clever people can continue to be fruitful on their own, or whether they need the support and stimulation and experience, and, indeed, the yardstick provided by many lesser mortals working in the same field before they can reach the heights. But perhaps the new fifth generation of 'thinking' computers we are promised will provide the intellectual competition needed by an increasingly shrinking (by reason of redundancy) regiment of the intellectually elite.

*

Coronary heart disease, strokes, and cancer will become preventable and treatable. New biological agents created by genetic engineering (quite different in kind to the chemical industry's present range of synthetic drugs) will be capable of halting and often reversing all kinds of fleshly aberrations, such as those producing arthritis, disseminated sclerosis, diabetes, and cataracts, in addition to the two major killers, cancer and CHD.

It may not prove possible, within the foreseeable future, to halt or slow the ageing process to any significant extent, but more and more people will, so to speak, stay healthy till they die, so that centenarians and nonogenarians will be commonplace.

The increasing numbers of old people will so disrupt traditional patterns of society (particularly by absorbing resources and occupying roles lusted after by their youngers) that pressures will build up for the imposition of a statutory age limit to the right of life. This could involve oldsters receiving on, say the occasion of their 85th birthday, a buff OHMS envelope (for the Royal Family will, of course, still exist), instructing them to attend their local euthanasia depot on the following Wednesday at 2.30 in the afternoon. Certain sorts of citizens, such as ex-prime ministers, bishops, Fellows of the Royal Society, members of the Order of Merit, ex-chairmen of the TUC and Unilever, and ex-editors and owners of *The Times*, would earn exemption from this sanction, thus making ambition and achievement (upon which the continuing prosperity of the nation so much depends) even more rewarding than it is today. More likely, perhaps, matters will be so arranged that the less important and influential among the very old will simply have a 'Not To Be Resuscitated' or its equivalent mark added, on due date, to their personal, centrally computerized files. State pensions will stop, free travel cards will be withdrawn, entitlement to free or subsidized medical attention will cease, and, in many another way, the undistinguished old will be 'encouraged' to fade away. None of this will be announced as part of a deliberate policy to rid the nation of the costly old. The various measures will be introduced upon various excuses designed to conceal their true intent. If this particular prediction appears unthinkable or ridiculous, I would remind you of the confidential government report, leaked by the *Guardian*, which suggested that any effective measures against smoking would result in an intolerable increase in the number of citizens surviving to old age.

*

The world population is rocketing upwards. This is the biggest existing threat to the survival of the species, because too many people demanding a rich share of inadequate resources must create pressures of a kind likely to tempt national leaders to use nuclear weapons in an attempt to gain control of minerals, farmlands, sheer space, and other finite commodities provided by the planet Earth which are essential to the sustenance of Man. And by the turn of the century every fanatical and tinpot regime will have its arsenal of megakilling rockets.

Perhaps that fact will provide the final solution, and there won't be any people any more, but if the destruction of the race is to be avoided there will have to be rigorous controls imposed upon population growth. That means rigorous controls imposed upon the reproductive proclivities of individuals. This will probable involve the administration of a long-term contraceptive imposed upon all (or perhaps only men or only women) at the time of puberty, and reversible only by some positive act, with official permission being required for this to be done.

*

Despite the success of a new generation of drugs in preventing and curing much disease there will still be some faults in organs like livers and kidneys and hearts beyond their control, and spare part surgery will become routine, not simply as a life-saving measure, but to improve efficiency (like replacing spark plugs and oil filters in a car). The rejection problem will have been overcome. This branch of the trade will no longer be entirely dependent upon salvaging parts from the brain-dead victims of traffic accidents and suchlike, because there will be a wide range of man-made artificial organs available, and it will be possible to grow supplies of tissues, if not entire organs, on the laboratory bench.

But brain-dead bodies may be kept alive specifically to

provide a support system. Karen Quinlan's womb could right now be used to rear somebody else's bench-manufactured embryo. I don't apologize for this tasteless and obscene suggestion, because it is necessary that those of us still sentient should be jolted into recognizing what is possible and what, therefore, somebody, sooner or later, is bound to attempt.

The Warnock committee, reporting in 1984, recommended that the transplantation of human embryos into the wombs of other animals should be made a criminal offence. The trouble is that the law never has been and never will be an effective instrument for the prevention of happenings. No doubt, before long, we shall be told of the birth of a child developed in the womb of an ape (or, more likely, a pig). The law on abortion, prior to 1967, didn't prevent abortions taking place. It simply ensured that they happened underground, and with the maximum chance of damage to all concerned.

In any case, currently emotive issues in this field, such as womb-leasing and surrogate motherhood, will have become a matter of historical interest, because it will be possible, and comparatively inexpensive, to rear bench-made embryos to maturity in an artificial womb. The Huxley baby factories will exist, and so will all the consequences he foresaw. No more disabled infants will be spawned. Cloning will be routine, so that human animals of a type and with characteristics deemed to be desirable will be bred, with the exclusion from the race of mavericks.

Some time before that happens (indeed, probably within the next few months) Robert Edwards will have perfected a means for allowing his customers to choose the sex of their test-tube babies, and not long afterwards parents reproducing by the natural and God-given techniques will enjoy the possibility of deciding whether to bud a daughter or a son. Since even a quite tiny change in the balance of the sexes would have the most profound effects upon society, governments might feel they had a duty to require parents to produce either a son or a daughter, or one of each, or two of one and one of the other, according to the pattern of a national plan. It remains to be seen whether the calculations of politicians, civil servants, and their 'expert' advisers will prove to be as felicitous as those worked out by Nature.

(Giving parents the opportunity to choose the sex of an

offspring will be justified on the grounds that certain pretty rare hereditary diseases, like haemophilia, only cause trouble in boy children, so that the carriers of such destructive genes should be able to opt for only having girls. But, of course, the facility would also be used for quite other reasons.)

*

Drugs will be developed capable of influencing attitudes. Not drugs of the present crude variety, which simply make you dreamy, or sleepy, or careless, or excited, but drugs of a more subtle kind which will home in on particular brain circuits, evoking specific emotional and intellectual responses, such as feelings of tenderness or compliance or aggression, or an enlargement of the individuals' capacity to concentrate or make objective judgements.

The citizens of Huxley's *Brave New World* were given a regular ration of 'soma' (a drug which possessed 'all the advantages of Christianity and alcohol, and none of their defects') to help them tolerate life under the system, but soma only provided a brief trip to nirvana, from which the traveller returned without any bodily or intellectual hangover. People do and always have used drugs to escape, and do enjoy drug-induced fantasies and emotional holidays, but they also want something that can help them handle the real world. The new range of psychotropic pharmaceuticals will serve both ends, and by abolishing the need for indulgence in alcohol and tobacco will do more to improve the public health than all the current products of the pill trade put together. But I hope they wouldn't entirely displace the delights of Burgundy and hock.

The question will arise as to whether such balms should be available on supermarket shelves, or whether they should be 'prescription only' medicines. It is vain to hope for a non-addictive pleasure pill, since pleasure is itself addictive, so that the risk would be created of having half the population permanently 'under the influence', thus being rendered careless or incapable of stern duties, such as cutting the grass or filling in tax returns.

But there is nothing about the wisdom or experience of doctors which would make them suitable judges of who should benefit from the new mind shapers, and to what extent, and

when. Dr Matthew Huxley, son of Aldous, who works at the
National Institute of Mental Health in the USA, is one of the
knowledgeable scientists who now feel that his father's soma
idea should be taken seriously. He has suggested that the pills
might contain an emetic, so that an overdosage would be
self-defeating. Alternatively they might contain a dye which, in
sufficient quantity, would tinge the skin, thus exposing over-
indulgers to ridicule. Some kind of controls would have to be
devised, but let it not be left to the medical clan. (Churchill and
Eden kept themselves going on amphetamines, with the conni-
vance of their physicians, and not perhaps to the ultimate good
of either the individuals or the state.)

*

Thus Huxley's *Brave New World* is now technically within our
grasp, together with many wonders the novelist never imagined, and our task must be to establish the means for
avoiding the horrors and reaping the benefits of our growing
capacity to manipulate the body and the mind.

The medical trade will certainly have a part to play in this
tightrope trick, but not as the final, or even the principal arbiter
of what should be done, and what would be best left undone.

I foresee a radical redistribution of authority and responsibility within the profession, which will be divided into two
distinct groups.

On the one hand there will be the medical scientists and
specialist clinicians who invent new therapies, and methods of
diagnosis, and ways of preventing disease, and procedures for
modifying mental and physical functions and behaviour, and
who undertake manoeuvres requiring their special skills, but
who will only have controlled and limited access to patients.

Their activities will be supervised and utilised by the second
and larger group, which will consist of medical 'priests', who
will make it their business to be fully aware of what the experts
are up to, but whose principal role will be to act as the patient's
friend, to counsel and console, and to suggest which of the
wondrous remedies and manipulations available might benefit
the client, and which, in any particular case, might generate
more grief than joy.

In other words, the profession would be split down the

middle, just as today, but with the big difference that, for the sake of the commonweal, the medical priests – the family doctors – would largely run the show, and, together with their clients, would call the tune.

The message I have tried to convey is that good health springs from the good society, and that we are asking too much of the medical profession if we look to the quite ordinary mortals who fill its ranks to cure or alleviate all our ills, and that it's hardly surprising if they often fail in this impossible task, or if, in making the vain attempt, they sometimes desperately pretend to powers and wisdoms they do not possess.

Doctors are not gods, and function best as loyal, devoted, skilful servants, advising, persuading, supporting, but never usurping.

The best doctor is a kind of Jeeves.

Index